BOUND BY PASSION

Skyler tightened his hold on her arm. "I can't believe you've actually agreed to marry David," he hissed, angry with her, but more with the pain he felt at the thought.

"What difference should that make to you?" Arden countered, her own tone thick with hurt. "Why do you care who I marry or what I do?"

"I don't know," he replied, his voice softer now. "I just do." He pulled her close to him. "Maybe it's because I know you don't love him," he whispered as he lowered his lips to hers. "Maybe it's because I know you love me."

Arden felt mesmerized by his words and his gaze, completely powerless in his grasp. She knew what would happen when he kissed her, yet she could not pull herself away.

He drew her back, away from the house and into the shadows of the garden. She followed him willingly, telling herself that he asked nothing of her she was unwilling to give. She pressed close to him as his arms enfolded her and let her body melt into his as she felt the heat growing between them. . . .

CAPTURE THE GLOW
OF ZEBRA'S HEARTFIRES

AUTUMN ECSTASY   (3133, $4.25)
by Pamela K. Forrest

Philadelphia beauty Linsey McAdams had eluded her kidnappers but was now at the mercy of the ruggedly handsome frontiersman who owned the remote cabin where she had taken refuge. The two were snowbound until spring, and handsome Luc LeClerc soon fancied the green-eyed temptress would keep him warm through the long winter months. He said he would take her home at winter's end, but she knew that with one embrace, she might never want to leave!

BELOVED SAVAGE   (3134, $4.25)
by Sandra Bishop

Susannah Jacobs would do anything to survive — even submit to the bronze-skinned warrior who held her captive. But the beautiful maiden vowed not to let the handsome Tonnewa capture her heart as well. Soon, though, she found herself longing for the scorching kisses and tender caresses of her raven-haired BELOVED SAVAGE.

CANADIAN KISS   (3135, $4.25)
by Christine Carson

Golden-haired Sara Oliver was sent from London to Vancouver to marry a stranger three times her age — only to have her husband-to-be murdered on their wedding day. Sara vowed to track the murderer down, but he ambushed her and left her for dead. When she awoke, wounded and frightened, she was staring into the eyes of the handsome loner Tom Russel. As the rugged stranger nursed her to health, the flames of passion erupted, and their CANADIAN KISS threatened never to end!

Available wherever paperbacks are sold, or order direct from the Publisher. Send cover price plus 50¢ per copy for mailing and handling to Zebra Books, Dept. 3428, 475 Park Avenue South, New York, N.Y. 10016. Residents of New York, New Jersey and Pennsylvania must include sales tax. DO NOT SEND CASH.

SUSAN SACKETT
DESIRE'S CHAINS

ZEBRA BOOKS
KENSINGTON PUBLISHING CORP.

ZEBRA BOOKS

are published by

Kensington Publishing Corp.
475 Park Avenue South
New York, NY 10016

First printing: June, 1991

Printed in the United States of America

Chapter One

New York, 1882

"I don't know that I'd like the job any better than reporting the week's murders. Frankly, I think you're wasting my talents."

Skyler Trask kept his sharp blue eyes riveted on the slightly myopic ones of his new employer, not the least put off by the fact that they didn't waver under his stare, not one iota.

"Never underestimate the reading public's taste for violence, Trask. A good little war is worth a ten-percent increase in circulation. And from all appearances, the Turks intend to provide one on Crete in the near future."

Forbes Devereaux dismissed Sky's objections without another thought. His reporters either did what they were told to do, or they could find employment elsewhere . . . not that he would like to lose the man. He had lured Skyler Trask away from the *Tribune* for an unconscionable salary to come to the *New York Sun*. But Trask was by far the most talented writer he had come across in a long time, and Forbes was willing to pay for quality when the need arose.

Forbes removed his spectacles and then drew a white

linen handkerchief from his pocket, not taking his eyes from Sky's the whole while.

"I've no argument with that. It's the thought of wasting my time until something happens. Why don't we wait for the war to begin before you send me over there?"

Sky realized his tone was painfully polite. He was beginning to feel as though he had made a mistake accepting Forbes's offer to work for the *Sun*. He'd heard the old man was a hard man to deal with, but the salary offer had been too good for him to turn down out of hand. Unfortunately, his editor at the *Tribune* had not been as impressed as Sky had been by the money, and the two had parted under strained circumstances.

In short, Sky had burned his bridges behind him, and he was essentially stuck taking Forbes's orders, for a while at least. The only problem was that he seemed congenitally incapable of taking orders. He worked best alone, letting his own judgment lead him to a good story. Having people tell him what to do and when to do it only made him uncooperative and ill humored.

"Because then we'll have missed most of it," Forbes replied as he continued to polish the perfectly spotless glasses. "It will be a little war, I think, but a decidedly complex one. The Turks are a vicious lot, and the Greeks unbending. And our readers like all the unpleasant details."

"You can always write up a few pieces about this madman Schliemann if you get bored while you're waiting." Harry Stoning, the *Sun's* editor in chief, tried to sound cheerful. He was not in the mood to have his new star put off by old man Devereaux's lack of tact. "Maybe you could send us back a journal, like that man Clemens did when he traveled to Italy for the *Boston Mirror*."

Sky turned to Stoning and let his lips compress sharply. With his round, pink-cheeked face and equally round body and thinning hair, Stoning gave the impression of being an extremely large infant. The antithesis of the tall, wiry, sharp-featured Forbes, he was expected to be little more than the man who stood by the old man's side, smiling, trying to make Forbes's orders more palatable to his underlings. Had Sky not known that Stoning was a power in his own right, he would have accepted appearances as fact at that moment.

"I don't write charming or amusing pieces, Harry," he countered. "I doubt anyone would be remotely interested in any articles I might write about this Schliemann of yours."

"Oh, he's not mine," Stoning told him. "He's a crazed German merchant who's taken it into his head that Homer's poetry can be taken literally. He's been racing around the countryside, digging holes in the ground, convinced he's going to find the ancient city of Troy."

"And Helen and Paris, too, no doubt," Sky responded with more than a shade of sarcasm.

"Helen and Paris? Is that all you gentlemen have to do, talk about the illicit affairs of mythical lovers?"

All three men turned to find a tall, slender young woman standing in the open doorway. The two older men noticed that she was quite smartly turned out in a moss green velveteen suit nipped artfully to reveal a narrow waist and embellished with a good quantity of black and gold braid. Sky, however, after a quick appraisal that assured him that all the expected curves were properly if a bit compactly represented, found himself staring at a pair of dark green, slightly almond-shaped eyes that returned his stare with decided curiosity.

Arden Devereaux was thoroughly accustomed to the stir she made when she took the opportunity to enter her father's offices. After all, she often told herself, she was the one source of sunshine most of those who labored under her father's rather despotic rule ever encountered, and she considered it almost a sacred duty to remind them occasionally that more pleasant aspects of life existed outside the door of the *New York Sun*. But if she was used to the adoring glances of such as Harry Stoning, she was decidedly not accustomed to the sort of appraising look this handsome, dark-haired stranger leveled at her. She suddenly found herself unaccountably flustered, a feeling that was not at all common to her. And to add to her confusion, she found she had to force her eyes away from his.

Sky had no hint that his glare had had any effect on her. In fact he found himself occupied with a consideration of the potent effect her eyes had had on him. It wasn't until she pulled her gaze away and started into the room that he noticed that those peculiarly intoxicating eyes were set in a heart-shaped face with strong and decidedly attractive features, the whole framed by a thick upsweep of soft, honey-blond curls.

"Frankly, I think living lovers are of far greater interest," he replied as she swept by him on her way to her father's desk.

Arden stopped at his words and turned to offer him a second glance, entirely ignoring her father's warning look. What was it about this man, she wondered, that made her feel so on edge? She forced some control on herself and smiled at him.

"My sentiments entirely, Mr. . . . . ?"

Sky quickly rose and offered his hand.

"Trask," he said, before either Forbes or Stoning had the opportunity to provide the introduction. "Skyler Trask."

"Trask?" She knew that name, and when she found the reference in her memory, she pounced on it. "Not the famous Skyler Trask who so diligently exposed the malfeasance of William Tweed? I *am* impressed." She turned to her father, finally managing to throw off the effect of his stare and settle herself. "You've stolen Mr. Trask

8

away from the *Tribune,* Papa? How perfectly brilliant of you!"

Sky glanced at Forbes and realized that for the first time the old man seemed to have lost control of the situation. Forbes might be the iron-fisted ruler of the *Sun,* he thought with a certain amount of pleasure, but this young woman apparently controlled him in his domestic environment. And, more to the point, it was obvious that Forbes did not at all like the tone of the conversation Sky was having with his daughter.

Forbes cleared his throat, apparently not completely comfortable at being forced to continue with the introductions.

"As you've obviously surmised, Trask, this young woman is my daughter. Arden, this is indeed the former *Tribune* reporter, Skyler Trask. And I rather dislike the insinuation that I'd have a hand in anything so mean as larceny."

Arden laughed. "Papa, where the *Tribune* is concerned, you'd stoop to larceny or anything else that would give you an advantage."

She darted another glance at Sky. He wasn't at all what she would have expected. Most of her father's reporters were either like Stoning, round and pleasant and entirely lacking in the ability to rouse any thought of romance, or else sharp-nosed, sharp-tongued men who tried to force her out onto the veranda alone with them at the annual Christmas party Forbes gave for the employees of the paper. More than anything, they left her feeling that she would never want anything more of life than to spend it entirely alone.

Skyler Trask, however, was neither round and pink nor sharp-nosed and unappealing. On the contrary, he was tall and blue eyed and very handsome. There was something about the way that single dark curl fell down across his forehead and the disturbingly mischievous

9

look in those blue eyes that made her think a walk alone with him on the veranda might not be an entirely unpleasant venture.

Forbes cleared his throat a second time, this time with a good deal more determination.

"I had no idea you would pay me a visit this afternoon, Arden." He looked up at Stoning and Sky's amused expressions. "If you gentlemen will excuse me for a few moments?"

"Oh, that won't be necessary," Arden broke in quickly, before either man could make a move toward the door. "Aunt Clarissa demanded my company on an expedition to the milliner's and as you forgot to mention if you'd be home to dinner tonight, we decided to stop by on our way and inquire." She watched as her father's eyes drifted to the open door and grew slightly perturbed. "Don't worry," she was quick to assure him. "I told her you would be far too busy to entertain us, and she's waiting patiently outside, doubtless harassing Mr. Oates about the dust and printer's ink that cover all the desks and entertaining ideas of sweeping down on the milliner like a great bird of prey."

After that description, Sky could not keep himself from venturing a quick glance to the outer office through the still open door. He immediately spotted a short, gray-haired woman with an excessively ample bosom. She was clothed entirely in brown. He thought she looked like a very large sitting hen.

"Yes, Arden, I shall be home tonight to dinner," Forbes was saying, his tone edged now with strained patience.

Arden waved this intrusion on her thoughts quickly aside despite the fact that it was ostensibly the information she'd come to seek.

"Why were you people discussing Paris and Helen and Troy?" she demanded abruptly. Her eyes narrowed and her expression grew suddenly sly. "Papa, you aren't going off to write about the doings of Herr Schliemann, are you?"

Sky frowned. "Does everyone except me know about this German?" he muttered.

Arden seemed bewildered at his question. "Certainly," she said. "He's the cause of a great deal of speculation at the Museum," she confided. "Half the curators think he's deranged, and the rest aren't quite sure if he's merely simple or a genius."

Forbes groaned. "My daughter helped organize the ball for the opening of the new wing at the Metropolitan," he explained. "The exposure has left her with an undue reverence for old pots and stones and the misguided souls who muck about with them." He wished now that the conversation had never taken this particular tack. He had an uncomfortable feeling he knew where it was going, and he was not at all sure he liked it. "Actually," he said, turning his attention back to Arden, "Mr. Trask was on his way to Crete to cover the unpleasantness there."

"But there is no unpleasantness," Arden objected. "At least not yet. And what a wonderful idea to write about Herr Schliemann's research. I find it absolutely fascinating. And there's Sir Evans, pottering about in Crete."

"Evans?" Sky asked, feeling himself completely out of his element.

Arden nodded. "Sir Arthur Evans. He's one of the more distinguished members of the Royal Archaeological Society." She said these words with the sort of offhand disdain that suggested such knowledge ought to be part of everyone's repertoire.

Sky shrugged. He had been right: he was out of his element.

"A farmer found some interesting stones in the middle of one of his fields last year, and Sir Arthur has organized an exploratory dig," Arden continued, rea-

11

lizing she was pleased by his attention. "He thinks he may have discovered a great palace at Knossos. He claims it is the palace of King Minos, perhaps out of spite for Herr Schliemann's claims he will find Troy." She grew thoughtful, then smiled and shivered with delight. "It's too delicious just to think of seeing it." Almost, she thought, as delicious as the idea she'd just had.

"I'm afraid I don't share your enthusiasm, Miss Devereaux," Sky said. "As I was just telling your father, I hardly was enthusiastic at the prospect of sitting around waiting for a war to begin with nothing to do but watch some aged German dig up old pots."

"Oh, but you're mistaken, Mr. Trask. It would be, I think, most intriguing. Perhaps not to you, but most certainly to me." Arden turned to her father, her smile turning just a bit sly as she considered the best way to approach the subject, and settled on the direct frontal attack. "Papa, I have an absolutely brilliant idea. You could take me to Greece and I could cover the story of Herr Schliemann's pots for the paper while Mr. Trask devotes himself to the unpleasantness, as you call it. We did have plans to visit London and Paris this fall. . . ."

"I am well aware of that fact, Arden, however . . ." Forbes broke in.

Arden gave him no time to further his objection. She turned to Sky, hoping to enlist his help even though she realized he was obviously not the sort of man she might easily manipulate. "Papa intends to find some poor earl or duke, marry me off to him, and simplify his life by leaving me to pine away in some drafty castle. Don't you think that a miserable fate, Mr. Trask?"

He couldn't keep himself from smiling at her. "Horrible," he agreed.

"Arden," Forbes interrupted sharply.

"Well, I think it's perfectly logical, Papa. You yourself

12

have said I write well enough to work for the *Sun*, if only I weren't your daughter and a female, that is. And this is one way to put all those years of expensive ladies' school education to some use."

"Actually, it isn't such a bad idea," Stoning offered before Forbes could completely reject it. Arden, he saw, was delighted with his words. His round cheeks grew a shade pinker. "The ladies love that sort of thing, and, if you will remember, Mr. Devereaux, it is to the ladies that the majority of our advertisers sell their goods. I think they'd applaud a series of articles written by one of their own."

If Forbes did not seem to accept his words with any enthusiasm, Arden certainly did.

"You see, Papa, it's a perfectly wonderful idea. Mr. Stoning says so."

Sky suddenly realized that however attractive he might find Forbes's daughter, he did not at all like the prospect of having either her or her father too close by when he was expected to work. Pleasure was one thing, and he would be the last to suggest that looking at Arden Devereaux was anything but a pleasure, but work was something entirely different.

"I'm afraid I must insist that I work alone, Miss Devereaux," he said, and found himself not displeased by her father's reception of that sentiment.

"And we wouldn't want to encumber Mr. Trask in his labors, Arden," Forbes added.

Arden felt a wave of regret that Skyler Trask seemed so willing to dismiss her. She was not, however, willing to be put off so easily. With a wave of her hand she dismissed any objections as mere fluff.

"I'm sure we can accommodate Mr. Trask, Papa," she said. Then, turning to Sky, she added, "Perhaps we could discuss the matter over dinner, Mr. Trask? Tomorrow evening?" She offered Stoning her most charming smile.

"And you, too, of course, Mr. Stoning," she added.

"With great pleasure, Miss Devereaux," Stoning accepted, grinning widely, anticipating the prospect of watching Arden defeat both Sky's objections and her father's even more than the excellent meal he knew he would be served.

"Excellent." Arden felt the glow of impending triumph and relished it. She turned back to her father. "Aunt Clarissa will be getting bored," she said, "Even the fascination of dust and printer's ink eventually pales."

"I'll escort you out," Forbes said in a tone that implied he wouldn't be entirely comfortable until he saw her safely out of the building. He rose and took her arm.

"Mr. Stoning. Mr. Trask," Arden said with a smile for each of them. She paused as her eyes found Sky's, aware that she found herself relishing the opportunity to relieve him of his objections. "Until tomorrow evening. We'll expect you at seven."

Sky couldn't recall having accepted the invitation, but nonetheless he found himself smiling back at her, nodding, and saying, "Until tomorrow evening, Miss Devereaux."

It wasn't until she and her father were out of the room that he realized he was not at all sure he wanted to get into the habit of seeing Arden Devereaux. It suddenly seemed to him that she was the sort of woman he found a bit too appealing for his own good, and that, he told himself, combined with the fact that her father employed him, was a decidedly dangerous combination.

Stoning considered Sky's expression as he watched Forbes lead Arden into the outer office. Although he seemed to be struggling to hide it, Sky's expression hinted at confusion, a feeling Stoning was willing to admit he himself often felt after a meeting with Arden.

14

Not that he found the feeling at all unpleasant. In fact, any time he spent in Arden's company left him feeling entirely pleased with the world, no matter how much she managed to bewilder him.

"A fascinating young woman, don't you think, Sky?" he ventured.

Sky turned to face him. "I suppose that's one word," he said with a smile. "She does dart from subject to subject with a bewildering flow of logic."

"But with agility and grace," Stoning interjected.

"With decided grace," Sky agreed with a smile. He suddenly grew serious. "You don't think she'll really convince him to take her to Greece, do you?" he asked.

The edges of Stoning's lips curled, and for a moment he turned into the image of an oversized and entirely pleased cherub, one who lacked only wings.

"Oh, she most certainly will," he replied. "In fact, I'd be willing to put money on it. She can convince him to do just about anything."

Stoning did not allow himself to dwell on the thought that if Forbes were to leave on the proposed European trip with Arden a few weeks early, there would be that much more time for him to run the paper as he saw fit. As much as he liked his job, he liked it far better without benefit of the meddling hand Forbes was entirely too willing to interject when it was least wanted.

"Damn," Sky muttered.

Stoning smiled. "Publishers," he said with a shake of his head. "You can't live with them and you can't live without them."

Sky was marveling at the enthusiasm with which Harry Stoning was consuming a second serving of chocolate soufflé—a miracle, Sky thought, considering the fact

15

that Stoning had done more than justice by the excellent dinner they'd been served—when Clarissa Devereaux suddenly dropped her napkin on the table, nodded to her brother, to Stoning and to him, then left the room without saying a word. Bewildered, Sky turned to watch her halt once she was just outside the room. She called to Arden to come, then started off once again, disappearing into the corridor beyond.

He was surprised, he realized, to discover himself feeling a stab of regret when Arden put down her spoon, took a last sip of her champagne, and then stood to leave.

"If you gentlemen will excuse me," she murmured, then followed after her aunt.

Sky watched her go and realized he'd lost all interest in food. It had been more than a bit pleasant to sit across from her at the table and stare at her throughout the meal, just as he'd known when she'd greeted him a few hours before. From the moment she'd entered the drawing room that evening he'd had trouble keeping his eyes from her. She was dressed in a deep turquoise silk dress that hugged her slender waist and dipped just enough to give a hint of what Sky thought was a decidedly pleasing cleavage. Around her neck she wore a delicate collar of tiny emeralds and pearls set in elaborate gold filagree, the green of the stones picking up the color of her eyes and sparkling in the candlelight.

He must have shown his disappointment, for Stoning raised his champagne glass and offered him a knowing smile.

"Miss Devereaux is a devoted niece," he told Sky. "Each evening she reads her aunt an inspirational passage."

Forbes groaned. "My sister tells me she finds the devotional words of the illustrious Reverend Trillingbee soothing in an unsettling world and suggests I ought to

16

join her in her moments of devotional frenzy. I'm afraid I've demurred, leaving Arden in the clutches of all those pious words. I've never quite taken the effort to learn who this worthy Trillingbee might be, perhaps because of a deep-seated fear that familiarity might lead to contamination with my sister's fervor, but I do know his sermons are bound up in a number of impressive-looking volumes, so one assumes he must be someone."

Sky grinned, then shrugged. "I'm afraid I can shed absolutely no light on the matter," he said, noticing that Forbes appeared to be not the least put out by the admission. "And Miss Devereaux?" he asked. "Will she be rejoining us?"

Forbes cocked a brow. He was not at all sure he liked the idea of his employee and his daughter exchanging the sort of glances he'd seen throughout the evening.

"Perhaps," he said, hoping she wouldn't, but entirely sure that she would. "In the meantime, might I interest you gentlemen in a friendly little game of pocket billiards?"

Sky glanced quickly at Stoning, who had warned him of the probable suggestion of a game, and turned back to Forbes.

"With great pleasure, Mr. Devereaux," he agreed.

"Excellent," Forbes said as he dropped his napkin to the table and pushed his chair back.

Sky lifted his champagne glass, drained it, and followed suit.

Stoning groaned. "I predict abject humiliation in my future if you insist I play as well," he said.

Sky laughed, but Forbes seemed to find nothing humorous in the words. He frowned, his look pained, as though he were considering the folly of employing a man who lacked confidence in his skills.

"Be a man, Harry," he said as he started for the door.

17

"Porter," he called as the butler started forward to clear away the dessert dishes, "Bring along some brandy, will you? And the Havanas."

Stoning groaned once more, quite volubly, and then he and Sky followed along after Forbes.

"I'll take that for you, Porter."

The butler showed no surprise to find Arden apparently lying in wait for him in the corridor just outside the billiard room. He was, after all, a gentleman's gentleman of the old school, trained in London and apprenticed in his youth in a titled if nearly impoverished house. A practical man, he had eventually left behind him the lure of being a member of a duke's household in favor of the more practical considerations working for Forbes Devereaux provided. And he had to admit, even from the start, the effort of civilizing the Devereaux house was a challenge entirely worthy of his talents.

At that moment he would no sooner have shown evidence of surprise—or any other emotion, for that matter—than he would have had he encountered a herd of elephants rampaging through the halls of the Devereaux mansion. In his years there he'd learned to expect the unexpected in any house where Arden Devereaux resided. There hadn't, of course, ever been an invasion of elephants, but he recalled with painful clarity the afternoon when eight-year-old Arden had guided her pony through the halls, up the stairs, and into her bedroom, later explaining that she intended to make him the guest of honor at a dolly tea party.

He placed the tray bearing a decanter, a siphon, and three glasses in the hands she held out to him without betraying any hint of surprise.

"The gentlemen have retired to the billiard room, Miss

18

Arden," Porter intoned, despite the fact that she was obviously aware of that.

"So it would seem, Porter."

"Shall I fetch the cigars, Miss, or will you be presenting those as well?" he asked with his usual stoicism.

Arden shook her head. "Oh, I don't think I should overdo, Porter," she told him. "You might bring along another glass when you bring the cigars." She crumpled her brow, a sign, he'd long ago realized, that indicated deep thought. "And perhaps another siphon. Papa wouldn't approve of my drinking his brandy, I think. Or any brandy for that matter. Men are strange creatures, Porter," she added with a note of seriousness that might have accompanied a discussion of the true meaning of life. "What is perfectly fine for them they consider, for some unfathomable reason, unacceptable behavior in a woman."

"Indeed, Miss," Porter agreed with a sage nod.

Arden considered for a moment the way Skyler Trask had looked at her all during dinner, the smiles they had exchanged, and then thought about the way he'd opposed her the previous afternoon in her father's offices. He was, she decided, more unfathomable than most, but a challenge nonetheless, and she was not about to shrink from a challenge.

"A small inquiry, Porter?" she asked.

"Certainly, Miss Arden, if I can."

"Do you think me capable of taming a den of lions?"

"If any young woman of my acquaintance is capable of such a feat, Miss Arden, it is certainly you."

Arden considered his expression, decided it sufficiently sincere, then smiled. She found his confidence in her settled the unpleasant feeling of uncertainty she'd felt nagging at her since she'd first met Skyler Trask.

"Thank you, Porter." She glanced at the tray. "It

19

would appear that I am adequately armed for the fray," she said. "You might open the door for me, please."

"Certainly, Miss."

He moved quickly to the heavy mahogany door that would have been, in any civilized house, the gate to an all-male precinct, pulled it open, then stepped aside to allow her to pass.

Holding the tray dramatically out before her, Arden sailed into the billiard room with the stateliness of a minister bringing the crown jewels to his monarch. She was rewarded with a bewildered glance from Skyler Trask and the knowledge that her presence was distraction enough to put him off his game. His cue met the ball slightly off center and sent it to make an unproductive foray, ricocheting off the five and the twelve and able to convince neither of them to make even a moderately convincing attempt on the far corner pocket.

"Tough luck, Trask," Forbes said, despite the fact that there seemed to be very little regret in his expression as he watched the play. He lifted a piece of chalk and applied it to the end of his stick. "Now maybe someone else can get into the game."

"I do hope I haven't broken your concentration, Mr. Trask?" Arden asked as she set the tray down on the table beside where Harry Stoning sat comfortably considering the situation.

"Not at all, Miss Devereaux," Sky told her, although he was well aware that it was not the truth. He glanced at her and found her green eyes smiling at him, telling him only too plainly that she was perfectly aware of the reason he had missed his shot.

"Your Aunt Clarissa all tucked in for the night, Arden?" Forbes asked as he leaned forward to survey the nine or ten colored balls that remained on the table. "You're down awfully quickly."

"She decided she was too tired this evening to pay

proper attention to the good words of the Reverend Trillingbee," Arden replied. "Blessedly," she added with a smile.

Forbes darted an arch glance up at her. "Arden!" he chastised, even though it was quite apparent he couldn't raise any real enthusiasm for the task.

She smiled at him sweetly. "Oh, I'm perfectly delighted there's one devoted soul in the family, Papa. I just can't understand why she insists upon trying to make it two."

"Messianic fervor," Forbes told her as he decided on a shot. "Nine ball, side pocket."

She raised a skeptical brow. "And I don't understand why I'm the target when we both know I lead a blameless life compared to your rather, shall we say, more interesting one."

"Arden!"

The exclamation came at the same instant the cue stick met the white ball, and once again Arden realized she'd been the cause of a misdirected shot.

She shrugged. "Well, I don't, Papa."

"Because you're the youngest," Forbes told her as he reluctantly stepped back from the table. "And the only one she has any hope of reforming."

Arden shook her head and turned. "Some brandy, Mr. Stoning?" she asked, already beginning to pour, well acquainted with his habits and taking his acceptance as a given. "Aren't you playing tonight?" she asked him as she handed him the snifter.

He swirled the glass and lifted it to the lamplight to watch the almost oily drops fall slowly back down the side of the glass. He always appreciated the food at Devereaux's table, and even more the offerings from the cellar.

"I've decided to leave the honor of the *Sun's* employees in far more capable hands," he told her, nodding toward Sky. He sipped the brandy, letting the first taste linger in his mouth before he swallowed, then sighed appreciatively.

Arden filled two more glasses, adding some soda to one before she handed it to her father. Stoning watched her as he had all through dinner, silently considering her. She had been thoroughly charming, and he had noticed that Sky Trask was not completely immune to her charms. He was also aware that Forbes had been watching Arden with interest equal to his own, yet for entirely different reasons.

Stoning was aware of Devereaux's determination to see his daughter married to a member of the society which had so far spurned him despite the fortune he'd made with his newspaper. He was not sure if it was a matter of spite or true desire to be accepted, but Devereaux was determined to become a member of the select group of families that ruled New York, to see Arden get for him what his money could not. He'd have thought it cruel if he had not known Forbes genuinely cared for his daughter and she for him. All of which meant that Forbes was not entirely pleased that Arden had been rather more charming than necessary with Skyler Trask, the fact of which was not lost on Sky himself.

But Sky, he thought, despite his willingness to consider Arden's more apparent attributes, had seemed on edge, waiting for mention of the proposed trip to Greece, doubtless ready to voice a half-dozen logical reasons why she and Forbes ought not to go. Stoning, who was more or less accustomed to the domestic habits of the Devereaux household, knew that nothing capable of rousing more emotion than a consideration of the weather would ever be discussed in the presence of old man Devereaux's sister Clarissa. He'd been thoroughly aware of the staid Clarissa's habits, including her rather unique method of departure.

Despite the pleasure he'd taken in the food and his consideration of the oddities of the Devereaux household, Stoning knew the best part of the evening was yet to come, and, unless he was mistaken, it had been heralded by Arden's arrival. He made himself comfortable in the wide leather chair, sitting back and leaning his head so that he might observe the whole of the scene without being forced to undue movement, and happily sipped his brandy.

This time Arden waited until Sky had made his shot before she interrupted. When he'd sunk the nine ball, she smiled at him and brought him his snifter of brandy. His fingers brushed hers as he accepted it from her. The contact left an odd tingle in her hand, and Arden found herself wondering why the room suddenly seemed warm to her.

"I've been thinking about our trip to Greece, Mr. Trask . . ." she began.

"I'd thought that not an entirely agreed-upon matter, Miss Devereaux," he replied. He sipped the brandy, his blue eyes intent on hers.

"Really?" She hoped her expression was completely innocent.

"First, I think you might consider the danger. If there is a war, people will be killed." He put down the snifter and leaned over the billiard table. The room sank into a duly reverent silence as he made his shot.

"But we're Americans, Mr. Trask. No one ever kills Americans," Arden said once he'd sunk the previously uncooperative five ball.

"May I assume you've sorely neglected the study of recent history, Miss Devereaux?" he asked. "Is it possible you've remained ignorant of the small fracas the southern states instigated over the matter of secession?"

Arden scowled, but she made no effort to speak as he made another shot, successfully disposing of the seven ball. Sky seemed to ignore her as he quickly surveyed the

23

remaining balls on the table, then, with an efficiency born of expertise and natural talent, quickly cleared them.

"I never said Americans never kill other Americans, Mr. Trask," Ardèn said when he'd done and deigned to look up at her. "Just that any war in Crete does not concern us, and therefore we stand in no danger."

"I regret to inform you, Miss Devereaux, that passports are not examined on a battlefield." He stared at her, determined to end the matter there.

"Good game, Trask," Forbes interrupted, hoping to defuse the bomb he saw about to ignite inside his daughter. "I don't suppose you'd care to give me a second go, this time without benefit of any interruptions?" He darted a warning glance at Arden.

"Why, Papa," Arden said with a saccharine smile. "I think you'd prefer I'd absent myself and leave you gentlemen to your own company."

"Certainly not, Miss Devereaux," Stoning offered before Forbes had the opportunity to agree. "There is far too little beauty in this world even to consider banishing it. Don't you agree, gentlemen?" He smiled as he beamed up at Forbes and Sky. He had no intention of being robbed of his entertainment.

"Here, here," Sky offered with a smile as he retrieved the balls and returned them to the table. It was against his better judgment, but still he was intrigued at the thought of bettering Arden, and he realized he was not yet prepared to relinquish her company.

Arden seated herself on a straight chair beside Stoning's, her head held regally, her glance clearly insisting that she was above any suggestion that her presence brought with it even the merest thought of dissension.

"I shall sit silently here beside Mr. Stoning." She offered her father a cherubic smile. "I relish the thought of your providing Mr. Trask a lesson in billiards, Papa."

She kept her word, sitting quietly and watching. This time, without her interruptions, the game was far more evenly matched. Both men were good—her father's style a trifle more studied, more intent, Sky's play a bit more daring, but both about equally skilled. And while she watched the play, Stoning watched her, marveling at the control she seemed to be exhibiting, wondering if he'd misjudged her. But as the game drew to a close and it became obvious that Sky was a shade more adept than Forbes, he noticed a look of settled determination in her green eyes and told himself that she would not disappoint him after all.

Sky cleared the last ball from the table.

"Excellent game, Trask," Forbes said, holding out his hand in congratulations.

"Yes, excellent," Arden agreed as she stood, lifted the bottle of brandy, and refilled the men's glasses. She stared up to Sky as he lifted his snifter. "It would seem that Mr. Trask has some unexpected talents."

Forbes nodded. "So it seems," he agreed with only a shade of wariness to his tone.

Arden returned the decanter to the tray, then turned to her father with her wide-eyed, innocent smile.

"I have an excellent idea, Papa," she said and waited until those words had the expected effect of making his brow wrinkle. "That is, if both you and Mr. Trask consider yourselves sporting men."

"Arden?"

"A game, Papa," she explained. "A game and a wager."

Forbes's eyes narrowed. "Just what do you have in mind, Arden?"

"A simple way to settle this matter of our going to Greece, Papa," she replied. "I'll play a game of billiards with Mr. Trask. If he wins, I promise to forgo the excursion without further argument. Should I win, on the other hand, you must agree to the trip." She paused and turned to Sky. "That is, of course, assuming Mr. Trask does not find it beneath him to pit his skills against mine."

"You play, Miss Devereaux?" Sky asked, frankly surprised.

She nodded and offered him the same innocent smile she'd given her father. "A bit," she replied. "I've prevailed upon Papa in his weaker moments to give me a lesson or two."

"Let me warn you, Trask," Forbes interposed. "She's good."

"Why, thank you, Papa," Arden exclaimed, once again all sweetness. Her eyes were sharp, however, and she kept them firmly on Sky's.

The man was not at all put off by Forbes's warning. As Stoning had told him that old man Devereaux was proud of his game, Sky had held himself back, purposely allowing an occasional shot he ought to have made somehow to elude him. He'd not played so badly as to be obvious, but he was far better than he'd so far demonstrated. He had no question that he could handily beat Arden; that would be the end of the proposed trip to Greece and he'd be free to work on his own.

He sipped his brandy, then offered Forbes a tolerant grin. "I've no objection to making a small wager with Miss Devereaux if you'd like to, sir."

Forbes shrugged. Despite his apparent opposition, he'd given the matter a good deal of thought since the previous afternoon, even gone to the trouble of having some of his more important advertisers polled. And as Stoning had suggested, they'd all accepted the idea with a good deal of enthusiasm, some even suggesting they might stock Greek and Turkish items, fabrics and rugs and pottery, and advertise them to take advantage of the interest the stories were sure to generate. Forbes had just

26

about determined that his daughter's fanciful idea might prove profitable to him, and he was not a man to ignore the possibility of profit.

Sky, however, seemed to consider the match won. He was good, Forbes thought, good enough to beat him fairly. And he was not sure that Arden's skill was quite up to the opposition. He looked at his daughter, however, and managed to stifle a smile as he brought his snifter to his lips. Arden would win, he decided; whether she had to use fair means or foul, she would win. He knew his daughter far too well to think she would allow anything or anyone to keep her from doing something she'd set her mind to do.

"Very well," he said, and handed his cue stick to Arden. "Let the games begin," he added with a smile. Then he skirted the table to settle himself beside Stoning.

Arden reached for the mahogany rack and set it on the table. "Mr. Trask," she said, nodding to him, moving past him intending to retrieve the ivory balls from the pocket at the far end of the table.

"Allow me, Miss Devereaux," he said.

Arden glanced up at her father and Stoning as Sky returned the balls to the table. She smiled and returned Stoning's wink.

Arden decided to take no chances. From the very start she took advantage of the fact that she could disturb Sky's concentration. She allowed herself to brush his arm lightly as she moved by, turned to stare up at him a moment as she leaned forward over the table before she made a shot, and even moved close enough to him when he leaned forward to shoot so that he could not avoid the scent of her perfume or the warmth of her body.

Part of her regretted this behavior, and she could not ignore the voice inside her that told her she was far better

27

than that, that she was above playing such foolish games to get something she wanted from a man. But the voice was answered by another, one equally strong, that countered by telling her he deserved whatever she gave him, that his arrogant assurance that he could better her warranted her using every weapon she had in her arsenal.

Still, despite the fact that Sky was far from immune to her, it was a decidedly close game. When only three balls remained on the table, he led by two. Arden cursed herself for having missed her shot and scanned the nearly completely open table. He would clear it easily, she decided, unless she found some way to stop him.

"It would seem you are about to dash my hopes, Mr. Trask," she said as she backed away from the table and watched him chalk his cue.

"I regret being forced to disappoint a lady, Miss Devereaux," he replied and grinned at her, "but you leave me with the advantage. Perhaps you will find some comfort in the knowledge that some disappointments are purported to be beneficial in life as a means of bolstering character." He raised a brow, and his glance had a touch of superior mocking about it. "And this was, after all, your idea."

Arden felt an angry flush rise in her cheek. He's been letting me keep up with him, she thought, seeing the truth now in his eyes, suddenly realizing that he had been playing with her when she thought it was she who was playing with him. And then she realized that he had been playing with her father as well, allowing Forbes to keep that game, too, fairly close when he could have easily won it. Skyler Trask, she realized, was far more complicated than he presented himself to be. She was not at all sure she liked that.

She forced herself to smile.

"I shall have to content myself with the reports you send back to the paper, Mr. Trask," she told him, her tone light as she watched him lean forward. She waited until he'd positioned the cue, until his expression told her he was concentrating and ready to make his shot. "Of course," she went on, "you will have much to relate to the *Sun*'s readers. I believe it was Catullus who claimed Cretan hetaerae were the most accomplished in all the civilized world. You will have to give us your doubtless expert opinion."

"Arden!"

Forbes, it seemed, was duly shocked with her.

A thick, sputtering sound came from Harry Stoning's throat, suggesting that he had nearly choked on his brandy.

Sky could not stifle the gasp of laughter that erupted from him, nor could he keep himself from missing the shot that had seemed impossible for him not to make.

Arden smiled sweetly at Sky as he straightened up and turned to her.

"Touché, Miss Devereaux," he laughed.

"Oh, dear," Arden murmured. "I haven't said anything to distract you, have I, Mr. Trask?"

Sky shook his head. "Certainly not." He motioned to the table. "It would seem you have been granted a last chance."

Stifling the satisfaction she felt, Arden leaned to the table, and quickly cleared all but one remaining ball.

"It seems I may win after all," she told Sky with a smug smile.

"So it would appear," he replied, not all that pleased about the prospect. He glanced at Forbes for a moment, then back at Arden as she leaned forward to make the last shot. A shame, he thought, matters could not have been arranged differently. "Of course, I'll probably still have the responsibility of reporting to the *Sun's* readers about the value of this person Catlus's claim."

Arden was just barely able to keep the stick quiet in her

hand. He's trying to do to me what I did to him, she thought. She turned and looked at him.

"Catullus, Mr. Trask. Gaius Valerius Catullus. A Roman lyric poet. I'm afraid your classical education is as lax as is mine of modern history." With that, she again leaned forward to her stick and sank the last ball.

"Bravo!"

Harry Stoning's exclamation seemed to have escaped his lips unintended. He colored, then pushed himself out of his chair.

Forbes, too, rose. He had known Arden would somehow manage to win. He wasn't at all sure he approved of her method, but still he was proud of her. She was, after all, his daughter.

"It seems we will soon be traveling companions, Trask," Forbes said, then emptied his snifter. He put the glass down and started for the door.

"Excellent game, my dear," Stoning said, smiling as he grasped her hand. He managed to collect himself when he saw the less than friendly look Sky directed at him, decided retreat was in order, and followed after Forbes.

"You surprise me, Miss Devereaux," Sky said as he took the cue from Arden's hand and put it and his own in the two empty places in the mahogany rack.

"Really, Mr. Trask?" she asked. "I should think you the sort of man who would be very hard to surprise."

He turned back to face her. "It would seem you are far more adept at games than appearances would indicate," he replied.

She shrugged. "Oh, just a bit of luck, I think."

He shook his head. "No, no luck was involved." He stared at her, letting his eyes find hers and hold them for a long moment. "I think you like games," he continued slowly. "And I think you like winning."

She cocked her head. "Perhaps I do," she agreed. "Is there something wrong with that?"

30

"The problem with that, my dear Arden," he began, then paused for a second. "I may call you Arden, now that we're about to become traveling companions?"

She nodded, suddenly wondering what it was about his expression that had changed. It seemed a good deal less benign than it had until that moment.

"Good," he went on. "The trouble, as I was saying, is that when you play games and don't play by the rules, Arden, it encourages your opponent to do the same." He put his hands on her shoulders. "And that, you see, sometimes becomes a bit more dangerous than you may expect. You may find yourself playing games you weren't quite expecting to play."

With that he pulled her to him, wrapping his arms around her and pressing his lips against hers with a sudden rough movement that took her by surprise. If she'd had time to consider the act, she would certainly have made some movement to protest, to push herself away from him. But as it was, one moment she was standing there facing him, and the next she was locked in his arms, his lips warm and sure against hers.

The air in the room seemed unaccountably close. She felt herself grow dizzy with the heat, yet the feeling was surprisingly pleasant. And more surprising still, she realized she had absolutely no intention of trying to pull away from him.

She'd spent a good deal of that afternoon thinking about him, thinking about how different he seemed from the other men who worked for her father's paper, even wondering what it would be like if he were to suggest a short walk on the veranda come the next Christmas party. She'd even gone so far as to decide that she might let him kiss her were the situation to arise. But those thoughts had been merely idle musings. This, she realized, was an unsettling reality.

Not that it was unpleasant, she decided. His arms held

31

her close, without any apparent thought that she might prefer her freedom, and his lips tasted of the brandy he'd drunk, slightly sweet and heady. There was something strange about their knowing contact, however, something that ignited thick, hot rivulets like molten honey in her veins. She considered the sensation for a moment, decided it was far from unpleasant, then gave herself up to it, letting it sweep through her and fill her. She let herself melt against him, let the unexpected and strangely narcotic feeling drift through her body.

Sky had expected to take her by surprise, had even expected to stifle her protest as a way of showing her that she was not quite as masterful as she had obviously thought when she'd managed to steal the game of billiards from him. But things were not quite as he had expected them—not the sharp reaction he had to the feel of her body close to his, and certainly not her kissing him back.

He lifted his lips from hers with decided reluctance.

Arden stared up at him and tried to ignore the sudden thumping beat that had sprung up inside her.

"Why did you do that?"

He was as surprised with her question as he had been with her response to his kiss.

He shrugged. "Because I wanted to," he said simply.

"And do you always take what you want, even if it isn't offered to you?"

His lips formed a sly grin. "Only if I've earned it," he told her.

Arden saw his amusement and realized he was playing with her again, just as he had been when he'd let her challenge him at billiards. She'd managed to outwit him then, she realized, but he would not let himself fail so easily a second time. And he had been right when he'd told her there was danger in playing games with opponents who did not play by the rules. This was one game, she told herself, at which he obviously had a great deal more experience than she did, a game she stood no chance of winning.

"It's stealing, nonetheless," she told him, her tone sharp now, and filled with an anger that confused her. She was not quite sure why she felt it.

Her anger seemed only to amuse him. He pulled her close to him once again, and when she raised her hands to push him away, he simply caught them in his own, pushed them to her back, and held them there.

"Release me this instant," she hissed at him.

Again, the sly smile.

"I think not, Arden," he told her. "I haven't quite collected payment for all I've earned this evening."

She squirmed, but he pulled her tighter until she finally quieted. Then he lowered his lips to hers once again, and this time kissed her slowly, the pressure of his lips taunting as he recognized her growing anger. But he released her when he realized that this time she was not melting, not acquiescing. Somehow the game had lost its savor for him.

He let his hands fall away from hers, half expecting her to flee from him. She didn't. Instead, she stood facing him, her green eyes glaring.

"You are no gentleman, Mr. Trask."

The condemnation in her voice had absolutely no effect on him.

"I quite agree with you, Arden," he said. "You would be wise to keep your distance from me, perhaps even decline the sojourn to Greece." His smile turned smugly superior. "I warned you, I think, about playing games. Like you, I like to win."

Her eyes narrowed and she took a step back, away from him. "I think one of us is about to be disappointed, Mr. Trask. I don't intend it to be me."

He reached out for her again, but this time she moved

out of his grasp before he could touch her.

"Is something wrong, Arden?"

She looked up to find her father standing in the door-way. His expression was one of thoughtful displeasure as he considered the two of them. She realized he did not approve of her being alone with Sky.

She forced herself to smile.

"Of course not, Papa," she replied. "Mr. Trask and I were simply discussing the finer points of the game."

With that she darted a sharp glance at Sky, then swept past him to the door.

Chapter Two

Forbes Devereaux had the pleased and complacent attitude of a man at peace with his world. He drained his glass of champagne with a sense of contentment that he rarely had the opportunity to experience and watched his daughter sweep across the dance floor of the White Star Passenger Line ship *Arcadia* on the arm of a young man who gave every indication of being completely besotted with her.

"Quite a coincidence, don't you think, Trask?" Forbes asked as a waiter hurriedly refilled his glass. "Who'd ever have thought this little excursion Arden insisted we take would lead to an acquaintance with one of the Boston Trumbulls?"

Sky made a noncommittal grunt in reply, then buried his lack of enthusiasm in his own glass. He was a good deal less impressed than Forbes with David Trumbull and the Boston Trumbulls—or any other Trumbulls, for that matter. He was, as a matter of fact, uncategorically bored with the Trumbull in question, with his clipped Beacon Hill accent, his perfectly tailored yet understated clothing, and his way of looking at people, Sky in particular, in a manner that indicated he was staring at something vaguely distasteful. But most of all, Sky had had his fill of

Trumbull's stories about his great grandmother's girlhood friendship with Abigail Smith and conjectures about what might have been if dear old great granny hadn't passed over a beau named John Adams, practically depositing the gentleman in question into Abigail's waiting arms, rather than keeping him for herself, thereby making her great-grandson the descendent of the second President of the United States.

Now that he took the time to think about it, Sky decided it was first class passage in general that bored him, not just the aforementioned Trumbull. He was on edge around people who seemed to find the need to mention their lineage in almost every conversation, and he highly resented the necessity to dress formally each evening before he was allowed his dinner. It was as close to torture as he could ever remember having been, and he was thoroughly tired of enduring it with smiling good grace, almost as tired as he was of hearing Forbes Devereaux constantly pointing out to him how lucky he was to be granted this luxury by his employer's largesse. He would have much preferred the less stilted company of the lower class dining room below, which he could have enjoyed without the encumbering necessity of evening clothes.

"Excuse me?" Forbes leaned forward to Sky and smiled at him with strained patience.

Sky cleared his throat, gathering the necessary forces to expand upon the grunt and provide Forbes with the agreeing words he seemed at that moment to require. Not for the first time since the *Arcadia* had sailed he regretted his own greed. If he had stayed with the *Tribune*, he might have been a good deal poorer, but he would certainly have been substantially happier than he was at that moment.

"I said, yes, it was a coincidence," Sky replied. He quickly swallowed the remaining whisky in his glass, then gave it an accusing look for daring to be empty.

Forbes's expression grew a bit unfocused. "You can't understand, of course, but having a daughter like Arden is not always an easy thing."

"Oh, I certainly do understand," Sky muttered as he caught a glimpse of Arden on the dance floor.

"Hmm?" Forbes returned his attention to Sky's bemused expression.

"I said, I think I understand."

Forbes waved his hand, dismissing Sky's words. "You look at her and see a beautiful young woman, which she certainly is, but I see much more, my boy," Forbes told him in a fit of champagne-induced camaraderie. "She's strong-headed and stubborn, just like her mother was. Not that that's all bad, mind you. And not that a man can't learn to deal with that sort of thing. I've been dealing with peculiar women all my life. Now my mother, there was a peculiar woman, until the day she died a spectacularly peculiar woman. Made my sister Clarissa seem almost normal by comparison. But Arden, she's something different—never quite know what she'll get up to from one minute to the next." His eyes narrowed. "Doesn't understand what's good for her and what's not."

"Like Mr. David Trumbull of the Boston Trumbulls?" Sky asked with a humorless smile.

"Precisely," Forbes said, nodding vigorously.

For an instant Forbes almost admitted that until David Trumbull had appeared, he'd had an uncomfortable feeling about the way his daughter acted when she was around Sky, but his better sense took hold of his tongue and modified the effects the quantity of champagne he'd drunk seemed to have had on it. He was feeling decidedly warmhearted toward Sky at that moment, and he saw no reason to disturb what he considered to be their flowering friendship.

Instead, he just smiled, and added, "David Trumbull would make an excellent husband for Arden. And from the way he's acted the last few days, I've a feeling that he's beginning to think the same way."

Sky nodded. There was something about this conversation that made him uncomfortable, like an itch in the center of his back that he couldn't quite reach. He told himself that it was simply the fact that he was not altogether comfortable with the unlikely spurt of friendship Forbes was showing him, but if he'd been honest with himself he'd have admitted that it was the current topic of conversation that made him uneasy.

"Yes, he does seem to hang around her with that lost puppy look in his eyes," he agreed.

Forbes seemed oblivious to the note of sarcasm in Sky's tone as well as the look of dislike that settled over his features as he turned to consider the look in question as its bearer began to escort Arden from the dance floor.

"Precisely," Forbes agreed. "I wouldn't be surprised if everything was settled before we reached Greece."

"But you're forgetting the fine Mr. Trumbull's commitment to that archaeologist on Crete." Sky took a certain amount of pleasure in the perturbed look his words roused in Forbes. "You forget, this particular Trumbull insists that he has determined to dedicate his life to scholarship."

"A temporary aberration, I'm sure," Forbes insisted. "Men with the sort of resources Trumbull's family can provide have no need to dedicate their lives to anything." He grew suddenly thoughtful. "Although I suppose having an interest can't be entirely detrimental to a man."

"Definitely not," Sky agreed with a smug smile. "Keeps a man from being a philanderer. Wouldn't want to marry your daughter off to a philanderer, even if he is the scion of one of the first families of Boston."

Forbes considered Sky's expression, not quite sure if what he saw in it was irony or merely attentive involvement. "Certainly," he said, pronouncing the word very slowly.

"Certainly what, Papa?" Arden demanded as she and David Trumbull joined them.

Her cheeks were slightly flushed, a most becoming shade of pink, Sky thought as he wondered what had caused the color—the heat of the room, the champagne she'd drunk with her dinner, or perhaps the presence of the estimable Trumbull's gallant display at the waltz.

"Your father and I were just discussing philanderers."

Sky let his gaze drift to Trumbull's face and was rewarded by the look of distaste he had come to expect to find there, only this time a bit sharper than usual, due, no doubt, to what any full-fledged member of Boston society could only consider the vulgarity of his last word.

Arden smiled prettily at him, thoroughly aware that he was trying to bait Trumbull.

"What a strange topic for conversation," she pronounced. "I do think you ought to take a bit of exercise. It's this lazing about on deck in the afternoon staring at all that water that doubtless affects the thought processes. Don't you agree, David?"

Trumbull nodded enthusiastically.

"I believe I've suggested much the same thing to Mr. Trask once or twice," he said. "Exercise cleanses the mind and strengthens the body."

Sky grinned at Trumbull. "I suppose that means I'll be forced to challenge you to a game of shuffleboard tomorrow? Perhaps we could make the game a bit more interesting by the addition of a small wager?"

"I don't believe in wagering," Trumbull replied with what Sky took to be his best version of a withering glance.

"Now why doesn't that surprise me?" Sky asked. He turned his attention back to Arden. "It occurs to me you

39

may be right about the exercise, though, Arden," he said. "Perhaps a dance would cleanse my rather musty mind?"

Arden laughed and took the arm he offered her.

They had been dancing in silence for several minutes. Arden had had ample time to decide that she quite enjoyed the way Sky's arms felt around her, despite the fact that both her father and David Trumbull were glaring at them, openly disapproving of how closely he held her. She darted a glance at David, then turned quickly away, at that moment entirely disinterested in his opinions. She decided a bit of stewing might be good for him.

"Just what is it that you see in him?"

She looked up, startled for some reason at Sky's sudden impulse to speech.

"I'm sorry?"

"I asked you what you saw in that fatuous Boston snob," he told her.

"Do you really think he's fatuous?" she asked him thoughtfully. "A Boston snob, certainly, and possibly— no, decidedly arrogant and self centered. But I'm not quite sure about fatuous."

He almost grinned. "All right, I'll accept arrogant and self centered in lieu of fatuous. That doesn't answer my question."

"Why, Sky," Arden breathed slowly and with obvious relish. "I do believe you're jealous!"

Her tone nettled him, all the moreso as it occurred to him that she might be right. He shook his head.

"Just bewildered," he told her firmly.

"I don't believe you."

He shrugged. "Suit yourself. But if jealousy *had* been my motive, I might have revealed to the fine, upstanding, and I might add, decidedly straight-laced Mr. Trumbull

40

something about you that might set him off the scent and leave the path clear for my own amorous advances. You will note I have not done that."

She shook her head, unperturbed at the suggestion. "Aren't you sly?" she asked. "I'm afraid this smells faintly of blackmail, Mr. Trask."

"I suppose it does, Miss Devereaux," he agreed. "Although we both know that, like Caesar's wife, I'm above reproach."

"In certain circles, perhaps," he agreed.

"But not Boston?" she asked, intrigued now.

He nodded. "Not Trumbull's Boston, at least."

She grew silent, wondering what he might consider a lack in her character. After a moment's concentration, she decided he really was not privy to any of her truly weaker moments.

"No," she pronounced finally. "I've taken into consideration the worst of my past and decided you know nothing of those character traits that could be thought anything less than sterling."

He grinned. "I think you've forgotten your penchant for wagers, Arden. I wonder what our good Mr. Trumbull would think of that?"

She gave him a bemused look. "Wagers?" she asked.

"I'm afraid the more recent history, the weaker your recall, Arden," he told her, reminding her of his criticism of her that evening at her father's house. "You haven't forgotten the little wager that provided you with the very opportunity you now find yourself enjoying, have you? Surely the good Mr. Trumbull would frown on a woman indulging in so unladylike a sport as billiards. I daresay that would raise a few brows in Boston. Not to mention the wager."

Arden smiled up at him seraphically. "Tell David," she replied. "I shall merely suggest that you have a tendency to untruths. I'm sure he'll accept that explanation as he

41

already considers you contemptible."

"Really?" Sky asked as he considered her pleased expression. "I'd not have thought him that perceptive." He seemed to find the possibility amusing.

"Just one more of many things of which you seem to be totally ignorant, Mr. Trask."

"I'll accept your judgment. But this tendency of yours to unladylike conduct bothers me, Arden," he added, and the look he gave her grew suddenly sober. "It would seem you've just suggested compounding your sin of gambling by adding a lie. What would the good Trumbull think of that?"

"I find myself agreeing with David's evaluation," she replied. "You *are* contemptible."

Despite her words, there was absolutely no hint of rancor in her tone or expression. She was quite enjoying Sky's company, she told herself. Talk with David was a much more complicated matter. With him she needed to weigh every word. With Sky she found she could say whatever came to mind . . . although she was not really sure why she insisted on taunting him. She wondered if he really might be jealous of the attention she showed David, and even more why that possibility seemed to please her.

"Decidedly." He grinned. "You still haven't answered my question. What do you see in him?"

"Papa likes him," she replied after a moment's thought, not really able to give him any better answer now that she seriously considered the question.

"I'd thought you too independent to marry someone like Trumbull just to satisfy your father's desire to buy his way into society."

Arden stopped dancing. A sudden anger began to well up inside her. Despite the little cat-and-mouse game they had been playing, he really hadn't said anything to her that was seriously offensive until that moment. But he

42

had no right to say such things about her father. No right at all.

She tried to pull herself from his arms.

"Your opinions are of absolutely no interest to me, Mr. Trask."

He saw her anger even though he did not understand the cause. Still, he refused to release her. For some reason not entirely clear to him he wanted her to see just what it was she was doing.

"Simply an observation, Miss Devereaux," he told her.

He pulled her firmly back into his arms and once again began to move with the music. Arden found she had the choice of either following him or making a scene.

She followed.

They finished the dance in a strained silence. When it ended, Sky escorted her back to where Forbes and Trumbull waited.

"A great pleasure, Miss Devereaux," he said, bowing to her with mock gallantry as he placed her hand on her father's arm. He could feel her anger with him, welling out at him, pushing him away. It left him feeling slightly numb. "But now, if you will excuse me, I've an appointment with a deck of cards in the Gentlemen's Lounge." He grinned at Trumbull. "I'd invite you to come along, Trumbull, but I know your attitude about gambling." He nodded to Forbes and then Arden. "Mr. Devereaux. Miss Devereaux."

Arden bristled at the hidden amusement she heard in his tone as he spoke to David, as his eyes found hers when he made his reference to gambling. But despite the urge she felt to offer him some scathing word or another, she found she had none readily accessible.

"Good evening, Mr. Trask," she muttered, managing to control her anger and feeling entirely dissatisfied with her suddenly diminished verbal powers.

Despite the fact that Trumbull was watching her expectantly, waiting for her to turn her attention to him, she found herself staring at Sky as he made his way from the room.

Sky stared at the pile of chips heaped onto the green baize of the card table in front of him. He could only scarcely remember the string of hands that led to his winning that mass of money, and he was completely bewildered with his suddenly unshakable good luck.

"Well, Trask, are you in or not?"

Sky looked up to find the five other men sitting at the table with him staring pointedly and waiting for him to make his bet. He tossed his chips into the small pile in the center of the table without even looking at the hand of cards that had just been dealt him.

"That shows a bit of unnecessary arrogance, don't you think, Trask?" one of the others asked. "You might at least look at the cards before you decide you've won."

Sky's lips turned up in wry amusement. "It seems I can't lose this evening, even if I want to." He gathered up the cards and looked at them.

The other man laughed. "So it does. Well, I'm content. You know what they say, unlucky in cards, lucky in love. I consider it a fair enough trade."

He was a big man, tall and well built, sporting a thick gray beard and absolutely no other hair on the whole of his head. His unbuttoned jacket revealed a large expanse of a wine-colored silk vest and a good deal more of pristine white linen. Sky laughed as the others did at his comment. It was obvious that no one considered him much of a ladies' man.

"In that case, that young Trumbull fellow must be the most unlucky card player on board," one of the others said when the laughter had subsided. He threw a half dozen

44

chips on the pile. "I'm in." He pursed his lips as he considered his hand. "Perhaps we should be playing with him, not Trask here. We could all make a killing."

"From what I've seen, he's about to win a prize catch," another agreed. "Fold." He dropped his cards to the table. "I must say, I find Miss Arden Devereaux an absolutely ravishing young woman. I'd be willing to lose a fortune at cards if I knew I would enjoy the wedding night Trumbull has to look forward to."

There was a murmur of general agreement and a bit of slightly lecherous laughter.

"You're an associate of her father's, aren't you, Trask?"

Sky found himself feeling the same uncomfortable itch he couldn't quite reach that he'd felt when he'd been talking with Forbes. This time it carried along with it a wave of anger that he couldn't understand any better than the feeling. He knew only that he heartily disliked listening to these men talk about Arden in this way.

"Not quite an associate," he replied. "I work for Forbes Devereaux, providing his paper with lurid stories of murders and battlefield deaths, and he, in exchange, provides me with the means to indulge my own more bestial appetites." He lifted a handful of the chips he'd won and let them fall through his fingers back to the heap in front of him. "An effort you gentlemen have very kindly improved upon."

Sky watched the faces of the men seated around the table grow suddenly remote with distaste. He realized he had spoken quite purposefully in a manner they would consider coarse, and he wondered why he had willfully alienated them. He knew the amount he had won from them, fortune though it might seem to him, was little more than pocket change for them, and their losses were of no concern to them. Apart from the fact that they happily gambled with him, providing him not only with

45

entertainment but with a substantial enlargement of his purse, they were the least stuffy of his traveling companions. He fleetingly wondered if he was unconsciously providing himself with the necessity of finding his company amongst the lower classes, a not unappealing thought.

There was a moment of uncomfortable silence followed by the sound of uncertain laughter.

"It's getting late, I think," one of the card players said as he pointedly removed his watch from his vest pocket and stared at it. "After midnight."

"Really?" another asked as he pushed his chair back from the table. "I'd no idea. Time to turn in."

One by one the men dropped their cards onto the table.

"You don't want to finish the last hand?" Sky asked, thoroughly aware that they'd all refuse.

"Not much need, Trask. We all know you'll win. Perhaps we'll play again."

There was a quick reckoning, losses paid, mostly to Sky, and then they stood, made a few more remotely polite remarks as they pocketed their own winnings, and left. Sky surveyed the heap on the table in front of him told himself that he was glad to be alone.

As he gathered together the stack of bills, he forced himself to consider just why it was that the discussion of the possibility of a pairing between David Trumbull and Arden had so disconcerted him, why the references to their wedding night had angered him enough to push him to offend his fellow gamblers. His first reaction was to tell himself that Trumbull simply annoyed him, that the man's arrogant manner was enough to make Sky consider him unworthy of any prize, let alone Arden Devereaux. Not that he had even the slightest interest in her himself, he told himself firmly. It was just that Trumbull was far too great a fool to be granted all life had already given him. He surely didn't deserve anything more.

46

Sky wandered over to the bar and ordered himself a brandy, then took the snifter with him, leaving the lounge for the comforting darkness of the deck. He stood leaning on the rail, staring off into an unbelievably dark, star-bedecked sky and listening to the sounds the waves made against the *Arcadia's* hull. He sipped his brandy and thought.

What he thought about, much to his own consternation, was Arden. He thought about the way she'd felt in his arms when they'd danced, remembered the oddly potent reaction his body had had to her when he'd pulled her close to him and kissed her that evening after their strange game of billiards. He smiled as he remembered that, telling himself that whatever she might be, she certainly wasn't boring. That, he realized, was a good deal more than he could say for most of the women he'd known.

And he'd known a good many women in his life. His career had given him the opportunity to make the acquaintance of actresses and shop girls and even an occasional whore. Over the years his looks and the agreeable manner he could manage when he found reason to had helped him make more than his fair share of conquests. But the memory of those conquests somehow seemed indistinct to him then, face blurring into face until he realized he couldn't remember even one of them with any great clarity. By contrast, he realized, Arden remained stolidly unique, her image unalterably clear in his mind.

He found his thoughts suddenly disturbing, not at all the sort of thoughts that would leave him ready to find a restful night's sleep. He swore under his breath, raised the snifter to his lips, and drained it.

Arden Devereaux was the last thing he needed, he told himself with a vehemence that seemed entirely out of proportion to the relatively remote relationship they shared. She was a woman whose interests lay, like her father's, in finding a place in the "right" sort of society. He scowled. He was, as he would be the first to admit, certainly not the "right" sort, not any sort of society at all. She was the last thing he needed, and he was the last thing she wanted. The subject ought to end there.

"And it does," he muttered angrily.

But it didn't and he knew it. He found himself thinking about the way she'd felt when he'd held her in his arms, the way she'd looked when she'd stared up at him, the way her lips had tasted when he'd kissed her. Although it pained him to admit it, he had been thinking of those things since that evening in her father's house. And the uncomfortable feeling he got at the talk of her marrying David Trumbull could have only been caused by the fact that he was not satisfied to let her slip away from him without at least determining that the taste he'd had of her hadn't been some aberration, or one wildly enhanced by his imagination.

He pushed himself away from the rail, deciding that what he needed was a comfortable bed made acceptable by another brandy. He grinned inwardly. An accommodating female to share it with might not be unpleasant either. But the chances of finding that particular comfort in the middle of the Atlantic Ocean were rather dim, and he decided he'd have to do with mere alcohol.

"I really should retire now, David. It's gotten quite late, I think."

"A last toast, Arden?" he suggested.

Before she could reject his offer, he turned to fill their glasses from the bottle of champagne he'd had a steward leave on the table near where they stood by the rail. The night was pleasantly balmy, the sky a deep, endless black, punctuated by innumerable bright stars and a round disk of moon that begged, or at least so it seemed to him, to overlook something momentous.

A perfect night to make a proposal of marriage, he decided after a quick glance at Arden.

He returned to where she stood staring out at the reflection of moonlight on the water and handed her one of the two glasses he carried.

"To us," he said, his eyes finding hers as he raised his glass. "To us, and to wonderful beginnings."

Arden had an uncomfortable feeling as she hastily murmured the reply. "To us," she said and wondered why that particular toast left her feeling so unsettled. She raised the glass to her lips and sipped the wine.

It was entirely obvious to her what David was about to say to her. His intentions were written on his face. He was going to ask her to marry him, and instead of being delighted at the prospect, as she ought to be, she was feeling uncomfortable and uncertain.

This is all Sky Trask's fault, she thought, turning away from David and pretending to stare out at the reflection of the moon on the waves. If he hadn't said those stupid things earlier, if he hadn't accused her father of using her to further his social ambitions, she would be perfectly happy now. But his words seemed to haunt her, forcing her to consider her intentions in a way she never had before.

David was certainly good looking enough, she told herself—tall, and blond, with regular if not spectacularly handsome features. In fact, if she were to characterize him, she would undoubtedly call him distinguished looking, with an attractiveness that would only grow as the years passed. And he was well educated and from a rich and respected family, all of which meant that he was ideal material for a husband. What more could she want?

She darted a glance at him. If she was delighted at the prospect of becoming Mrs. David Trumbull, why

49

couldn't she turn back to face him? Why was the prospect of staring into his eyes so frightening to her at that moment?

She forced herself to smile up at him and then, to cover the confusion she was afraid she might show, she once again lifted the glass to her lips and this time drained it. Almost instantly the alcohol had an effect, no doubt intensified by the number of glasses she'd consumed in a more moderate fashion earlier.

David smiled as though he took her gesture to be enthusiasm for the toast and quickly followed suit, emptying his glass, then taking hers and setting the two of them down on the table alongside the now empty bottle.

"It's been a lovely evening, hasn't it?" she asked, her words sounding brittle and too quickly spoken, even to her own ears. This isn't like me, she thought. She was never this uncertain, never felt this awkward. She realized she was used to feeling comfortable around men, used to expecting them to be the ones who were unsettled in their attempts to please her.

"Wonderful," he told her as he turned back to face her. "I can't remember having enjoyed one more."

Arden was aware that he was putting his hand to her wrist and drawing her to him. Still, the exercise seemed strangely remote to her, as though it were happening to someone else while she stood by and watched. She had to force herself to concentrate, to keep her mind on him as he kissed her.

She closed her eyes, let him press his lips to hers, and told herself that surely his kiss would chase away all the confusion. She waited for the contact to produce some sort of reaction deep within her, the reaction she remembered having felt when Sky had kissed her that evening in her father's house. She searched desperately within

50

herself, longing to feel the heated rush, the sweet liquid fire inside her.

And then she found herself wondering why she seemed to feel nothing at all. The realization bewildered her. Surely, she told herself, all other things being equal, one man's kiss could not be so terribly different from that of any other. And, she insisted, all things were equal, better than equal. David was certainly as attractive as Skyler Trask, more so, and he intended his kiss to be a prelude to a proposal of marriage, not a lesson in his own superiority, as Sky had intended his. Surely his kiss ought to leave her breathless and trembling.

Yet the only change she felt within was a slight muddling, induced, she was sure, by the quickly consumed glass of champagne. It appalled her to think that David's kiss roused absolutely no response within her.

"Ahem."

Arden opened her eyes as David released her. The two of them turned to find Sky standing not fifteen feet from them, staring at the two of them with the sort of amused look that told Arden he had been there more than long enough to watch the rather passionless exchange between her and David.

David's expression, unlike Sky's, showed absolutely no humor. He stared at Sky with a look that said that given the chance, he would only too gladly shed Sky's blood.

Chapter Three

"I hope I'm not interrupting anything?" Sky asked blandly as he moved forward along the dim deck toward them. After a quick glance at David, he pointedly ignored him, turning instead to Arden.

"Of course not," she assured him promptly.

Arden realized with more than a little surprise that she was glad to see him. If nothing else, his presence at least allowed her to avoid the necessity of facing David's proposal, something she realized she was at that moment entirely unprepared to do. She supposed she ought to resent his sudden appearance as David so obviously did, but she realized she greeted it with more than a little relief.

David, however, was less willing to forgive the interruption. "Have the cards ruined you, Trask?" he asked, his tone more than a shade perturbed.

Arden could see the edge of Sky's lips twitch, and she knew he was amused by David's tone. She felt a twinge of regret at her own betrayal as she realized she felt the same way.

"Actually, they've been quite kind to me this evening," Sky replied. "It's nights like this that tempt a man to leave respectability and follow after Lady Luck."

"Billiards, cards," Arden told him with a sharp smile. "Is there no end to your dubious talents, Mr. Trask?"

"It would seem there is not, Miss Devereaux," he replied.

"Then you're just out for a late evening stroll, I take it?" David said, not at all liking the way Sky, for the second time that evening, was stealing attention that he felt ought to be entirely his.

"Wrong again," Sky answered. He darted a glance at David, grimaced slightly, then returned his stare to Arden. "Your father asked me to bring him a brandy out here." He held out the snifter of brandy he'd brought from the bar as though to verify his words, then glanced around the deck, apparently searching for the missing Forbes. "He hasn't been here and left, has he? I had the feeling he might have been just the least bit uncertain. I think he might have already had one or two before I happened along."

He turned his glance to the snifter and stared at it with an admonishing look, apparently bemoaning the depths to which such an apparently innocent liquid might plunge even the strongest and noblest of men. He put the glass down on the table beside the empty champagne bottle, giving it a final condemning look of distaste.

Arden's reaction to his words was immediate and sharp. Forbes had a considerable capacity for alcohol. She had never once seen him drink enough to make him appear even the least bit unsteady. She shook her head and looked around the deck.

"No. No, he hasn't been here."

Sky regretted the story as soon as he saw her troubled expression. "Perhaps he was here before you arrived?" he ventured.

"No," she told him. "We've been here for some time." She started to move forward to a less well-lit portion of the deck. "I wonder if he might not be unwell?"

Both David and Sky followed after her.

"I'm sure he's fine," David assured her, more than ready to dismiss the interruption. He reached for her arm but was not quite able to grasp it as she turned away, totally unaware of him with her preoccupation that Forbes might be ill.

"Perhaps Miss Devereaux and I ought to locate him and make sure he finds his way to his stateroom," Sky suggested, seeing an opportunity to turn the situation to his advantage.

"Oh, yes, thank you, Sky," Arden murmured as she started forward towards the aft deck.

David was less than enthusiastic for the exercise. This was not at all the way he saw the evening ending, and he had to force himself to swallow his disappointment. Added to that was the unpleasant prospect of finding Forbes Devereaux well into his cups, something not the least appealing to him.

"Well, I'll come along with you," he said without much enthusiasm.

"No need to bother, Trumbull," Sky told him. "I'm sure Miss Devereaux and I can handle the matter easily. Besides," he added, leaning close to David and lowering his voice so Arden couldn't hear, "we wouldn't want to embarrass the old man unnecessarily by causing a row searching for him. He probably took one too many and will feel bad enough in the morning as it is."

"I suppose you're right," David replied reluctantly, but showing signs of relief that he would not be forced to impose upon one of Forbes Devereaux's less than laudatory moments. He told himself that after they were married Arden would find little time to spend in New York in her father's company. He would see to that.

"Well then, I'll wish you good evening, Arden," he said, his voice raised now, loud enough to cause her to stop and turn to face him.

"Yes, of course, David," she said, and offered him a weak smile. Her thoughts were on her father, and she had nearly forgotten David was still there.

He moved to her, took her hand, and held it between his own. "Until tomorrow, Arden," he said softly.

"Yes, certainly, David," she replied.

He tried to hold her eyes with his but quickly realized the effort was useless. She was darting her glance around the deck, peering into the shadows. He released her hand and turned to Sky.

"Trask," he muttered, then shrugged and started off, moving briskly along the dimly lit deck.

"Do you think he might have gone back to the Gentlemen's Lounge?" Arden asked Sky. "Perhaps you might go back there while I search out here."

Sky darted a quick glance to where David was just disappearing into an interior corridor, then put his hand to Arden's arm and smiled.

"I really don't think that will be necessary, Arden," he told her. He found himself itching to grin and couldn't quite control it. He decided it wasn't worth the effort of fighting the inclination and allowed himself a broad grin as he turned back to face her.

"I hardly think this is amusing, Sky," Arden snapped at him. "Papa does not drink too much, not ever. I'm worried about him. Perhaps he's ill. We *have* to find him."

"There's no need to worry," he said. "Actually, I've a good idea where he might be."

"Where?" she demanded, exasperated now and bewildered by his apparent amusement.

"Tucked up in his bed, I should think, all safe and sound," he said.

"But you said . . ."

"I lied," he told her with a shrug, apparently completely unconcerned with the gravity of that particular sin.

"But, but why?" she demanded as she tried to back away from him.

He tightened his hold on her arm, then slowly began to draw her close to him.

"Because when I happened upon you and our friend Trumbull, it occurred to me that he was incapable of doing both you and this beautiful night justice, Arden," he told her.

"And just what is *that* supposed to mean?" she demanded.

"It means this," he told her as he wrapped his arms around her, pulled her close to him, and pressed his lips to hers.

For a moment she struggled with him, pushing against his chest with her hands, angry with him for the games he chose to play with her. But even as he pulled her near and stifled whatever words of contempt she might care to offer him with his kiss, she knew that she was struggling as much with herself as she was with him.

She had wanted this, to feel his arms around her, to taste his kiss once again. She had known it the moment she had realized David's embrace left her indifferent, known that she needed to find out if what she'd remembered of Sky's kiss was simply another game, one of her own imagination.

It wasn't. The first touch of his lips to hers proved it. From the instant he touched her, she felt the soft, warm flood begin inside her, felt herself melting as though she had been cast into a forge.

She stopped struggling, letting her hands first fall, then slowly snake their way to his shoulders. It was as though they were moving without her direction, as if her whole body were moving, pressing her closer to him, without her command. She closed her eyes and gave herself up to the sweet narcotic feeling.

Sky lifted his lips from hers with obvious regret but was rewarded with the knowledge that she was breathless and trembling. He stared down at her as she slowly opened her eyes.

"Now," he said softly, his eyes on hers, "tell me his kiss made you feel this way."

For a moment she didn't understand the words, couldn't think whose kiss she was meant to compare with his. And then she remembered what he had done so that he could put her in a position to make the comparison. It had been cruel of him to say the things he had about Forbes, callous of him to frighten her that way.

"It did," she said in a spurt of spite. "His was better."

He smiled at her. "Now *you're* lying," he told her as he pulled her close to him once again.

This time she didn't make even a pretense of trying to push herself away from him. It was folly to pretend she didn't want this. She knew she did, and she knew he knew it as well. She let herself melt against him, let the feeling of his arms holding her, his body close to hers, his lips touching hers, let it all sweep through her.

She felt a slow, insistent probing of his tongue against her lips. This was something strange to her, something she had never encountered. For all her apparent worldliness there had been only a handful of times she had allowed a man to steal a kiss, and none of them had ever led to this.

But the sweet, thick flood inside her told her to admit the probe and, after a second's hesitancy, she complied. The touch of his tongue to hers was electric, setting adrift radiating fingers of fire within her.

This time when he released her, neither spoke. Sky put his arm to her waist and led her back to the rail where she had stood with David. It seemed strange to her that the sky had taken on a luster she had not noticed before, that the moonlight seemed so much more beautiful reflected on the water. She stood beside him, aware of the warmth of him close to her, of the strength of his arm at her waist. She turned and stared up at him and waited for him to kiss her once again.

But Sky realized that he had made his point to her, showed her that she felt nothing for David Trumbull. And now that he had accomplished what he'd set out to do, he was not sure in which direction he ought to proceed.

Had she been a woman of experience, he knew that second kiss would have led directly to his bed. But she was not that sort of woman, and he found himself feeling suddenly guilty for what he was doing, and even more for what he wanted to do.

He turned away, let his eyes fall on the snifter of brandy he'd left on the table beside the empty champagne bottle and glasses. He wondered then just how much champagne she'd had that evening, how much of what she had allowed him he could attribute to the alcohol. He lifted the snifter and tasted the brandy.

"It's quite late, Arden," he said after a moment's silence. "Perhaps I ought to escort you to your cabin."

At first she felt only surprise at the ease with which he seemed willing to dismiss her after the effort he'd so obviously taken to be alone with her. Then it occurred to her that he was playing games again, that he had wanted only to show her how hollow and passionless David was, and what a fool she would be to marry him. She told herself that she hated him, that he had no right to kiss her, to hold her the way he had, and then to treat her as though she meant absolutely nothing to him.

"I'm not quite ready," she told him as she put her hand to the glass he held and took it from him. She considered the golden amber liquid, then sniffed at it tentatively. "This has always been a mystery to me," she murmured, more to herself than to him. "Men hold so much as fit for themselves yet not quite proper for a woman. Like this brandy: it's perfectly acceptable for a man to drink, even to excess. Some consider drunkenness nothing but a minor failing. Yet the world is aghast to see a woman in such a condition. Men, it would seem, have managed to make their vices mere follies and still keep them sins if a woman dares to engage in them." She looked up at him. "Can you tell me why that is, Mr. Trask?"

He was puzzled by her sudden thoughtfulness and by the remote way in which she spoke. For a moment he wondered what it was she had on her mind, what she really intended to do.

"Perhaps they want to protect their ladies," he suggested.

She shook her head. "No," she told him firmly. "They have no desire to protect us, for they have nothing from which to protect us save themselves. I think it is only to assure themselves that they are superior to us." Her eyes narrowed as she stared into his. "Surely you understand the feeling, Mr. Trask, the desire to show a woman how weak and foolish she is, and how very superior you are compared to her."

With that she raised the glass to her lips and took a long swallow of the brandy. It filled her mouth with heat. As she swallowed, the fire spread down her throat and to her stomach. She gasped.

Sky put his hand to hers and took away the snifter. She'd nearly drained it, he realized, something that was decidedly less than wise, especially as she'd been drinking champagne with Trumbull before he'd happened upon them.

"That was supremely foolish, Arden," he told her, cross with her and not sure why.

"Of course it was foolish," she told him. "I'm simply a

poor, inferior woman. Whatever I do is bound to be foolish." Her tone grew cold with sarcasm. "How lucky I am to have you to show me the error of my ways."

"Enough, Arden," he said. He put his hand on her arm. "You're going to bed."

She tried to wrench her arm free, but he held it tight in his grasp.

"You're despicable," she hissed at him. "You're cruel and malicious and without conscience. I think you are contemptible."

He seemed shocked at her words. It hadn't occurred to him until that moment that he might have hurt her. And now that he realized he had, he had absolutely no idea how to mend what he'd done.

She stared at him with revulsion for a moment, then felt as though she were crumbling inside. Unaccustomed to the brandy, she felt her body reacting swiftly and with vehemence. She felt dizzy and foolish and thought she might cry.

Sky saw the look of anger leak away from her eyes to be replaced by one of bewilderment and uncertainty. He put his hand out to her but she pulled back, afraid of what his touch might do to her, unwilling to let him see just how vulnerable she was. He released her and she turned away.

But the alcohol had had its effect, and she moved with unaccustomed clumsiness. She stumbled and would have fallen had he not caught her. For a moment she tensed at his touch and then, suddenly, seemed to collapse. He put his arms around her and she fell against him.

He held her for a moment, his lips buried in the silken luxury of her hair. He closed his eyes and inhaled her perfume and the sweet, undefinable scent that he knew came from no perfume but from her. Then, still silent, he put his arm to her waist and led her to her door.

Sky pushed the cabin door open.

"Good night, Arden," he whispered.

She stared into the dimly lit cabin and then turned to gaze up at him. She knew she ought to feel something—remorse for what she'd said to him, regret for having drunk the brandy, perhaps shame for getting tipsy. For she was, for the first time in her life, inebriated; of that she was certain.

The feeling of dizziness had passed, however, and whatever effect the alcohol was having, she was not at all sure it was something she ought to reject. She found herself suddenly free of all those feelings she knew she ought to feel, a realization which baffled her. Even more puzzling, she found herself unburdened as well of all those inhibitions her upbringing had impressed upon her as absolute prerequisites. She felt light and almost floating, and, for the first time in her life, entirely, incontestably free.

"Good night, Sky," she said.

Despite the words, she made no move to leave him. Instead she reached her arms up to his neck and pulled him down to her.

Her action took him completely by surprise. He would have expected almost anything else from her at that moment but this freely offered kiss. He was not so surprised, however, that he was unable to react to it. He put his arms around her and pulled her close.

Later, when he was to think about it, he could not remember having pulled her into the cabin and pushed the door closed behind them. He realized that he'd done those things, but he could not remember actually performing the tasks. All that he could remember was the feeling of her in his arms, the sweet, honeyed taste of her lips on his, and the surprising surge of desire she had so effortlessly ignited in him.

Arden forgot everything—the anger she'd felt with him at the game she'd convinced herself he was playing

62

with her, the way he'd accused her of allowing herself to be used to further her father's social ambitions. A small voice inside her told her that unlike David, Skyler Trask cared nothing for her save to show her her own failings, to raise himself in his own eyes by diminishing her. It insisted that she ought to be disgusted by him, that his touch should be the last thing that should bring her any pleasure.

But it was a lie and she knew it. She stilled the voice, ignoring its cries for attention, telling herself that it was no longer time for thought. She pressed herself close to him, forcing away any stray thought of her father or David and letting herself become lost in the sweet, liquid feeling that filled her at his touch.

Something was happening to her, she realized. Somehow, some part of her she had never known even existed was stirring, wakening, coming slowly to life. She let her thoughts dwell for a moment on that fact, the realization that buried deep inside her was a being who had waited until that instant, until Sky's touch, to be roused. She had never imagined she could feel as she did at that moment, never contemplated what Sky's hands and lips made her feel. She felt dizzy, far dizzier than even the brandy had left her. But this derangement did not frighten or offend her. On the contrary, she realized she wanted only to cling to the feeling, to hold it fast for as long as she could.

He bent his head to bring his lips to her neck. The sensation sent rivulets of sweet fire through her. She let her head fall back and put her hands to his hair, twining her fingers through the thick curls at the nape of his neck.

Sky tasted the soft, warm skin of her neck, like cream and honey to his tongue. He felt the heightening throb of her pulse beneath his lips and knew it echoed his own. For just an instant he hesitated, his conscience calling out to him, reminding him she was in no condition to know just what it was she really wanted, that she had had too much to drink and was incapable of making decisions. For him to do anything at that moment but turn away, to get away before something unalterable occurred between them, was simply taking advantage of her.

He pulled himself from her with regret, putting his hands to her shoulders and staring into her eyes until she opened them and stared back at him.

"Is this what you want, Arden?" he asked her softly. "Is this what you really want?"

He wondered what he would do if she turned away from him and told him to leave, wondered if he could still the racing fire in his veins, wondered if he had the strength to do what he knew he ought. He waited, his eyes on hers, searching in them for some indication of what it was she wanted from him.

It seemed an eternity to him, those seconds while she stood motionless, staring up at him. And then she put her hands to his cheeks and slowly pulled him to her, bringing her lips to his, parting them in invitation as they met his. Any thought he might have had of turning away disappeared in a flood of desire for her. He wrapped his arms around her and pulled her close.

Arden stood motionless, almost afraid to breathe. He'd helped her with her buttons, disrobing her with what would have seemed unlikely ease had she been of a mind to consider it, an ease born of much practice. But her thoughts then had been far from any consideration of his previous experience with women. Instead she'd watched his expression, thinking it much like that of a child on Christmas morning who unwraps an especially longed-for present that he'd really had no thought he might receive. She found herself gratified by that expression of

64

delight, realized it made her feel very special, very precious.

She stood naked, her feet surrounded by the silken pool of her gown. She wondered what it was she was supposed to do, then realized as her eyes met his that he found pleasure in simply looking at her. This, too, brought her an odd sense of delight and a small thrill of power over him, something she'd never thought to feel.

Sky dropped his jacket to the floor and stood for a moment longer simply staring at her. Her body shone pale in the dim lamplight. It might have been carved from marble or alabaster, it seemed so perfect to him, a flawless sculpture fashioned by a master's hand. He knew he had never wanted a woman as much in his life.

He went to her and put his arms around her, this time kissing her gently, slowly, letting his lips warm hers. More than anything he wanted to feel in her the insistent throb he felt in his own veins, to know she wanted him as much as he wanted her. He let his lips drift to her ear and then her neck, and, feeling the sharp, steady beat of her pulse beneath his lips, realized that she had given him what he had searched for. He pulled her close, hungering for the touch of her skin, smooth and warm, beneath his hands. He kissed her again, then lifted her in his arms and carried her to the bed.

Arden lay back against the small heap of pillows and raised her arms to him as he followed her. She was adrift, she realized, not at all certain where she was or what it was she was doing, but nonetheless sure that whatever happened that night, wherever it was he was to take her, it was a path she was destined to follow.

He kissed her once more, this time his lips hard and urgent against hers, before he stood and pulled off his own clothing, then once again lowered himself to her.

He pressed his lips to her neck and then to the warm

valley between her breasts. Arden closed her eyes and let herself float on the sudden tide of strange, wondrous feeling that swept through her, a tide that was sweet and hot and pulsing in her veins, completely unlike anything she had ever felt before. She brought her hands to his shoulders, let them slide along his skin, and felt the muscle beneath, hard and strong. She felt a sudden awareness of the strength that lay beneath her hands, and the knowledge made her feel terribly vulnerable, yet oddly safe. She let herself drift, let herself fill with the undulating waves of liquid heat that the contact of his hands and lips and tongue roused inside her.

He began to kiss her, his lips warm on her bared breasts, his tongue gently teasing the nipples until they grew hard with want. Arden put her hands to his neck, then slowly snaked her fingers through his dark curls, pulling him close to her, not at all sure what caused this magic he had released within her, but knowing she was unwilling to lose it. Nothing had prepared her for the fires he ignited within her, for the surging tides his touch released.

His lips and tongue were touching her, she realized, moving from her breasts to her belly and downward, to the soft thatched vee between her legs. She tensed for a moment at the unexpected contact, then gave herself over to the wave of liquid fire that it released. Her body seemed a strange and alien thing to her, more his ally than her own, for he seemed to know how to release the deep secrets it had kept from her all her life. She could only wonder at his ability to do these things to her, to fill her with such strange and unbearably sweet fires.

He raised himself once more to her, letting his tongue find the lobe and then the inward spiral of her ear.

"I want you, Arden," he whispered as he spread her legs with his own and slid inside her.

It was like an explosion of sweet fire within her, an explosion that snaked its way through her body, melting her until it seemed that there was nothing left but the feel of him inside her. Arden pressed herself close to him, trembling with the reverberations of that first wondrous thrust.

Sky encircled her with his arms, holding her gently, cradling her in his embrace as his lips found hers. Then, slowly, he began to move inside her.

She followed as his hands guided her, then suddenly realized some part of her deep within, some instinct that had lain buried inside her, already knew the dance. She gave herself up to the music of it, pressing her hips to his as the tides grew stronger and more urgent within her.

Arden was floating, drifting on a sea of passion as the waves grew ever stronger and more potent within her. She felt herself melting, becoming one with him, giving him part of herself. Never had she thought it possible to feel this way, to be so joined with another that she could not distinguish the place where her own body ended and his began.

She felt a moment of panic, a sudden fear that never would she be able to find herself again, that somehow this act tied her to him in a way that could never be undone. And then thought drifted away from her, beyond her grasp, as the tides seemed to fill her and she felt as though she were drowning. She abandoned herself, surrendering the last of herself to him, letting him take her wherever he wanted, knowing only that she was powerless to do otherwise.

He began to move faster, each thrust stronger and more urgent. And the tides grew stronger inside her until they overwhelmed her completely. She felt herself exploding, shattering, until she was nothing more than a pure, clean shaft of light, and then that too scattered and fell in a million tiny bursts that slowly faded. She found herself clinging to Sky, trembling and panting, not sure of what it was that had happened to her, knowing only that she was irrevocably changed.

Sky felt her trembling release, and with it came a wave of satisfaction that he had given her this rapture. The knowledge somehow dissolved his control, and he found himself following her, falling into a well of pure pleasure.

Sky held her close, cradling her in his arms, letting his fingers splay her long, golden curls on the pillows. His heart was still pounding and his breath was ragged and short, and he held her still, not wanting to leave her yet, unwilling to end the moment. Never had it seemed so right to him before, never had the pleasure been so overwhelmingly complete. That realization puzzled him, but more than that it pleased him. This woman, he realized, had a strange, potent effect on him that was a mystery he could not comprehend, and yet that mystery was one he embraced with a sense of wonder and delight.

Arden stared up at him, searching in his dark eyes for some sign, some explanation of what had happened to her. A tiny face with bemused eyes, her own face, stared back at her from each of his blue eyes.

She put her hand to his cheek, then smiled when he grasped it in his own and brought it to his lips. The pressure of his kiss against her palm sent a tiny shiver through her.

"What happened?" she asked him when she'd managed to catch her breath.

He smiled, somehow pleased at the naiveté of her question.

"I suppose that depends on whom you ask, Arden," he replied.

Her eyes darted around the cabin as though for just an instant she feared there might be someone else there to provide an answer. She was relieved to find there was not.

"I asked you," she said, and answered his smile with one of her own.

"Then what happened is what was intended to happen between a man and a woman," he replied. "We made love, Arden, wonderful love."

"And is it always like that?" she asked thoughtfully. "Like stars exploding?"

He smiled again, this time wryly. "It should be," he told her.

She sighed, and smiled up at him, content and happy. She reached up and put her hands to his shoulders, still intrigued by the way his shoulders and chest felt beneath her hands, fascinated by the muscles, hard and strong and a complete mystery to one who had never touched another unclothed body.

"And if I asked someone else?" she persisted, this time not really interested in what he might answer, only in the sound of his voice, the feel of his words rumbling deep in his chest. "Would the answer be so different?"

He shrugged. "Your friend Trumbull, I suppose, would say I've ruined you."

Arden felt suddenly sober. A chill seemed to sweep into those parts of her that had been warm and liquid, leaving in its wake a trail of ice. Her hand froze and she stared up at him, looking in his expression for some hint that what had happened between them had had some meaning for him as it had for her. All she saw was an absent amusement.

"What has this to do with David?" she asked.

Sky shook his head. "Nothing," he said. "Only to prove to you that you can't possibly marry him," he told her. "I don't think Boston scions accept damaged goods."

"Damaged goods?" she asked, her voice a whisper, her thoughts suddenly confused.

He smiled. "Never fear. I'm willing to make an honest woman of you."

It was only after he'd uttered the words that he realized he had just offered to marry her. It came as a shock to him to realize that he didn't want to take back the words, that the idea, however sudden, left a pleasant afterglow in his imagination.

Arden, however, couldn't believe the offhand way he spoke, as though he were discussing the weather, or the complacent grin that flickered across his lips. It really had been nothing more than a game to him, she realized, a way to best David, a way to belittle her. She felt crushed and used. She turned away from him, unable to look at his face any longer.

Sky put his hand to her cheek, found it moist, then pulled her chin until she was again facing him.

He leaned forward to her, and tried to kiss her on the lips, but she jerked away from him.

"What is it, Arden? What's wrong?"

She bit back the tears, not wanting to give him the satisfaction of them as well.

"I think you should go now," she told him.

He was more than a little bewildered by her sudden change. To Arden he had spoken words he'd assiduously avoided all his life, and he was shocked to see them received not with delight, but with apparent disgust.

"Arden, tell me what happened."

"Nothing happened," she replied. "I just want you to go. Now."

"Damn it, talk to me."

But she didn't. She refused to so much as look at him. Instead she turned to face the wall.

Sky pushed himself from the bed. "If that's the way you want it," he said as he grabbed up his clothing from the floor and angrily began to climb into them.

I should have known better, he told himself as he pulled on his trousers. All she wanted was a socially acceptable name, a place in society. Well, if that was what she wanted, then damn her, let her have it. Let her have David Trumbull and go to hell with him.

He stood for an instant by the door, his hand on the knob, and turned to look at her.

"Arden?"

She didn't answer.

He clenched his hands into fists, wishing for something he could strike at.

"I hope you and your precious Trumbull will be happy," he hissed as he turned the knob. "You deserve one another."

Arden didn't turn away from the wall until she heard the door to her cabin slam behind him. She lay and stared at it for a long, miserable moment, then gave herself over to tears.

Chapter Four

"The work I'll be doing with Sir Arthur will have great impact on the knowledge we have of the society of the ancient Minoans on Crete. If we can believe, as does Herr Schliemann, that Greek myth can be accepted as history, then I will actually walk where Theseus walked, touch the place where he did battle with the Minotaur."

Arden stood at the boat's rail and stared at the approaching shoreline of Heracleion. Part of her was paying scant attention to David's words, enough to realize he seemed terribly impressed with himself and the work he would be doing at Sir Arthur Evans's dig at Knossos, but she found it almost impossible to force herself to concentrate on what he was saying. Her mind, she found, was busy with other matters.

One other matter, actually—a matter by the name of Skyler Trask. She darted a quick glance forward to where he stood in thoughtful solitude by the rail, apparently studying the coastline with an intensity of attention it hardly deserved. But when he turned to glance down the deck to where she stood with her father and David, she quickly looked away. The last thing she wanted, she told herself, was for him to think she had the slightest interest in his existence.

He had carefully avoided her since that night, which was, she told herself, just fine with her. Actually, "that horrible night" was the way she classified it when she allowed herself consciously to consider what had happened between them. Mostly, she told herself she just wanted to pretend the whole awful thing had never happened. As for him avoiding her, the greater the distance between herself and Skyler Trask, the happier she would be. That night had been a mistake, something that never would have happened if she hadn't had all that champagne and brandy. He had taken advantage of her, she told herself, and she would never, ever forgive him for that.

She felt his eyes on her, and she turned to David, determined to be attentive to him to show Sky that she hadn't the least interest in him or his opinions or anything else about him. And she didn't, she told herself firmly, she didn't care where he went, what he did or what happened to him just so long as she didn't have to think about him. The only emotion she felt in connection with Skyler Trask was disgust.

"And you, David?" Forbes was asking. "Do you believe these myths can actually be treated as something more than fables?"

He darted a cross look at Arden, one that chided her as effectively as any words, and told her that although he was doing as much as he could to take up the slack in the conversation, she was being rude to David by so openly ignoring him.

Arden accepted the unspoken criticism meekly, knowing her father was right, silently admitting she was being rude to David and forcing herself to regret it. She listened carefully as he answered her father's questions.

"Frankly," David was saying in his most pontificating tone, "I am hardly given to such fanciful interpretations. But it would be foolish, I think, to ignore any theory that might eventually be proved true. And as Sir Evans has already uncovered part of what can only be called a palace at Knossos, perhaps it would be best to maintain an open mind and consider the possibility that it might once have actually been the palace of King Minos."

"Well, regardless of fact, I think I'd rather accept the possibility," Arden said. "It's far more romantic to think that a great hero could actually have existed than it is to think heroism beyond mere mortal mankind, something to be invented for us to revere."

David turned to her—surprised, perhaps, by her sudden show of interest, but pleased by it.

"Is it a hero, then, that you would seek, Arden?" he asked her softly.

She shook her head and offered him a brilliant smile. "No," she replied. "Think of Ariadne, left abandoned by Theseus; Antiope, killed in battle with her own people because of him; and Phaedra, driven mad, torn by her love for his son and her duty to him. Heroes, I think, are far too hard on their women. I will happily content myself with a mere mortal."

He put his hand on hers where it grasped the rail.

"Speaking as a mortal myself, I'm delighted to hear that," he told her.

Arden turned away from the questioning look she saw in his eyes and once again pretended interest in the steadily nearing port of Heracleion. He had finally managed to ask her to marry him the evening before. She'd not quite accepted, but then she hadn't rejected his offer either. Life, at that moment, her own in particular, seemed terribly confusing.

"Well, whether truth or myth, it will all make fascinating stories for the *Sun's* readers, don't you think, Arden?"

"Certainly, Papa," she replied. "I've already begun to

study the book of myths David gave me. I consider it research for my articles."

"Hence the sudden authority on the many loves of Theseus?" Forbes pushed, his lips curling into a grin.

"Color, Papa," she replied with a laugh. "I prefer to think of it as color."

She glanced at David, expecting him to be laughing, too, only to find him considering her proposed articles for the *Sun* with an expression of disapproval.

"Do you really think it quite proper, Forbes, for a young woman to pursue endeavors outside of the home?" he asked.

Forbes shook his head and tried to look grave. "Certainly not," he replied. "But Arden considers it a pastime, not a duty. And I think I remember it was her excuse to take this little excursion. Her enthusiasm for the task stems, I think, from the lack of a husband to whom she might devote her attentions." Then he turned to Arden and smiled mischievously.

"Papa, really!"

"It is a lack," David interjected as he, too, turned to face her, "that is, I hope, soon to be remedied."

Arden found herself blushing, although she wasn't quite sure why. She was grateful for the flurry of activity as they docked, and the turning of the men's attention from her to the more immediate consideration of the ship's crew as they scrambled along the deck, throwing lines to be caught on the pier.

Arden left them and went to her cabin to collect her purse and the parasol she had been warned would be needed against the Cretan sun. When she left it, prepared to face the rigors of the less than extravagant hotel in which she had been warned she would be staying while in Heracleion, she found Forbes by the door, waiting for her.

"Well," he began as he took her arm and began to lead

76

her to the gangplank, "when do you intend to accept David's proposal?"

Arden pulled her hand from his arm and stopped. He turned to face her.

"How do you know he proposed to me?" she demanded.

"He told me. How else?" Forbes shrugged. "As a matter of fact, proper Bostonian that he is, he asked my permission beforehand."

"Which you, of course, granted with enthusiasm."

"Certainly. Is there some reason I oughtn't to have?" She shook her head. "No, Papa. No reason."

Forbes took her hand and replaced it on his arm. They began once more to walk to the gangplank.

"I should think you'd be ecstatic, Arden. He's rich, attractive, from a good family, and obviously besotted with you. Why didn't you accept him immediately?"

"I don't know," she replied. She felt suddenly subdued, uncertain. "It's just that I'm not sure I love him, Papa."

"That will come, Arden, believe me. Life isn't the way it seems in fairy tales, no heroes on white chargers, no thunderclaps that strike you with undying passion." He patted her hand. "But if it suits you better to take a while to consider, then do as you like. You both have time." He turned and grinned at her, then lowered his voice so that it seemed conspiratorial. "Besides, it wouldn't do to let him believe we're too eager."

He sounded, Arden thought, as though he were planning strategy for a military attack. She was not at all sure she approved of the attitude, nor of her father's apparent belief that her marriage was a matter of mutual decision. It was not as if he would face the prospect of spending his nights in David Trumbull's bed, as she must.

"Ah, Trask."

77

They had reached the gangplank and Arden looked down to find Sky standing on the pier, apparently waiting for them. Forbes waved to him and started to hurry down. Arden hesitated, not at all certain she was prepared to face him, but her father turned to her and she obediently followed.

"I only intend to stay in Heracleion overnight," Sky told Forbes without preamble. "I thought I'd scout around the countryside, see if I can't learn something, even if it's nothing more than the feel of the place."

Forbes nodded. "As you like, Sky. I have every confidence in you."

"Then I'll say good-bye to you now."

"You won't dine with us this evening?" Forbes asked.

Sky shook his head and let his eyes stray to find Arden's. "No," he replied, turning back to Forbes. "I think it best if I start out early tomorrow morning. I'll have an early dinner and turn in. I might just as well take my leave of you now."

"As you like." Forbes offered him his hand. "Good luck."

"Thanks." Sky shook hands with him and once again let his glance stray to Arden. "Miss Devereaux."

He seemed so cool, so smugly superior. Arden bridled at the indifferent way he stared at her as though he were a complete stranger to her.

"Mr. Trask," she managed to respond.

He nodded and then turned away. Arden followed him with her eyes as he made his way through the crowd on the wharf, aware that she was feeling suddenly unsteady, as though she'd been struck and found herself unable to breathe.

Forbes was oblivious to her distress. He scanned the mass of milling humanity on the wharf, ignoring a half dozen dirty children who darted boldly among the foreigners, their voices raised to a thin whine as they begged for a few drachmas.

"Ah, there's David," he told her, forcing her attention away from the retreating form of Skyler Trask. "He's found a hansom for us."

He put his hand to his pocket, pulled out a dozen pennies, and threw them to the children, who shouted as they raced after the coins. Then he put his hand to Arden's arm and began to move forward, through the crush of people.

Feeling as though she'd gone numb inside, Arden let him lead her to David and the waiting cab.

That afternoon, David sent a message to Sir Arthur Evans in Knossos, informing the archaeologist that he had arrived in Heracleion and planned to travel to the dig the following afternoon. In his note, David also informed him of Forbes Devereaux's arrival and mentioned the publisher's interest in Evans's work, implying that if Forbes and Arden were to be welcomed at the dig, Evans could expect some very favorable coverage in the *New York Sun*.

"Archaeologists are never averse to good publicity," he informed Forbes and Arden that evening when they met in the hotel dining room for dinner. "We're the sort who are always looking to universities and scientific societies for funds to finance our work. I'm sure Evans will welcome you both with open arms, especially if he thinks your coverage in the *Sun* will lead to some backing."

"I don't see why it shouldn't," Forbes replied. "I think I might even be persuaded to have the *Sun* lead the list of contributors."

David smiled at that, as though to give his benediction to this good thought. His attention, however, was not really on Forbes but on Arden, who was staring absently at the plate of eggplant salad that had been set in front of her, poking the heap of vegetables with her fork, but making no real effort to eat any of it.

"I agree with you, Arden," he said with a commiserating smile as he took a small piece of flat bread that was smeared with a pale-colored concoction consisting mostly of fish eggs from the plate in the center of the table. "I find the food here virtually inedible, not at all like that at home. I'm already hungering for a good American steak or a properly prepared Boston scrod that isn't sitting in a puddle of something distastefully red." He looked at the bread and his own plate of *baba gannoj* with distaste, then around at the small, less than elegant dining room. "Nothing is like it is at home," he went on. "I'm afraid we'll have to make do, however difficult that may be." He smiled at her. "A small sacrifice to make for science."

Arden bridled at his tone, at the implication that nothing could possibly be as fine as what he was accustomed to having, that he and his were somehow innately superior to anyone else.

She lifted a forkful of the salad to her mouth and ate it. Spicy, she thought, but good.

"I quite like it," she told him firmly. "Both the food and the hotel. I think people who are unwilling to be open to new experiences when they travel ought to stay at home."

"Well, if you wish to define accepting a lukewarm bath in barely adequate facilities as being open to new experiences . . ." Forbes interjected.

He knew his daughter's moods only too well. He could also see David draw back at her tone. It bothered him that she seemed almost entirely too ready to disagree with David, that she seemed to be taking absolutely no pains to be pleasant. The thought that she seemed willing to destroy what could very well be her best chance at making a good marriage left him bewildered and angry with her. He shot her a warning glance and saw her turn away from it, obviously intending to ignore it, which only irked him all the more.

David looked away, pretending he hadn't heard Arden's criticism. He lifted the glass of retsina the waiter had poured for him, tasted it, and then set it back down with a look of displeasure on his face, but without uttering another word.

Forbes, though, was determined to take his part. He tasted his own retsina, grimaced, and put the glass down. "Hardly Château Margaux, eh, David?"

"I'm sure with a bit of time we'll become accustomed to it all," David replied, determined to make himself agreeable to Arden.

She, however, seemed determined to ignore the conversation. She addressed her dinner with undivided attention.

"Have you ever met Evans before, David?" Forbes asked.

"Once, two years ago, in London. A most agreeable and knowledgeable gentleman," David replied. He stared across the small table at Arden, then reached over and grasped her hand. "It would be a great pleasure for me if I could introduce you to Evans as my fiancée, Arden."

Arden was startled into attentiveness. She looked up at him, surprised to see his dark eyes firmly fastened on hers.

"I hardly think this is the time or place to discuss this matter, David," she said. She drew her hand away.

"Why not?" he prodded. "Your father is well aware of my proposal. And I'm certainly not ashamed of my intentions." He leaned forward and took her hand once more in his, this time holding it firmly.

Arden stared at his intent expression, then glanced at her father. Both of them, it seemed, wanted her to settle

81

the matter, to say "yes" to David and be done with it. And she had to admit that David had really done nothing wrong, nothing to rouse the feelings of antagonism that she seemed to feel lately. This is all Skyler Trask's fault, she told herself.

"I'm sorry, David. I think I'm just tired from the trip. I don't mean to be cross with you, or to behave the way I find myself behaving lately." She lifted her napkin from her lap and placed it beside her plate. "I think what I really need is to get some sleep."

With that she pushed her chair back and stood. David was forced to release his hold on her hand.

"Good night, David . . . Papa." She nodded to the two men, turned, and left.

They watched her depart in silence. It was only when she'd left the room that David realized she'd once again avoided answering his question.

He lifted the glass of retsina and swallowed it without even tasting the resin that had so put him off a few minutes earlier.

"The Greeks invented Stoicism, my boy, so I suppose it wise to learn it at the font," Forbes said in a commiserating tone. "Have a bit of patience, though. I know her. She just needs a bit of time to see what's apparent to us, that you would make the perfect husband for her. She'll come round soon enough."

In his own mind, Forbes was certain that Arden would eventually accept David Trumbull's proposal, a prospect he found pleasing. The trip, he decided, would definitely be a successful one for him, both for his business and for his personal ambitions. If David was a bit uncertain at that moment, it was only to be expected. In the end, though, it would all turn out quite well, his desire to marry Arden entirely sympathetic to Forbes's own.

That matter settled in his own mind, Forbes returned his attention to his dinner. If he wasn't as charmed by

Greek cooking as Arden had said she was, he wasn't as put off by it as David seemed to be, either.

"Have you tried this ground lamb, David? It's not at all bad."

Arden drew the door to her room closed behind her. It was, as her father had said at dinner, barely adequate by the standards to which she was accustomed—a narrow wrought-iron bed with a faded cotton spread, a dark wooden armoire with a dark, imperfect mirror, a single comfortable chair, and a small table with a scratched and stained top set by the only window in the room.

If the accommodations were not quite luxurious, however, the room was made more inviting by a large terra cotta vase filled with roses and sprigs of jasmine and heliotrope. A handful of wild thyme rested by the bed, a charm, the maid had told her, to fend off any night-roaming *kallikantzaroi*—small, roguish, hairy creatures, as local legend held, who were to be blamed for unexpected bad luck. From her window she could survey the incredible view of the water, the Venetian port with its small fort that had been built in the fourteenth century, and the solid Venetian walls raised to protect the city against the Turks, all of which David had pointed out in his most pompous manner as they'd driven past them on their way from the wharf to the hotel that afternoon. Without exception the people had been friendly and helpful. All in all, Arden decided she quite liked it.

But her pleasure with Heracleion and the Hotel Zenia could not mask the decided feeling of discomfort she had when she allowed into her thoughts the question of marrying David Trumbull. And that, she realized, was because the thought of such a marriage somehow seemed inevitably to lead her to thoughts of Skyler Trask.

She had spent the greater part of the afternoon considering Sky's brusque departure from her and her father, and each time she ended by telling herself that his manners, like his morals, were decidedly lacking. But then, she asked herself, what would she expect from a man who would do as he had done—let her drink too much and then taken advantage of her when she was in no position to defend herself, a man who had callously used her and then was cruel enough to openly scorn her?

More times than she could count, she told herself she hated him. Still she found she could not keep herself from thinking about him, about the moments she had spent in his arms. And as much as she disliked the idea of listening to it, she could not quite still a persistent voice inside her that told her she had been as much at fault as he, that he hadn't forced himself upon her. All she knew for certain was that something had happened to her that night, and, right or wrong, it had changed her forever. Try as she would, she could not forget it.

She crossed the room and stared at her reflection in the dark, uneven mirror, considering what she saw with a critical eye. She realized she was searching for the flaw that had made her so completely unacceptable to Skyler Trask. Despite the mirror's deficiencies, however, she could find no glaring lack in her reflection. Whatever it was about her that had offended him was not to be found in the mirror; her scrutiny gave her no clue.

She turned away from her reflection, shedding her clothing quickly and climbing into the small bed. She extinguished the lamp, then lay back, staring up into the night darkness, thinking. If she had an ounce of sense, she told herself firmly, she would force herself to forget Skyler Trask. She would be a fool to let her life be soured by one experience, one night. The only rational course to take was to convince herself that it had never happened.

Tomorrow, she vowed, she would apologize to David, beg his forgiveness for having been rude to him. Perhaps she would claim the rigors of the voyage as an excuse and hope he would accept that explanation. Whatever the words she used, however, she would make him understand that the wall she had erected between them was the result of some sort of temporary derangement, some passing fever of which she was finally cured.

Perhaps she would give him the answer he'd seemed so anxious for that evening, the answer both he and her father so obviously expected from her. After all, he, unlike Skyler Trask, wanted to marry her; he was, as Forbes had pointed out to her that afternoon, clearly taken with her. It was only common sense to return the love of a man who cared for her rather than to spend her life miserable over one who so obviously thought of nothing and no one but himself.

Her decision made and her resolve firm, Arden told herself she should sleep. She closed her eyes firmly and tried to clear her mind of all thought. Despite her determination, however, sleep steadfastly avoided her. Finally resigned, she rose, relit the lamp, and found her lap desk among her luggage. If she could do nothing else, at least she could make an attempt at the articles she had promised her father for the *Sun*'s lady readers.

She propped up the pillows, resettled herself on the bed, and pursed her lips in thought for a long moment. Then she took up her pen and began to write:

The voyage is a long one, and when the boat docks at Piraeus the traveler wishes for nothing more than a night's rest amidst the luxury of the Athenée Palace Hotel and then leisure to explore the ancient wonders of Athens. But this trip has been dedicated to adventure, and so we barely stop to pay homage to the Acropolis before we board the packet, promising that we will return soon and see those marvels we have so callously ignored.

85

The Island of Crete rises up before us out of the deep blue waters of the Aegean Sea like a mountain at the end of a long plain, the city of Heracleion heralded by a four-hundred-year-old fort the Doges of Venice built to protect their interests against invasion. It takes only a cursory inspection to realize this place is rich with the evidence of the civilizations of centuries, and yet it is not these evident artifacts that we have come to see but those that lie buried deep in the Cretan soil, the adventure to reveal mankind's most ancient past. . . .

If David Trumbull was disappointed with the simple offerings of Cretan hospitality, Skyler Trask found himself perfectly content with it. Rather than retiring early, as he had told Arden and Forbes he intended to do, he had taken himself to the outskirts of Heracleion, to an area by the water where he found fishing boats pulled up on the beach. The air was heavy with the scent of fresh-caught fish, and the feeling of the place was thick with the rough-and-tumble of the fishermen who labored unloading the last of their catch and setting out their nets to dry on the sand.

Sky walked along the beach until he found a *taverna* clinging to a rocky ledge just above the sand with a wide, open veranda that looked out on the sea. The place seemed reasonably noisy, with two overworked waiters who raced between the tables where the fishermen ate and drank and gambled on games of backgammon. The activity and the scent of roast lamb coming from the rear of the taverna was evidence of good food to be found in the place, Sky decided. He crossed the narrow stretch of beach, climbed the stone steps of the ledge, and made his way to an empty table among those set out on the open veranda facing the sea.

He looked around as he settled himself in a chair, considering the dark tanned and intent faces of the fishermen. It didn't take him long to decide that he had found just the sort of place for which he'd searched.

He ordered himself a *mastika,* then sat watching the moonlight on the water and listening to a game of backgammon being played with much comment and obvious passion at the next table. For a while the fishermen avoided him, apparently unused to having strangers here on their modest home ground. From time to time Sky noticed one or another of the men eyeing him and realized there was more than a hint of suspicion in their glances. He realized that his clothes marked him as alien in this place, and he began to wish he'd thought to outfit himself with the sort of rough worker's shirt and trousers the fishermen wore.

But it didn't take him long to come to the conclusion that even if he had been dressed like them, he'd still be an outsider in this insular environment. He didn't belong here, wasn't part of the family, and a change of clothing could hardly change that. He would simply have to be patient, he told himself. He reminded himself of the much heralded curiosity of the Greeks, as well as their innate sense of hospitality to strangers.

When he'd finished the first small glass of *mastika,* he ordered another, and with it a plate of *dolmades,* by pointing to the contents of a platter several men at a nearby table were consuming as a way of compensating for his lack of Greek.

As Sky had expected, one of the fishermen eventually drifted to his table and stood at the far side, glass in hand, facing him.

"Kali spera."

87

Sky looked up and smiled. "I'm afraid I don't understand," he replied, then shrugged by way of expressing his regret for his ignorance of the language.

There was a quick change of expression to the fisherman's face, but it disappeared too quickly for Sky to decide whether he was pleased by the admission or not.

The man's dark hair was peppered with gray, and his bushy moustache and darkly tanned skin were evidence of a life spent largely on the water. His body was small and wiry, but with the well-muscled arms and chest a fisherman earns from hauling up heavy nets in rough seas. But there was something about his dark eyes, about the intelligently inquisitive look he leveled, that suggested this particular fisherman was a good deal more than a strong arm on a fishing boat. It confirmed Sky's supposition that he had come to the right *taverna* after all.

"Good evening," the fisherman translated.

Sky motioned to the empty chair across from him and at the plate of stuffed grape leaves on the table.

"Will you join me, friend?" he offered.

The other man nodded politely in thanks, then pulled out the chair and seated himself.

"You are English?" he asked, his accent thick but not unschooled. "We are not honored by the presence of many Englishmen here. Not many foreigners at all, actually. They tend to keep to the fancier places in town. You are, as you must have realized by now, quite a curiosity amongst us."

Sky smiled. "I'm afraid you still don't have an Englishman," he replied. "I'm American."

The man returned the smile, and for the first time Sky felt that he might not be such an unwanted intruder after all.

"Here on Crete we revere you Americans," the man

said with enthusiasm. "We admire the way you took your independence, the way you honor liberty."

Sky nodded. "The lesson was our fathers'. I fear many of my countrymen have forgotten the philosophy of liberty, even to the point where we fought a war amongst ourselves over it. If you revere us, you give us credit we hardly deserve."

The other quietly sipped his drink and considered Sky's words. Then he put the glass down on the table and leaned forward.

"But still, you fought your war and came to terms with your philosophy. And now you live the life to which we aspire. To us you are proof that what we yearn for is attainable if we are willing to pay the price." He reached out his hand to Sky across the rough wood of the table and smiled at him, baring a row of even, white teeth. "I am Spiros Petropoulos. In the name of all Cretan patriots, I welcome you to Crete."

Sky smiled in return. "Skyler Trask," he introduced himself. "I thank you for your welcome, Mr. Petropoulos."

Petropoulos shook his head. "No, no . . . we are friends. You must call me Spiros."

"With pleasure," Sky replied, amused by this sudden adoption, feeling as though he were being welcomed like a stray puppy who'd wandered into the *taverna*. "And I am Sky to my friends." He raised his glass. "To friendship."

Petropoulos joined the toast. "To friendship," he said as he too raised his glass. "And freedom." He tossed back a mouthful of the liquor.

"And freedom," Sky agreed as he drank. "Your English is excellent, Spiros."

"Thank you," Petropoulos replied. "My father had ambitions for me beyond the fishing boats. He spent his life working on them so that I would not have to." He shrugged. "Not every ambition is fated to be fulfilled. But I still have the education he gave me, the excellent English."

"I wish I could say the same for my Greek," Sky said. He grinned. "I wish I could say anything in Greek."

Petropoulos returned the grin. "We will have to teach you while you are here." He lifted his glass again. "*Yasas!*" he said. "To your health." He drained his glass.

Sky grinned. "*Yasas!*" he repeated before he emptied his own glass.

"Now," Petropoulos said as Sky motioned to the waiter to bring more *mastika,* "you must tell me how it is you have come to join us here to watch the sun set behind our boats."

Sky set his glass down carefully before he answered. "I write for a newspaper in New York," he began.

"Ah, New York," Petropoulos interrupted enthusiastically. "I have a cousin who went to live in New York." He leaned forward and lowered his voice. "There was this small matter of a knife fight, you see, which my cousin had the good fortune to win. It was, however, his misfortune that the man who lost died, and that man was a Turk, and one of influence. In any case, my cousin thought it wise to leave Crete, however much he loved it, and eventually he found a new life for himself in your very city!" He gave the impression that this coincidence was of great import. "A great city, New York." He leaned back as the waiter set a fresh glass on the table in front of him. "To New York," he said as he lifted it.

Sky took his own glass of *mastika.* "To New York," he replied gravely.

The toast completed, Petropoulos again leaned forward to Sky. "What is a writer for a newspaper in the great city of New York doing in an out-of-the-way *taverna* in Crete?" he asked.

Sky shrugged. "My publisher thinks there will be war

90

here soon. He thinks the Turks will fight the Greek forces for control of Crete."

Petropoulos sobered. "You come here to look for a war?" he asked, looking under the table, around at the other tables, and then to the beach where the fishing boats lay on the sand in peaceful silhouette against a round yellow moon.

Sky shook his head. "I come here to ask an honest Cretan what he thinks of this war that may or may not happen."

Petropoulos shrugged. "Foreigners have come to fight wars here for hundreds of years," he said. "Arabs, Venetians, Turks—greed brought them all to us. We fought them, but we were few and their numbers endless, and eventually they took what they wanted from us. But of them all, the Turks, they are the worst. And so now we ask the Greeks to help us throw off a yoke we can not bear."

"Then my publisher was right. War will come?"

"Yes, war will come, my friend." For a second Spiros seemed undecided, as though he were not quite sure he should speak. Then his expression hardened and he leveled his gaze at Sky. "Many Cretans prefer a Greek yoke to a foreign one. But there are still patriots amongst us, men who believe any master is a master over slaves, men who refuse to be shunted from one bondage to another. Yes, there will be war. And when it is over, both the Greeks and the Turks will have learned a lesson about men who yearn for their liberty." He motioned to the men around him. "To liberty!" he shouted and held up his glass.

The other fishermen turned to face Petropoulos. For an instant the noise subsided; even the backgammon game sank into silence. And then there was a low chorus that slowly swelled as the others lifted glasses and joined him.

91

"To liberty," they repeated again and again, the sound of their voices rising until it was a thick, basso chorus.

Sky listened to the swell of the chant and retreated into thought. Forbes Devereaux had brought him to Crete to report on a remote clash between two armies as if it was a play being enacted for the *Sun*'s readers' entertainment. Whatever he had anticipated, Sky realized then that he had stumbled onto a war that could prove to be a good deal more dangerous than anything he'd thought to find.

He'd seen enough violence to know that this war on Crete was no game. Men dedicated to a cause had a stake here, and a cause, Sky knew, whether for good or evil, could be deadly to anyone who happened to stumble into its path.

Chapter Five

"It's a pleasure to welcome you."

Sir Arthur Evans held out a large, bony, and decidedly dusty hand to Forbes. A tall, gangly man with thinning, sandy blond hair, he seemed entirely in his element, perfectly at his ease in wrinkled khaki that seemed far more appropriate to the setting, Arden thought, than her father's and David's dark suits and collared shirts.

"We're delighted you were willing to allow us to impose on you this way, Sir Arthur," Forbes said. "There is a great deal of interest in the States in the work you've begun here."

Arden turned away from the others, entirely bewitched by the incredible scenery. They were standing on one of the hills that surrounded a huge mound of earth whose edges had been partially dug away. The gashes into the mound were irregular, almost haphazard, it seemed to her, irregular brown slashes invading the green of the untouched areas. It seemed as if some monster had stood at the mound's rim and nibbled, taking a small bite here and a larger bite there, tasting some and moving on. Where the excavations had been begun lay partially exposed pieces of walls and columns, a small hint, she realized, of what must lie beneath the great heap of dark earth.

"Do you really think it could once have been the palace of King Minos?" she asked absently, more to herself than to any of the others, a hint of awe in her tone as she considered the expanse of the mound, the possible size of the place.

Evans turned to look at the site as she did, then shrugged. "It was surely someone's palace, Miss Devereaux," he told her. "Even if you wish to consider Minos only a legend, this place was undoubtedly the palace of some very powerful king." He smiled then, a smile that somehow managed to change the otherwise rather austere look of his face, making him seem far younger, far less aloof. "Personally, I find legend appealing. It pleases me to believe that Theseus might actually have slain the Minotaur, that Daedalus and Icarus might actually have escaped from the labyrinth with wings."

"Looking at all this, it is hard to believe anything else," Arden agreed. "This land seems to be a womb for legend, a place where heroes ought rightly to have lived."

Her words seemed to please Evans, and perhaps even echo his own thoughts, and he nodded in agreement. He had no chance to reply, however, for the wind chose that moment to blow a haze of golden soil into a small funnel, lifting it into the air above them before releasing it to settle over and around them in a thin dusting. Evans laughed as he saw Arden's amazement at this curiosity and then Forbes's expression as he cast a distasteful glance to the deposit on his shoulder.

"In Delos they call this wind *meltemi,*" he said, "and there it blows throughout the whole of the summer, making everyone's life fairly miserable. But here in Crete there is only an occasional afternoon of it. The local farmers say it is good luck to be greeted by it when you start out upon a journey."

"Then I shall take it as a good omen," David said.

He turned to survey the excavations, considering them

with a look Arden could only describe as greedy. His manner since they had arrived at the site had surprised her. If he was ordinarily aloof, he'd grown far more so, and he spoke with a pedantic, donnish air that rivaled anything even Evans could muster.

"I did not know how long you intended to stay," Evans was saying to Forbes. "As you've doubtless discovered, the distance from Heracleion, as the crow flies, is not great. Unfortunately we are not crows and must travel by the less than perfect Cretan roads. I assumed that you and your daughter would prefer not to try to attempt the trip each day, and so took the liberty of taking rooms for you both in the house of the farmer where I myself am boarding. Hardly luxurious, but clean. Considering what is available in Heracleion, I don't think you'll notice the difference much. I can introduce you to the farmer's wife now, if you like, and let you get settled. Then, I'm afraid I must return to my work." He turned to David. "You might just spend the afternoon looking around and we'll get down to real work for you in the morning."

"Certainly," David agreed.

They turned from the hillside and descended the far side to a small stone house fronted by a pleasant little garden and bordered by a large barn. Chickens chased each other among the flowers of the garden and scratched in the soil searching for grubs. The sound of bleating sheep drifted to them from the fenced field on the far side of the barn.

A middle-aged woman exited the house as they approached it. Arden had the feeling that she had been watching them, waiting for the proper moment to make her appearance. She was a tall, large-boned, and amply bosomed woman dressed in a heavy black skirt, a crisp white linen blouse, and, despite the warmth of the after-noon, a flowered shawl, obviously her best, worn in honor of the newcomers' arrival.

Evans made the introductions with due gravity and formality, to the obvious delight of Kiria Spirtos, then translated her small welcoming speech into English. The formalities completed, Evans smiled by way of encouragement, then departed, leaving the three Americans to cope with the Greek matron as best they could on their own.

Kiria Spirtos took her role as hostess very seriously, herding them into a dark parlor filled with heavy, overstuffed, and apparently rarely used furniture, then pressing on them small cups of dark, thick coffee and plates of honeyed pastries, talking in Greek the whole while, despite the fact that neither Arden, Forbes, nor David understood so much as a word of it.

"Are you certain you don't understand anything she's saying, David?" Arden asked in a whisper when Kiria Spirtos left them for a few moments to refill her coffeepot. "I don't see how a classicist could not possibly understand Greek."

David scowled at her. "Modern Greek is entirely different from ancient Greek, Arden," he hissed in return. "I've already told you that."

She had but a second to return the scowl before their hostess rejoined them, bearing along with the coffee another plate of sweets.

Arden wished she had been less appreciative of the first helping of pastry. Kiria Spirtos seemed to interpret her enthusiasm as a request for more, an impression that took a good deal of hand waving and regretful smiles to dismiss without causing insult.

When Kiria Spirtos was finally satisfied they had all sufficiently exhausted their need for sweets, she finally showed them their rooms.

They climbed the stairs after her to a bare, low-ceilinged second floor, where they peered into the rooms she had made ready for them. The rooms were all small, spare, and stark with blank, unadorned white walls, but spotlessly clean, each equipped with a narrow brass bed covered with a white coverlet, a single straight chair, a table, and a small chest.

Arden wandered into the room Kiria Spirtos had assigned to her, went to the narrow window, and stared out at a field where sheep grazed. She turned back, smiled, and nodded appreciatively at Kiria Spirtos's hopeful glance, murmuring, *"Efcharisto,"* thank you, one of her few recently mastered Greek words.

The word of thanks was apparently encouragement enough, for it seemed to please Kiria Spirtos sufficiently to set her off once again into a stream of talk. Arden nodded, and smiled, and managed to make her escape to find David and her father waiting for her in the garden to the front of the farmhouse.

"I feel as though I've just listened to the chorus of a play by Euripides, in the original," she laughed to Forbes. "I wonder what she was telling me."

"Probably to watch where you step," Forbes said dryly as he wiped the sole of his shoe on the grass and glared at the brood of chickens roaming freely in the garden.

"Shall we take a look at the dig?" David asked. "I'm eager to see what they've found out there."

"Oh, yes," Arden agreed enthusiastically. She realized she had begrudged the time politeness dictated they spend with Kiria Spirtos. She was filled with curiosity about that huge mound of dirt they'd overlooked and what might lie beneath it.

"You two run along," Forbes said as he settled himself onto a wooden garden chair set in the sunshine. "After that pastry, I think I need a bit of a nap." He smiled at the prospect of such self-indulgence, then gave David a small, conspiratorial wink.

David held out his arm. "It would be my pleasure, Miss Devereaux," he said, "to provide you with escort."

Arden's eyes narrowed as she turned to her father. "Papa?" she asked, sure he had conspired with David to leave the two of them alone together.

But Forbes ignored her glance, settling himself in the chair, resting his elbows on the arms, and twining his fingers together before letting his hands settle on his stomach.

"Have a pleasant walk, Arden," he mumbled, then closed his eyes.

Resigned, Arden put her arm through David's. Well, she thought, perhaps this is the time to settle matters with David. She wondered why she felt no excitement at the prospect, why she felt, in fact, nothing more than a vague sense of resignation.

It was like a treasure hunt, Arden thought as she surveyed the huge green mound that Evans believed held within it the remains of King Minos's palace. It seemed almost like a search for El Dorado or buried pirate booty. The very air felt tense to her, charged with a strange excitement, a feeling that something momentous was happening in this place. The weight of it amazed her. She could almost taste it on her tongue each time she drew breath.

The dig was a flurry of activity, with dozens of men wielding picks and shovels and carting away the loosened dirt in huge woven baskets. The workmen seemed barely conscious of her and David as they scrambled through the heaps of rubble that waited to be loaded into baskets and carried away.

"Evans must have hired every farmer in the area to be his spade men," David commented as he considered the activity. "He must be concerned about the possibility of war and eager to accomplish as much as he can quickly."

"But who oversees what they do?" Arden asked.

"Surely Evans can't personally direct all this work himself."

David nodded. "That's the sort of thing I'll be doing. I'm sure Evans has a half dozen others like me, young men just starting out in the field." He pointed to a tall, lanky form leaning into a crevice that had been dug into the mound while two workmen, holding shovels, lazed behind him, waiting. "Like him," David said.

Just as he spoke, the man withdrew itself and straightened up, spoke a few words to the two workmen, then looked in the direction of where Arden stood staring at the procedure. He waved.

"Welcome to Wonderland."

The words were loud and booming, a surprise coming from so narrow a chest, Arden thought as she watched him approach. Tall, thin, and bespectacled, with watery blue eyes and bright red hair, he moved quickly, crossing over a heap of rubble and making his way to them.

"Charles Langford," he said when he reached them, offering his hand to David and a surprisingly pleasant smile to Arden. "I take it you're David Trumbull. The old man told us to expect a new boy." He watched David's reaction to the last two words and held up a calming hand. "British public school term . . . I forgot you were American. No offense intended."

David nodded. "None taken," he replied.

"Good," Langford said. "We can certainly use an extra pair of hands around here." He turned his glance to Arden. "And it's even more welcome now that I see it comes accompanied by a lovely lady." With that he reached out for Arden's hand, grasped it in his own rather dusty one, and brought it theatrically to his lips. "Welcome, beautiful goddess, whoever you are."

Arden laughed at his flamboyance, unaware of the anger Langford's gesture had managed to rouse in David.

"Arden Devereaux, Mr. Langford . . ."

99

"My fiancée," David interrupted, reaching for Arden's arm and pulling her back, close to him.

Langford put a hand over his heart and groaned. "My heart is broken," he moaned with proper melodrama. "I've come to Greece and found a goddess, and in the time it takes to draw breath she is snatched away from me." He grinned and winked at Arden. "But I've heard it's better to have loved and lost," he added philosophically. He nodded to David as though looking for affirmation of his statement, then back to Arden when he realized he wouldn't find what he was looking for.

"Kirie Langford!"

Langford turned to the workman who had called for him, then back to David and Arden.

"My services, it seems, are needed. There is no rest for the struggling young archaeologist here," he said, and started to move off. "Enjoy your afternoon," he called back as he climbed through the heaps of rubble. "Tomorrow it begins for you, too, Trumbull."

David took Arden's arm and began to walk in the opposite direction. His expression settled into one of pained control.

Arden found herself amused by his anger. "He seems quite nice," she said, knowing he wouldn't agree. "I liked him."

"I did not," David said through tight lips.

"So I noticed," Arden replied. "And it also did not escape my notice that you introduced me to him as your fiancée."

David stopped walking and turned to face her. "I didn't like the way he looked at you," he said. "The way he spoke to you."

"Really, David. He was only making an effort to be amusing."

"*I* wasn't amused." He stared at her for a long moment before he seemed to realize he might have done some-

100

thing wrong. "Surely you aren't angry with me?"

Arden considered his expression, wondering if there might be a hint of regret in it. She couldn't quite decide.

Finally she shook her head. "No, David, I'm not angry with you."

He put his hands to her shoulders. "Arden, I know I told you I wouldn't press you, that I'd wait for you to make your own decision. But back there when Langford took your hand that way I realized I simply can't wait any longer. I must know now. Will you marry me?"

She hesitated a moment, not really sure what she ought to say. But then she reminded herself of the decision she'd made the previous night, told herself again that she would be a fool to do anything else.

"I suppose it wouldn't be fair for me to be the cause of Mr. Langford's believing you a liar, David," she replied slowly.

There, Arden thought . . . it's done. She waited for a surge of feeling, excitement or delight, but found after she'd searched vainly for it within herself that she had managed to find only a dull sense of accomplishment, the sort of feeling she might have after having completed some odious but necessary task.

It seemed to take a few seconds for him to decipher her words. Then his lips formed themselves into a satisfied smile. His grasp tightened on her shoulders.

"I'll make you happy, Arden," he told her. "You'll see. We'll be married when I've finished the six months' work I've contracted to do here. After that we can take a tour of the continent as a wedding trip, if you like. You've made the right decision."

She wasn't sure if he was trying to reassure her or convince her, but it really didn't matter. She'd made her decision, and she intended to stand by it.

"I know I have, David," she told him, then waited.

He started to lean forward to her but hesitated, first

looking around to the workmen who labored nearby. For a second Arden found herself wondering what it was he'd intended to do that could not be done in front of those men. Surely, she thought, a kiss would not be thought so great a transgression, not even back in Boston. She lifted her face to his, expecting he would come to the same conclusion.

He didn't. He pressed his lips chastely against her forehead, then quickly drew away from her, releasing his hold of her shoulders and stepping back. Then he gave her the crook of his arm, waited while she put her hand in it, and started forward again.

"Look there, Arden," he said, pointing to fragments of painted plaster that had been exposed by the workers, the rubble managing to hold it upright as though it were still the wall of some great room. Its surface bore a still colorful fresco of what appeared to be monkeys amid a jungle of greenery. "Isn't it incredible?"

Arden turned to the piece of exposed wall, wishing she could summon some interest in it, but unable to find any at that moment.

"Yes," she agreed. "Incredible."

While Forbes Devereaux was busy organizing the carriage to take David, Arden, and him to Evans's dig at Knossos, Skyler Trask was already on horseback, well to the east, following the old road to Mallia. By early afternoon he found himself sitting on the grass on a plateau overlooking a row of picturesque windmills, built by the Venetians he would learn a few hours later when he had descended into the town, and disused for centuries, remnants of other, supplanted masters on Crete—and all the while he found himself thinking, despite his own better wishes, about Arden Devereaux.

He'd told himself when he'd taken leave of her and

Forbes at the dock the previous afternoon that it was in his own best interest if he managed to avoid seeing Arden again. He'd managed to arrange his existence precisely to his liking. The last thing he needed was a woman, especially a shallow, status-hungry, rich woman. His life was just fine as it was—free, uncluttered, and uncomplicated. In short, Arden Devereaux was decidedly the worst sort of excess baggage.

It was a litany he'd repeated to himself more times than he cared to count. Despite the repetitions, however, he'd hardly managed to convince himself. He found himself thinking more and more about her, about the way he'd felt when he'd held her in his arms, about the way he'd felt when he'd made love to her. As long as they had been together on the *Arcadia* and he had had her in view, all too often with that fool David Trumbull in tow, he'd had no trouble dismissing her. Let her play her little games with Trumbull, Sky had told himself. Let him have her. They deserved one another.

It was far less easy, he found, to dismiss the image he held of her in his mind.

Sky grunted in disgust. This is foolish, he told himself as he removed from his mouth the piece of grass he'd been chewing and threw it to the ground. He turned to stare into the shade, where his horse nibbled at the grass beneath the tree where Sky had tied him, apparently more than happy to end the long walk by spending the remainder of the afternoon just as he was.

But Sky had other plans. He had a job, he reminded himself as he pushed himself to his feet. And despite the limited expectations he had had when he'd started out on the trip to Greece, he realized from what he had learned the night before that there really was a story for him to find here, something far more compelling than the jockeying of two governments involved in a skirmish over a relatively small piece of real estate in the middle of the Aegean. The people who had become pawns in that skirmish were not to be as easily dismissed as he had expected them to be.

There had been skirmishes between the Cretans and the Turks for more than two decades, skirmishes that had grown bloodier as the years passed. And now it seemed the Greek government was finally stepping in to help the people of Crete force the Turks off their island. Sky would have assumed Petropoulos would have welcomed the help. But he did not.

"We will only exchange one yoke for another," Petropoulos had said. "A less odious yoke, perhaps . . . but a yoke nonetheless."

Petropoulos had told him of acts of defiance against the Turkish rule that seemed incredibly heroic to Sky. Among them was a story that had seemed almost biblical in its fervor: not twenty years before, while his own countrymen were busily engaged in their own war to decide if one man had the right to lay claim to another, the local Cretan peasants had risen up against an increasingly odious Turkish rule. Eventually they had entrenched themselves in the monastery of Arkadi, and, along with the monks, held out against a siege by Turkish troops. When it became obvious the monastery would soon be taken, the Abbot Gabriel had ordered the monastery refectory blown up, killing not only the defenders, but also three thousand armed Turkish assailants as well.

"We revere such bravery," Petropoulos had told him. "We honor men who choose freedom over mere existence. Go to our towns, talk to our people. Then go back to New York and write about us. Tell the world that heroes still dwell in Crete, men who fight against unbelievable odds, and all for the sake of liberty."

That, of course, was exactly what Sky had intended to do, the first part at least, to go to the towns and talk to the people. But armed as he now was with a list of names of

Petropoulos's "cousins," (and they could not possibly all be cousins), that task should be, Sky realized, a good deal easier than he had first anticipated.

Sky was hardly so great a fool as to think he had been accepted by Petropoulos. On the contrary, he was sure the Cretan was hoping to use him, to use his voice in a fairly well-known American newspaper to champion the separatists' cause. But Sky found he did not resent the patriot-fisherman's manipulation. He would, he realized, have done the same thing were he in Petropoulos's place. Crete had been the pawn in other countries' ambitions for hundreds of years. Sky could easily understand why Petropoulos would be willing to misuse a stranger's trust if he thought it would help his cause.

He looked down at the long row of windmills one last time and found himself confronted by the fleeting thought of how pleasant this place might be were he able to share the view and the sunshine with Arden. He closed his eyes and imagined what it would be like to have her lying there on the grass beside him, to celebrate the beauty and the solitude of the place with an embrace— even, perhaps, to make love with only the uncluttered blue sky above them.

His thoughts grew painful with the knowledge that none of it would ever happen. He chased the pleasant image away, telling himself it was useless to torture himself. Then he went to the tree where he'd tied the horse, loosened the reins, and swung himself reluctantly into the saddle.

He looked regretfully back at the impression he'd made where he'd lain on the grass. It would have been pleasant to simply spend the afternoon lying in the sun watching the old windmills, he thought. Or perhaps not. Perhaps his mind would have become mired in thoughts of Arden Devereaux. Perhaps it was just as well he had other matters to which he must attend.

He turned the horse back to the road that led down from the plateau toward the town. He was hungry. When he reached the town he would find a *taverna* and get something to eat. Hopefully the food would be delivered along with some information as to where he might find one of the people on the list of names Petropoulos had given him.

A few hours later Sky found himself in the center of a small town square trying to decide in which of three *tavernas* he would eat. They all seemed pretty much the same, except for the fact that one of them appeared to enjoy the patronage of soldiers, Turkish soldiers, while the two others did not.

He found himself wondering why there seemed to be so many soldiers in such a small town, for as he looked around he saw a good number of them, many more than he had seen in all of Heracleion. The townfolk, especially the women, appeared to make every effort to avoid them, and there were unpleasant looks on both sides. The air was thick with a tension that seemed completely at odds with the pleasant warmth of the late afternoon sunshine that glinted off the brick of the square, the white walls of the buildings that faced it, the scattering of flowers that tumbled out of windowboxes, and the branches of a huge almond tree that dominated the center of it. Only the children, playing noisily in the center of the square, darting out amongst the small amount of traffic that moved through the street and to all appearances totally ignored by it, seemed entirely at their ease.

Sky settled his moment of indecision by electing to avoid the *taverna* where the soldiers congregated. He headed instead to the one at the far side of the square, wondering as he walked if the distance meant the café's patrons were at the opposite end of the town's political spectrum.

He found a table at the edge of the veranda, dropping his canvas bag at his feet as he sat. There was not so much noise here as there had been the previous night at the *taverna* in Heracleion, no game of backgammon, no noisy fishermen growing mellow over a glass of *retsina*. The few customers who sat at the tables talked quietly among themselves, leaning forward so they might speak to their companions in low voices as though they feared being overheard. The loudest sound came from the clicking of the stone beads they shunted from hand to hand. This unconscious fingering of amber beads was a habit, Sky had grown to realize, that seemed to infect all Greeks, including those of Crete. The noise from the *taverna* at the far side of the square where the soldiers congregated was loud and raucous by contrast.

"*Kirie?*"

He looked up to find a waiter had materialized at his side. The man seemed less interested in him, however, than in the activity at the *taverna* across the square.

"I'd like dinner," Sky said. Then, seeing the waiter's perplexed expression, he searched his memory for the few words of Greek Spiros Petropoulos had managed to teach him the previous night. After a moment's casting about, he managed to find the word. "*Fagito,*" he said. "Food."

The waiter's stare hardly encouraged him, and Sky wondered if he'd mispronounced the word, perhaps sworn at the man or even worse. But the waiter turned and began to move inside. After a step or two he turned back to Sky and motioned for him to follow.

A bit perplexed, Sky rose and followed the man through the small front room of the *taverna* and into the kitchen. A short gray-haired woman wearing a large

107

white apron around her considerable middle was standing at a work table chopping vegetables. She looked up and smiled at him.

"Kali mera, Kirie," she said, greeting him with a wave of her knife. Then she motioned to the half dozen large pots that sat atop a heavy black stove. She moved back, clearing the way so that he might pass her.

Bewildered, but willing to be cooperative, Sky inspected the contents of the pots. Most appeared to contain fish in one sort of preparation or another, and all but two held a fair proportion of tomatoes in varying states of decomposition. As the waiter was staring at him, Sky assumed he was to indicate his choices, which he did rather haphazardly, aware as he was that he was hungry enough to find almost anything palatable.

The task completed, Sky wandered back to the veranda and reseated himself on the chair he had vacated. Then he leaned forward to where his bag lay on the ground, opened it, and removed the paper Spiros Petropoulos had given him, the list of names of "cousins." He put it on the table and ran his finger down the list, searching for the one that had the town name Mallia printed beside it. He found it, and by the time the waiter had returned bearing his food, he'd returned the list to his bag.

The waiter set the plate down in front of him, as well as a small basket of bread and utensils wrapped in a white linen napkin.

"Retsina?" the waiter asked, but with a tone that implied agreement was a forgone conclusion.

Sky nodded. "And perhaps you can tell me how to find a man named Nikolas Constatin?"

For an instant Sky thought the man would drop his tray.

The waiter's eyes darted to the veranda of the *taverna* across the square, then back to Sky.

108

"Nikolas Constatin?"

"His name was given to me by Spiros Petropoulos," Sky added, knowing the man didn't understand the words, but hoping he might recognize the name.

"Spiros Petropoulos?" The waiter shook his head.

Sky realized he was only adding to the confusion. "Constatin?" he asked again. "Nikolas Constatin?"

The waiter grimaced and once again darted a glance across the square. Then he backed away from Sky as though he'd been bitten.

Sky scowled, aware that he'd made a muddle of things somehow. But his stomach was growling, and he decided to eat before he made any attempt to rectify the situation.

"Lack of sustenance," he muttered to himself as he lifted his fork, "makes the brain weak."

He'd hardly made a dent in the food on his plate when a thin young man with dark hair and steely eyes slid into the chair beside his. Sky stared up at him, rather surprised at this unexpected and uninvited guest at his table.

"If you're looking for a handout, you'll have to tell the waiter to fetch another plate," he said in a dry tone, sure the young man had no idea what it was he was saying. "I'm too hungry to share."

The young man's expression grew pained, and Sky realized he'd made his second mistake of the afternoon.

"On the other hand," he added and attempted a smile, "I'd be more than willing to stand you a glass of *retsina* if you can get the waiter to bring mine."

"I did not come here to beg from your plate or drink with you," the young man hissed. "What do you want with Nikolas Constatin?"

"You speak English?" Sky asked, the question now unnecessary.

"We are not all boorish peasants," the man shot back.

"I did not mean to imply that you were," Sky said,

hoping to calm the obviously ruffled feathers.

"What do you want with Nikolas Constatin?" the man demanded a second time.

"Are you he?" Sky asked.

"I'm his brother, Theo. Why do you come here looking for him?"

Sky put down his fork and leaned across the table to him. "While I was in Heracleion, I met a friend of his, Spiros Petropoulos. He told me to look up your brother if I should find myself in Mallia."

His explanation seemed to have absolutely no effect on the younger man's suspicions. Constatin darted a glance across the square, then returned his gaze to Sky and glared at him.

"Why should I believe you?" he demanded in a hoarse whisper. "How do I know you aren't an agent sent by the Turks?"

Sky shrugged. "Why would I be?" he asked as he reached for a piece of bread. He took a bite of it and chewed it slowly, wondering just what it was he had wandered into in this strangely wary little town.

His companion gave him no answer. He seemed to be trying to keep his eyes on Sky, but they kept straying, off toward the *taverna* at the far end of the square. Sky found himself bewildered and followed the younger man's gaze. It was only then that he realized the square had grown suddenly quiet. The children had disappeared, and there was no one, not a wagon, not a single man on foot, on the streets surrounding the square. The only noise was from the *taverna* at the far side of the square, from the soldiers who still spoke with the same noisy boisterousness. One of the soldiers called out loudly for a waiter to bring him more wine and swore with equal vigor when none seemed forthcoming. Sky could see no waiters among the men who lazed about the place. It seemed they too had disappeared.

110

Sky dropped the piece of bread. He turned his gaze back to his suspicious companion.

"What's going on here?" he demanded sharply. He reached out and grasped the front of the young man's shirt.

Constatin put his hand to Sky's and tried to push it away, but his attention was still riveted on the far end of the square. Sky turned back, realizing that whatever was going to happen would come soon. He got a quick glimpse of a black-clad figure kneeling at the side of the veranda, then rising and fleeing.

He didn't know what it was that made him understand, but at that moment he knew. He started to rise, and a cry of warning rose to his lips. The explosion occurred before he had the chance.

The very earth of the square seemed to rumble and shiver. The roar was deafening, and with it a huge ball of flame rose from what had only seconds before been the veranda of the *taverna* where the Turkish soldiers had been sitting. The force of it, even from such a distance, was great enough to throw Sky to the ground.

Chapter Six

Forbes Devereaux looked up at his daughter's expectant face.

"Well, Papa?" Arden demanded.

She found herself involuntarily holding her breath, not at all sure why his opinion of her work meant so very much to her, but realizing that she would be crushed if he did not approve of the article she'd written.

He purposely drew out the moment, savoring the power he held over her at that instant, something he felt far too rarely, he thought. Then he allowed himself to smile up at her.

"It's quite good, Arden," he told her.

Arden let out the too long held breath.

"Is it? Is it really, Papa?" she demanded as she dropped onto his bed, bouncing as she sat. It seemed almost as though the feeling of relief weakened her, and her legs were not quite able to hold her.

He nodded. "Your style is a bit flowery for my taste, but Harry Stoning tells me the ladies like that sort of thing. And your descriptions of Evans and of the dig are excellent." He grinned. "If I'd known you had such talent I'd have set you to work long ago. And if I wasn't certain you'd eventually agree to marry David Trumbull,

I think the editor of the *Sun* might consider making a star reporter of you."

Arden looked down at her ink-smudged fingers and found herself smiling with pleasure at the possibility. But then she shook her head.

"I doubt that, Papa," she told him. "I think you'd be afraid I'd grow too accustomed to the sense of independence it might give me." She looked back up at him and realized from his expression that she had inadvertently found a hidden nerve, that what she had said was precisely correct. "In any case, I've promised to earn my bread, or, in our case, my *baklava* on this trip." She momentarily felt a twinge in her teeth at the mention of the sweet pastry, an uncomfortable aching feeling at the prospect of consuming more of it that evening at dinner. She'd never cared very much for sweets and could not quite understand the Greek taste for them. "And, any engagement to David notwithstanding, I must admit I find the prospect quite pleasing."

Forbes could not miss the hint of bitterness in her tone as she mentioned David, and he found himself wondering if he was doing the right thing, if in urging her to accept David's proposal he had not in some way failed her. He found himself reaching out to grasp her hand, wanting her to cling to him, to make him feel as though she still found him as infinitely wise as she had thought him when she was a child. Before he could take her hand, however, she stood, turned, and moved away from him to peer out the window. He found himself holding nothing but air, and he looked down at his empty hands with regret. It was only then that he realized what she had just told him.

"Did you say engagement to David?" he demanded.

She turned back to face him and nodded, oblivious to the discomfort that lingered in his expression. "Yes," she told him. "We settled the matter this afternoon. As soon as he's finished with his work here, we'll be married."

Forbes let the pages of foolscap drop to the floor as he pushed himself out of the chair and moved to her. Whatever feeling of regret he'd had disappeared in a wave of delight.

"But why didn't you tell me immediately?" he demanded as he put his arm around her and offered her a fatherly kiss on the cheek.

Arden shrugged. "I was just eager to get on with the article, I suppose," she replied. She pulled away from him, crossed back to the chair he'd vacated, and knelt to gather up the scattered pages from the floor.

For an instant Forbes found himself wondering why she seemed so disinterested in the prospect of her own marriage, why she showed none of the nervous, girlish delight he'd have expected under the circumstances. But he told himself quickly that Arden wasn't that sort of a young woman, that despite her age there was very little about her that was girlish or uncertain.

"Have you met the others, Papa?" she asked him as she sorted out the pages and arranged them for him.

"Others?" he asked. He had some difficulty following her train of thought, her sudden change of subject as though the matter of her marriage had been completely exhausted with the few words they'd exchanged and other, more pressing topics had come to mind.

"Yes, there are three others who will be working with David. A Charles Langford, an Englishman, and two more, also English, I suppose, although I haven't met them yet." She left the neatly arranged article on his table where he could not forget to mail it off to Harry Stoning for publication in the *Sun*.

He shook his head. "I've been promised that particular pleasure at dinner this evening, along with an introduction to the formidable husband of Kiria Spirtos."

115

"Is there a husband?" she asked. "Of course, I suppose I knew there must be, as Kirsi Spirtos doesn't dress entirely in black like a good Greek widow, but somehow I can't picture a husband." Just as she could not picture herself with a husband, she thought, at least not if it had to be David Trumbull.

He laughed. "Indeed there is. As well as three strapping sons, according to Sir Arthur, all of them cheerfully involved with the dig when they are not otherwise occupied in the family orchards. As for the sons, it would seem we are literally sleeping in their beds. We've apparently usurped their rooms and they've moved themselves out to sleep in one of the barns."

"Oh, but that's terrible, Papa."

He nodded. "So I suggested to Sir Arthur. But he was quite firm in insisting we not even suggest leaving. It would insult our host. The Greeks apparently hold a classical view of the obligations of hospitality."

Arden laughed. "Yes, David told me a story about Nestor, who told his servants to go after a departing guest and force his return."

"A tale Kiria Spirtos takes to heart, I'm afraid. She twice approached me with sweets while you were off with David this afternoon."

"You must find some occupation while you're here, Papa. You must come out to the dig tomorrow."

"In self-defense, I suppose you're right, Arden. If I stay here, I'm sure Kiria Spirtos will stuff me the way the French do their geese to make foie gras."

She laughed again. But before she had the chance to offer any comment as to his similarity to a goose, there was a knock at the door.

"Ah, there you both are," David said as he pushed the door open and poked his head inside. "I think they're waiting dinner on us."

116

"Dinner? Is it that time so soon?" Forbes groaned softly.

Arden laughed. "Be brave, Papa," she told him as she took his arm and started with him toward the door.

Kiria Spirtos had set out a long table in her garden, one large enough to accommodate not only her own family but the team of archaeologists and Forbes and Arden as well. The others were already assembled in the garden when Arden arrived with David and her father. She hesitated a moment as they approached, feeling almost as if she were walking into a sea of strange, tanned young men.

Sir Arthur, carefully scrubbed now, dressed in freshly laundered, crisply pressed linen and dark suit and seeming as formal to Arden as Forbes, took pity on her and greeted her.

"Langford has been extolling your beauty to the others for the last quarter hour, Miss Devereaux. They are all eager to meet you."

"I fear Mr. Langford has a vivid imagination, but I sincerely appreciate the flattery," Arden laughed. "But you, you've changed, Sir Arthur."

"Changed?" Evans offered her a confused stare.

"Arden has described you in her article as an explorer, Sir Arthur, dressed in khaki and holding the dust of the ages in your hands," Forbes explained as Evans took her hand.

She laughed. "Indeed," she agreed. "It hardly seems fair of you to change so completely before I've settled my description of you into print."

Evans smiled. "Should I ever go to New York, Miss Devereaux, I promise to wear only clothes that have been properly steeped in reverently ancient dirt," he told her

117

with mock seriousness. "I most certainly would not want to disillusion your readers."

"Don't let him fool you, Miss Devereaux. He's only dressed like a gentleman in honor of your arrival, as are we all."

Charles Langford had appeared at Evans's side, as scrubbed and neatly attired as his superior, his pale eyes peering merrily at her from behind his spectacles, his red hair still damp and slick from the brushing it had received.

"Of an ordinary evening," he added in a slightly hushed tone as though he were imparting a secret of great import, "we are more than apt to dine like the beasts we actually are, dressed in little more than bear skins and an occasional fig leaf."

Arden couldn't keep from laughing. "I think, Mr. Langford, fig leaves might prove a bit drafty for an evening."

He considered her words thoughtfully. "Perhaps," he acceded. "But we are willing to suffer for our science, Miss Devereaux."

Evans remained aloof during this exchange. When it was completed, he cleared his throat.

"As it would seem you've had already the pleasure of making Charles's acquaintance, Miss Devereaux, please allow me to introduce you to my two other assistants."

With that he took Arden's arm and led her to where two other young men stood patiently waiting their turn.

James Blake and Franklin Hobbs seemed serious, rather dry individuals, with none of Charles Langford's humor. Even as Evans made the introductions Arden could not help feeling that she would confuse the two of them in her mind despite any efforts to the contrary. David, on the other hand, seemed to find their conversation more than interesting as they spoke of finding the

118

outlines of what they believed to be a barrow tomb just to the south of the main part of the dig.

"Did you hear that, Arden?" he asked, turning to her. "A barrow tomb. If it houses the remains of a king of Knossos, who knows what treasure it might contain?"

Arden thought the prospect roused the first real enthusiasm she had ever seen in him.

"Blake and Hobbs are burning to get inside it," Langford said to Arden. "Probably hoping to do a bit of bag work, and make off with an ancient treasure or two to compensate them for the money their fathers donated to the dig."

Both Blake and Hobbs scowled at him, ignoring his grin, obviously not in the least amused by his sense of humor.

"For pity's sake, Langford," Hobbs hissed. Then he turned to Arden. "My apologies, Miss Devereaux."

Langford wasn't the least put off. "I don't see why you two won't admit we're all of us simply ne'er-do-wells whose families are happy to spend small fortunes for the simple luxury of being rid of us. Not that I resent the fact in my own case . . . the old man's put out a fortune of his own to fund the dig. I can't blame him for wanting to know his assistants are at least marginally committed. And our careers have a good deal to gain from the investment."

Before either Blake or Hobbs could offer any counter to Langford's levity, Evans returned with Alexander Spirtos at his side. This introduction Evans performed with all formality, just as he had earlier that day when he'd introduced Kiria Spirtos. The Greek farmer was a big man, tall and broadly built, with dark hair and eyes and a pleasant smile.

"I welcome you to my house," he said in careful English. "It is a great honor to receive you." He then introduced his three sons, tall, dark-haired, dark-eyed men like himself, strong and strapping and eager to wish the pretty foreigner welcome.

Later, as they sat at the table over plates heaped with roast lamb and eggplant stew, Spirtos grew philosophical. He seemed eager that the Americans get to know him.

"When I was Niko's age," he said, pointing to his youngest son, "I thought to leave here, to get away from the Turks and everything they did here. My father told me to wait, to stay here and work in his orchards, that nothing lasts forever. But I was an eager young man, as all the young are, I suppose. I signed on as a seaman to an English merchant ship and spent the next few months washing decks and heaving overboard." He laughed at himself. "Can you imagine, a Cretan who has no tolerance for the sea? But then my father grew sick, and by the time the letter found me and I returned, he was already dead. So I had my adventure and returned home for good, to live here and work in my father's orchards, all by the time I was twenty." He looked along the length of the table to his wife. "I've not regretted it," he said as he smiled at her. "That year taught me many things, a bit of English, how to tie nautical knots, but mostly how to appreciate what is most important in a man's life."

"Here, here," Forbes offered in agreement.

"I hope only to live long enough to see the Turks driven out of my home," Spirtos added, and raised a glass of the pale *retsina* they all had been served.

"For my part, I would rather things remain peaceful here as they are now," Evans said. "I've heard of acts of violence in the villages to the east."

Spirtos nodded. "If things go on, I think the Greeks will finally agree to come to our aid."

"But if war breaks out, think what might happen to this beautiful place, to your home and your orchards," David countered. "Isn't it better to keep peace with the Turks? Life seems pleasant enough here."

"It is easy for you to talk, someone who has always been free," came a low growl from the far end of the table. "You would feel differently were it your home that was held hostage by a filthy Turkish sultan who has only one interest, his own pockets."

"That is enough, Kostas," Spirtos hissed angrily at his eldest son. He turned to David. "You will be kind enough to excuse my son," he said. "There is something about this time that brings out the madness in young men."

Kostas stood and threw his napkin to the table. "I can make my own apologies when they are called for," he told his father angrily. "While we sit here and talk about how pleasant our lives are, men are dying. What sort of men are we when we think more of our own comfort than of our countrymen? Because you gave up and accepted a life in your father's vineyards does not mean we are all cowards."

Spirtos rose. "Kostas!" he shouted.

But Kostas had turned and stalked away, and Spirtos found himself staring after his son's back. His face was dark with anger, and Arden could see his hands were balled into fists. It took him a moment, but he managed to calm himself, to keep his own emotions from his guests.

"He has reason," Langford said gently as Spirtos reseated himself. "I've heard the Turkish officials had five men killed in retribution for an accident that took a Turkish soldier's life in a town near Dikte. If there are many more acts like that, the Greeks are sure to send troops and there will be no avoiding a real war here."

"Crete has been fighting wars against outsiders for more centuries than I can count," Spirtos told him. "I fear our young men know little of life without the prospect of war hovering close by. They talk of bravery and death as though it meant nothing to them, as though dying were some minor event in their lives."

"But surely you would welcome the help of the Greek government," Arden asked. "They could help you force out the Turks."

Spirtos nodded. "We have petitioned them for years, and it seems they may actually come to our aid at last. Most of us will welcome them if they do come. Most would wish to become part of Greece, as our closest ties, even from antiquity, are with Greece. But there are still many young men, hotheads like Kostas, who see Crete only for Crete, who wish us to stand alone in a world that will not let us. Between the Greeks and the Turks, we can do little but sit and wait for our destruction."

Arden raised her glass to her lips and sipped her wine. Alexander Spirtos and his sons were hardly the simple farming family she'd thought they would be when she'd sat in Kiria Spirtos's parlor and eaten her pastry. And life in Crete was far more complicated than she'd imagined. The possibility of war grew steadily less benign than the image she'd had when she'd persuaded her father to bring her to the island.

She hoped for all their sakes that Spirtos's words were not a prophecy.

Sky lifted his head and stared across the square. Where the *taverna* had stood there was only rubble. The soldiers who had sat closest to where the bomb had been set were gone, so much charred refuse amongst the burned remains of tables and chairs and the still smoldering structure of the *taverna* itself. But the force of the explosion had blown some of the soldiers out to the center and far sides of the square. Some were still alive, and the sound of their cries sent shivers along his spine.

There was a hand at his shoulder, shaking him.

"Get up. We have to get out of here."

Sky turned and looked at him. It took him a moment to realize the hand and the voice belonged to Theo Constatin, his suspicious companion.

"We have to go. Now," Constatin hissed at him, obviously not pleased that Sky had made no move to do as he had ordered.

Sky only shook his head.

"Why?" he demanded.

The cries of the wounded seemed to have grown sharper, more pathetic. Sky turned away from Constatin and got to his feet, intending to see if there was anything he could do to help.

Again he felt the young man's hand on his shoulder.

"Are you deaf? We must get out of here."

"Why?" Sky asked again.

Constatin shook his head in disgust. "Because there will be soldiers here in a few minutes."

"Why should that concern me?" Sky demanded. "I've done nothing."

"You've been seen with me," Constatin replied.

"That's no reason for the Turks to concern themselves with me," Sky protested.

"It will be more than enough reason for the Turks. Either you come with me now, or you'll find yourself in prison before the sun sets."

His words finally made an impression on Sky, who looked back at the square one last time as the younger man snatched up his canvas bag and then put a hand to his arm.

"This way," Constatin hissed. "Now, or I leave you

123

here to convince the Turkish soldiers of your inno-
cence."

Realizing he had little choice, Sky turned and followed
him through a narrow street and out of the town.

Sky followed along behind Constatin, climbing the
hills behind Mallia in the growing darkness.

"Did I forget to tell you I have a horse stabled back
there?" Sky asked, his voice breaking an uncomfortable
silence. "We could be riding now instead of walking."

"If you have an ounce of brains you'll leave the horse
where it is and let the authorities think the man who rode
it into town was killed in the explosion."

"I don't suppose you'd care to tell me where we're
going?" Sky asked.

"Where you wanted to go," Constatin told him. "To
find my brother."

"And I don't suppose either you or your brother had
anything to do with what happened back there?"

"Ask your questions of Nikolas. If it were up to me, I'd
kill you and be done with it."

Sky considered the young man's face as he spoke those
words, looked in his eyes for some sign that the words
were nothing more than bravado, a young man's show of
manhood. He found none. Theo Constatin, he realized,
would quite probably kill him as easily and with as little
remorse as he had shown when he sat and watched the
Turkish soldiers being murdered in the town square in
Mallia.

"Would you consider, perhaps, telling me how much
further?" Sky asked.

"We're almost there," was the only reply Constatin
deemed fit to offer, for he quickened his pace then,
leaving Sky to accept that response or not as he chose,

but giving no indication that he intended to offer anything further.

It was almost completely dark and fully an hour more before Constatin finally halted. Sky realized they had climbed a good distance, for the air here was cool and sharp with the taste of pines. Constatin pointed. Sky squinted into the darkness until his eyes picked out a small structure surrounded by a grove of tall cedars a good deal further up the hillside. A muffled light barely managed to edge its way from the cabin's single window and was quickly swallowed by the darkness.

"Fine home you've made for yourselves, you and your brother," Sky said and was rewarded with a scowl.

"This way," Constatin told him, then started forward once again, leading Sky to the cabin's door.

Constatin knocked once, then called out softly, "It's me, Theo."

The door opened an inch. Sky could not help but notice that the dark-eyed man who peered out at them held a pistol ready in his hand. But the weapon was quickly dropped and the door pulled fully open.

Nikolas Constatin had the same dark features as his brother, but none of the younger man's boyishness. This man was strongly muscled and mature, and there was a thick line of scar down the length of the side of his left cheek that gave him an unsettlingly malign air. But it was not the scar that startled Sky when he stared at him. It was dark clothing and the way the man held himself that caught his attention. He had seen this man before, he'd seen him that afternoon, kneeling by the *taverna* that had been destroyed.

"Why are you not alone, Theo?" he hissed when he spotted Sky standing in the darkness.

"I had no choice," Theo replied, then stood back and motioned to Sky to precede him into the small cabin.

Nikolas stood back with a show of reluctance, but he made way and Sky walked past him into the cabin. He was surprised by the relative comfort the small room offered. Out of the night wind, and warmed by a small fire that burned in the hearth, the air was pleasant with the smell of wood smoke and food that cooked in a pot hanging on a grate in front of the fire. Two narrow beds lined opposite walls, made from roughly hewn wood but comfortable looking, each topped with a bright cotton blanket. In the center of the room was a rough plank table, set for two and surrounded by a half dozen stools.

When the door was closed behind them, Nikolas turned and stared at Sky. "Who are you?" he demanded.

"My name is Skyler Trask," he told him, keeping his eyes riveted on Nikolas's. "I write for a newspaper in New York, one that has become interested in the coming war here. I happened to meet a friend of yours while I was in Heracleion, Spiros Petropoulos. He suggested that I might find talking with you interesting." Sky's expression hardened. "What he didn't tell me was that you were a terrorist, that you set bombs that kill innocent people."

"Innocent?" Nikolas almost laughed. "You can't be so great a fool as to think any of those Turks was innocent." He shook his head. "They were all guilty, and they all deserved to die."

"At your decision? By your decree?" Sky asked.

"Mine, and that of others like me."

"And have you managed to make a bomb that kills only Turkish soldiers?" Sky demanded. "There were children in that square. And men and women on the street. And those who worked in the *taverna*, the waiters. Do you mean to tell me your bombs do not harm them as well? Or in your eyes are they guilty, too?"

"They were warned," Nikolas replied. "Only the soldiers were hurt."

Theo pushed his way past Sky to face his brother.

126

"Why do you bother to argue with this fool, Nik?" he demanded.

"Because, my impatient little brother, Spiros Petropoulos would not send him to us if there was not good reason." He turned then and smiled at Sky. "I think it will be easier to find that reason with our bellies filled," he said. "Sit." He pointed to the stools by the table. "Give me the opportunity to answer your questions."

They moved to the table. It was only when Nikolas set a plate in front of him that Sky realized he'd had the chance to eat only a few bites of the food he'd been given in the *taverna*, that in the intervening hours since he'd fled with Theo his stomach had grown tight with hunger.

"You met Spiros?" Nikolas asked as he settled himself across the table from Sky. "He must have been impressed with you or he would not have given you my name."

Sky shrugged. "I don't think he had much of an opinion of me one way or another. I think he simply wants me to write about your cause, to rouse public interest in you."

Nikolas grinned. "As I said, he must have found you intelligent."

Sky ignored him. He leaned across the table toward Nikolas. "If he expected to convince me to champion your cause, he never should have sent me to you. What I saw today does not sit well."

Nikolas put down his spoon and stared at Sky.

"Listen to me, Mr. Skyler Trask of New York City," he said. "Less than two weeks ago a farmer was driving his wagon to market in Dikte, a town about twenty kilometers south of here. When he was near the town, his wagon became mired in mud. He was trying to urge the horse to pull the wagon free when a soldier came by, deciding to help because the wagon was blocking the road. His idea of helping was to take a whip and start to beat the animal. The horse, a good Cretan animal, reared

127

up, striking the soldier with his hooves, killing him."
Nikolas put his arms to the table and leaned forward toward Sky. "The Turkish authorities decided this was an act of aggression. Not only was the farmer killed, but five others as well, so that the townspeople could learn a lesson. It was the soldiers you saw in that *taverna* this afternoon who did the killing."

"If they took six lives for one in Dikte," Sky asked, "what do you suppose they will do in Mallia? How many did you kill there? How many more will die to pay for what you have done?"

Nikolas pushed himself away from the table, then stood and went to a cupboard near the door. He opened it and removed a bottle and three glasses from it before returning to the table.

"This is war, Mr. Trask," he said evenly. "People die in wars. It is unfortunate, but it is a fact of life."

Sky shook his head. "Soldiers die in wars," he said. "And that is unfortunate. But soldiers at least know what might happen to them. They recognize the dangers they face. Women and children who happen to be in the way of your bombs, they have not been told they are part of a battle, that they must die for a cause. And the farmers who will be killed in retribution for your act have no chance to make a choice, to decide if your cause is their cause. You have no right to take their lives along with those of your enemies."

Nikolas uncorked the bottle and poured some of its contents into each of the three glasses.

"Do you think I like any of this?" he asked as he pushed one of the glasses across the table to Sky. "I have no choice. People must know what the Turks do here, must know how they have taken what isn't theirs to take. Word of what happened today will go beyond Crete. The world will learn about us."

"And what if the world decides it doesn't care?" Sky asked.

"Then we will find another way to tell them, a way that will make them care." His eyes narrowed. "You, for instance, Mr. Trask. What would your American government do were it to come to their attention that a famous reporter like yourself was killed as a result of Turkish armed aggression here in Crete?"

"You overestimate my importance," Sky countered.

"I think not," Nikolas replied.

"Are you threatening me, Constatin?"

The Cretan shook his head. "Certainly not, Mr. Trask. Frankly, I think you could be of far greater use to me and to Crete's cause if you were to remain alive and well. I was simply making a point."

Sky considered Nikolas's expression, the emotionless way he spoke of death. He had made his point, made it all too clearly. A highly visible foreign victim would bring home to the rest of the world the extent of the discontent that seethed in Crete. And the most visible group of foreigners on the island, Sky knew, and no doubt Nikolas knew as well, was Evans's party at the dig at Knossos.

"You'll end up killing more of your own than Turks," Sky murmured as he reached for the glass and pulled it across the table to himself. His hands, he realized, seemed a bit unsteady. He let the glass lie where it was on the table in front of him and stared into the pale liquid.

"Do you think there is any satisfaction for me in any of this beyond the knowledge that each man the Turks kill adds fuel to the fire of hatred they have already kindled in every heart in Crete?" Nikolas demanded.

"And what do you expect all that hatred to win for you, Constatin?" Sky demanded. "Just what is that raging fire expected to burn?"

"It will destroy the Turks who come here to rule us," Nikolas told him.

"Or it will lay waste to Crete," Sky countered.

"Either way the Turks will be gone."

There was no answer to that, Sky realized, no possible response. He stared first at Nikolas, then at Theo, and saw the same look of determined certainty in both their expressions. These men had a score to settle, a cause for which they were willing to die. And their own dedication was such that they were more than willing to condemn others to death if that was the path to which their cause forced them.

His eyes on Nikolas, Sky lifted the glass and emptied it, then dropped it back to the table. Flashes of what he had seen that afternoon passed through his mind, gory memories of the burnt and broken bodies he'd seen after the explosion at the *taverna*. He'd had no time to be sickened by the sight that afternoon, no time to be anything more than a remote observer. But now he found himself growing ill at the thought of how many more bodies would soon lie across the countryside, how many would die before the killing would end.

He could not keep himself from thinking about Arden, and for the first time in his life Sky realized he was truly afraid. Crete was a tinderbox just waiting to ignite, and she was sitting right in the middle of it. He could repeat the litany of what he saw as her sins all he wanted, but the thought of her being trapped in a vise of violence from which she would find no escape left him filled with a strange new fear.

There was a good story for him to uncover in Crete; Forbes Devereaux had been right. But before Sky could do that, he had to go to Knossos and somehow convince Forbes that he had to get Arden out of Crete before it was too late.

130

Chapter Seven

Arden looked at the narrow opening into what appeared to be nothing more prepossessing than a small, perfectly round mound of hillside. Had the field around it not been so resolutely flat, it would have blended indistinctively into the surrounding countryside. It was hard for her to believe that this particular bit of farm field might hold within it secrets as old as civilization on Crete.

The workers were busily digging, clearing away the baskets of dislodged soil with a stoic manner that Arden found utterly baffling. She was forced to admit to herself that she was nearly bursting with curiosity to see what lay within the tomb.

For it was a tomb, of that David had assured her as soon as the first bit of dirt had been scraped away to reveal the stone understructure. The hillside had been made by man centuries before, far into man's antiquity, built and then sealed to lie closed and untouched for more years than she could imagine.

"No one knows how these tombs were built," David was saying, "how people with only the basest tools could manage to erect these circular stone mounds that can withstand the weight of the thick layer of earth on top of them, yet are so perfectly engineered that if the single stone at the peak of the tomb's roof is removed the whole structure will collapse."

Arden nodded. She'd heard this lecture several times in the preceding few days. Since Evans had given the task of opening the tomb to him, David had become consumed with the topic, unable to discuss anything else.

In a way, that single-mindedness had been a comfort to her, distracting her from thinking about their engagement. It was not as though she was displeased at the prospect of marriage, she found herself telling herself again and again. It was just that she wasn't yet quite comfortable with the idea, that she needed a bit of time to acclimate herself to the realization that she was soon to become some man's wife.

At that moment, however, she was thinking not of her own future but of the past, the distant past, and what might lie within the barrow. And as for David, even if he seemed to be playing the part of the bombastic don just now, she knew that just beneath the veneer was a curiosity that more than rivaled her own. In the previous few days he had spoken of treasure that was often buried with ancient royalty, growing more and more eager to see what lay inside as the work progressed. She had the distinct impression that he was burning to see what the tomb held, to be able to consider himself the one who had uncovered a treasure of the ancient Greeks and bring it to modern light, to make an enviable start to his career.

It had taken a good deal of labor merely to find the entrance to the tomb, clearing away the earth that clung to the barrow's sides, all the work done with great care and patience so as not to disturb any of the stones of the tomb wall. When the arched top of the entry had finally been located early that day, Arden had been certain that the door would finally be cleared away and she would be witness to the opening of the tomb before nightfall.

But now the sun was already low on the western

horizon, tinting the sky with orange and red fingers of fire, and still the entryway had not been entirely cleared.

Arden was just managing to resign herself to being forced to wait another day to see what might lie within the tomb when there was a loud cry of triumph from one of the workers. Others soon followed suit. David began to force his way forward through the crowd of shouting workmen, who moved good-naturedly aside to let him pass.

Arden saw him stop and stand motionless for a long moment, simply staring at an enormous stone door that blocked the opening. Finally he reached for one of the picks that lay on the ground, dropped there by one of the workmen, and lifted it to put it to the stone's edge, trying to use it as a pry bar. The pick scraped against the stone, and Arden could see David straining, could see his arms shaking with the effort, but the stone didn't budge and finally he was forced to drop the tool.

Arden thought he would give up the effort then, that he would leave the work until morning. Instead, David called to the workmen, directing them to do as he had done, to bring picks and pry bars against the edges of the huge stone. They did as he directed, at first scraping away the encrusted dirt that sealed the stone to the wall of the tomb, then using the openings they made to wedge the tools between the two stone surfaces and lever them apart.

The work went on for more than two hours. By then darkness had fallen and lanterns had been lit to cast a flickering, dancing light on the side of the barrow. Evans stopped by to see how the work was progressing, quickly evaluated the situation, and joined in the effort. Langford was the next to arrive, and then Forbes, Blake, and Hobbs.

It wasn't long before the remaining workmen had also gathered around, their hunger and thirst temporarily forgotten, their curiosity piqued enough so that they didn't mind working the extra hours after the day had officially ended. It was more than apparent that now that the tomb was nearly open, everyone had become infected with the same curiosity that Arden felt. All were now eager to be part of the breaching of the tomb. As one man tired, another stepped forward willingly to receive his pick or shovel and take his place.

The stone door finally loosened and when it was pulled free there was a great roar from the gathered crowd of men. Evans snatched up one of the lanterns, David took another, and the crowd fell suddenly silent as the two stepped into the tomb.

Arden watched David disappear, aware that she felt slighted, as though his failure to include her was an intentional sign of neglect. She found herself wondering if this was a feeling to which she must accustom herself in her marriage to him, if she would always be left outside what he determined to be his own realm and expected to remain strictly within those bounds he deemed acceptable for his wife.

"That man should be drawn and quartered."

She didn't have to turn to realize Charles Langford was standing behind her.

"A prospective wife can't hope to compete with a man's immortality," she replied, her tone dry, without bothering to turn to him.

"A decidedly ungentlemanly attitude," Langford said.

"Don't tell that to Trumbull. You've accused him of the greatest crime of which his rather crimped imagination could conceive."

This, too, was a voice Arden recognized. For a second she froze, and although her eyes remained on the flickering light emanating from the mouth of the barrow, it seemed to fade and blur until she could no longer see it at all.

"Sky?" she whispered.

She found she had to muster her courage before she could turn to face him. She had tried not to admit it to herself, but since she had accepted David's proposal of marriage she had found herself thinking more and more about Sky. Her father had not been alone in wondering about her rather disinterested attitude toward the prospect of becoming David's wife. She'd been unable to keep herself from wondering if she would feel as she did if it were Sky Trask she were to wed rather than David Trumbull.

When finally she did turn to him, she found he was staring at her, his blue eyes quickly finding hers in the dim light. To Arden they seemed almost to emit sparks, tiny fires that flowed from him to her and sank into her, leaving eddies of liquid heat in their wake. She did not understand why she was having this strange reaction to his unexpected presence, why the mere sight of him could have such an effect on her.

"So you do know this person, Miss Devereaux?" Langford was asking. "He claimed acquaintance and demanded to be brought to you."

Arden did not know why, but a thick lump had leaped into her throat at the sight of Sky, and her heart began doing strange things, things she was sure it ought not to do. She realized Charles Langford was talking to her, but she found herself unable to decipher the words, completely incapable of offering him an answer.

"I think Miss Devereaux would prefer not to admit to my acquaintance," Sky said, "at least not in polite company. You see, as steadfastly as her friend Trumbull nurtures and cleaves to his reputation as a gentleman, I long ago shunned mine as needless baggage."

His words and the suddenly playful expression on his face as he turned to face Langford had the expected result: the Englishman roared with laughter.

"Then I think I have found a soul mate in you," he said finally when the laughter had ebbed. He held out his hand. "Charles Langford, struggling archaeologist, black sheep, and general ne'er-do-well."

Sky laughed as he shook Langford's hand. "Skyler Trask," he introduced himself. "The best I can say for myself, I'm afraid, is that I am in the employ of Miss Devereaux's father."

"A reporter?" Langford asked. "The old man will be in seventh heaven. The thought that Mr. Devereaux is publishing articles about the dig has Evans absolutely eating out of Miss Devereaux's hand." He grinned pleasantly at Arden. "A second reporter to write about his dig will nudge him in the direction of complete ecstasy."

Sky sobered. "I'm not here to write about the dig," he said, whatever amusement had been in his words before now completely gone. "In fact, after what I've learned in the past few days, I'd advise Evans to shut everything down and get out of here before any serious harm has been done."

Arden finally found her tongue.

"What are you talking about, Sky?" she demanded. "And what are you doing here?"

He took her hand and put it on his arm. "Let's find your father, shall we? It'll be easier to say it all just once."

"He's here," Arden said, looking about in the darkness, unable to distinguish one form from another. "Somewhere . . ."

"There," Langford said, pointing to the opening that led into the barrow. Forbes was entering the tomb along with the two young archaeologists, Blake and Hobbs. "I think the second-class ranks are being admitted. We might as well be part of it."

He started forward, leading the way while Arden followed with Sky.

"Why *are* you here?" she asked Sky, even as she tried to convince herself she wasn't in the least happy to see him. "I thought you were off in the countryside, looking for your war."

"I came to realize that I simply couldn't live without you, Arden," he replied.

For a second she thought he meant it. The prospect set her heart thumping, making those odd sounds it had made when she'd turned and found him standing behind her. And for an instant she wished that she'd never agreed to marry David, wished more than anything that Sky would sweep her into his arms and kiss her and tell her that he loved and wanted her. She found herself thinking of the way he had made her feel when he held her, the way his kisses left her breathless and trembling while David's left her coldly indifferent.

But then she saw the laughter on his lips, the amusement in his eyes. The thumping of her heart suddenly ceased as she realized he was playing with her, taunting her. It was all a game to him, she told herself, nothing more important than the desire to win, to show her that he could beat her at the same game she'd first thought to best him that night they'd played billiards. He'd warned her that evening, but she hadn't listened, hadn't had any idea just how dangerous his games could be.

There was a sharp stab of hurt so deep and painful it astonished her. She pushed it away and replaced it with anger. He had no right to do this to her, she told herself, no right to make her wish for something that she would never have, no right to make what she did have seem less in her own eyes than it ought to seem.

"The Cretan hetaerae are not to your liking, Mr. Trask?" she hissed as she pulled her hand from his arm.

She didn't wait for an answer but stalked ahead of him, moving first to Langford's side and then past him, too, and into the opening in the hillside, into the entrance of the tomb.

She wasn't in the least prepared for what she found there. She was thinking of Sky and her anger and wanted only to get away from him. But the sight of the interior of the tomb pushed aside thoughts of her anger with Sky and her ambivalent feelings about David. She was quite literally struck dumb with awe.

The inside of the tomb was lined with gold. Flowers, their petals made of thin sheets of beaten gold, were fastened to the stone of the dome, a field of hundreds of glittering blossoms turning the barrow into an unbelievable underground garden. The light of the lanterns skimmed off the gilt blooms and was reflected thousands of times over by the petals, each sending the light that shone on it off in a different direction to be reflected yet again. Arden turned slowly around, staring upward, feeling as if she'd somehow wandered into a giant's jewel case.

"Do you believe it?"

Even in his excitement David's voice was hushed with awe. He'd come up beside her when he'd seen her enter and now stood with his hand on her waist. Arden's reaction to the gold-encrusted dome was so great, however, that it wasn't until he spoke that she realized he'd approached her.

"Is it real?" she whispered, afraid to raise her voice in this place.

She began to look around, her glance settling on the enormous, strangely painted earthenware jars, a half dozen or so, that occupied the center of the room. Around them was a litter of smaller jars, as well as wooden chests and plates and bowls, all containing offerings of one sort or another, gifts to the dead who had occupied the barrow for more than two thousand years.

"Oh, yes, it's real," David said as he took her hand and

138

pulled her to the center, to where the huge jars were. "Kings lie here, Arden," he told her. "Kings of ancient Knossos." He got his hand on the rim of one of the jars and peered reverently inside.

Arden raised her hand to touch the jar, realizing it reached nearly to her shoulder, and for an instant wondered what it could possibly have contained. So large a vessel filled with grain or oil would surely have been too heavy to move. It was only then that she understood what David had said and she pulled her hand away as though it had been burned by the clay.

"You don't mean . . . ?"

Her voice trailed off into silence. She stared at the jar and felt a sudden wave of revulsion sweep over her.

"Yes, certainly," David told her with an impatient wave of his hand, dismissing her squeamishness as unimportant. "Think about it, a king of Knossos, perhaps even legendary Minos himself."

She backed away from the huge clay pot, her movement upsetting a half dozen offering bowls and sending their contents skittering along the stone floor. Beads made of gold and precious stones scattered underfoot and rolled in every direction, mixing with other offerings, golden coins, small clay figures, bits of bone, and some whose identity had long ago been lost and now appeared to be nothing more than a handful of dust.

"Really, Arden!"

David was decidedly peeved. She looked down at the mess she'd made and felt like a clumsy oaf, realizing that he saw her as an interloper, someone who had entered his domain without his express leave and then proceeded to lay waste to it. She was bewildered that she felt so little regret at that fact, that she cared so little about what he thought of her.

"I'm so sorry, David," she murmured with no great conviction, but dutifully knelt and began to collect the scattered beads from the floor.

"Oughtn't to let a young woman stumble onto the body of a legend, Trumbull. It's apt to leave her a bit disoriented."

Charles Langford had entered the tomb and obviously seen Arden's reaction to learning that the jars held the remains of corpses. Rather than standing and glaring at her for her clumsiness as David was doing, however, he knelt at her side and began to help her sweep up what she had spilled.

"I'll be damned."

Sky, too, had entered the tomb, and his reaction, although more blunt than that of the others, was no less amazed.

Evans was the only one of them who seemed to be totally organized at the revelation of the contents of the barrow, a fact which allowed him to turn to the newcomer and see him as a possible thief. He pointed toward Sky.

"Who is this man?" he demanded sharply. "What are you doing here?"

"Don't worry, Sir Arthur, he's not a grave robber," Forbes said as he too turned toward Sky, who stood by the entrance of the tomb. He started forward, his hand extended. "Trask—good to see you. I hope you won't think it untoward of me to ask you what the hell you're doing here."

Sky tore his glance from the dome's golden interior and turned it on Forbes.

"I came here to tell you that if you value your lives, you have to get out. You all must leave Crete as quickly as possible."

The tomb, for the first time since it had been broached, settled into the absolute silence it had offered the bodies

140

that had lain in it for those long, empty centuries. Arden and Langford slowly stood and turned to stare at Sky in disbelief, a feeling that was quite obviously mirrored by the others.

Sky found them all staring at him, Forbes and Trumbull and the four Englishmen, all of whose names—except for Evans—escaped him at that moment. The only eyes that seemed of any consequence, however, were Arden's green ones, and they, like the rest, were intent on his and filled with disbelief.

"You can't be serious."

Evans's words shattered the silence, seemed even to make the thin petals of the golden flowers on the dome that surrounded them shake with his vehemence.

Sky turned to face the man.

"I've never been more serious in my life," he replied. "But look at what we've found here. You can't expect us to turn our backs on a treasure like this. And there's more, much more, waiting to be discovered." He gestured in the direction of the main dig, the excavation of the palace.

"Is even a hoard of gold worth your life?" Sky asked him. "Or the lives of any of the others with you?"

"I'm not talking about gold," Evans fumed. "Do you take me for a filthy miner, grubbing about in the dirt for a few hundred pounds' worth of metal?" He waved his arm at the contents of the tomb. "This is civilization's history, man. Does that mean nothing to you?"

Sky remained unmoved.

"It's been here for centuries," he said. "It can lie where it is a few years more."

Evans shook his head. "No. The authorities weren't anxious to allow the work to be begun. If we leave it now, who knows if we'll ever be able to return?"

"Look," Sky said, moving forward to Evans, trying to keep himself calm, to make his argument sound reasonable. "I've spent the past few days in some very nasty company. I saw a squadron of Turkish troops blown up in a *taverna* in Mallia. An act of revenge, they said, for killings the Turks had done, and those killings, in turn, revenge for other deaths. These people no longer think of killing as anything more than a gesture, a show that they will not stop until they have what they want. And believe me, your people here are becoming a more and more attractive target as time passes."

Evans shook his head. "Nonsense," he replied. "The authorities have given us leave to be here. Besides, why should the Turks want to make a target of us? They have much more to gain from letting us do our work here in peace."

"Not the Turks," Sky fumed.

"Certainly not the Greeks?" David asked. "The government hasn't even agreed yet to send troops. But even if they do, they can only want to protect us. What lies here is Greek history, the legacy of Greek forebears. They would have no reason to want to destroy it or interrupt what we're doing."

"There is more involved here than the two governments," Sky told him. "There is a population on this island that has endured the rule of foreigners for a long time. They may just have had enough."

"Impossible," Forbes interjected. "We've seen nothing but the warmest hospitality from everyone here."

"Not every man born on Crete is a friendly farmer," Sky returned. "There are others, men who don't care anymore who gets in the way of what they want, of what they think is right."

Evans shook his head once more. "I think this isn't the time or the place for a debate," he said. "Langford, why don't you post a guard? We don't want any light-fingered grave robbers to get any ideas tonight."

142

"I'll do better than that," Langford suggested. "Why don't I post a half dozen men to guard the place and spend the night here myself? I've always wanted to sleep with kings."

He darted an amused glance toward Arden, one that said his words ought not to be misconstrued, then started to the barrow's entrance to find workmen willing to earn a few extra drachmas by spending the night on guard duty.

But David didn't seem as willing to put off the argument as were the others. He watched Sky turn his glance to Arden, and as he did his expression hardened.

"What right have you to come here trying to frighten us off with these ridiculous tales, Trask?" he demanded as he moved to Arden's side and put his hand on her arm.

Sky watched David and felt an irrational anger growing within him. There was something about the way the Bostonian put his hand on Arden, about the proprietary way he seemed determined to handle her, that evoked a kind of fury in Sky he never remembered having felt before in his life.

"What are you afraid of, Trumbull?" he asked. "If I'm wrong, you get to spend a few months on holiday roaming around the continent, doing whatever it is you do. If I'm right, you don't get killed. It seems to me that you have nothing to lose."

"How noble of you," David shot back, his voice dripping with sarcasm. "Coming here, the hero, saving us all from our doom."

Sky shrugged. "Stay if you like. And if you want the truth, I don't give a damn about you or your old pots. If it weren't for Arden and Forbes, I wouldn't have bothered to come to warn you."

"Miss Devereaux is none of your concern, Trask. And in the future you will not refer to my fiancée in such a way."

Sky's first reaction to David's red-faced anger was amusement. But the amusement disappeared quickly as he realized what David had told him.

For all the times Sky had told himself Arden and David deserved one another, he realized he'd never really believed she would actually agree to marry the Bostonian. He let his eyes find hers once again, though this time he realized he was looking for something from her, something that would tell him what David had said wasn't true. A deep pang of regret filled him as he realized that what he was looking for wasn't there, that all he found in those beautiful green eyes was regret and perhaps a hint of sadness.

She pities me, he thought . . . damn her, who is she to pity me?

The glitter of the gold-lined dome faded from Sky's view as if it were no longer there. All that existed for him were her eyes, staring at him, tearing into him with that look that told him only that she regretted the hurt she caused him. He found himself backing away, edging toward the exit of the tomb, sure only that he wanted to be away from those eyes, from the knowledge that he was only then coming to accept: that he loved her.

Arden's eyes popped open and she found herself staring up into the darkness. There was an instant when she felt unsettled, waking as she did, torn from sleep so abruptly to find herself completely awake.

She strained to peer around the room, into the night-blackened corners, wondering what it was that had wakened her. And then the noise came again, a small clatter behind the drawn curtain of her window, and she realized that it must have been that. Bewildered, she swung her feet out of bed and stood, then crossed the few paces to the window. She drew back the light curtain and

144

let a thin stream of moonlight find its way into the room. She stepped forward to the window, and as she did, she felt a sharp pain in her bare foot. She knelt down and retrieved the pebble that had caused it.

There was another clatter, and another small stone landed on the bare floor where she knelt. This one, too, she retrieved; then she stood and peered out the window and into the garden.

He was down there, looking up, standing in the one thin patch of moonlight that the garden foliage did not interrupt. For a moment she stared down at him, wondering why he appeared so vulnerable to her, a descriptive that she had never before associated with him. He looked rumpled, his shirt was wrinkled, his hair was mussed, a thick dark curl hanging low over his brow nearly to his eye, and he carried his jacket over his shoulder. But it couldn't be merely his uncharacteristic lack of grooming that made him seem so different. He smiled up at her with boyish glee. Arden thought he must have been drinking.

"What are you doing down there?" she whispered into the night.

He waved an arm. "Come down, Arden."

"*Shh*," she hissed. She looked around at the windows on either side of hers, the windows to Forbes's room and David's. After the way Sky and David had spoken to each other earlier, she needed little imagination to know what would happen if Sky woke either of the others. "Be quiet! You'll wake someone."

"Then come down," he told her, raising his voice enough to make her realize he really didn't care if he woke everyone in the house.

She shook her head. "No. Go away."

"Come down," he called, raising his voice again.

"Why should I?" she demanded.

He smiled up at her—a foolish, silly, charming smile. "Just to talk," he said. He put his right hand over his

145

heart. "I swear, Arden, just to talk."

"Then you'll leave?"

"If you tell me to," he agreed.

She scowled. "Wait there."

Why was she doing this, she asked herself as she found her robe and slippers and put them on. She'd had enough of his games, more than enough. He'd proved his point, proved he could hurt her. Why on earth was she slipping out into the hall, taking great care to walk silently to the stairs, making the effort not to wake anyone or be heard?

There was no possible reason why she ought to agree to see him at this hour alone in the garden. But still she realized she was going to him, descending the stairs as if she were a thief determined to slip away without being discovered. There must be some part of her that wasn't quite certain she hated him as much as she'd told herself she did, wasn't quite so convinced that she was better off if she never saw him again.

She pulled the door opened carefully and slipped outside and found him standing on the small stone step, waiting for her.

He stared at her for a long moment in silence, his expression strange, as if he wasn't quite sure if she was really there. And then he put his arms around her, pulled her to him, and kissed her.

For an instant she let the fire fill her. For just a moment she let herself melt against him and let the liquid heat fill her. But she came to her senses quickly, told herself that it was nothing more than a game to him, a game she could only lose. She pushed herself angrily away from him, balling her hands into fists and hammering them against his chest until he dropped his arms and freed her.

"*Liar,*" she hissed. "You said *talk.*"

She started to turn back to the door, but he caught her arm with his hand and held her.

She stood and stared up at him in silence for a moment, and realized that he had been drinking, that his eyes weren't quite clear, that there was the scent of alcohol on his breath. She was tempted to try to wrench herself free from his hold, to tell him she thought him disgusting to come to see her like this, when he spoke.

"Yes," he told her slowly, "yes, I've been drinking, Arden." She jerked her glance away from his then, wondering how he managed to be able to read her thoughts. That seemed to amuse him, for he smiled at her. "Let me assure you," he went on, "I'm most certainly not drunk."

"Why did you come here?" she demanded.

"To talk to you, to convince you that you must leave Crete, that you must convince your father to go."

Her anger disappeared. "You really *do* think something is going to happen here," she whispered, surprised to think that there might actually be some danger, as he had told them earlier.

"I'm fairly certain, Arden. And I don't want to think of you getting caught in the middle of it."

She shook her head, refusing to believe anything so calm and peaceful as the garden in which they stood might come to harbor danger.

"But David said . . ."

"David be damned," he interrupted, his tone harsh. His eyes narrowed as he considered the surprise he saw in her expression as the words faded and silence settled around them.

"Please, Sky," she whispered finally, turning away.

His hold on her arm tightened. "I can't believe you've actually agreed to marry that fool," he hissed, angry with her, but more with the pain he felt at the thought.

"What difference should that make to you?" she countered, her own tone hard and thick with hurt. "Why do you care who I marry or what I do?"

147

"I don't know," he replied, his voice softening, the anger nearly gone from him. "I just do." He pulled her close, holding her arms with his hands, waiting until her glance found his. "Maybe it's because I know you don't love him," he whispered as he lowered his lips to hers. "Maybe it's because I know you love me."

Arden was mesmerized by his words and his eyes, completely powerless in his grasp. She knew what would happen when he kissed her, knew she ought not to allow him that freedom, yet she could not pull herself away. She knew what he had said was true: she didn't love David. If she'd been honest with herself, she'd have realized that from the start. And she did love Sky; she knew it as he pressed his lips to hers and felt the liquid fire coursing through her veins.

He drew her back, away from the house and into the shadows of the garden. She followed him willingly, telling herself that he asked of her nothing she was unwilling to give. She pressed herself close to him as his arms enfolded her, let her body melt into his as she felt the heat growing between them. He pulled her close, felt the soft curves of her body pressed to his as he kissed her.

"You won't marry Trumbull," he told her, whispering the words into her ear before he pressed a kiss to the soft flesh of her neck. "Promise me you won't marry Trumbull, Arden. Say it."

"I . . ."

She got no further. The air was suddenly filled with a dull ripping sound. The noise grew until it was a roar and then ended with a loud, earthshaking crash.

Chapter Eight

Arden felt the ground beneath her feet vibrate. She'd never experienced this, never heard such a noise as that which preceded the movement, almost as if the earth were tearing itself apart.

"What was that?" she cried.

"I don't know," Sky muttered angrily, as though the noise and whatever it was that had caused it were nothing more than a badly timed interruption. But he recovered quickly. "I think it came from the direction of the tomb." He thought of all that had brought him to the site of the dig in the first place and with the thought came the realization that he was suddenly stone-cold sober. "Oh, God," he murmured. He pushed Arden away. More than anything he wanted to stay there with her, to forget the noise and the earthshaking tremor and simply pretend he hadn't heard or felt anything, but he knew he could not. "I have to find out what happened."

She saw the look of concern in his eyes and knew that he feared the disaster he had promised had come all too soon.

"I'll go with you," she said.

He shook his head. "No," he told her as he pushed her toward the house. "You stay here. I'll be back."

"Sky!" Arden shouted.

But he was already running away from her, toward the barrow. She hesitated for a moment, wanting to follow, then realizing she couldn't go running through the countryside in her robe and slippers. She turned reluctantly toward the farmhouse.

She felt cheated. He'd appeared out of nowhere and made her realize just how much she loved him, and now it seemed he was disappearing again, as though being with her was an afterthought for him, something to do when nothing better presented itself. She told herself that she hated him, that she was a fool to let him play with her emotions, but she knew it was a lie. She couldn't marry David, not now, not knowing how she felt about Sky. He'd done what he'd intended, made her realize that. But simply knowing what she didn't want in no way brought her any closer to what she did want.

She'd only just neared the door when she saw the men racing out, Forbes and David pulling on their dressing gowns, Alexander Spirtos quickly buttoning up the trousers he had quite obviously just donned. Kiria Spirtos trailed after her husband, firmly tying a dark wool robe over her white cotton nightdress, her long hair wild around her face, making her look more than a little like an evil spirit out of one of the old Greek tales Arden had been reading in the previous weeks.

Arden stepped back into the shadows and let them pass, not wanting to face the necessity of explaining either to her father or to David just what it was she'd been doing in the garden dressed as she was at that hour. When they'd rushed past her to the edge of the garden, she stepped forward, pretending she'd just come down the stairs.

"What happened?"

David and Forbes both wore the worried expression of

150

a person who is lost, who is incapable of accepting the unexpected.

"Could it be an earthquake?"

Forbes asked the question with a good deal of trepidation. He was aware that such phenomena occurred on Crete, and the prospect apparently terrified him. His expression changed from one of fear to surprise when he felt Arden's hand on his arm.

"Papa."

He turned to face her and stared at her accusingly.

"Arden. Why didn't you answer when I knocked at your door?"

"I was still half asleep, Papa," she replied, regretting the unaccustomed lie, yet not quite knowing what else to do. She could feel the blood rushing to her cheeks and thought he would surely see it too, that he would see the lie in her eyes and know.

But Alexander Spirtos distracted his attention.

"No, not an earthquake," Spirtos said as he turned back to face Forbes. His expression was one of concern. "I think the noise came from the tomb. If you would be so kind as to keep watch over the women, I will go and see if I can learn anything."

"We want to go, too," Arden said.

Spirtos's expression hardened. "It would not be acceptable for you to be seen dressed as you are, *despinis*," he told her, addressing her formally with the Greek word for "Miss." His disapproving glance told her quite clearly that certain things might be allowed in America but would not be countenanced here, not with a proper Greek hand to keep her from her womanish folly.

"Mister Spirtos is right, Arden," Forbes told her. He put his hand on hers where she held his arm and nodded to Spirtos. "Let us know if there is anything we can do," he said.

The farmer nodded. "I will send word if I can not come myself."

He turned to his wife then and spoke to her in Greek. Arden didn't understand the words, but she could read the emotion in both their faces. She remembered that their sons had been among those who had stayed at the tomb to serve as guards and understood their concern.

She moved to Kiria Spirtos's side and stood for a moment, watching the older woman's husband as he disappeared into the darkness at the far side of the garden to be swallowed by the shadows of the orchard beyond. Then Arden turned to the Cretan woman and considered her, watched as Kiria Spirtos struggled with emotions she was too proud to show. Arden understood the woman's fear and wished she knew of some way to comfort her. She found she could no longer dismiss what Sky had told her about men who didn't care about death, who cared only about their own cause. Somehow she knew that something had happened at the tomb, something terrible. And she realized that somehow Kiria Spirtos knew it, too.

Arden put her hand on the older woman's arm. "Don't worry," she whispered. "I'm sure they're safe."

She knew Kiria Spirtos didn't understand her words, but the emotion that had prompted them was apparently well conveyed. Kiria Spirtos put her hand on top of Arden's and squeezed it, then forced herself to smile at her.

"Perhaps we should wait inside," Forbes suggested.

"Yes," David agreed. "No need for us all to take chill in this night air."

Arden didn't know why the sound of David's voice seemed to grate at her; she knew only that it did. It took her just a second to decide that she could not sit around in Kiria Spirtos's parlor and wait for news of what had happened.

She accompanied the others inside, then waited until

Kiria Spirtos was busying herself preparing some tea.

"I see no reason to sit up," she said abruptly. "I think I'll go to my room. Good night."

She moved off, refusing to acknowledge the questioning glance her father directed at her, starting up the stairs before he could question her.

Once in her room with the door closed, however, she had no intention of going to bed. Instead she lit a lamp and quickly slipped into her skirt and blouse. No one, not even Alexander Spirtos, can accuse me of impropriety if I'm properly dressed, she told herself as she donned her shoes. She knew it wasn't quite true, that neither Spirtos nor her father would approve of her roaming around the countryside alone in the middle of the night, but she didn't care. Sky was out there, and there was a sick feeling in the pit of her stomach. He had been right, she told herself. Something terrible had happened, and she had to find out what it was.

It was dark, much darker than Arden had anticipated. There had been moonlight earlier, and she'd thought she'd be able to see by it, but once away from the garden by the house and into the orchard that surrounded it there seemed to be no light at all. She'd wished she'd had the foresight to bring a lantern, but it was too late for that. She couldn't go back to fetch one, and there didn't seem to be anything for her to do but go on.

She stumbled forward into the darkness, wondering what could have caused that terrible noise, what could possibly have made the earth tremble so. Sky had said something about an explosion at Mallia, about Turkish soldiers being killed. But surely nothing like that could happen in so peaceful a place as this. Surely no one would plant a bomb to destroy the barrow tomb.

She wished she could convince herself but she knew

she could not. There had been something in Sky's expression before he'd left her, something that told her that it could happen here.

She stumbled on a root, nearly fell, and ended by cursing her own clumsiness as she regained her footing. She didn't remember the walk through the orchard being all that long, but it was impossible for her to judge distances in the darkness. She told herself she had to stumble blindly on just a little farther before she'd come out onto the open field where the barrow stood. She refused to allow herself to be cowed by her own fear of the darkness, telling herself she was acting like a child who saw monsters beneath his bed when the light was extinguished.

Still she could not deny the relief she felt when she saw the glimmer of a light through the trees.

"Sky?" she called out. "Is that you?"

She began to run toward the light, her movements steadier now that she had the point of light to guide her. There was no answer to her call, but she didn't stop to consider that, didn't think who else might be out there if it wasn't Sky who held the lantern. Her fears and the darkness of the orchard had unsettled her enough to sweep any thought of caution from her mind. Her only thought now was to reach the light and find Sky.

The lantern, when she got close enough to see it, was sitting on the ground at the foot of one of Alexander Spirtos's ancient olive trees. The flame bobbed in the night breeze, making the light move along the canopy of branches above her head, shadows leaping forward and back, eerie wraiths in the night sky hovering just beyond the reach of her fingertips but threatening to come closer.

She stopped when she was perhaps thirty feet from the lantern and stared at it. The orchard seemed entirely deserted. The only movement was the flutter of the dark leaves overhead as they stirred in the night breeze.

"Sky?" she called again as she took a tentative step forward. And then, "Is anyone here?"

There was no answer. She was staring into the shadows, searching them, when an arm reached out from the darkness behind her.

A hand was clamped over her mouth and she was drawn, struggling and terrified, into the darkness.

Sky didn't need the first pale light of dawn to show him the enormity of the destruction. He'd been working for hours by the flickering light of lanterns, laboring side by side with the dozens of hastily assembled farmers who had answered the call for help at the barrow tomb. The fact that three of their own as well as the Englishman Langford were missing and thought to be buried beneath the rubble of stone was spur enough for them to work feverishly to pry away and remove the stones. The need precipitated by the unexpected disaster bonded strangers more effectively than years of friendship.

Alexander Spirtos and his two older sons were among the most tireless workers. Spirtos's youngest son, Niko, was nowhere to be found. It was feared that he might have entered the tomb for some reason and been trapped by the collapse. Neither Spirtos nor his other two sons would rest until all the stones that had formed the dome of the barrow had been pulled away, until whatever bodies that might lie beneath had been recovered, until they knew if Niko was among the dead.

By mid-morning the field surrounding the tomb was strewn with heaps of stones that once had formed the tomb. Bright spots of gold clung to the stone. Sky knew they were the remains of the intricately worked golden flowers that had lined the roof. They were crushed now as an ordinary bloom might be, but still the gold reflected sharp points of sunlight. The men who labored with the small mountain of stone seemed impassive to the lure of the metal, ignoring the bits of gold and intent on more important matters, only occasionally rubbing their eyes when they lifted them and felt the sting caused by the reflected light.

Like Sky, they were all grimy and covered with sweat, close to exhaustion but unable to leave or even rest. This was a small community, and what happened to one happened to them all.

As the morning wore on, more men and women from farms and orchards neighboring Spirtos's land arrived to offer their help, almost all claiming kinship of one sort or another to the missing men. Black-clad old women stood at the field's perimeter, staring at the work. Occasionally Sky turned his glance to them for an instant and found himself shivering at the sight of them, as though they were sentinels, guardians of death, their presence almost more ominous than the destruction that lay all around him.

When the first body was recovered the keening began, the old women's cries nearly as chilling as the sight of the mangled human flesh that had been pulled from beneath the mountain of rock. Ironically one of the gold leaf flowers clung to the smashed chest, flattened and stained with blood, but clearly recognizable, the metal shining bright and brittle in the hot Cretan sunlight.

Sky found the old women's wails almost harder to endure than the prospect of finding more bodies in such horrible condition. The others, however, seemed not to notice, or if they did, took the cries as homage befitting the dead. Sky told himself that stoicism was part of the Greek heritage: the work continued, the men oblivious to the old women who knelt by the body and keened.

Eventually there were four bodies laid out on the grass, Niko Spirtos's and Charles Langford's among them.

Sky sat on a heap of the ruined stone and drank some of the water that one of the women had brought to him, and poured the rest over his sweat- and grime-laden face and neck. He had never been especially squeamish, and surely the sight of the explosion back in Mallia ought to have inured him to anything he would see here. Still, the sight of those four bodies, especially Langford's, left him with a gut-wrenching feeling of revulsion. He realized he had known this man, spoken to him only hours before, liked him. Now Langford lay on the grass, crushed and broken like a piece of discarded pottery, and the sight of it gave him greater knowledge of his own mortality than any stranger's might.

Sky could not help but think what might have happened had the barrow collapsed a few hours earlier, when he and Arden had been in it as well. The thought of her lying there, her body smashed like the others, left him wet and shaking with the thick, sour sweat of fear. Even the specter of his own death could not compare to the reaction he had to that image. He shivered despite the heat.

He lurched to his feet, suddenly filled with the need to see her, to assure himself that she was alive and well. He remembered having seen Evans and the other members of the dig arrive along with the first of those who had come to help. He'd ignored Evans then, not wanting to speak with him for fear he might accuse the Englishman of being a fool not to have listened to the warning he'd given. Sky could not, however, remember if Forbes or Arden had been with them. He cursed himself for being so unobservant, then set about finding Evans.

He found himself racing from one group of men to another. They lay exhausted on the grass or sat, dazed and spent, on the heaps of stone that dotted the field. Some looked up at him curiously, but mostly they ignored him. Sky's own muscles ached, but the feeling of exhaustion had fled. He was filled with an energy that could have been generated only by fear.

When he finally found Evans, he was shocked to see the change in the Englishman's manner. Gone was the air of certainty, the slightly arrogant facade of a man used to being listened to and obeyed. His eyes were dazed and distant. It took him a long moment to recognize Sky.

"You, Trask," he said finally, acknowledging Sky's greeting. "You were right."

The admission was obviously painful to him—not so much, Sky thought, because he had ignored the warning, but more with regret for all that had been lost.

"That's not important now. Have you seen Miss Devereaux?"

Evans thought for a moment. "I think her father was here somewhere. She must be here too." His gaze drifted to where the bodies lay on the grass, covered now with a sheet, but no less ominous. "I don't understand how they knew." He shook his head in bewilderment.

Sky didn't want to stand there talking any longer. If Evans couldn't give him the information he wanted, then he wanted to be off, searching for Arden. He started to move away, but then turned back to face Evans, his curiosity bitten by the man's words.

"How who knew what?" he demanded.

Evans gazed up at him as though he were simple.

"How your madmen knew how to destroy the tomb," he said simply.

Now it was Sky's turn to consider the frailty of the human mind.

"They may be madmen, but they certainly aren't mine. And all they needed was a bomb," he said. "They certainly demonstrated that they knew how to use one in Mallia."

"No, impossible," Evans said flatly. His tone said he had no question in his mind that Sky's supposition was false. "Look around you," he said. "Do you see any evidence of an explosion or a fire? Anything burnt?"

Sky stared around him at the ruin. Funny, he thought . . . he hadn't even given the matter any thought but had simply assumed it had been a bomb. But Evans was right, he realized. There were a few shattered stones, but most of them were still whole. There were no scorch marks, no evidence whatsoever of an explosion.

"Then how?" he asked.

Evans shrugged. "Simple. All they would have had to do would be to pry up the keystone, the stone at the very top center of the dome. That would precipitate a collapse."

Sky's eyes narrowed. "Who knew that?" he demanded.

"All the workers. They'd all been warned." He shook his head again. "But apart from them, no one. How would these madmen of yours know?"

"How indeed?" Sky muttered.

It suddenly occurred to him that anyone could have caused the collapse, even one of the workmen. There was no reason to assume it had been Nikolas Constatin, no reason to assume that there were not others who believed what Constatin believed right here amongst the men Evans had hired to work the site.

He turned away, muttering, "I have to find Arden," leaving Evans to contemplate his loss and his folly.

The need to find Arden had suddenly become more pressing, more urgent. Anyone might be the murderer, he told himself. Arden would have no reason to know that, no reason to suspect, to be cautious. And she could be anywhere, the perfect victim just waiting for the killer to reach out and snuff out her life.

There were people milling everywhere; the field was dotted with them. Sky found himself walking past them, staring into faces, and turning away in disappointment.

His movements became more and more agitated as he searched for her and couldn't find her. A dull terror began to fill him. He had to find her and convince her to leave Crete. Nothing was more important than getting her away to someplace safe.

Alexander Spirtos stood in his parlor and stared at the body that had been laid out on the table he'd set in front of the fireplace. They'd done what they could, washed Niko and dressed him in his best suit, but still Spirtos could feel no kinship to the mutilated flesh, could not think that that had been his son. He had loved Niko, perhaps more dearly than his other sons, but still he found he could not mourn this battered body. He would weep for the loss of the image in his memory, but what lay on the table in front of him was not his son.

He darted a glance at his wife, who sat by the body, clad in black and weeping softly now, numbed, he thought, by the horror, her grief temporarily muted. She reached out and touched Niko's hand. At the sight of the gesture, Spirtos found he could not help but wonder how it was that she did not feel the same remoteness he felt, the same lack of compassion for the alien-seeming flesh.

"Do you still think we can hide here in our orchards? Do you still think we can sit here in comfort and ignore the fact that we have Turks as our masters?"

Spirtos turned slowly to face his oldest son. He'd not even heard Kostas enter the room. He realized that he had been mourning after all, that he'd lost touch with the reality around him in his thoughts of Niko. That was small comfort, to realize that he had not completely separated himself from Niko's flesh, to know that despite everything, still it was part of him. But as he considered Kostas's words, those thoughts fled and were replaced with anger.

"The Turks had no part of this," he hissed. "There had been no soldiers here for weeks."

Kostas shook his head as if this reasoning were foolish and flawed. "Still, they are the cause of this," he insisted.

Spirtos bared his teeth in anger. "No," he said. "This is the work of your friends, the ones who spit on the Turks and the Greeks alike." He made a movement toward Kostas almost as though he meant to attack him. "Did you tell them to kill your brother?" he cried. "Is your cause so great that you are willing to pay for it with Niko's life?"

"*Ochi*, no, Alexander, please," Kiria Spirtos begged softly.

She looked up at her husband, her expression pleading that he not fight here, now, that he at least let his anger with Kostas lie until Niko was decently at rest. Spirtos took pity on her, turning his back on his son, hoping the anger would die.

Kostas turned away, keeping back the biting words he'd intended to say, the condemnation of his father as a weakling, one grown too accustomed to his own comfort to fight. But he could not argue with his father now, not in front of Niko's battered body, not in sight of his mother's grief.

The others, the ones who had come from Mallia, had promised that only the Englishman would die. When he had wavered, uncertain, they had told him that this act would bring the world's attention to the cause, that the death was necessary. And he'd smiled and suggested that it be the American instead, the arrogant one, the one who slept in his bed and laid claim to the pretty American woman. But there had been only this one opportunity, and so it had been decided that it would be the Englishman instead.

He'd told them how it might be done, how Evans had warned them all that lifting the stone at the dome's center would cause the whole structure to fall. They'd liked the idea, thinking it fitting that one of the foreigners die under the weight of their own discovery. And Kostas had agreed, accepting their assurances that it would be only the Englishman who would die, not knowing that his friends and his own brother would go into the tomb at precisely the wrong moment.

It was not his fault, he told himself, trying to rid himself of guilt. How could he have known?

But now he stood facing his brother's body and his father's wrath, and he knew he was as much the cause of this as the others, that although it hadn't been his hands that had raised that single stone, he was stained with Niko's blood nonetheless. He'd never questioned his own dedication before that moment, his own willingness to give up his life for what he believed. Now he could only ask himself if he had ever had the right to make that decision for his brother.

But backing away from his father would be admitting his guilt, and that Kostas could not do. If he did, he would carry it to his grave.

"We don't know who did this. We know nothing," he said, dismissing his father's accusation.

His words made no impression. Spirtos turned back to him, and his face was contorted with his fury.

"*I* know," Spirtos roared at him. "You, your friends . . . *you* killed Niko!"

He raised his fist in rage, but his wife stood and ran between them.

"You can't do this," she shouted at them, her voice unexpectedly forceful, no longer begging, but demanding that they listen to her. She was strong, and she would bear what she must, but the sight of them fighting, here, in front of Niko's body, that was too much.

Kostas backed away, glared angrily at his father one last time, then turned and stormed from the room. He

162

brushed against Sky as he passed him in the hallway beyond, but gave no indication that he was even aware of a stranger present in his home.

Spirtos did not lower his fist until his son was gone, until he had transferred his glance to Sky, who stood in the doorway.

"*Signomi,*" Sky murmured, "excuse me. I regret the necessity of intruding on your grief, Kirie Spirtos, Kiria Spirtos." He stood respectfully, waiting to be invited in, giving no indication that he had seen or heard what had passed between father and son.

Kiria Spirtos backed away from them, and once more settled herself at her place beside her dead son's body. Spirtos nodded to Sky, apparently indifferent about whether he entered or not, but unwilling to transgress on the laws of hospitality by turning him away.

"What is it?" he asked.

"I've searched everywhere for Mr. Devereaux and his daughter. No one has seen them, not since last night."

Spirtos shrugged. "I fear I can not help you."

"Perhaps your wife," Sky ventured. "Perhaps she remembers what happened after you left her last night, something that might help."

Spirtos stood silent for a moment, then turned to his wife and spoke to her, translating Sky's question.

Kiria Spirtos looked up at Sky, her dark eyes thoughtful. Then she spoke to her husband and he translated her words for Sky.

"*Despinis* Devereaux went to her room soon after I left. That was the last my wife saw of her."

"And Mr. Devereaux?" Sky asked.

Again the translations and Spirtos answered, "He left before dawn. Someone came with a note for him, he went upstairs, and my wife heard him enter his daughter's room. A few minutes later he left without saying a word."

"A note?" Sky demanded, exasperated now that he

was forced to this roundabout means of communicating with the farmer's wife. "What note? Who brought it? Did Arden leave with him?"

Spirtos obviously did not like Sky's tone or the way he pressed, but he turned to his wife and they spoke one last time. He turned back to Sky.

"She did not see who brought the note and does not know what happened to it nor what it contained. She does not think *Despinis* Devereaux left then. She knows nothing more."

This bit of information baffled Sky. Who would have reason to send a note to Forbes, he wondered. He was sure Devereaux knew no one on Crete with the exception of himself and the members of Evans's team. None of it made any sense to him.

"May I look in their rooms, please?" he asked Spirtos. When the Cretan nodded, he said, "*Efcharisto,* Kiria Spirtos, Kirie Spirtos." Then he left the room.

Once he was in the hall, his apparent calm disappeared. He ran to the stairs and took them three at a time.

He went to Forbes's room first. It didn't take him long to realize there was nothing there for him to see. The bed was still unmade, and a robe and nightshirt lay where they had been dropped on a chair. All the room told him was that Forbes had been roused from his sleep by the sound of the tomb collapsing and that he had dressed hurriedly and without any attempt at neatness.

He left the room disappointed and went to the next one, the room Arden had occupied. Here, too, was a rumpled bed and cast-off night clothes. He lifted her robe, recognizing it as the robe she'd worn when she'd come down to meet him in the garden. It surprised him to realize it had been the night before. It seemed like months since he had stood in the garden holding her in his arms, but he realized it had been barely a day. Her robe still seemed warm to his fingers, as if she had cast it off moments before.

"Put that down!"

Sky didn't have to look at him to know that David had come into the room. He made no pretext of trying to mollify David's anger. Instead he raised the thin silk robe to his nose and sniffed the flowery hint of her scent that still clung to it.

David crossed the room and snatched away the robe. "I told you to put that down," he hissed. "What are you doing here? You have no right to be here, to touch my fiancée's things." He sneered at Sky's generally dirty and disheveled condition. "Keep your filthy hands away from her belongings."

Sky felt a wave of disgust as he realized that despite the tragedy at the tomb, David had managed to find the time to make himself comfortable, to bathe, shave, and don clean clothing. It seemed that his own comfort was paramount to the Bostonian, coming before the consideration of such minor matters as Forbes's and Arden's disappearance.

"Haven't I, Trumbull?" Sky asked absently, clearly uninterested in what David thought he did or did not have a right to do. "I don't suppose it's occurred to you that both Forbes and Arden are missing, has it? Or is that small matter simply too unimportant for you to waste energy considering?"

His words seemed to disconcert David enough to temporarily muffle his anger.

"Missing, what do you mean, missing?"

"To put it simply, in terms even you can not misunderstand, Trumbull, they are nowhere to be found. I've been searching for them since this afternoon, since the last of the bodies were found at that damn tomb of yours." He paused for a moment, searching David's expression for some sign of responsibility, some show of grief for what had happened. He could find none. "No one has seen either of them. And as you can see," he motioned to the untidy state of the room, "Arden hasn't been here."

"That's absurd. They must be here somewhere."

"Have you seen either of them?" Sky demanded.

"No, but that doesn't mean . . ."

"Have you seen either of them?" Sky interrupted as he turned away and began to rifle through the litter of papers on the table by the window. He was aware of David watching him, apparently undecided about whether he ought to stop him from searching through Arden's belongings or simply ignore the situation. Had the circumstances been different, had he not been tortured with thoughts of Arden, he might have even enjoyed David's confusion. "Have you even thought of them? Of *her?*"

Sky could find nothing of interest among the papers on the table. It was obvious that this was where Arden had been writing her articles for the *Sun*. There were a half dozen sheets of foolscap covered with her handwriting and filled with crossed-out words and corrections. He smiled at that, well aware of how much work was really required for a good article. There was also the start of a neat final copy. At any other time he might have stopped to read a bit of it, but his mind was too occupied even to consider such a distraction. He looked through everything on the table but found nothing that could possibly be the note of which Kiria Spirtos had spoken.

"You've no right to be doing this," David murmured. His objection, however, was half hearted. Now he seemed more perplexed than angry. "What are you looking for?" he asked, almost as an afterthought.

Sky ignored him. He turned then and let his glance drift to the small table beside the bed.

There was a single sheet of smudged paper beside the lamp. Sky felt the hairs at the back of his neck rise the second he saw it. This, he realized even before he'd touched it, was the note for which he'd been searching.

He crossed the room, oblivious to David's bewildered gaze, and lifted the sheet.

"Damn it, I demand to know just what is going on here," David hissed at him finally.

"I'm shocked, Trumbull," Sky said dryly. "Do they know back in Boston that you use such words as damn? I'm sure they'd all be duly disgusted."

He looked down at the note and scanned the few lines that had been printed in neat block letters. The hint of amusement he had felt at the sight of David's clearly irked expression vanished.

"Well?" David asked.

Sky's expression grew fixed and hard as he held out the sheet to David.

"What is it?" David demanded.

"Read it yourself."

David took the sheet from Sky's hand and read:

I have your daughter. Come to the large cypress on the rise overlooking the Englishmen's dig at full light if you want to see her alive again.

Chapter Nine

Sky started for the door.

"Where are you going?" David demanded.

"To find them," Sky murmured angrily, thinking the answer ought to have been obvious enough, even to someone of David's limited observational capacity.

"I'm going with you," David told him.

"Sure you have enough time, Trumbull?" Sky asked, his tone dripping sarcasm. "I wouldn't want to interrupt your schedule or delay your dinner. And you might get your polished boots dirty."

David swallowed. He obviously was trying to keep his temper under control and found the exercise almost beyond him.

"Look—you don't like me and I don't like you," he said. "As his employee, you may owe Forbes some loyalty, but Arden is going to be my wife and that makes her my concern, not yours. And it seems to me that two of us working together stand a better chance of finding her quickly than even you would have alone," he added with his own healthy dose of sarcasm. "I'm going with you to find her."

He pushed his way past Sky and out into the hall. Sky could hear his footsteps advancing toward the stairs. For an instant Sky hesitated, considering letting him go on his own, but then decided that as much as he hated to admit it, David was probably right. Two of them working together would have an easier time of it.

"Want to tell me where you're going, Trumbull?" Sky called out.

The footsteps in the hall ceased, and after a moment's hesitation, began again, but this time they returned. David stood just outside the room and glared at him.

"To the rise above the dig," David said.

Sky shook his head slowly. "I don't believe you, Trumbull," he said. "Do you mean to tell me you really think that whoever asked Forbes to meet him there at sunrise will still be standing around waiting for you to decide to go after him? You can't really be that stupid."

David's cheeks colored. He immediately realized Sky was right, and that only increased his anger. "Well, who do *you* think has her? And why?"

"I told you last night, but none of you would listen," Sky replied.

"These separatists of yours?"

"Hardly mine," Sky replied dryly. "I wonder if they have any friends in the neighborhood."

"Probably a lot. Even Spirtos's oldest son was talking some sort of nonsense about the Greeks and the Turks the other night at dinner. He and Spirtos started a small row over it."

Something went clink in Sky's head, like the tumblers of a safe falling into place.

"Spirtos's son, is he tall, dark haired?" he asked.

"They're all tall and dark haired," David snapped, smug in the knowledge that there was finally something he knew that Sky did not.

Sky just nodded. He really didn't need David's confirmation. He'd seen Spirtos and his two sons working among the rubble at the tomb. There was no question

170

that the man he had seen arguing with Spirtos downstairs in the parlor was the older son.

"What is it?" David demanded. "Damn it, what's going on?"

"Tsk, tsk, Trumbull," Sky said. "I really think this tendency toward profanity is growing."

"I don't have any experience in this sort of thing," David said.

He was excusing himself, Sky realized. The response seemed habitual, as though the necessity had been inbred. He almost felt a twinge of pity for David. Almost, but not quite.

"Well, I do," Sky told him. "I earn my living by getting information out of people. So for the duration, why don't we just agree that I'll do the thinking for both of us?"

It was obvious that David wasn't pleased at the prospect, but he nodded a reluctant agreement.

"If not the meeting place, then where?" he asked.

"That, I think, is what we're about to discover," Sky told him cryptically as he edged by him and made his way to the stairs.

"But why Spirtos's son?" David demanded.

They were walking toward the barn where Spirtos's three sons had taken up temporary residence while the Americans occupied their rooms in the farmhouse. For a moment Sky considered not answering and letting David stew, but then he decided his responses would have an even more unsettling effect.

"Because I overheard a rather unpleasant exchange between him and his father earlier," he said. "I think he may know something."

"What did they say?" David demanded.

"I don't know." Sky grinned. "It was all Greek to me."

171

The grin, along with the hint of amusement that had caused it, disappeared quickly as Sky reminded himself that Arden was in real danger.

"Then how do you know what they were talking about?"

"I've got a feeling," Sky said.

"A feeling? You don't mean to tell me you intend to find Arden on the evidence of a feeling?"

"I don't mean to tell you anything, Trumbull. Scientist that you are, you can draw your own conclusions."

Sky sped up, leaving David to mull over his words as he followed.

The door to the barn, Sky found as he approached it, was ajar. He pushed it open a bit further and entered.

"Spirtos?" he called out.

There was no answer. He made his way past the two empty stalls to the rear of the enclosure where three cots had been set up with dormitory neatness. Sky decided there was ample evidence of Kiria Spirtos's presence. The floor was swept clean and the place was terribly neat, far too neat for three young men.

"*Malista?*"

David came up behind him just as Christos, Spirtos's middle son, entered by way of a door at the far end of the barn. He was bare chested, and water dripped from his hair as he wiped himself with a towel. He eyed David and Sky.

"Yes?" he asked again, this time in English.

"We were looking for Kostas," David said.

"He's at the house with my parents," Christos replied.

"We've just come from there. He's left."

"Well, he's not here, now, is he?" Christos said, making a motion to the bare room. "Unless you can find him hiding under one of the beds."

"It's important that we find him," David pressed.

Christos threw the towel onto the bed, then skirted

172

around the three cots to the far wall to retrieve a shirt that hung on a hook.

"Maybe he's gone off into the hills." He began to pull on the shirt, turning away from David as though he would be just as pleased to ignore him.

"Where?"

Christos turned back to face David. There was anger in his eyes now, and he made no effort to disguise it.

"Our brother was killed last night in your damn tomb. Can't you leave us be? Or is there some little task you want us to do, something so important it can't wait while we mourn our brother?"

David stiffened, obviously affronted. "This is important . . ."

Sky waved him to silence. "I apologize for imposing on your grief," he said.

Christos turned to consider him for the first time since he'd entered. After a moment he nodded. "You were there," he said finally. "You helped me pull the stones off Niko." That fact seemed to mollify him.

Sky nodded but said nothing.

"Who are you?" Christos asked.

"My name's Skyler Trask," Sky replied. "I work for Forbes Devereaux."

Christos darted a distrustful glance at David, then turned back to Sky.

"What do you want with Kostas?"

"To talk with him, nothing more," Sky told him. "His politics are none of my concern."

Christos's eyes narrowed. "Politics? What has this to do with politics?"

This was the time to gamble, Sky realized. He was holding very little in his hand, and in the face of Christos's antipathy, he doubted he'd get very far unless he seemed to be dealing from strength.

"Don't think me a fool, Christos," Sky said. "This is all

politics. The destruction of the tomb was politics. Your brother's death was politics. And unless Kostas talks with me, and soon, he'll be so mired in it he'll never escape."

"Niko's death was an accident!"

Sky shook his head. "Maybe as far as Kostas was concerned. But it was no accident, believe me. And unless someone makes him understand who he's dealing with, he'll be as guilty as they are."

Christos was breathing hard, as though he were struggling with himself.

"Why should you want to help Kostas?" he asked finally.

"I don't," Sky replied flatly. "But his friends have kidnapped Forbes Devereaux and his daughter. If he helps me, I can help him."

Christos looked away. "He's just left."

"Where is he going?"

"To Neapolis, he said. It's a town just to the east of Mallia. He was to join the others there."

Sky turned to David. "Let's get going. We can still catch him."

The horse stopped.

Arden was bruised and exhausted and terrified. She had no idea how long she had been riding, but was certain it had been a very long while. She'd never been so sore or tired in her life.

She felt the hands reach up and untie hers from the pommel, then pull her from the saddle. Her legs, numb from the long ride, seemed to crumple beneath her as her feet came in contact with the ground, but a hand reached out and kept her from falling.

"Where are we?" she cried. "Why are you doing this?"

Her questions were ignored, just as the others had

174

been, and she sank once again into a resigned and weary silence. She wished he would remove the blindfold, wished she could at least see his face. She was certain she would know whether he intended her harm if she could only see his eyes.

The hand on her arm nudged her forward, and she moved along awkwardly, almost stumbling with her uncertain footing. Only a few steps, though, and the path became smooth and flat. She realized the breeze had suddenly ceased to touch her skin. We're inside, she thought as she heard the echo of footsteps against stone . . . wherever it is he was bringing me, we're here.

"Sit, Miss Devereaux."

The hand was moved to her shoulder and pushed her downward. Too weary to protest, she sat.

"I don't think we'll need this any longer."

He untied the blindfold, and for a moment the glare of lamplight, after the hours of total darkness, blinded her. She lifted her hands, still tied together at the wrists, to her face until the stinging ebbed and her eyes had become acclimated to the light.

She dropped her hands finally and looked up at the black-clad, wiry man who stood in front of her. He was staring down at her with a look of amused superiority.

"Who are you?" she demanded. "Why are you doing this to me?"

He smiled, his amusement increasingly evident. "It is late, Miss Devereaux. I fear our journey has taxed you unduly," he told her. "There will be more than enough time to answer your questions tomorrow. For now, you should eat," he waved toward a table where a tray had been set, "and then sleep."

With that, he took a knife from the sheath on his belt and held it out. Arden stared at the blade in terror, her eyes fixed by the way the lamplight glinted from it. Finally, she tore her eyes from it and looked up at him.

"What are you going to do?" she whispered in fear as she tried uselessly to back away from him.

He stood for a moment, and Arden had the distinct feeling that he was savoring the fear he saw in her. The thought disgusted her.

"Ah, I am disappointed, Miss Devereaux. I fear you think me a monster." He laughed then, and smiled at her. Then he leaned toward her, grasped her bound hands in one of his, and neatly slit the cord that tied them. He released his hold and stepped back.

She sat for a moment, rubbing away the numbness from her hands and wrists, and watched him return the knife to its sheath.

"Eat something, Miss Devereaux," he told her. "And then sleep. I wish you pleasant dreams."

With that, he turned and crossed the room to the door. He stopped, though, with his hand on the knob and turned back to face her once more. He stared at her, and Arden realized his look frightened her almost as much as the knife had.

"Until the morning, Miss Devereaux," he murmured before he left the room and pulled the door shut after himself.

Arden felt her heart pounding in her chest. The sound of it nearly muffled the dull metallic thud of the bolt falling. It took her several seconds to realize that she had been imprisoned.

"I don't understand why we don't simply overtake him. What good is following along after him like this?"

Sky put his hands on the pommel of his saddle and leaned forward. The view of the road and the surrounding countryside from this vantage point was impressive. Even the first pale light of dawn was enough to illuminate

176

the road. He could clearly make out the small, dark figure that was Kostas Spirtos.

He would have liked to ignore David, to simply pretend he wasn't there. In the previous hours he had come to think that allowing the Bostonian to come had been a mistake, that not only would he not be of any help, but he might actually prove a hindrance.

"I told you, Trumbull, it's easier to follow him than to try to make him talk to us."

"But this is foolish, trailing after him until he makes his camp. Up before dawn to make sure he doesn't steal away. It would have been far easier simply to confront the man."

"You're right, Trumbull, it would have been easier," Sky conceded. "And it would have been equally easy for him to tell us that he knows nothing and suggest we find our way to Hades."

"But you could threaten to go to the authorities with what you know about what happened at the tomb. It was enough to frighten his brother . . ."

"His brother knew nothing," Sky interrupted. "That made it easy to make him think we knew a good deal more than we actually do. But if Kostas is working with men like the ones I met, then he will know enough not to betray his friends. And, most likely, just in case we were foolish enough to follow him, he might just decide to spend a week or two roaming the hills by way of discouraging us from looking for his people. We might never find Arden and Forbes."

"We don't even know that he's going to meet the people who have them," David protested. "All this might be a waste of time and effort."

"True," Sky admitted. "But then, I can't think of anything else to do, so we might just as well follow Spirtos."

"And let the real kidnappers do whatever it is they

intend to do with Arden," David accused in a huffy tone. "For God's sake, she might already be dead. Doesn't that disturb you?"

Sky resettled himself in the saddle and turned to face David. If he hadn't been firmly convinced that left to his own devices David would go blundering off and do more harm than good, he'd have invited him to take up the search on his own. It would be a good deal less annoying than having to listen constantly to his complaints and trying to make him see reason.

Not that David's suggestion the kidnappers might already have killed Arden wasn't a thought that hadn't tortured him. It was, after all, what he'd first imagined they intended to do. But logic told him that she was still alive. That, and something deep within him that told him he would know if she were dead, he would know because a part of him would die with her.

"She's not dead!" he nearly shouted. He saw David's startled expression and realized he was giving away something that should remain hidden. He lowered his tone. "If they intended to kill her or Forbes, they would have done it at the dig and then made sure the bodies would be found quickly. They'd have no reason to keep them hidden."

"But why would they take her? Or Forbes?"

"Can you think of anyone else who might be interested in taking an American hostage?" Sky demanded. "Especially an American who happens to own a fairly powerful newspaper? Who else would be so desperate for the press to present their story to the world? Surely not the Turkish government. And the Greeks haven't even decided if they'll bother to step into this mess. That leaves Constatin or some other separatists."

"If they want Forbes's support, they ought to be courting him. Surely the last thing they'd do would be to kidnap his daughter," David persisted.

178

Sky felt the last of his patience beginning to fade. "Look, Trumbull—even you have to recognize this isn't Boston. These men have neither the time nor the inclination to be polite. Arden is their insurance. If Forbes isn't accessible by means of persuasion, they can always use threats."

"I can't believe you're serious, Trask," David insisted. "According to you, first these men destroy the tomb in an attempt to call attention to their plight, then they kidnap Arden in order to kidnap Forbes. You make them sound as though they're playing a game of Robin Hood. And why should America or England—or anyone else, for that matter—care what happens on a little island in the Aegean?"

"If you ever took your nose out of your old pots, Trumbull, you'd realize this 'little island' could be extremely useful for a country with a strong navy and the desire for trade throughout the Mediterranean, which pretty much describes both England and the United States. And as far as these men are concerned, believe me, they aren't playing."

He stared at the slowly receding shape of Kostas Spirtos. "Unless," he added as he dug his heels into his horse's side to start him on the road, "you think death is just a game."

Arden balanced on the small table she'd pulled up against the wall and stared out the barred window. The glimpse she had of the hillside to the left told her that grapevines grew in the pale ocher soil. But what really interested her was the tall stone wall that broke up the sharp rise immediately to the front of her window.

She could see figures, black robed and dark bearded, pass through the iron gates in the wall. They carried hoes and rakes and moved with a determined, plodding step that seemed uninterested in the path they followed, as though their minds were too busy to be bothered with matters so mundane as their surroundings, or even, for that matter, the menial tasks they were about to perform. Of one thing she was only too certain: they were unable to be roused by her cries for help. They made their plodding way to the fields of vines, ignoring her shouts as if they had not heard them. Eventually she gave up the effort and simply stood staring out at them, dark, lank creatures who edged their way through the rows of vines, prodding the pale soil with their hoes and rakes as though it were an enemy they were intent upon subduing.

She'd hardly slept all night. Even as exhausted as she'd been after the long ride, she'd been too frightened to really rest. At first she'd prowled the room, but the walls, bare white relieved only by a carved wooden crucifix, gave her no clue to where she might be. Unsatisfied, she'd put the tray of bread and cheese on the floor, dragged the table to the place beneath the barred window, climbed on top of it, and stared out. The darkness of the night, relieved only by a thick scattering of stars, told her as little as the white walls.

She'd tried to eat some of the dark, thick-grained bread and pale, crumbly cheese she'd found on the tray, telling herself that it was stupid to starve when she had food within her reach. But despite the fact that her stomach growled with emptiness, she found herself unable to force down more than a few bites. The uncertainty of what she faced had tied her stomach into knots that refused to be calmed. In the end she'd returned the tray to the floor and sat on the edge of the narrow bed staring at the crucifix, considering the tortured face of Christ.

When finally the small amount of oil in the lamp had burned itself out and she was left in darkness, she'd felt almost relieved. She'd forced herself to lie down on the narrow bed. Eventually she'd fallen into an uneasy sleep.

But the first fingers of light had roused her, and once again she'd took up the place by the window, clinging to the bars as she stared out. Soon after she'd seen the first dark-robed men and cried out to them. Her cries went unanswered. She did not know why she continued to stand there and stare out at that steep, harsh landscape and the surrounding vineyard. Perhaps, she decided, it was better than sitting and staring at the blank white walls or the small carved face that spoke only of agony.

She was startled to hear the sound of the bolt being thrown and the door to the room being pulled open. She turned.

"Ah, Miss Devereaux. Up and about, I see. I hope you have made yourself quite comfortable. I should have thought you'd still be asleep."

It was him, the one who had come out at her from behind the shadows of Spirtos's orchard, the one who had brought her to this place. Once again, as he had the previous night, he offered her his amused, superior smile.

"I suggest you come down from there. I don't think that table was made to serve as a pedestal even for one so lovely as yourself."

She slowly climbed down from the tabletop.

"There, that's better," he told her when she stood on the floor and faced him. He glanced down at the tray she'd left on the floor. "It seems you did not care for your dinner last night," he said as he considered the barely touched food.

Arden, too, looked down at the tray of bread and cheese. The night before she'd been too frightened to eat any of it, but now she was hungry enough to eat despite her fears. Her stomach was telling her that a few bites of the cheese would be a welcome diversion.

She tore her glance from the food to her captor. "Who are you?" she demanded.

"Ah, your questions. I promised to answer them this morning, didn't I?"

He grinned again. Arden had the feeling her confusion and fear fed his amusement. She determined to provide him with as little as she could. She straightened her shoulders and stared directly at him.

"You may call me Constatin," he told her.

Her fear of him, she realized with surprise, had already begun to fade. And his superior smile was beginning to rouse an anger in her that was completely out of proportion. She let it grow unchecked, telling herself that if he'd intended to harm her, he'd had more than ample opportunity and would have done it by now.

"I can think of a good number of things to call you, thank you," she told him tartly. "Who are you? What is this place and why have you brought me here?"

His smile disappeared. "I must warn you that I do not appreciate a woman with a sharp tongue, Miss Devereaux," he told her.

"And I do not appreciate being kidnapped and held against my will, Mr. Constatin," she snapped.

He stared at her a moment, his eyes blazing, and then he laughed.

"Perhaps I missed the joke?" she asked.

"I was just thinking that were circumstances different you and I might become friends, Miss Devereaux."

She shook her head. "I make it my business never to become friends with kidnappers."

He sobered. "As you like. I would prefer our relationship to be a bit less hostile, but if you insist upon thinking of me as your enemy, I have no way to change that. In answer to your questions, you are in the guest house just outside the walls to a monastery. Just for now, I will keep its name and location from you, if you don't mind. If you insist that you are my enemy, that information might prove dangerous to the monks here."

"Those men are monks?" Arden asked.

He nodded.

"Are they all deaf?" she asked. "I called out to them for help, and they acted as though they heard nothing."

"The monks here are very devout, Miss Devereaux. You are lucky that this particular monastery is fairly modern. Others on Crete would not allow a woman so close to its walls. There are some where only steers are raised, and roosters, so that the monks need not be defiled by the knowledge that their food comes from a female. In any case, they would not respond to a woman's cry."

Arden shook her head, bewildered. "Would they have answered a man's calls?" she asked.

"I am afraid the monks of this particular monastery are not only devout, they are also extremely determined to be rid of the Turks on Crete. They are sworn to help our cause."

Arden considered his words and recalled what Sky had told her and the others about the Cretan separatists.

"Why have you brought me here?" she asked him after a moment's silence. "What have I to do with you or your cause?"

"You are here to ensure that your father listens to me, Miss Devereaux," he replied. "Nothing more."

"My father?" she demanded. "What has any of this to do with my father?"

"Your father, Miss Devereaux, is a very appropriate means for us to tell the United States government that, with the proper encouragement for our cause, they could enjoy certain military and naval accommodations in an extremely propitious location in the Aegean."

"Encouragement, I assume, is your euphemism for arms and munitions?" Arden asked.

Constatin shrugged. "Encouragement is encouragement, Miss Devereaux."

"But why my father?" she asked. "Surely the embassy in Athens would provide you with the means to reach officials in Washington."

He scowled, his amusement gone. "The official position is one of wait-and-see, Miss Devereaux. Your government will stand aside as long as the Greeks still consider fighting the Turks here and annexing Crete themselves."

"And you don't want that?" she asked.

"No," he conceded, "we don't need to exchange one master for another, even one that shares our heritage."

"My father can't change any of that," she told him. "He owns a newspaper. He has nothing to do with the government."

"His power is greater than you think, Miss Devereaux. Governments have been known to change their positions if there is a loud enough outcry from the populace. And in your country the way to excite the populace is to rouse them through the newspapers."

"Surely you don't think my father would ever support you after he learns what you have done to me!" she said.

"Ah, but you have not been harmed, Miss Devereaux." He motioned with his hand. "These accommodations are quite comfortable by local standards. Our only aim was to assure ourselves of your father's attention. When we have explained this to him, I am certain he will forgive us this little ruse."

"And that is why you have kidnapped me?"

"Under the circumstances, it seemed the most expedient means, Miss Devereaux. A ragtag group like ours, it would seem very unimportant to a man like your father, just as we seemed unimportant to his reporter, Mr. Trask."

Arden gasped. "You've spoken with Sky?" she asked.

"I'm afraid he thought his publisher would be unwilling to accommodate us," Constatin replied. "I think now, however, I have the means to prove him wrong. I think now your father can be induced to listen to us."

Arden shook her head. "My father will not be blackmailed," she told him flatly.

"Blackmail is such an unpleasant word, Miss Devereaux. I've sent your father a note telling him that I have taken you. He is to meet my brother, who will invite him here and then bring him to me. I am sure he will decide that the cost of a bit of his time is well worth the pleasure of being reunited with you. They should be arriving quite soon."

"And what if my father has refused to come with this brother of yours?" she asked. "Or what if once he gets here he tells you he won't help you?"

Constatin's expression stiffened. All traces of the humor he'd shown her were gone.

"Let us hope for both our sakes that he does not refuse," he said. "You are a very handsome young woman. It would cause me great distress were I to be forced to kill you."

Chapter Ten

Sky sat down at a table at the far side of the veranda of the small *taverna* where Kostas Spirtos had decided to take his midday meal. Sky was more than a little pleased at the respite offered by the cool of the shadows cast by a large plane tree that obscured the table. The ride to Neapolis had been a long one, dry and hot. He was quite content to sit for a while in the shade and enjoy something cold to drink. He hoped that Kostas took his time over his meal.

"He'll see us here," David hissed as he slumped into the chair beside Sky's.

Sky shook his head. "He isn't acting as though he thinks he's being followed. Besides, he barely saw me at Knossos. Keep your back to him and he won't notice either of us."

David slid his chair so that his back was to Spirtos. "At last, something to eat," he muttered. He'd never before missed two consecutive meals, and the absence of dinner the previous night followed by a breakfast consisting of a drink of water from the stream they'd camped near had given him a new appreciation of hunger.

Sky considered him with a touch of amusement. David's veneer of carefully groomed superiority had crumbled the further they'd ridden from Knossos. He found himself wondering if Forbes Devereaux would be quite so eager for a union with the Boston Trumbulls if he could see David in this less than socially presentable condition.

"I thought you realized my life wasn't civilized, Trumbull," Sky told him dryly. "Meals aren't always available at a specified hour as they are in Boston."

David ignored his words and the slightly superior smile that accompanied it. "I wonder if there's anything decent here," he sniffed doubtfully as he eyed the plates of food that were being consumed by the other patrons at the tables around them.

"If you're hungry enough, you'll eat whatever they give you," Sky told him, watching David's dully accepting expression and realizing that he was indeed that hungry.

The waiter approached the table and set down a small basket filled with round, flat bread. *"Parakalo?"* he asked.

Sky pointed to the next table, where two men sat eating plates of sliced grilled meat and rice. *"Dio,"* he said, and held up two fingers.

The waiter apparently understood. He nodded, said, *"Efcharisto,"* and made his way through the maze of tables to the kitchen.

David turned and darted a glance at Kostas Spirtos. "Do you think he came here to meet one of them?" he asked Sky.

"I think he came here to eat," Sky told him flatly as he watched Kostas make a furious attack on the plate of food that had just been set in front of him. "He's as hungry as we are, I should think."

"But he's supposed to meet his friends here," David said. "That's what Christos said."

"In Neapolis," Sky corrected. "Not necessarily in this

188

taverna." He took one of the small rounds of flatbread, broke off a piece, and chewed it thoughtfully. "He'll have a place and a time," he said finally. "If he misses one day, he'll be able to go there the next. We just have to keep an eye on him until it's time for him to make his connection."

David considered his expression. "You seem to be well versed in this sort of thing, Trask."

Sky shook his head. "It's just logic," he said. "He wouldn't be told where the headquarters are. That way, if the authorities for some reason took an interest in him, he'd have nothing to tell. He'd just have someplace to go, a public place, most likely, and someone who can recognize him to meet him there. Once he makes his connection, then our real work starts."

The waiter neared the table and Sky fell silent as they were served.

When he'd gone, David leaned forward. He considered the food on the plate that had been set before him as he spoke.

"We might be chasing him for nothing, you know. He might have nothing whatsoever to do with Arden's disappearance."

Sky was not interested in his opinion. "If you think that, you're free to go back to Knossos, Trumbull," he said as he lifted his fork. Keeping an eye on Kostas, he directed his attention to his food.

David watched Sky eat with what appeared to be single-minded attention. He hated being ignored, hated even more Sky's ability to make him feel inadequate. Eventually, however, his hunger overcame his animosity, and he took Sky's cue. He, too, ate silently—and ravenously.

Sky darted a glance at him and felt a hint of amusement to see hunger had overcome David's usually impeccable table manners. He wondered if the Bostonian had ever missed a meal before.

A few minutes later a church bell rang the hour, one o'clock. Even from across the veranda, Sky could see Kostas start at the sound of it, as though he had not been quite prepared for it. The Cretan lifted his glass and quickly drained its contents. Then he dropped some coins on the table and stood.

Sky put down his fork and he, too, got to his feet.

"What is it?" David demanded.

"Pay for the food, Trumbull. Our rabbit is about to bolt."

"Damn," David muttered as he considered the still half-filled plate. But he did as Sky told him, quickly paying for their meal and then starting across the crowded town square after Sky.

"As I promised you, she is unhurt."

Nikolas Constatin dropped the piece of wood that covered the tiny window in the door to Arden's room.

"I want to talk to her," Forbes fumed. He put his hand on the latch.

Constatin laid his hand on Forbes's arm, keeping him from drawing back the latch.

"I repeat, Mr. Devereaux, I sincerely regret the worry I have caused you, just as I regret the necessity of this unpleasant ruse. It is only the greatest of need that has forced me to this action, the need to see you and explain to you, to convince you to help us."

Forbes's expression hardened. "*After* I have spoken to my daughter."

Constatin lowered his head. "If that is your wish, Mr. Devereaux, certainly. But I think we both realize that young women have no understanding of politics. This is a subject for rational minds, for men. A woman's hysteria can only cloud the important matters we have to discuss."

190

Forbes hesitated a moment, then raised his hand from the latch. He lifted the wooden shutter and stared through the small window a second time. Arden was pacing the room, but from what he could see, Constatin hadn't lied. She looked fit and unhurt.

"Arden?" he called out.

She started at the sound of his voice and then ran to the door.

"Papa? Is that you, Papa?"

"Arden, are you all right?"

She stared out the small window at him, and then saw Constatin standing just behind him.

"Papa, he's a murderer!" she cried. "Be careful."

Forbes turned a puzzled look at Constatin. Although the note he had received regarding Arden's disappearance had been threatening, he'd been treated quite courteously, and Constatin had more than amply explained his motive for giving the appearance that he would use force. In fact, the man had been decidedly deferential since Forbes's arrival. It was obvious that he regretted what he had done, that he had acted as he had only out of direst need.

In view of this, Arden's words seemed more hysterical than anything else. Not that he blamed her—after all, the experience had doubtless been unpleasant. But he was inclined to dismiss her words and give Constatin the benefit of the doubt.

The Cretan returned his stare with a shrug and an expression that said, "I told you so, women are far too emotional to consider such grave matters seriously."

Forbes turned back to his daughter. "Arden, have you been hurt?" he asked her.

She shook her head, bewildered by the terseness in his words, by the distant, authoritative tone of his voice.

"No, Papa," she admitted. "I haven't been hurt. But that man is a terrorist. He's . . ."

Forbes cut her off by turning back to face Constatin. Perhaps the man is right, he thought. Perhaps the talk the Cretan had gone to such great trouble to have with him was best left to just the two of them.

"Very well, sir," he agreed. "I will listen to what you have to say.

"Papa, you can't be serious!" Arden shouted as he turned. "Papa!"

"Be patient, Arden. This will not take long," Forbes called back to her.

Then both Forbes and Constatin were turning away, leaving her locked in the featureless room, and she stared after them in bewilderment.

Constatin put his hand on Forbes's back in a comradely fashion.

"Papa!" Arden shouted as she watched them near the end of the corridor and turn, passing out of her view. She could hear Constatin's voice drone on.

"I appreciate this, Mr. Devereaux," Constatin said. "There is a fine Byzantine arched garden in the monastery. Are you a student of architecture? No? Well, it is cool, and we can talk there without being disturbed. I think we might even be able to sample a bit of the monastery wine."

Arden put her hands on the knob and tried to shake open the door, but the effort was useless. The door was heavy and the latch secure.

"Papa!" she screamed one last time, but that, too, was useless.

Constatin led the way outside and up the hill to the monastery walls. He kept up a stream of amiable chatter, pointing out the old Byzantine architecture to Forbes as they were admitted onto the monastery grounds. Forbes walked along with him, nodding, smiling at Constatin's small jokes. He wondered only for a moment why he had agreed to this man's request. But his questions dis-

192

MORE PASSION AND ADVENTURE AWAIT... YOUR TRIP TO A BIG ADVENTUROUS WORLD BEGINS WHEN YOU ACCEPT YOUR FIRST 4 NOVELS ABSOLUTELY *FREE*
(AN $18.00 VALUE)

Accept your Free gift and start to experience more of the passion and adventure you like in a historical romance novel. Each Zebra novel is filled with proud men, spirited women and tempestuous love that you'll remember long after you turn the last page.

Zebra Historical Romances are the finest novels of their kind. They are written by authors who really know how to weave tales of romance and adventure in the historical settings you love. You'll feel like you've actually gone back in time with the thrilling stories that each Zebra novel offers.

GET YOUR FREE GIFT WITH THE START OF YOUR HOME SUBSCRIPTION
Our readers tell us that these books sell out very fast in book stores and often they miss the newest titles. So Zebra has made arrangements for you to receive the four newest novels published each month.

You'll be guaranteed that you'll never miss a title, and home delivery is so convenient. And to show you just how easy it is to get Zebra Historical Romances, we'll send you your first 4 books absolutely FREE! Our gift to you just for trying our home subscription service.

BIG SAVINGS AND FREE HOME DELIVERY

Each month, you'll receive the four newest titles as soon as they are published. You'll probably receive them even before the bookstores do. What's more, you may preview these exciting novels free for 10 days. If you like them as much as we think you will, just pay the low preferred subscriber's price of just $3.75 each. *You'll save $3.00 each month off the publisher's price.* AND, your savings are even greater because there are never any shipping, handling or other hidden charges—FREE Home Delivery. Of course you can return any shipment within 10 days for full credit, no questions asked. There is no minimum number of books you must buy.

GET
FOUR
FREE
BOOKS
(AN $18.00 VALUE)

ZEBRA HOME SUBSCRIPTION
SERVICE, INC.
P.O. Box 5214
120 BRIGHTON ROAD
CLIFTON, NEW JERSEY 07015-5214

appeared quickly as he realized his fears for Arden had been satisfactorily quelled and he found his curiosity had begun to outweigh his anger.

After all, he told himself, this Constatin was pleasant and charming. Neither he nor Arden had anything to fear from such a man. As they settled themselves in the comfortable cool of the monastery garden and sipped the potent wine the monks made from the grapes they cultivated on the surrounding hillside, Forbes's questions slid into silent abeyance until they were superseded by thoughts of an entirely different sort.

Constatin was, he realized, offering him the opportunity to do something important, something more far reaching than he had ever thought to do. The *Sun* had always espoused his rather conservative political views, but he had frankly considered the paper a means to fortune, not power, and so tended to avoid any real political controversy that might have an adverse affect on either advertising or circulation. Until Constatin had begun talking to him, he'd never seriously considered the possibility that he might, simply by espousing its cause, affect the fate of a country. And according to Constatin, the cause was one of freedom and democracy, a populist cause that could not possibly lower his own stature.

Constatin's words quickly began to raise an image in Forbes's mind, one of himself as a standard-bearer for liberty, someone who molded history. It was an image he found more and more appealing as their talk continued, until the questions he had about Constatin were dismissed as easily as he had Arden's warnings.

"Santos Cyrill."

David sounded out the Greek letters that were incised in the stone beside the church's arched doorway.

"Bravo, Trumbull," Sky whispered. "Your classical

education has equipped you magnificently for life on Crete."

David scowled. He was perfectly well aware that Sky had picked up more of the language in the few days they'd been on Crete than he had. He himself might be able to read and translate an ancient Greek tablet, but the modern language seemed completely beyond him. Sky, however, seemed to have a natural ear for languages and an easy ability to make himself understood.

He followed Sky, slipping beside him into the dark cavern of the church. Candles flickered at the front, near the altar. The light from them shone on a gold-leaf triptych that dominated the apse but faded quickly, leaving the nave in virtual darkness. Paintings of saints, their faces stern and reverential, gazed upward from the side walls of the altar. The place smelled of incense and the damp. It was not at all like the austere church his family attended in Boston, and David was not at all sure he liked it.

He stood for a moment staring into the darkness, searching along the rows of pews for Kostas Spirtos. It was only when a hand reached out, grabbed his arm, and tugged on it that he realized he was making himself far too visible. He hurriedly slid into the seat beside Sky.

"Kneel and keep your head down," Sky hissed at him.

"What?"

David had always had a proper Bostonian Protestant suspicion of Catholic rite. The idea of kneeling in a Greek Orthodox church seemed somehow sacrilegious to him.

"Damn it," Sky hissed, "do as you're told."

Realizing that the few others in the church, mostly old women, were kneeling and appeared to be absorbed in penitent prayer, David decided that Sky was probably right, that particular position would probably be the least obvious. He slid down on the rail and lowered his head, occasionally allowing himself a surreptitious glance around as he tried to decide which of the others in the church might possibly be Kosta Spirtos.

Sky had no such difficulty. He recognized Kostas's broad back immediately and kept his eyes firmly on the young Cretan where he sat alone to the side of one of the front pews. He wondered how long it would be until Kostas's meeting would take place. Two men kneeling in the rear of a church in the middle of a weekday afternoon would not go unnoticed for long.

He hadn't long to wait. A few minutes after Kostas had settled himself, a small, black-robed, bearded man entered the church from a side entrance. He genuflected, stood by the altar for a long moment in what seemed like reverent prayer, then turned and scanned the occupants of the church.

Sky had paid him little attention until that moment, for he seemed just another of the countless monks he'd become accustomed to seeing since he'd arrived in Crete. But the way he looked at Kostas seemed strange to Sky, the look far too intent to be casual, and Kostas's reaction seemed even more intense.

The monk walked toward the confessional, and Sky assumed Kostas would follow immediately, but he didn't. One of the elderly women rose from her knees, crossed to the stall, and entered. She seemed to take an extremely long time confessing her sins, and Sky found himself wondering what such an old woman could possibly have done in her life to warrant such an extended search for absolution. He kept his eyes on Kostas and saw that the young Cretan also seemed to have a deep curiosity about the old woman as he constantly turned to watch for her to leave the confessional.

Eventually she left the stall and knelt before the altar, her beads busy in her fingers. Kostas wasted no more time: he quickly made his way to the door of the stall, opened it, and went inside.

Sky rose silently and, skirting the nave by way of a side aisle, made his way to the wall of the confessional. He waited, leaning close, trying to hear what was happening inside.

The talk was entirely in Greek. The only words he understood were *Haghios Nicodemos*. It was a monastery, he knew, located about halfway between Neapolis and Cape Yoannis, perhaps five miles from the town. There was a bit more talk and then the sound of stirring. Sky barely had time to slip into the pew before Kostas appeared.

Unlike the old woman who had preceded him in the confessional, Kostas seemed to have merited no penance. He strode directly to the rear of the church without so much as glancing back at Sky. Before he had left, Sky was on his feet and following.

"What's happening?" David asked as he trotted up behind Sky.

Sky darted a glance at him. He'd almost forgotten about David, and at that moment wished he could.

"I thought I'd sample some monastery wine," Sky told him. "If you're coming, I suggest you move a little faster."

The sergeant examined the papers David and Sky had given to the soldier who had stopped them on the road and demanded identification. Sky looked up to see Kostas Spirtos disappearing in the distance and swore under his breath.

"Why are you here?" the sergeant asked them in English that, despite his heavy accent, did not in any way disguise his displeasure at the sight of foreigners in the area. "An American newspaperman and an archaeologist . . . what do you two find so interesting in the countryside here?"

"I'm with Sir Arthur Evans's party at Knossos," David told him in the same supercilious tone to which Sky had recently grown accustomed.

The sergeant raised a disinterested brow. "You're a long way from Knossos here," he said, and stared at David in a way that made it clear he was not impressed.

"We're searching for my . . ."

"My colleague is trying to explain," Sky cut in quickly, "in his own rather unique manner, that he's on an expedition to scout out likely sites for Evans's further archaeological examination."

The sergeant frowned. "There is nothing authorizing that here," he said, tapping the papers impatiently with his hand. "And what does a journalist have to do with archaeological sites?"

"My publisher wants me to write about the latest discoveries in Crete," Sky told him, "all the ancient wonders Evans is digging up. In America there's a lot of interest in the past." He grinned his rather dull-witted, unsophisticated American smile. "For you, living with the past is everyday. For Americans, who have so little past, artifacts are a matter of great curiosity."

The soldier shook his head. "Then I suggest you go back to Knossos and write about the pots Evans has dug up," he said. "You may go no further toward the coast."

"But," David sputtered, "you let that farmer pass!" He pointed to the tiny dark dot that was Kostas Spirtos disappearing into the distance.

The soldier spat. "A Cretan farmer. Let him get in the path of battle. There will be one less to deal with. You Americans, you go back to Knossos."

"Battle?" Sky asked. "What do you mean, battle?"

The soldier's eyes narrowed and he peered at Sky suspiciously. "You have not heard?" he asked.

"Heard? Heard what?" David demanded.

The sergeant shrugged. "The Assembly in Athens has

decided to intervene here on Crete. They are sending troopships, and we are told they may be landing near Cape Yoannis." He scowled. "The fools think they can fight us here. We'll be waiting. Already the soldiers are coming from Mallia and Phaistos. And more leave Izmir to join us." He smiled slyly at Sky. "But you are not interested in such matters," he said. "You are simply looking for ancient pots."

"Then there will be war," Sky mused softly.

The Turkish soldier shook his head. "Not war. A battle or two, perhaps, but hardly a war. It will not take much to send the Greeks back to Athens with their tails between their legs." The prospect seemed almost to depress him, as though a short struggle meant he would be cheated. "But as you Americans will have no desire to become casualties of those battles, you will return to Knossos until the matter is resolved. Later you may come to look for your old pots."

"We're willing to take our chances," Sky told him.

The soldier's expression grew grim. He nodded to the other soldier who had originally stopped Sky and David, indicating he should take aim. Then he lowered his own rifle and pointed it in a threatening manner.

"You will return to Knossos," he said. "You may go no further toward the coast." His expression grew sharp. "Unless you have other business on Cape Yoannis that has nothing to do with buried bits of clay."

"No, we have no other business," Sky replied slowly.

The soldier held out their papers. "Then you will take these and return to Knossos," he said.

Sky took the papers and buttoned them into the pocket of his jacket. Then he turned back to his horse, remounted, and waited while David followed suit.

"Thank you, sergeant, for your kind concern for our well-being," he said.

"It is the least we could do for our honored American

visitors," the sergeant told him. Despite the words, there was no suggestion in his tone that he regarded them with anything but disdain, and he made no motion to the soldier to lower the rifle that was still aimed at them.

Sky stared for a second longer into the distance but realized that Kostas Spirtos had disappeared completely. There was no way of knowing if he was keeping to the road to Cape Yoannis or turning off somewhere ahead.

Sky turned his horse and, with David following, began to retrace his path from Neapolis.

Sky darted a glance back. They'd passed over a small rise, and the place where they'd been stopped by the Turkish soldiers was hidden now from their view.

He turned off the road and started toward a thick stand of trees.

"What are you doing?" David called, starting after him.

Sky stopped and waited for David to catch up.

"We're going around those damned Turks," Sky told him flatly.

"What do you mean, we're going around them?" David demanded. "They'll see us. And I have the distinct feeling they won't hesitate to use those rifles they were holding."

Sky grinned at that. At least David had gotten one thing right. "I had that feeling, too."

"Then what do you think you're doing?" David demanded.

"I'm following Spirtos," Sky said. "Or don't you remember what we started out doing? There was the small matter of finding Arden and Forbes."

"Spirtos is gone," he said. "He's disappeared by now and we'll never find him."

"But we know where he's going," Sky replied. "To the

monastery of Haghios Nicodemos."

David shook his head. "No, that's where you *think* he's going," David objected. "We don't know anything for certain."

Sky shrugged. "We don't have any other choice. We have to find Arden and Forbes. If they're at that monastery, or anywhere else between here and Cape Yoannis, for that matter, they're directly in the path the Turks are taking to meet the Greek troops."

"We don't know where they are," David said. "In fact, we don't even know they've been kidnapped. For all we know, Arden and Forbes are still back at the dig."

"That note," Sky reminded him.

"Means nothing," David insisted. "It's stupid for us just to walk blindly into the path of a battle. The wisest thing for us to do is return to Knossos. Perhaps they've already been found."

"Do you really believe that?" Sky demanded. "Or are you simply looking for a reason to act the coward?"

"You bastard," David hissed. "How dare you call me a coward?" He reached into his pocket for the small pistol he'd brought with him from Knossos.

But Sky saw the movement and realized what he was about to do. His hand slid to the holster he wore on his shoulder, and before David had drawn his weapon, Sky already had his gun in hand and aimed.

"I wouldn't do that, Trumbull," Sky told him. "There are some things for which you simply weren't properly prepared at Harvard." He motioned to the hand David still held in his pocket. "Leave it where it is."

A flush of anger colored David's cheeks, but he withdrew his hand without the pistol.

"You presume a great deal, Trask," he said.

"Actually, I presume very little, Trumbull," Sky replied. "I told you before, if you want to go back to Knossos, you're free to leave. I'd be the last one to stop you. If I might remind you, *you* were the one who wanted to come with *me*." He leveled a steely glance at David. "Perhaps you've decided that Arden's safety isn't quite as important to you as you thought."

David bridled. "I hope you walk into the middle of a bloody battle," he told him with more than a hint of rancor.

"Bloody? I think you've spent too much time with Evans and his Brits, Trumbull," Sky said. "Or were you being literal, hoping that blood, namely mine, might be spilled?" He didn't give David the chance to answer. "In either case it wouldn't be the first time. At least this time I've a real reason to go." He stared at David. "Or maybe you don't think Arden's and Forbes's lives sufficient reason?"

David glared at him. "You don't know that," he snapped. "They could be back at Knossos, for all we know."

"As you like, Trumbull," Sky said.

David hesitated as though he expected the argument to continue further, but Sky said nothing more.

"I won't let you get me killed for nothing," he said finally, then he turned his horse and trotted back to the road.

Sky watched him for a few seconds, then dug his heels into his horse's sides and started for the trees.

There was the sound of the latch being drawn. Arden looked up. She watched the door slowly swing open.

"I see you've decided to end your fast, Miss Devereaux."

Arden let her glance drift to the mug of tea that she held in her hand, then down to the remains of the bread, cheese, and olives that had been on her plate. She lifted the mug slowly to her mouth and swallowed some of the tepid liquid as she considered Constatin's amused smirk.

"I've decided I might just as well put you to the expense of feeding me," she told him finally as she returned the mug to the tray. "That is, after all, one of a jailer's responsibilities."

"Really, Arden. Mr. Constatin was only keeping you safe."

Arden realized her father's attitude pleased her no better than Constatin's did. She wondered if the Greek habit of displaying an exaggeratedly dominant masculinity was catching. Whatever the cause, Forbes seemed determined to treat her with as little respect as Constatin did.

"Certainly, Papa," she agreed in an acid tone, "if you consider locking me in this room and threatening to kill me keeping me safe." She reached for the mug again but kept her eyes on Forbes. She couldn't help but notice his look of doubtful disapproval.

"I think you've misunderstood, Miss Devereaux," Constatin told her with his superior smile.

"Think what you will, Mr. Constatin," Arden told him. She turned back to her father. She lost interest in the tea and pushed the mug away. "It would seem that you and this person have come to some understanding, Papa. Does that mean we are free to leave now?"

"We are free to leave whenever we wish, Arden," Forbes told her. "But Mr. Constatin and I still have a few matters to discuss. We shall spend the night here and return to Knossos in the morning."

"Does that mean I'm to remain imprisoned in this room until then?" she demanded.

Forbes turned to Constatin. "Is it really necessary?" he asked.

"Of course not," Constatin agreed. "But the monks would not approve of a woman wandering unescorted on the grounds. One of my men will be glad to serve as your escort."

"A guard, you mean, don't you?" Arden asked. "Or is 'escort' another of your euphemisms?"

"Really, Arden, you've made your point," Forbes told her. "I'm convinced Mr. Constatin intended neither of us any harm."

Arden scowled, but nodded in reluctant acquiescence. "As you think, Papa."

"Excellent," Constatin said. "Come. I think my brother Theo would consider it a great pleasure to serve as your guide for the remainder of the afternoon, Miss Devereaux." He moved to the door and held it open for her.

Forbes offered her his arm and Arden took it. The two of them preceded Constatin out of the room, then he took the lead, showing them through the maze of corridors to a small garden that fronted the guest house.

Constatin pointed to the thick stone wall Arden had seen from the window of her room. The iron gate was closed and locked.

"Of course you realize you may not trespass on the monastery proper," he told Arden. "Women are not allowed there."

Arden nodded. "Of course not," she replied with pointed politeness.

"Ah, and here is Theo."

Constatin waved and called out to a tall young man at the far side of the garden, near the stables. At the sound of his voice Theo turned. He didn't hesitate but started forward at a lope. He was smiling at Forbes when he reached them.

"Miss Devereaux, my brother Theo," Constatin introduced him. "Theo, Miss Devereaux has expressed a desire for a short tour. I didn't think you'd consider it an odious duty."

"On the contrary—a pleasure," Theo said. He grinned at Arden, obviously pleased with what he saw. But the distraction she offered was not quite great enough to

203

remove duty from his thoughts. He turned back to his brother. "I'm afraid there's a small matter you must tend to immediately, Nik," and he motioned in the direction of the stables.

Constatin darted a glance toward a tall figure who stood in the shadows beside the stable doors. He scowled but recovered himself quickly.

"This won't take long," he told Forbes before he started off.

Arden watched him approach the stables, then turned her attention to the second man, the one who kept to the shadows. He seemed familiar to her, but his features were obscured by the shade, and she could not immediately place him. Constatin spoke a few words to him. Then, noticing Arden's interest, he directed the second man inside the stable.

If his intention had been to keep Arden from recognizing his visitor, it would have been better for them to remain where they were. As he turned to enter the stable, the second man moved for a second out of the shadows and Arden had a clear look at his face.

She darted a glance at Theo. It would be foolish, she decided, to tell Forbes what she had seen while Constatin's brother could hear what she said. But she'd been certain from the first that whatever had happened back at the dig concerned Constatin. And now, with Kostas Spirtos there, she was even surer.

She turned to Forbes. "Papa," she asked, "what happened at the tomb?"

Forbes gave her a confused look. "What?" he asked.

"The tomb, David's ancient tomb. The night before last, there was that horrible noise. What caused it? Did something happen?"

Forbes shrugged. "I don't know," he told her. "I left before Spirtos returned to the house." He gave her a questioning look. "What does it matter?"

She shook her head. "Nothing, I suppose," she murmured.

But it did mean something, of that she was certain. If only she could work it all out, she thought, she'd understand just what it was Constatin really intended. All she knew at that moment was that whatever it was, it was not as innocent as he had convinced her father it was. He'd threatened to kill her, and she'd seen his eyes when he'd made that threat. He'd meant it. He was, she was certain, a man who would kill without remorse.

If only she knew what had happened back at Knossos and what part Constatin had had in it. All she knew for certain was that she and her father were in the hands of a man who had little or no conscience. And that, she knew, was a very dangerous place to be.

Chapter Eleven

Sky moved through the stand of trees. It wasn't deep, and he soon found himself on a hillside covered with ancient olives. The gnarled branches of the old trees reached nearly to the ground and were heavy with ripening fruit which glowed dark green in the sunshine. The air was heavy with the warm smell of earth and rotting leaves.

He climbed part way up the hill and then turned north again, toward Cape Yoannis, this time keeping well east of the road and the soldiers who had stopped him and David. The going was rough here, and slow, and he regretted the loss of time. He realized, however, he had little choice if he was going to try to bypass the Turkish soldiers and find his way to the monastery of Haghios Nicodemos. Were he to travel closer to the road, he would surely be seen and stopped by the Turks. And if nothing else, the slow going allowed him ample time for thought.

The more he considered his destination, the surer he was that he would find Arden at the monastery. He remembered those things he had learned over the previous weeks, remembered hearing about priests and monks who gave up their lives rather than submit to

Turkish domination. The monasteries harbored men who were often among the strongest supporters of those wishing to see the Turks expelled from Crete. If Arden had been taken by the separatists, a monastery would be a safe and secure place to keep her hidden, one that wouldn't be easily accessible to public view.

His one fear was that he would not reach the monastery before the Turkish soldiers did on their march to Cape Yoannis and their meeting with the Greek troops. The Turkish soldiers had a reputation for being vicious both in battle and in victory. There was no question in his mind as to what would happen to Arden were she to fall into their hands.

He wondered what had finally pushed the Greek Assembly to take the decisive step against the Turks— the killings in Mallia, perhaps, or the destruction of the tomb at Knossos? Whatever the reason, their timing could not have been worse for Arden and Forbes. He was certain of only one thing—he had to find them and help them get away before it was too late.

When he finally came to the end of the olive grove, Sky found himself overlooking a landscape of neatly tended fields edged by the road to Cape Yoannis and well to the north of the place where he had been forced to turn back. But he was not comforted by the fact that he had outwitted the roadblock. In the time it had taken him to work his way through the root-rutted olive grove the road had grown heavy with traffic.

He looked south and saw a thick stream of soldiers, a long, dusty line of them marching toward Cape Yoannis. The horizon behind him was filled with the dark moving ribbon of humanity on the road. The sergeant at the roadblock had been right, he realized; the Turks were more than prepared for battle with whatever forces the Greeks could possibly send against them.

He considered the landscape to the north. Rolling

hills, green with orchards and vineyards and neat fields of vegetables peaceful in the brilliant afternoon sun. It wouldn't be peaceful for long, he realized. Death was marching north along the same path as the Turkish troops.

He dug his heels into his horse's side, urging the animal down the slope and back to the road. He knew he had little time to find Haghios Nicodemos and Arden. And if he failed, he could very well be signing her death warrant.

Sky skirted the olive grove until he saw a farmhouse. Then he turned his horse and cantered it across a field to the small stone structure. A young woman who had been industriously sweeping the steps that fronted the house stopped and watched as he approached.

"Kirie?" she asked when he drew the horse to a halt in front of the house. She stared up at him, her expression half curious, half frightened.

Sky realized how strange it must be for her to see a stranger in this remote place. Not wanting to frighten her, he nodded and smiled reassuringly. Then he dismounted and walked slowly toward her. She was young, he realized, and very pregnant.

Before he had the chance to speak to her, a man came out of the house. He put his hand on the woman's arm and stared at Sky with suspicion.

"Kali mera, kirie," he said—Good afternoon, sir.

Despite the polite greeting there was distrust and the hint of a threat in his tone. Sky decided he had good reason to be wary on this particular afternoon with Turkish troops marching toward his farm.

"Milate ghalika?" he asked—Do you speak English?

The man shook his head and Sky cursed under his breath. He might be able to get himself fed in Crete with his few acquired words of Greek, but this was going to be a good deal harder.

"*Haghios Nicodemos? Pou?*"—Where?

The farmer understood. He pointed to a narrow, winding path that led in a more or less northerly direction, and spoke in very rapid Greek. Sky didn't understand a word, but he got the point and nodded.

"*Efcharisto*," he said as he turned and put his foot in the stirrup. But before he mounted, he turned back to the farmer and his young wife. "Turkish soldiers," he said. The couple stared at him in bewilderment, not understanding. "Soldiers," he said again, and he took his pistol from its holster and showed it to them while he pretended to march. "Do you understand? Soldiers. *Turks.*" The last word, at least, seemed to make an impression. "Turkish soldiers," Sky repeated, and he pointed to the road to the south.

The farmer's puzzled expression was slowly replaced by one of fear. He pulled his wife close to him, and nodded at Sky.

Sky realized he'd done what he could. "Good luck," he murmured as he mounted his horse. He turned and started off to the north, in the direction the farmer had showed him. After a few moments he looked back to see the man hitching an old nag to a wagon where the woman already sat waiting for him.

"Good luck to you," Sky wished them a second time. It occurred to him that they, like him, would probably need all the luck they could get.

"Watch your step here. The footing is uncertain."

Theo Constatin smiled at Arden as he held out his arm to her, expecting her to grasp it. She didn't. She had absolutely no intention of responding to either his studied politeness or the boyish charm he seemed determined to lavish upon her. She ignored him, moving carefully on the path, taking care not to lose her balance on the loose pebbles as she and Theo moved down the steep slope of the monastery vineyard.

The surrounding countryside was beautiful, she realized, the orchards and vineyards lay still and peaceful in the afternoon sun. Arden wished she were in a more receptive mood, one that would allow her to pay nature the homage she rightfully deserved. Instead Arden was plagued with fears and suspicions.

Theo stood watching her, not quite understanding the reason for her snub, then shrugged and hurried along behind her.

"That next rise gives a glimpse of the sea," he said, pointing to a steep hill just ahead of them. "We could climb it if you like before we return to the monastery."

She continued to walk, refusing to turn to face him or even acknowledge his suggestion. He was an intrusion on her thoughts, bothersome and irritating. She walked on in silence, aware that he had moved to her side, but making no effort to recognize his presence.

When they reached the foot of the hill she stopped and hesitated. The next hillside rose up almost immediately, the rise Theo had promised provided a view of the sea. It was still early afternoon, and there was no reason why she need consider ending the outing. The walk at least helped her relieve some of the tension that had built up inside her during the long hours she had been locked in the room at the monastery. If nothing else, she could manage to make herself tired. And with Nikolas Constatin now sure of her father's help, she knew she had nothing to fear from Theo.

She realized Theo was standing and staring at her with a slightly puzzled expression. It occurred to her that he was not accustomed to being ignored by women, that he probably was used to getting whatever attention he desired from them. Tall and dark and well built, he was, she realized, certainly attractive enough to have developed an expectation that his attentions would be at least pleasantly entertained. Such men, she thought, are bewildered by their own failure to charm simply because the circumstances arise so rarely.

She wondered if she might use the confusion she'd incited in him to her own advantage. She was, after all, not without charms of her own. And properly used, she thought, there was no reason why they might not help her learn something.

She began to walk forward toward the next hillside, but now her step was a shade slower, yet apparently less careful. There was a rough path through the fig trees that lined the hill, and the climb was steep. When her foot slipped on a stone and she found herself stumbling, she was not in the least surprised to find Theo eager to assist her with a strong arm at her waist.

She let him steady her, regained her balance, and then turned to face him.

"Thank you," she said.

"It's always a pleasure to help a beautiful woman," he told her with theatrical gallantry and a pleasant grin.

She made an obvious attempt at stifling a smile; then, with apparent reluctance, she let it escape.

"You *can* smile," he said. "I was beginning to wonder."

"I'm afraid I've lost the habit. I've not had much to smile about for the last few days," she told him. She started forward again, continuing the climb. "Your brother said he'd kill me if my father didn't agree to what he wanted."

Theo shook his head. "Nik talks like that. He didn't mean it," he said.

"No," she said slowly. "He meant it." She stared at him in silence for a moment, wondering if he really believed what he had said to her. "You're not like him," she said finally. "Why are you doing this?"

He grinned. "Because I find it pleasant to be in your company. Besides, Nik asked me to show you around."

She shook her head. "No, not this. Why are you part of what your brother is doing?"

He sobered. "It's what a man does—fight for what he believes in."

"And in just what *is* it that you believe?" she demanded.

"A free Crete," he answered vehemently.

"And you'd kill for that?"

He considered her for a long moment, his expression dark now, and serious. But then he smiled. "This is not the time nor place to speak of such unpleasant things," he told her. "Not on this beautiful day, and certainly not in the company of so beautiful a woman."

He lowered his face to hers, but before he could kiss her, Arden turned away. It's not going to be so easy as that, Mr. Constatin, she thought.

But she realized it would not be easy for her, either.

It wasn't long before Sky saw the hillside with its grapevines and the stone wall surrounding a collection of white-walled structures. The walls of the enclosed buildings were silent and still, waiting with a patience that implied they had been erected to shelter humanity for an eternity.

It could only be the monastery, Sky told himself. But it wasn't the handful of structures clinging to the hillside that held his attention; it was the sight of the road to the southwest that transfixed him, the main road that led directly from Neapolis. It was already thick with Turkish soldiers.

He realized he had taken a longer detour than he'd

anticipated in order to avoid meeting Turkish troops. He would reach the monastery only minutes before the soldiers. Even as he watched, a small scouting party broke off from the main body of the troops and started across the fields that separated them from the seacoast just to the north. It was obvious the Turks intended to be ready and waiting when the Greek troops disembarked at Cape Yoannis.

He had very little time. The Turkish forces would meet the Greeks on the shore as they disembarked, he realized, then back through the fields behind them until they could use the monastery as a screening fortification to hold the Greek troops at bay. The monastery would be the center of the worst of the battle, and no matter who was the victor, the monastery and its occupants would certainly suffer casualties.

It was not pleasant for him to contemplate the fact that Arden would be right in the middle of the battle.

Sky spurred his horse to a run. David Trumbull's wish, he realized, was about to come true: he was about to find himself in the center of a bloody battle.

He only knew he had somehow to extricate Arden from it before they both became cannon fodder.

"But what chance have you against an army of occupation?" Arden asked Theo.

They had climbed about two-thirds of the way to the top of the hillside and now began to slow their pace as the exertion coupled with the afternoon heat drained their energy. Arden had encouraged Theo's dissertation on the role of freedom fighters as they'd climbed, and with her encouragement his reluctance to talk about what he had previously considered proscribed quickly vanished.

"As long as we do not submit to the Turks, our people will support us," he told her.

214

He paused and seemed to be thinking as he leaned against one of the fig trees, reaching up to grasp two of the ripe fruits. He held one out and Arden took it. He bit into his first, then nodded to her, waiting and expectant, until Arden took a bite. They began walking once more.

"And we are not so few as you may think," he continued. "Many will fight with us when the time is right. Until then we strike where we can, however we can, to let the Turks know we will not be cowed by them."

"Mallia?" she asked. "The Turkish soldiers who were killed there?"

"It was a warning, to make them understand we will not stand quietly by while they murder our countrymen."

She stopped and turned to face him.

"And what happened back at Knossos? Were you part of that too?" she asked. She looked up at him with a mixture of curiosity and invitation. But when he reached out to take her arm, the invitation disappeared and her tone grew sharp, despite her intentions to keep it otherwise. "Was that how you fight for Crete's liberty?"

He let her back away from him. "I don't know what you're talking about," he said as he considered what he saw in her expression.

"Don't you?" she asked. She dropped the remains of her fig to the ground. "You were at Knossos. It was you who brought my father here."

"And what if I was?" he demanded.

She tossed her head. "Your brother said he'd spoken to one of my father's reporters, Skyler Trask."

She paused for a moment. She found it had been hard for her to utter Sky's name. She wondered where he was at that moment, if he was searching for her, if he even knew she had been kidnapped. It seemed impossible that a few nights before she had been standing next to him, had felt the warmth of his arms enfolding her. Everything had turned mad in the previous few days, and none of it made any sense. She forced herself to go on.

"As it happens, Mr. Trask returned to Knossos with the warning that something might happen to us if we stayed there, something unpleasant. Was that just coincidence?"

"Your father's man Trask is a fool!" Theo told her vehemently. "He left before Nik had the chance to make him understand, ran away like a cat afraid of its own shadow. He refused to listen, to understand what happened at Mallia."

"His job is to write about what he sees," she said. "He told us what he saw in Mallia." She tried to recall what Sky had said, but realized he had never mentioned any names. He'd not thought she or Forbes would ever come into contact with these men. She stared up at Theo. "Was your brother responsible for that explosion in Mallia?"

"Nik does what he has to do," Theo insisted.

"And you?" she asked him softly. "Do you kill, too?"

"I have killed," he replied, his words as calmly spoken as if he'd described the weather. He raised the remains of his fig to his mouth and ate it.

Arden shivered and turned away from him. He put his hand on her shoulder, this time refusing to allow her to slip from his grasp. He turned her to face him.

"I have killed Turks," he told her firmly. "I am a soldier fighting a war with other soldiers. It is not what I want, but it is what I must do."

"And your brother," she asked, "is it only soldiers he kills?" She stared up at him, letting her eyes find his. "Were soldiers his only victims at Knossos?"

She'd gone too far. She knew it as soon as she saw the look in his eyes, the anger that slid into them. And the cat-and-mouse game she'd been playing with him for the previous hour had all been for nothing. She had learned nothing, had nothing to tell her father save her suspicions, and Forbes had already made it sufficiently clear to her that he was not interested in listening to them.

"I think it is time we returned," Theo said coldly. It was obvious that the whatever flames she had lit within him and kept smoldering had been abruptly extinguished.

"You promised a glimpse of the sea," she said.

He shook his head. "It will be late when we return. Your father will be worried about you." He eyed her dispassionately. "And I have nothing else to tell you about Mallia—or anything else, for that matter."

He put his hand on her arm and began to turn back down the hill. Arden pulled her arm away from him, feeling like a fool for having been so clumsy, so transparent. He let her go, but kept his eyes on her as she turned and began to move rapidly back down the slope.

The sound of the shot was the last thing Arden expected. At first she thought Theo might have used his pistol to shoot in the air as a means of warning her not to try to run off. She stopped, then turned slowly around to face him.

But he wasn't standing behind her staring down at her. He had fallen and lay face down on the ground. There was a dark red stain on his back.

Arden ran back to him and knelt beside him. He was still alive. When she put her hand to touch his cheek, he managed to turn his head and look up at her. There was shock and disbelief in his expression, but that was quickly supplanted by pain.

Arden looked up to the crest of the rise above them. There were half a dozen soldiers standing there, staring down at her. One still held aloft the rifle he'd used to shoot Theo. The others were simply gazing at her with what could only be described as amusement.

217

She put her hand to her mouth, but it didn't help muffle the scream that rose to her lips. She froze, rooted by fear.

Above her the soldiers began to scramble down the slope, shouting with pleased excitement like a pack of wolves surrounding a cornered deer.

Sky had intended to go to the monastery, to demand to see the *higoumen,* the leader of the monastic order. He had little thought that he could convince the man to evacuate the monastery, to get the monks away before the impending battle, yet he was determined to find Forbes and Arden.

But when he approached the wall and looked through the wrought-iron gate, he saw two men walking just inside the grounds. Although their backs were to Sky, there was no mistaking Forbes Devereaux's tall, wiry frame, his gray hair, and the impeccable waistcoat Sky had seen him wear several times before.

He didn't bother to try to rouse the fat old monk sleeping in a chair in the shade whose duty it was to tend the gate. Instead he called out to Forbes.

Forbes turned, as did his companion. And when he saw the second man's face, Sky realized he knew him, too.

"Constatin?" he shouted. "For God's sake, do you know what you've done?"

"Trask? How did you know I was here?" Forbes asked as he began to retrace his steps to the gates.

Sky waved a hand. "There's no time for that. You and Arden have to get out of here."

Forbes and Constatin reached the gate. Forbes unfastened the latch and drew it open.

"What are you talking about?" Forbes demanded as Sky passed through the gate to enter the monastery grounds.

But Sky was not looking at Forbes or listening to his questions. He was staring at Constatin. "I should have known it would be you," he said.

Constatin offered him a humorless grin. "It would seem we are reunited, Trask. And it would also seem your employer is a good deal more reasonable than you were. Mr. Devereaux and I have come to an understanding that you and I could not reach."

"Understanding?" Sky asked. "I don't suppose you told him you were responsible for the death of four men back at Knossos?" He peered at Constatin's eyes, amazed at the way the man could hide any surprise, could so completely keep emotion from his expression. "I don't suppose you happened to mention that you were putting him and his daughter in the middle of a battle between the Turks and the Greeks."

Forbes's eyes narrowed. "What are you talking about, Sky?" he asked.

"The Assembly in Athens finally decided to send troops," Sky told him. "They're about to land on Cape Yoannis, a few miles from here. And the Turks have decided to send a few troops of their own to welcome them. In a very short time this whole area is going to become one vast battlefield, and you're standing in the middle of it."

Forbes turned to Constatin. "You knew about this?" he demanded.

Constatin shook his head. "No," he said. "And I'm not sure I believe any of it."

"Believe what you like," Sky told him. "But Mr. Devereaux and his daughter are leaving with me—now."

At the mention of Arden, Forbes suddenly became agitated. He turned to Constatin.

"Where did your brother take her?" he demanded.

Constatin shrugged. "Through the vineyards," he said. "Wherever she wanted to go."

Forbes turned back to Sky, who had turned to peer at the hillside.

"My God," Sky murmured.

"What is it?" Forbes demanded.

"I saw a Turkish scouting party start off in that direction about an hour ago," he said.

Sky didn't stop to wait for Forbes to respond to that piece of information. He ran through the gate, swung himself back into the saddle, and set off at a gallop.

Theo reached out a shaking hand to Arden.

"*Run!*" he cried out to her.

She could see the pain he suffered, could see the thick flow of red that grew steadily larger on his back and seeped onto the dark earth around him. Nothing made sense to her, not the sight of his blood or the cry of the Turkish soldiers racing down the hillside toward her.

"I can't leave you," she told Theo.

It was true. Her fear had left her trembling and without the ability to move, let alone run.

"*My pistol!*" Theo hissed. "*Beneath my jacket!*"

She stared at him, not quite believing he expected her to retrieve the pistol.

"*Hurry!*" he shouted.

He gasped with pain as he tried to push himself up and reach for the weapon himself, then collapsed forward once more.

His anger galvanized Arden. She put her hand to his shoulder and pushed him far enough over to reach the holstered weapon beneath his jacket. She withdrew it with trembling hands.

"*Aim it,*" Theo gasped. "*Shoot.*"

She turned to the hillside. The soldiers were little more than a hundred feet from them now. Her hands still shaking, she raised the pistol, put her finger on the

220

trigger, and squeezed hard. The sound of the shot seemed deafening, and the recoil, unexpected, startled her and nearly pushed her to the ground.

There was the sound of a scream, and one of the Turkish soldiers stumbled, grasping his leg. Arden could hardly believe she'd hit one of them. She'd never so much as touched a pistol before, and certainly never fired one. She began to tremble as she realized what it was she had done.

The other soldiers stopped for a moment to dart a glance at their fallen comrade. Then they turned back to Arden. The amusement in their expressions was gone now. With a wildly frenzied cry, they raced down the path toward her, more intent on their revenge than on any danger she might pose.

Arden again lifted the pistol. Holding it this time with both hands, she squeezed the trigger again and again and again. But although she continued firing, the shots went wild and there were no more anguished cries from the Turkish soldiers. Before she had time to think what she ought to do, one of the Turks was beside her, his black-booted foot raised to kick the pistol away from her hand.

She turned too late to stop the blow. A wrenching pain filled her arm and the pistol fell from her hands, dropping to the ground beside her. The soldier kicked the weapon away, then reached down and grabbed her, jerking her to her feet. He held her close to him for a moment, then pushed her into the waiting arms of the others. Two of them grabbed her, pawing her eagerly, while the one who had kicked her slowly raised his rifle.

Arden closed her eyes, wondering why he did not shoot, why he seemed to have no great eagerness to be done with it and kill her. Then there was the sound of a bullet being fired.

For a second she knew only shock, wondering why there was no pain. Then she opened her eyes and saw the soldier standing over Theo. The young Cretan was on his back now, spread eagled. His eyes were wide open and staring but they saw nothing. He was still, much too still. There was a thick red opening in his chest.

Arden uttered a strangled scream and struggled against the hands that held her, but they only tightened their grasp on her more. The men seemed to enjoy her fear and her feeble attempts to free herself. They laughed coarsely at her, and one grasped her breast with his hand.

Slowly her eyes rose to those of the Turkish soldier who had killed Theo. She no longer had any thought that he might simply kill her as he had Theo. He and the others had other plans for her first, and none of it would be pleasant.

He called out and then waved at the man that she'd wounded. She turned and saw him making his way painfully down the hillside, using his rifle as a crutch. He was staring at her with cold hatred in his eyes.

When he was a few feet from her, he reached for his belt and began to unbuckle it.

Chapter Twelve

As Sky rode through the still and quiet vineyard, he felt something tugging at him, urging him to the hillside beyond. He'd long ago learned not to question these odd urgings, for on more than one occasion in the past they had kept him out of danger or provided him with the means to information to which he otherwise would never have had access. This time he accepted the inclination without questioning it, knowing there was little time for him to mentally debate the issue. Instead he turned his horse to the slope without so much as slowing the animal's pace.

Sky glanced up at the fig trees that covered the rise before him. Like the vineyard, the orchard seemed calm and peaceful. He was forced to remind himself just how deceiving appearances could be. There was something inside him that told him Arden was somewhere on that hillside. It told him she was there and that the chances were far too great that she was in danger.

It was then that he heard a noise, sharp and short and loud. It echoed down the hillside, and Sky knew it could only be a shot. He hesitated a moment, wondering if the battle had already begun, if what he'd heard had been the echo of the first shot fired. But a battle, he quickly told himself, would be heralded by a thunder of rifle fire, not the sound of a single shot. And this shot could not have been so far away as the beach at Cape Yoannis. It was closer, much closer.

The sound sent a tremor of fear through him, and for an instant he pictured Arden as the victim of that single bullet. Then he heard the scream.

Unlike the shot, it lingered in the air, a chilling testimony to violence. A voice deep inside Sky told him it had been Arden who had cried out in terror.

He dug his heels into the horse's sides, forcing it up the steep hill. He had but one thought: to find her. It chased away any consideration of what he might find on that hill, any thought that he might be riding directly into the rifle sights of the Turkish scouting party.

The rapid succession of shots occurred when Sky had ridden nearly halfway up the slope. The noise of it was enough to startle him into a little caution. He realized he would be of little help to Arden were he to get himself killed.

He drew the horse to a halt, dismounted, and left the animal at the side of the path. Climbing on foot now, he kept to the shadow of the trees and away from the path as he ran. He was hardly conscious of the fact that he had drawn his pistol. He held it, as comforting as a part of himself, ready in his hand as he climbed.

He crossed over the root-rutted ground, climbing upward, listening for those sounds that would tell him he was getting close, scanning the shadows around him. He knew what would happen to Arden if the Turkish soldiers had her, knew what they would do to her before they would kill. The thought sickened him.

He found Theo's body first, the young Cretan lying dead, his unseeing eyes staring into the thin rays of bright sunlight that snaked their way through the canopy of branches overhead. Flies attracted by the scent of his blood were already feeding at the wound in his chest.

He skirted the body, sure he would find whoever it was who had killed Theo nearby. And he was equally sure they had Arden.

The first sound he heard was rough laughter. It was loud enough to nearly drown out her cries. He ran toward the sound, slowing his pace only when he saw the outline of the group of men through the shade cast by the trees.

The soldiers' attention was riveted on their prey. They didn't notice Sky as he crept up behind them.

What he saw set loose a thick surge of pulsing rage within him. Two of the soldiers held Arden's arms while a third was kneeling over her, kneading her naked breasts. She was pinned, unable to move, and nearly choking on her own tears.

Sky had seen violence, almost an endless stream of it, it seemed, since he'd come to Crete, but none of it had left him as filled with fury as this. It clouded his judgment enough to make him forget that they were six, and he only one. He had but one thought, that he had to stop this obscene thing they were doing to her.

He leaped out from the shadows of the trees, firing as he ran, felling three of the Turkish soldiers before they had the chance to gather their wits to find and raise their weapons to return his fire. But the remaining three soon had their rifles in their hands, and the air filled with noise as they returned his fire. Sky could hear their bullets hiss as they passed close by him to strike the ground or a tree trunk nearby.

Sky kept running, crossing the path, finally falling and rolling behind a tree trunk as the barrage of bullets continued. The Turks, too, retreated, running into the trees and leaving Arden lying on the ground between them and the place where Sky had taken cover. The gunfire continued for a moment longer, then stopped as both sides realized they had come to an impasse.

An uneasy silence filled the orchard.

Arden couldn't believe it had stopped, couldn't believe her hands were free and the Turk was no longer touching her. She was gasping for air, sobbing still, but she realized she could move freely. She pulled up her legs and tried to roll herself into a ball, tried to make herself as small as possible, as though the exercise might somehow make her invisible and safe.

But as the silence settled around her and she realized the shooting had stopped, her thoughts began to clear and she began to wonder what had happened.

She looked around and saw the bodies. She grew sick with revulsion as she realized she was surrounded by dead men. The scent of their blood assailed her nostrils and made her stomach begin to heave. She had to get away from here, she thought, get away from the bodies of these men and the red sea of their blood.

She began to edge her way toward the side of the path, toward the shelter of the fig trees. She'd moved only a few inches, however, when there was the sound of another shot being fired, and the dirt in front of her exploded in a spray that coated her face.

She shrieked in terror.

"Arden! Don't move. Stay where you are."

It seemed impossible, but that was Sky's voice. Impossible, yet he was here. Somehow he'd known, somehow he'd come to save her.

"Sky?" She'd been sure she was going to die, and now, for one shattering instant, she felt hope again. "Sky, is that you?" Her words were slurred with tears and her voice shaky with disbelief.

Dazed, she looked around and then began to push herself to her knees. He was here somewhere. He'd been the one to fire at the soldiers and make them free her. He was here and would save her.

Again there was the sound of a bullet being fired, and this one was even closer, grazing her arm and leaving a long red streak of blood on it. She cried out again, this time with pain as well as fear.

"Don't move," Sky shouted again. "Get down."

She realized then what he had realized, that the Turks did not want to lose her and with her their own amusement, but that they would kill her if she tried to get away.

She did as Sky told her, falling back down to the ground, trying to make herself melt into the dark soil beneath her. She closed her eyes, wanting to shut out the sight of the dead soldiers, the dark, thick red of their spattered blood. But even with her eyes closed she could still see it, could still smell it. She lay in the dirt, shivering and sobbing in fear.

"You, American. Is that you?"

It was the soldier, the one she'd shot. He was talking to Sky as though greeting an acquaintance on a street corner. His tone sounded pleasant, almost jovial. It all seemed too impossibly insane to her to be real.

"Let the woman go," Sky shouted. "The Greek troops will be here soon. If you don't leave now, you'll be killed."

"Ah, I thought it was you, American," the soldier replied. He laughed coarsely. The sound of his laughter made Arden shiver. "So it is not old pots you seek, but young female flesh. I do not blame you. She was very good. It gave me great pleasure to take her." There was more laughter, coarse and lewd.

"Then you've done with her," Sky replied, his voice thick with rage. "I'll take her from you now, and let you leave. I think we both would prefer that there be no more blood shed here."

The Turkish soldier laughed. "I think you are wrong, American. I fear there must be more blood spilled. It would not do for my men to think I failed to avenge the death of one of them, let alone three. And as for the woman, neither I nor my friends have yet had our fill of her."

His words cut through Arden like a knife. There were still three soldiers, three of them against Sky. There would be no escape for her, and now the knowledge that Sky would die there with her left her sick with remorse.

Again there was a barrage of bullets, and she wrapped her arms around her head, pressing her face against the ground. She heard the bullets as they sped through the air above her. The ground muffled her shriek of fear. After a moment the firing ceased as it had before, and once again there was a sudden, intense silence.

It took her a second to realize what that silence must mean, that Sky had been killed.

"Sky!" she shouted, filled with an agonized sense of loss.

There was no answer, and she began to feel as though she were being smothered. She pushed herself up, turning to stare into the shadows, gasping for air.

"Sky!" she cried, again frenzied with her own fear.

The sergeant waited a moment, apparently listening, then Arden heard him call out to his men.

"Jusef? Soltan? What happened?"

There was only silence for an answer. Arden stared at the Turk as he stirred, clinging to the side of a fig tree as he climbed to his feet, clumsy with the wound in his leg. He peered out across the open area the path made through the trees. She saw him glance at her for only a second, then concentrate on the shadows of the trees behind her. He was interested in other prey at that moment, not in her.

"Jusef? Soltan? Did you kill him?"

It seemed to Arden that he was getting nervous, that there was fear in his words. She kept her eyes on him as he leaned forward, apparently listening for a sound, a clue to tell him what had happened.

"Damn you, woman, be silent," he shouted.

Arden had no idea that she had been sobbing. His words startled her. She realized the air was filled with the sound and that it came from her.

She saw confusion in the Turk's expression now and realized it fed his fears, fears that only grew as the moments dragged on. There was no sign from his men that they had killed the American. That silence returned to her a small measure of hope and she began to dare to believe that Sky was still alive. But with the hope came the realization that his fear would make the Turk even more violent, that he would be easily goaded into killing her now. She tried to do as he had ordered but was unable to still the loud, wrenching sobs, the convulsive gasping for breath.

She stared at him wide-eyed as he raised his rifle and pointed it at her.

Sky realized as soon as he heard the Turk's voice that it was the sergeant who had forced him to turn back on the road just outside Neapolis. His presence had meant more than just a roadblock to keep the way to the north clear for the first of the Turkish soldiers. He and his men had themselves been part of the advance of the troops.

When he heard the Turk's boast about taking Arden, Sky fought down the rage the sergeant's words sent through him, knowing the soldier was trying to bait him into making a mistake. Despite the part of him that urged cool logic, however, Sky could not shut away the fury. He felt himself grow hot with the surge of rage the words left in their wake, but he forced the anger aside, telling himself the soldier was talking to him for a reason, that the man wanted to keep him occupied and distracted.

He turned, taking care to move silently, and peered into the shadows of the trees to the rear.

He was just in time to see the two soldiers circling around behind him. Already they had raised their rifles to shoot. Sky pushed himself away from the tree just in time. The trunk behind him splintered as the bullets struck it. Sky dived to the ground, firing his pistol as he landed.

It seemed the longest moment of Sky's life, the two rifles pointed at him, the sound of the shots filling the air, the taste of dirt in his mouth as he rolled across the dark earth. But when the moment was over, he was still alive and the two Turkish soldiers lay on the ground not a dozen feet from him. There was sharp pain in his left arm, and when he looked he saw a gory hole, but he had no time to consider that. He was alive and able still to keep the last Turk from Arden. That was all that mattered.

He crept silently to the two dead soldiers, taking the rifle from one man's hand and then starting around through the trees, following the path they had no doubt taken to circle around behind him. Arden's tortured cry tore at him, but he knew he dared not answer, not if he was to get them both away alive. The price of a comforting word to her at that moment might very well cost both their lives.

Sky had covered about half the distance between himself and the Turkish soldier when he heard the sergeant shout at Arden to be silent. He didn't know why, but he was sure the man was at the edge, ready to do anything. Sky knew he was wounded and now probably beginning to realize that his men might very well be dead. When he and his squad had happened on Theo and Arden, he'd probably never considered he might be left alone facing an armed enemy. Attacking a defenseless woman was one thing; having his men killed and facing the possibility that he might follow the same route was something entirely different.

Sky realized he wouldn't have the time to work his way around and behind the soldier. If he did, he would take the chance that the sergeant might fire at Arden in a frenzy of his own fear. She might very well be killed before Sky reached a safe, sheltered place from which he might deal with the soldier.

Sky abandoned stealth, running now toward the path, holding the rifle ready to fire. And the moment he saw the Turk, he realized it was none too soon. The man was taking aim at Arden.

Sky pulled the trigger twice in rapid succession. The Turk seemed to freeze for an instant, then the rifle dropped from his hands and he looked down at the blood on his chest. Sky moved forward, his own rifle still aimed and ready. There was no need for it. The Turk crumpled and fell to the ground dead.

For a long instant Sky simply stood there staring at the dead soldier. Then he dropped the rifle and ran to Arden.

He knelt beside her and pulled her into his arms.

She held herself stiff and still for a moment, as though she couldn't quite believe it was him. Then she fell against him and clung to him. Never had she seemed more precious to him; nothing had ever seemed sweeter than the feel of her safe in his arms. He could feel the pounding of her heart against his chest, and he gave silent thanks for the continuance of that steady, even beat.

"They killed Theo," she murmured through her sobs. "They were going to, to . . ."

She couldn't bring herself to say the words. She was quivering, trembling, weaker than she had ever felt.

231

She'd always thought she was strong and independent, that her person was inviolate. And now she had learned in the most painful manner how wrong she'd been, and how vulnerable she actually was.

Sky held her close. He put his hand to her head and stroked her hair.

"Shh," he whispered. "I know. You don't have to talk. You're safe now. We're both safe."

But even as he spoke the words he knew they were a lie. In the distance he could hear a deep rumbling like thunder. But it wasn't the sound of a storm that was moving inland off Cape Yoannis. Sky knew it was the sound of cannon fire he heard, the rolling thunder of war.

It took a few moments, but Sky finally managed to calm her, to quiet her trembling.

It seemed impossible to Arden that she was safe, that she was with Sky, that she felt his arms, warm and protective, around her. She thought she would never again want to move from that spot, never again want anything more but the feel of his arms around her.

"We have to leave here, Arden," he told her. "The fighting's already begun. Once the Greeks have made a beachhead, the Turkish troops will move back and the monastery will be in the middle of the battle. We have to go back, find your father, and get away from here."

She pulled away from him and stared at him bewildered, as though lost and unable to comprehend his words. She still could not understand what had happened, couldn't confront the reasons why the air was now filled with a dull, thundering roar that seemed to draw closer. But then she nodded, agreeing with him, willing to do whatever he told her must be done.

"Are you all right?" he asked softly, knowing full well she wasn't, that she was still shocked with what she had seen and been made to endure. He had no doubt that she was still filled with terror.

He wished more than anything that he had the ability to numb her memories of the previous hours, to somehow make them disappear. He wished he had at least the time to comfort her. But he had neither the time nor the power to help her deal with the terror she must feel. The one thing he did have, however, was the means to get her away.

She nodded in reply to his question, and he stood and helped her to her feet. While he retrieved one of the Turkish soldiers' ammunition belts, she covered her breasts with her torn blouse, tucking it into her skirt with shaking hands. She tried to ignore the burning in her arm where the bullet had grazed her, tried not to see what lay around her on the ground, tried not to think of death or the blood. She could, she told herself, convince herself that none of it was real, that none of it had ever happened.

But when Sky returned to her, she noticed for the first time the seeping hole in his arm and knew she could deny it no longer.

"You've been shot," she said.

He shook his head, put his hand on her arm and began to urge her down the hillside. "It's nothing," he told her.

"Don't be a fool," she said as she stared at the thick ooze that continued to spread over the sleeve of his shirt and drip in dark red droplets to the ground. "You're bleeding."

He hesitated for a moment, not wanting to waste time. But then it occurred to him that she was right, that if he lost too much blood he'd be able to do neither of them much good. Besides, she seemed to need to tend to the

233

wound, to have something on which to focus her thoughts beside what had happened. She needed to prove herself capable of helping him, of reaffirming her sense of independence.

"All right," he agreed, and found a rock on which he could sit. He settled himself and held out his arm to her to tend. "You're hurt, too," he told her, nodding toward the line of red on her arm.

She darted a glance at it. The blood had already dried on the long, narrow cut. It ached, but it was obviously not nearly as serious as Sky's wound.

"That really is nothing," she told him as she began to tear off a long strip of her petticoat. "Although when it happened, I was sure I was about to die." Her voice caught at the memory, and she had to force herself to some measure of calm. "I thought we were both going to die," she said in a hoarse whisper.

He touched her arm with his hand. "We're neither of us going to die, Arden," he told her quietly.

She raised her eyes to meet his. There were tears in them, he realized, and he could see she was struggling to keep some control over herself.

"Arden," he whispered and began to lean toward her.

She stood still for a moment, staring into his eyes, willing him closer. She thought that she wanted his kiss more than anything she had ever wanted before in her life, wanted to feel loved, cared for, needed. But the thought was chased away by the memory of what had happened to her, a memory that swept over her, bringing with it the feel of the Turk's hands on her body. His blood was still smeared on her breast, and it seemed to her a mark of condemnation. She was afraid she would never be washed clean of it.

She pulled away from him and forced herself to concentrate on tending his wound. She stared at the wrinkled, dirty bandage she'd made from her petticoat with a feeling of disgust.

"I wish I could think of something better," she told him, making a great effort to keep her voice as even and normal sounding as she could.

He grinned at her. "All you need do is press it to your lips, and just like in the fairy tales, you'll endow it with magical healing powers," he assured her.

"You're mad," she told him as she began to wrap the strip around his arm, but she nonetheless found some of the weight within herself begin to lessen and she smiled at his words. "I don't think I ever realized it before, but I am now absolutely certain you are a raving lunatic." She pulled the bandage tight.

Sky winced. "I'd not given it much thought, but you may be right." He nodded toward his arm. "Do you suppose you might take it easy with that? I know it's hard to think of lunatics as sensitive, but that's human flesh you're mangling."

This time she failed to be amused by his attempt at humor. She stared at his bloody arm as though she were seeing it for the first time. Her lip began to tremble.

"Oh," she said, and dropped the remaining piece of bandage.

He put his hand on hers, regretting his words, realizing that she was still unnerved and on the very edge of breaking down.

"You were doing the right thing, Arden. It's the only way to stop the bleeding. Can you finish and tie it up?"

She nodded, and bit her lip to hold back the tears that once again threatened. Then she carefully finished wrapping the bandage around his arm and tied it.

"Done," she murmured.

"Good," Sky told her and stood. "I think we'd better get moving."

He didn't mention it to her, but he was sure the sound of the cannon fire was getting louder, and that could only mean the battle was drawing closer.

It took Sky a good deal longer to find his horse than he had thought it would. The animal had wandered into the orchard, looking for the cool of the shadows and some new grass to eat. When Sky approached him, he looked up with baleful eyes, as though in reprimand for Sky's forcing him to further effort after the long run that afternoon.

Sky lifted Arden onto the saddle, then swung himself up behind her. She fell back against him, and it struck him that she wanted to be close to him, that he was her anchor and her security. The thought pleased him, enough to ease the aching in his wounded arm. If nothing else, he thought, he had come to mean something to her. That, at least, was a start.

He turned the horse toward the path, and they started down the hillside.

But Sky drew the animal to a halt before they reached the foot of the hill.

The noise of the battle had grown louder as they neared the valley between the two hills, and Sky realized the Greek advance had been faster than he'd expected. However strong the Turkish forces sent to repel them, the Greeks' strength had obviously been greater. The battle was coming closer, and that could only mean the Turks were falling back toward the monastery.

There was no way he could reach the monastery before the Turkish soldiers, he realized. And making the attempt would only put Arden and him in greater danger.

"I think we should find a lookout," he said. "To go stumbling into a battle would be more lunacy than that to which I would admit."

She turned back to face him.

"But Papa," she objected. "He's down there."

"He should be safe enough as long as he's inside the monastery," Sky told her. "Not even Constatin is so great a fool as to leave shelter while there are bombs exploding around him." He fervently hoped he was not telling her lies, but he knew the chances were great that neither of his statements was true.

Arden bit her lip, but she nodded and made no attempt to disagree with him. She knew what he said made sense, but she could not say that it pleased her. She realized her father was there and not safely back at Knossos because of her. The weight of her own responsibility for what had happened to her and what might happen to him grew heavier by the moment.

Sky dismounted, helped her down, then took the reins and began to lead the horse across the hillside into the orchard. It took a while, but eventually he found that for which he'd been searching, a projection providing a view of the valley and the next hill with the monastery at its crest. He left Arden and the horse under the cover provided by the fig trees, then crept out on the bare ledge to survey what lay below.

"What is it?" Arden asked. "What's happening?"

She tied the horse's reins to a tree branch and edged her way out onto the ledge until she was beside him. She peered down, trying to make some sense out of the havoc below.

There were soldiers everywhere she looked, swarming over the hillside, trampling the vineyard she'd watched the monks so industriously cultivate only hours before. And in the distance there were explosions—great dark clouds of black smoke that rose into the air to hover like an evil blanket above the battle. She'd never considered what cannon fire might look like. Now she knew.

"What's happening?" she asked again, only this time

weakly, as though the effort of the words had become more than she had strength to voice.

Sky pushed her back to the sheltering shadows of the trees. His expression was grim.

"We'd never have gotten through that if we'd continued on down," Sky told her. "The Turks are retreating and the Greeks are close behind them."

"But the monastery is right in their path," Arden cried. "Papa is there."

Sky could offer her no denial, no words of comfort.

"There's nothing we can do now but stay out of sight and wait," he told her.

"But there must be something," she cried, and started to move forward, back to the edge.

He caught her arm and pulled her back. She looked up at him with eyes that were filled with pain and remorse.

"You can't show yourself, Arden. You can't take the chance of being seen."

"Papa," she murmured. The word caught in her throat and ended with a small sob.

"There's nothing we can do now, Arden," he said, and pushed her back into the shadows of the orchard. She was frightened and worried, and more than anything he wished he could tell her something more hopeful. But there was nothing else for him to say.

"It's my fault," she whispered, looking past him, glancing back down at the swarm of soldiers below. "It's all my fault. If I hadn't made him come to Crete in the first place, if I hadn't run off that night . . ."

He put his arms around her and held her close.

"It's no one's fault," he told her.

There was the sound of the cannon's thunder again, but this time it was closer than it had been even moments before. They both turned to watch with horror as the side wall of the monastery began to crumble.

Chapter Thirteen

It seemed to Arden that the noise and thunder of the cannon fire went on forever, but Sky recognized that the battle was over fairly quickly. Before the afternoon had ended, it was obvious to him that although they outmanned the Greek soldiers by nearly two-to-one, the Turks were not prepared to face the number of cannon the Greeks had brought to use against them. The intense assault forced the Turkish troops to retreat back to the south, first to the monastery, and then, as the outer walls of the structure began to crumble under the cannon shot, into the countryside beyond.

Rather than pursuing the scattered enemy past a defensible line in the growing darkness, the Greek commander halted his army's advance at the monastery so that he might regroup his forces and allow his soldiers a much needed rest. As the sky began to darken, Sky and Arden could see lights glowing from the monastery. Confident it was now in the hands of the Greeks, Sky decided it was safe enough for him to agree with Arden's demand to be taken to the monastery gates to try to find Forbes.

They rode the rest of the way down the hill, guided by the muted moonlight that filtered from an overcast sky and campfires the bivouacked Greek soldiers had lit in the surrounding vineyards. Despite the campfires and a constant glow from the monastery itself, however, the night was still gloomy, the whole area blanketed by a thick, acrid haze that hugged the valley. Sky was thankful for the near darkness. It helped to hide from Arden the destruction that surrounded them once they reached the valley. He could make out the movement of soldiers in the darkness and knew that they must be burial details disposing of the dead. He was glad that at least that was hidden from her view.

Eventually they approached the perimeter of the Greek position, where they were challenged by the sentry on guard. Sky managed to make himself well enough understood to convey the information that he needed to see someone in the monastery. After a good deal of being handed from one soldier to another, they were eventually led inside the grounds.

Both Sky and Arden stared around them in dazed and regretful amazement. Early that afternoon the monastery had seemed so permanent, so immutable. That so much could have changed in the span of only a few hours seemed impossible.

The buildings now showed scars, as though each wall had been wounded in the battle. Most still stood, but few were unmarred, testament to the battle that had swept through. Here and there one of the smaller structures had been reduced to little more than rubble, and flames engulfed others. Obviously exhausted soldiers struggled to extinguish the flames to keep them from spreading.

"All these fires," Arden murmured to Sky.

He turned to her, saw her anguished expression, and knew immediately what it was she was thinking, that her father might have been inside one of those buildings, or that he might even have been killed by cannon fire.

"He's safe, Arden. We'll find him," he told her firmly. But he knew as well as did she that the words were intended as comfort and meant little. Surrounded as they were by so much evidence of destruction, it was impossible to think of anything or anyone as being safe.

Eventually, they were led into the largest of the monastery buildings, through a series of corridors and finally into a narrow, white-walled room dominated by a single desk and a large, excessively tortured crucifix on the wall behind it. The officer at the desk looked up when the aide showed them in.

"Parakalo?" he asked when he saw them.

He eyed the two skeptically, both of them dirt- and blood-smeared and rumpled. It was obvious they were not Turkish soldiers, but they seemed to have little else to recommend them to him. He allowed himself a small moue of distaste.

Sky ignored the expression.

"Milate ghalika?" he asked. Do you speak English? "We need to see someone who speaks English, who can help us."

The fact that they were foreigners seemed to give the officer little comfort. He had more than enough to do without having to cope with foreigners who had been inadvertently caught in the midst of the turmoil. His look of distaste turned into a full scowl.

"I speak English. I am Major Petsos. My aide will find you rooms for the night and provide you with some dinner." He darted a look at the bloody bandage on Sky's arm. "If you wish, I will have my medic attend to your arm. In the morning the aide will see you to a packet that will take you to Piraeus. From there you can petition your consul in Athens. I regret the inconvenience you have been caused, but these things can not be helped."

He seemed quite pleased with his speech, as though he were certain he had answered any possible questions they might have, and as though the interview, and the interruption to his work it caused, were therefore at an end.

He waved to his aide, then turned back to the heap of papers on the desk in front of him.

"We don't wish to go to Piraeus, Major Petsos," Sky said, forcing the officer to return his attention, however reluctantly, to him. "We need help finding someone here in the monastery."

Petsos's scowl increased. It was more than apparent from his expression that he was far from pleased at being forced to waste more time with them.

"Perhaps you had best explain," he suggested.

"My name is Skyler Trask. The young lady is Arden Devereaux. Miss Devereaux's father, a well-known and respected newspaper publisher from New York," Sky said these last ten words slowly, hoping they might induce a measure of cooperation from the Greek that had been as yet denied them, "was here, in the monastery, when the Turks retreated to it."

"What," Petsos demanded in a belligerent tone, "was an American publisher doing in a monastery in Crete?"

"Mr. Devereaux's paper is currently publishing a series of stories on the findings at Knossos and Crete's other antiquities. He came here to see if there might be some truth to a rumor that the monastery was built over the remains of another ancient castle."

Arden was startled by the calm way Sky told the lie, but she said nothing, aware that it would be foolish to inform Petsos that Forbes had been meeting with separatists who were as violently set against a Greek presence in Crete as they were against the Turks.

Petsos eyed them both. "I have never heard such a rumor," he said, but then he shrugged and seemed to dismiss his own objection. "But then I am no scholar of ancient history. Am I to believe the two of you made your way through battle lines to come for a visit?" he asked. He considered their appearance. "Although from the looks of you, I suppose I ought not to be surprised if you tell me that is exactly what you did." He nodded toward the rifle the aide had taken from Sky and now held pointedly, as though it were an exhibit at a trial. "And perhaps you might be so kind as to tell me how you come to be armed with a Turkish rifle?"

"We ran into a Turkish scouting party in the orchard on the next hill," Sky replied.

Petsos nodded at Sky's wounded arm. "A not entirely peaceful encounter, I presume?" he asked.

"I'm afraid not," Sky admitted. "Once the battle progressed this far south, we remained hidden on the hillside until the Turkish forces had retreated and we felt it safe to continue on here."

"And the scouting party?" Petsos asked, curious now. "How did you escape from them?"

"There are six dead Turkish soldiers in the orchard," Sky replied with little emotion. "As well as a young Cretan they killed."

"We just want to find my father and leave," Arden broke in. "He's here, somewhere, on the monastery grounds."

"I regret, *Despinis* Devereaux, there was no one alive in the monastery when we arrived."

"No!" Arden cried. "He can't be dead!"

She turned back to the doorway. The fires they'd passed, the ruined structures . . . she'd had the thought when she'd seen the destruction, but she'd been more than willing to accept Sky's assurances that Forbes was still safe, wanting it to be true and therefore letting herself believe.

Petsos stood and leaned forward, toward her.

"No, no—you misunderstand," he told her. "It seems the Turks entered the monastery and forced the occupants to leave just before we arrived, before the battle even began. They no doubt thought it would be an easy position to defend as long as there were no troublesome priests to get in their way. They did not anticipate that we would bring cannon with us, nor use them so well."

His words were not quite as comforting as he had thought. Arden stared at him with a look of frenzied fear.

"Where would they take them?" she demanded.

Petsos shrugged. "They'll hold them, perhaps as hostages. It is regrettable for you and your father, but I am afraid there is nothing I can do."

"But my father, he's American," Arden insisted. "They've no right to hold him."

"That is doubtless true, *Despinis* Devereaux," Petsos repeated, this time his tone less sympathetic, more irritated that she would persist this way, "but I am in no position to point this out to them. If you wish to lodge a protest, you must go to the American consul in Athens. He can no doubt see to your father's release."

"Athens!"

Sky put his hand on Arden's shoulder, pulling her back, trying to calm her.

"We appreciate your help, Major," he said.

Arden refused to be calmed. She turned on Sky.

"But Papa—the Turks have him, and there's no telling what they might do to him," she cried. Her lower lip began to tremble. "After today . . ." she murmured, remembering all too well the brutality of which those soldiers were capable.

"I am sure he will be safe as soon as they realize he is American," Petsos assured her. "Not even the Turkish government would be so foolish as to give unnecessary offense to America just now. Your consul in Athens can make whatever arrangements must be made." He nodded at Sky and offered him a commiserating glance, one that said he understood the irrationality to which women are often subject, how difficult it is to make them see reason. "I am afraid I can give you little more by way of infor-

244

mation. I can, however, offer you the services of my medics," he said, pointing at Sky's wounded arm, "and hospitality for the night."

He nodded to the aide, spoke very quickly in Greek, and then turned his attention back to the papers on his desk, obviously feeling he had given them more than enough of his time. Sky took the hint, taking Arden's arm and following after the aide, who showed them out of the room and through several corridors until he finally left them in front of two adjoining rooms that fronted a small, enclosed garden.

They were obviously monk's cells. Sky gazed into one tiny room with its bare white walls, rough wash table with plain white bowl, pitcher, and cup, straight chair, and a narrow, pillowless cot.

"I always knew I didn't envy the life of a monk," he commented dryly as he led the way into the cell. "Now I know why."

Arden, however, wasn't the least interested in banter. She'd managed to remain quiet and relatively calm since they'd finished the interview with Petsos, but now her reserve of control seemed exhausted.

She turned to Sky. "What are we going to do about Papa?" she demanded. "How can we possibly leave him in the hands of those monsters for the time it would take to go all the way to Athens to have the consul lodge a complaint?"

Nervous, she walked into the room but then turned to stand by the single narrow window that looked out on the cloister. She stared out at it, trying to concentrate on the regular pattern of dark shadows that must be neatly tended beds, on the sound of water that trickled from a fountain. The attempt, however, was useless, and her thoughts remained fixed on Forbes. She turned away to look once more at Sky.

"No," he agreed, "we don't go to the consul. Officials

have one speed—slow. Even if we didn't have to go all the way to Athens to lodge the protest, it would still take forever. No, we'll have to find another way."

"Then what *do* we do?"

"First we find out if he might not have left before the Turks arrived. It's not impossible that Constatin left with him when he realized the Turks would find him here. I should think he'd be less than delighted to find himself in a Turkish prison and in a position to be questioned about his own recent activities."

The thought brightened Arden somewhat. "Do you really think they might have gotten away?"

Sky shrugged. He really didn't think the possibility great, but he had no intention of admitting that to her. Besides, the only reasonable thing for him to do would be take her back to Knossos and leave her there, where she would be safe.

"Forbes would somehow get back to Knossos," he told her. "That would be the only place he'd go, knowing we'd go there too."

She turned back to face him. "And if he's not there?" she demanded. "What if he's here someplace, lying under one of those heaps of rubble? Or one of those lying out there," she gasped softly, hardly able to say the words, "on the hillside?" The thought made her tremble with fear.

He considered what he saw in her face and realized she'd seen more than he'd thought, understood what the burial parties were doing as well as he had. He shook his head.

"You heard what Petsos said. The monastery was emptied by the Turks before the fighting began. If they were taking hostages, they certainly wouldn't leave Constatin and Forbes behind."

She considered his words and decided they sounded

reasonable. "All right, they've taken him with the rest. What do we do?"

He shook his head. "I'm not sure," he admitted. "But something."

He dropped onto the cot, leaned his head against the wall, and closed his eyes. He could not remember ever having felt so tired. The wound in his arm throbbed, and he was beginning to feel warm and a bit disoriented. When he looked up, the ceiling seemed to spin ever so slowly. He wondered if his arm had become infected, if he was about to become ill. The prospect was not one he looked on with any pleasure. He'd had the experience before and had no desire to repeat it.

Arden stared at him for a moment, only then realizing he was in pain. She'd been angry with him just a moment before, wanting answers from him, assurances which she now realized he had no way to give to her. She felt guilty for badgering him when he was so obviously trying to do everything he could to reassure her.

She went to the cot and put her hand to his forehead. She realized she hadn't thought about the wound in his arm since they'd started down from the hillside, realized that her concern for her father had displaced the concern she rightly owed Sky.

"You have fever," she told him softly.

"The medic should be here soon," he said.

"I can at least wash your arm," she told him.

She crossed the room to the wash table, poured some water into the bowl, then returned to sit beside him on the cot. She leaned forward to him and began to unbutton his shirt. He smiled at her.

"I should get shot more often," he told her. "I like the attention."

"I was right before, when I told you you were a lunatic," she replied as she helped him strip off the shirt and

247

remove the filthy makeshift bandage. The torn bits of fabric around the wound stuck to the dried blood, and he winced as she pulled them away.

"I'm sorry," she murmured. "I don't want to hurt you. I suppose I don't make a very good nurse."

"I suppose there's a price to everything, especially a beautiful woman's attentions," he replied.

She stopped and looked up at him a moment, wondering what it was she saw in his eyes. They were very blue, so much like the sea that seemed welcoming on the surface but gave no hint of what lay in its depths. She was startled by the way his words affected her, by the possibility that he considered her beautiful. But she forced herself to draw back from the thoughts that began to creep up on her, thoughts of how frightened she felt and how comforting it would be to feel his arms around her. She told herself his words were just that, words, and they meant nothing. Besides, there were far more important matters to which she must attend.

She tore her glance away from his, then busied herself wetting a piece of toweling in the water and turning her attention back to his arm.

She was concentrating on the task, carefully swabbing the area around the wound to remove the dirt and dried blood. She hardly noticed when he put his hand on her shoulder, or when he moved it slowly to her neck. Then his hand was beneath her chin and turning her face to his and she knew what he was doing, and realized she welcomed it.

When he urged her forward, she moved willingly, letting him pull her to him, letting his lips find hers. She closed her eyes and gave herself up to the feel of his lips on hers, to the heat the contact sent through her. It dissolved her thoughts, left her without fear, without the unsettling fears or the terror of the memories the day had held. All there was for her was the feeling of his lips against hers and the warm liquid that began to flow through her at his touch.

It was a long, slow kiss, neither passionate nor disinterested, more seeking than anything else. A voice inside Arden cried out silently to him, answering the question his kiss had asked, telling him that she wanted this, too.

When she opened her eyes, she found he was staring at her and smiling.

"And this a monk's cell," he said with an amused grin.

Why, she wondered, why is it never anything more than a game to him? Or was it a joke, one that she was incapable of understanding? Didn't he see that she wanted more than anything for him to make to her the same admission he had forced from her that evening they'd stood together in Kiria Spirtos' garden? Or was it simply that it didn't matter to him that she loved him?

She felt a wave of remorse, thick and bitter and hurtful as it swept over her. It only intensified her feelings of loneliness. She wished that she could hate him, wished she could blame what had happened on him and feel herself blameless. But she knew she couldn't. She'd begun the game that evening they'd played billiards, made the first challenge. He'd even given her fair warning that she was more than likely to be hurt if she persisted with it. She wondered if he understood just how right he'd been.

She pulled away from him and returned her attention to bathing his arm.

"Arden?"

She found she couldn't trust herself to speak, not then at least. She was too full of hurt and far too conscious of her own need for him. She shook her head, dropped the piece of towel into the bowl, and stood.

"There is someone here needing medical attention?"

She turned at the unfamiliar, accented voice to find a

249

short, dapperly moustached, gray-haired man standing in the doorway. She realized she was more than a bit relieved at the interruption.

"I am Doctor Georgandis," he said with the sort of manner that indicated the words ought to have been unnecessary, that they ought to have known that already. "They didn't mention anything about a woman," Georgandis said and smiled at her. "An American, they said. But no mention of a woman."

"Mr. Trask is your patient, Doctor," Arden told him and pointed at Sky.

"You crush my fondest hopes, young lady," he told her. "I see you and my heart leaps at the prospect of having so lovely a patient. Now you tell me it is just another reckless male to whom I must tend."

He entered the room and stood for a moment staring at her and making no move toward the cot where Sky sat.

"What is this?" he said finally, putting his hand to the arm with the long line of red where the bullet had creased it, staring at it over the top of his spectacles. He frowned. "Not so grave, but you will give me the pleasure of letting me tend to it later, won't you?" He didn't wait for an answer, just flashed at her the sort of smile an indulgent grandfather might use with a disobedient but favorite grandchild, then turned to Sky. "Never become an army doctor, young man," he said. "The bane of an army doctor's life is that he sees only soldiers. Only men for patients. Can you imagine how uninspiring that is?"

Sky laughed. "I'll keep your advice in mind," he replied.

"Wise youth," Georgandis said. He set his bag down, drew up the chair, seated himself, and proceeded to inspect Sky's wound.

"It's become infected," he pronounced after a bit of prodding and poking. "But the bullet passed through the soft tissue, and that is good. It will heal well enough."

250

He opened his bag and withdrew bandages, disinfectant, and a handful of instruments. Once he had satisfied himself that he had everything he needed, he proceeded to wash the wound with far greater expertise than Arden had shown.

"I don't suppose you have any whiskey?" he asked when he'd finished with the preliminaries.

Sky shook his head.

"Ah, but that I did," he replied mournfully.

"Unfortunate. It would have made what I'm about to do a bit less unpleasant," the older man replied. He rummaged about in his bag, withdrew a bottle, then turned to Arden. "Would you be kind enough to fetch that mug, my dear?" he asked. He considered the nearly empty bottle. "Ouzo," he said. "It isn't as good as whiskey, but it will do."

Arden took the mug from the wash table and handed it to him. He proceeded to half fill it with the remaining contents of the bottle and held it out to Sky.

Sky took the mug, gave the liquid a less than confident glance, then quickly downed it. He gasped slightly as he handed the mug back to Arden.

The doctor nodded. "Good," he said. "I like a man who knows how to drink ouzo. Now lie back and we'll get on with it." As Sky complied, the doctor made ready to sew up the hole in his arm.

Arden watched the operation with horrified fascination. Georgandis's precise and practiced movements could in no way dull the realization that it was flesh he was sewing, not cloth. Sky remained stoically silent, but his clenched jaw and faded pallor attested to the extent of his pain. By the time Georgandis had finished, he was pale and shaking.

"I think you should try to get some sleep," Georgandis told Sky as he bandaged the wound.

"I thought I'd spent a bit of time talking to Miss

Devereaux first," Sky muttered in reply and attempted a lame smile.

"I should think you'd make less than ideal company just now," Georgandis said as he stood. He took a vial from his bag, then stood. "This will help you sleep." He put some of the contents of the vial into the mug, added a bit of water, and held it out to Sky.

Sky took the mug a second time, looked at its contents with even greater distrust than he had when it had held *ouzo,* then dutifully drank the mixture.

While Georgandis cleaned up his instruments, Arden watched Sky fight the drowsiness that quickly overcame him. Finally he let his eyes close, and she carefully drew up the blanket and spread it over him.

The doctor turned to Arden. "The one pleasurable task I shall have this whole day will be tending to your arm, my dear," he told her in a whisper. He lifted his bag, checked Sky one last time, then turned back to her. "Perhaps we should let Mr. Trask sleep."

She nodded, and left the room with Georgandis. They entered the room next to it, the one she'd been given, and he quickly set about cleaning and bandaging her arm.

"I'm afraid your Mr. Trask will spend a rather bad night," he told her as he worked. "And thanks to the afternoon's festivities, I have a number of other patients to tend, so I won't have time to watch him. I trust you'll be able to see to him?"

She nodded. "Certainly."

"Good. I'll give you some medication to help the fever. Make him as comfortable as you can."

He finished with her arm. "I regret I can spare no more time, my dear. My inclination would be otherwise, could it be honored." He grinned at her. "Were I a decade or two younger, I might even ignore my responsibilities to spend a few hours in your company."

Arden touched her ruined clothing, then put a hand to

her disarrayed hair. She smiled at him in return. "I think you are most gallant, sir. And far too dedicated to ignore a patient for any reason."

He nodded as he withdrew a small tin of powder from his bag. "My wife has suggested the same thing more times than I can count over the last thirty years," he told her. He handed her the tin. "A spoonful mixed with a bit of water, as often as he will take it," he directed. "If he's not better by morning, have someone fetch me. In any case I'll look in on the two of you sometime tomorrow."

"But we were to leave in the morning," she said.

He shook his head. "I assure you, Mr. Trask will be going nowhere tomorrow morning," he said. "Perhaps the day following, if the fever has abated."

Arden took the tin. "Thank you, Doctor." She flexed her arm. It was stiff with the bandage, and a bit sore.

He eyed her. "I think you could use some food," he told her as he snapped his bag shut. "And I'll have someone find some fresh clothing for your Mr. Trask and a clean shirt for you. I regret there is little chance of finding a clean skirt hereabouts."

Arden nodded solemnly. "Not in a monastery," she agreed.

He grinned at her. "I think your young man is very lucky, my dear," he told her as he crossed the room to the door. "Until tomorrow, my dear."

"Until tomorrow, doctor," she murmured in reply as he left.

Arden sat for a long moment, staring after him and mulling over his words, wondering why she had not corrected his mistake and told him Sky was not *her* young man, that she had no idea where her young man might be at that moment, probably safely back in Knossos, and without a thought to spare for her. She finally came to the conclusion that she hadn't said those things to Georgandis because she wished his version were the truth, that if she could make it happen, she would change matters so that it would be Sky she was to marry, not David.

It occurred to her that until that moment she hadn't given a single thought to David. She wondered why she felt no guilt at the realization, then decided it didn't matter. Whatever she might feel for Sky, whatever she might or might not feel for David, none of it mattered at that moment. The only thing that meant anything was finding a way to get her father away from the Turkish authorities who held him.

The aide appeared a few moments later, bearing the clothing and food Georgandis had promised. She waved him to leave it on the table and watched him, too, leave with the same absent consideration with which she had stared after Georgandis. She felt weak, almost as though she were incapable of standing, as though her legs could no longer support her. The day's events, now that she had time to consider them, overwhelmed her. She felt lost and alone and entirely incapable of coping.

She stood finally and pulled off her torn and blood-smeared blouse. Half naked, she went to the wash table, poured some water into the washbowl, then proceeded to scrub away as much of the grime from her face and body as she could. She stared at the dirty water that she left in the bowl with disgust. The disgust, however, turned quickly to a feeling of anger and guilt as the sight of the water flooded her with thoughts of what had happened on the hillside. She began scrubbing her skin, rubbing it with the dampened rough toweling until it was red and irritated, hardly aware of what she was doing to herself until she found herself sobbing and clinging to the edge of the rough wash table to keep herself from falling.

She dropped the towel, then stood with her back to the

wall, her fists pressed into her eyes. It took a few minutes, but finally she managed to fight off the desperation and loss that had gripped her. She dried herself and pulled on the clean shirt that the aide had brought, throwing her own torn and filthy blouse into the bowl of water. Then she ran her fingers through her hair in an effort to bring it into some order. She was glad that monks' cells are devoid of such frivolities as mirrors. She was sure she would not find her own reflection even remotely acceptable.

Then she gathered up the tin of powder Georgandis had given her, the tray of food, and the clothing the aide had brought. Thus burdened, she returned to Sky's room.

The night was a long one for Arden. As Georgandis had predicted, Sky's fever quickly worsened. He dozed fitfully, and during the short periods when he was awake, he was disoriented and irrational. She did what she could, pressing the medication Georgandis had given her on him when he was awake and could be urged to drink, the rest of the time bathing him with cool water and holding cold compresses to his feverish skin.

She was glad of the occupation, glad she hadn't the time to think. It was far easier to center all her attention on Sky, especially as he was incapable of forcing her to realize that that attention was not reciprocated. While he was ill she could at least imagine that he needed her.

The fever, however severe it had been, was short lived. When the first fingers of daylight began to lighten the gloom of the cloister garden beyond the window, Arden realized dawn had broken and Sky was sleeping with a peacefulness that had evaded him all through the night.

She pushed her chair away from the cot and stood. Sky obviously did not need her beside him any longer. She wondered if she was exhausted enough to drop off to sleep without being plagued with unpleasant thoughts. But the movement seemed to wake him, and when she saw his eyes open, she returned to him.

"Am I dead?" he asked as he stared up at her.

She took the compress from his forehead and gently wiped his cheeks.

"No," she told him softly. "You're quite alive, Sky."

He managed a crooked smile. "Then you're not an angel?" he asked. "You look like an angel."

She returned the smile. "Appearances, they say, are often deceiving." She took the mug with his medicine and held it to his lips.

He put his hand on hers. "Not this time, I think," he said when his eyes found hers.

She rewarded him with a faint blush in her cheeks. "You're hallucinating," she told him.

He pushed himself up to his elbow, accepted the liquid in the mug, then lay back again, spent by the effort. In moments he was once more asleep.

This time when Arden rose he did not stir. She looked out at the cloister, still and peaceful, awash in a golden glow of early dawn light. It was soothing to consider that peacefulness, soothing to think herself one with it.

But a voice inside her cried out that it was a lie. Her life was in tatters—she'd agreed to marry a man for whom she had no feeling while her heart ached for another who wasted no opportunity to show her that he was simply playing with her. It was only more painful for her to think she had no one to blame for her situation but herself. And now her father was held prisoner, God only knew where, and she had only herself to blame for that as well.

Chapter Fourteen

Arden went to her own room and slept for several hours. When she woke, the sun was high and bright, intruding into the small room through the uncurtained window. She had slept fitfully, her sleep filled with dreams, and she woke lost and disoriented. It took her several minutes to remember where she was and why she was there.

She rose from the narrow, uncomfortable cot with little regret. Although she could not remember any of the dreams clearly, certain images had stayed with her: the memory of being surrounded by blood and dead men, and, the most horrifying, the face of the Turkish sergeant staring down at her, leering at her, telling her what he was going to do to her.

For a moment she felt herself weak, in the grip of the hopelessness that had nearly overpowered her the previous afternoon. She couldn't move, and she sat, weak and shaking, on the narrow cot. She was filled with a desperate need to be held and comforted, to be told that what had happened the previous day didn't matter, that it hadn't been her fault and so she could bear no guilt. She wanted more than anything for Sky to come to her and put his arms around her and tell her that he would get

Forbes away from the Turks and assure her that that, too, hadn't been her fault. More than anything, she needed him to tell her he loved her.

But all that, she realized, was impossible, and giving in to the weakness she knew could only make matters worse. She told herself she was behaving deplorably, that until she had come to Crete she would have considered anyone who acted as she now was with disgust. She couldn't allow herself to succumb to her terrors as long as Sky needed her help, as long as there was still some chance that she might somehow be of use in freeing her father. That, she decided, was the only way she'd ever escape the feeling of guilt that gnawed at her, ever reconcile herself to the knowledge that if Constatin had not had her to use as a tool, Forbes would never have come to this place, never have become a prisoner of the Turks.

Still, the images from the dreams bit at the edge of her consciousness. She swore to herself she would not let herself sleep, told herself she would sooner live with total exhaustion before she would give in to such dreams again.

After washing quickly and pulling on her clothing, she slipped out of the room and into Sky's.

Two faces turned to greet her as she pushed open the door to Sky's room.

"*Despinis* Devereaux. Come in, come in. The sight of you will not only cheer our patient, it also reminds me that I am not as old as I usually think myself."

Doctor Georgandis beamed an elfish grin at her, and Arden honored it with a warm smile of her own. Despite her own feeling of gloom, it was hard not to return the older man's warm good humor. Somehow his manner made the situation seem, for a few moments at least, less dire than she knew it actually was.

258

Once the pleasantries were concluded, however, her eyes turned to Sky.

He was sitting up with his back against the rough white plaster of the wall. The fresh bandage Georgandis was wrapping around his arm seemed very white against his skin. Although his face still appeared a bit drawn to her, the color had returned to it and he seemed perfectly content as he stared back at her.

Arden found herself fighting the urge to run to him, to ask him to put his arms around her, to hold her. That was all nonsense, she told herself. She must somehow make herself immune to him, somehow keep herself from feeling anything for him, at least for as long as it took for them to get Forbes back. Once that was done, she could face the hurt the knowledge of his rejection would bring to her, but until then she must simply not let herself feel anything at all for him.

"Just how is the patient doing today, doctor?" she asked, trying to sound brisk and nurselike.

"As you can see," Georgandis replied, "much improved. Due, in equal measure I am sure, to my doctoring and your fine nursing, my dear."

"To your doctoring, at least," Arden agreed.

"I think it callous of the two of you not to consider the fact that I am an exceedingly good healer," Sky interposed.

"Well, then, we divide the credit equally," Georgandis said as he finished with the fresh bandage. He returned his glance to Arden and noticed the dark circles beneath her eyes. "Have you slept enough, my dear?" he asked. "I think you could use a bit more rest."

Arden shook her head. "I'm fine," she said. She had not the least desire to abandon herself once again to her dreams.

"But you can not have slept very long. Mr. Trask tells

me he remembers an angel sitting beside him when he woke at dawn. That tells me you were here at least until then."

"I think Mr. Trask was more ill than you anticipated he might be, doctor. He was subject to visions caused, no doubt, by the fever. There was no angel," Arden replied.

Georgandis smiled. "But it is not difficult to understand the confusion. There is no face I have seen, even in this holy place, more angelic than yours."

Arden found herself blushing at the compliment. "Blasphemy, doctor," she replied lightly. "And in a monastery!" she added with a small laugh.

He scowled, but with humor. "I assure you, my dear, it is only the atmosphere of the place that keeps you safe from my pledges of undying passion," he told her with mock solemnity. He stood then, and pointed to the chair he had vacated. "If you would be so kind as to let me look at your arm?"

Arden rolled up the sleeve of her shirt as she sat, then extended her arm to Georgandis. He cut away the old bandage, nodded with approval at the way her arm had already begun to heal, then washed and rebandaged the cut.

"I pronounce you both on the mend and prescribe food and rest for the remainder of the day," he said when he'd done. He closed his bag with a crisp snap. "And with that, I regret that I must leave you to return to less enjoyable tasks."

"We both thank you, Doctor," Sky said.

"It has been a pleasure," Georgandis said with a smile at Arden as he started to the door. "God speed you both."

"And you, Doctor," Arden replied.

When he'd gone, Arden turned to Sky. "Shall I leave?" she asked. "Do you want to rest some more?" She suddenly found she could not look at him, not and hold onto the shred of control she'd been carefully nurturing. It had been one thing to be near him, to touch him, while he was weak and feverish. But now he looked only too healthy to her, and, she told herself firmly, she could not afford to place herself in a position to be hurt by him.

She stood, and crossed to the window, leaning forward to stare out at the cloister.

He shook his head. "No, no more sleep. I feel as though I've slept for a month. Do you suppose you might assist an invalid on a short walk in the garden? I'm not used to being cooped up like this."

She turned back to him. "If you like," she agreed.

"Good," he said, then threw off the blanket that covered him and stood. He began to look around for his clothing.

For a short moment she stood where she was, staring at his naked body. Obviously he assumed it didn't matter, that she'd seen him once before naked and now need not bother with the niceties of normal modesty. Or perhaps he simply didn't bother to think of her at all. Treating her like a piece of furniture, after all, was the clearest way there was to show her just how little he thought of her.

Whatever his intention, it could not diminish the interest she had in the sight of his body. It seemed odd to her, the fascination it held for her, the way the muscles of his shoulders moved, the way his chest melted into the narrow vee of his belly, the thick dark thatch and that mysteriously masculine part of him between his legs. After only a moment's consideration of it, she felt the image of his naked body seem to burn itself into her memory.

After that moment, however, she began to feel as though she were doing something wrong. Surely, she thought, she ought not to enjoy the sight of his naked body, surely there was something unnatural, something perverse in that. She turned away, glad he hadn't noticed

261

her stare, and concentrated on the flowers in the garden. She quickly realized what she had not noticed in the previous night's darkness, that here, too, the effects of the previous day's battle could be seen. With the cloister illuminated by stark daylight she could see that the blooms and the carefully clipped and tended shrubbery all were dulled with a thin coating of dark soot, a remnant of the fires she had seen burning the monastery outbuildings the night before.

"I don't suppose you've seen my trousers?" Sky asked. The sound of his voice broke her revery. She turned to find him casting about amongst the clutter of rumpled bedclothes, searching for the trousers, and becoming a bit perturbed when they didn't immediately present themselves to him. "A man gives up his trousers for a few hours and they somehow manage to disappear."

Making a point of not looking at him, Arden crossed to the wash table, lifted the neatly folded trousers and shirt the aide had found for him the evening before, and dropped them on the bed. He stared at them without recognition.

"Your things were all torn and stained," she explained. Then, vexed at her discomfort and hating the fact that she could not dismiss it, she added, "I'll wait for you outside."

She turned away from him, wondering as she did how she could have possibly thought herself capable of being immune to him. She suddenly felt as though she were crumbling inside, weak from the hurt generated by the events of the previous day and the need for him that hurt seemed to have released within her. Her voice was quivering, she realized, and she knew her determination to remain calm and controlled had been useless. She bit her lip to hold back the tears she felt threatening and started for the door, wanting to get away from him before she lost her self command completely.

But Sky saw the trembling of her lip and the strained expression on her face. He reached out for her and caught her arm, holding onto it, staring at her as her face began to crumble and the first silent tears began streaming down her cheeks. He realized that she'd been hiding this hurt since the previous day, afraid to let herself give in to it. She'd carefully nursed his wound, but had kept her own secret and unattended.

He put his arms around her and then pulled her to him, holding her firmly until she gave in and put her head to his chest. Arden realized that it would do her no good to fight him, that he was offering her the sympathy and compassion she desperately needed. For a while she simply gave herself over to her tears, relieved, finally, to be able to shed them.

Once begun the tears seemed to pour out of her, a torrent of them, and with them great, gasping sobs. It was a wonder to her how cleansing they seemed, what a wondrous release they generated within her. She was dimly aware of the sound of his voice, of the gentle words he spoke, but somehow they seemed apart from her. All she felt was the hard, strong wall of his chest against her cheek, the pleasant warmth of his body closer to hers, and the sure knowledge that as long as she was in his arms she was safe.

When finally the well of the tears had emptied itself, she raised her head, sniffed loudly, and drew the back of her hand across her cheek.

"That was stupid," she muttered, feeling foolish now, and once again angry with herself for the display of weakness.

He shook his head. "No," he told her. "It was necessary."

Then he put his hand to her chin and pulled her face gently until she was looking up into his eyes. Very carefully he wiped her cheeks with the palms of his hands, then leaned forward to her and dried them with his lips.

Arden closed her eyes and stood still beside him, conscious of the gentle press of his lips to her skin, of the warmth of his body close to hers. It had been stupid of her to think she could ignore this need for him, stupid and useless. This was what she had wanted from him, had needed from him. No matter that he had not told her he loved her. If this was all she could have from him, it would be enough. She simply knew that she had exhausted her strength and now she needed to find it again in him.

She raised her arms to his neck and pressed herself to him, more acutely aware now of his growing tumescence even as she felt the liquid heat begin to surge within herself. Let tomorrow bring what it would, she told herself. For now, if only for a few moments, this was right.

She returned his kiss with an ardor that surprised her even more than it did Sky. She'd never thought to feel this way, never suspected she might find such raw need, such a gnawing yearning, within herself. She parted her lips, inviting his tongue, breathless with anticipation.

Her mouth was like honey to his tongue, thick and hot and sweet. For a moment, as the first hard surge of passion filled him, he fought against it, telling himself he hadn't intended any of this, that he'd meant only to comfort her. But the protestations were weak, and he knew it was a lie he'd told himself, knew that he'd wanted nothing more than this for weeks.

He put his hands to her waist, expertly unfastening the hooks on her skirt and letting it fall to the floor even as his lips found her ear and then her neck. And then he unbuttoned her shirt, his lips following his fingers as the vee of exposed flesh slowly grew, each kiss sending waves of eddying pleasure through her. When he'd done, Arden quickly shrugged it away, then slowly moved back until she was beside the narrow bed.

264

He released her then, as though asking her if she was sure this was what she wanted. She answered by sitting, staring up at him, and putting her arms around his hips.

"Arden," he whispered as he placed his hand on her hair.

But she shook her head, afraid of what he might say, and even more afraid of what she knew he would not say. "Later," she whispered. "Not now . . . later." And then she tore her eyes from his, leaned her head forward, and kissed him.

The feel of his belly was strangely sweet to her lips, and she thought of how the sight of it had so fascinated her only moments before. He stood, quiet and still, his hands just barely touching her hair. But as she brought her lips to his belly and then downward to that part of him that had seemed so foreign to her, so alienly male, he dropped his hands to her shoulders, held her close to him, and uttered a low moan of pleasure.

She looked up at him, at the strangely tense expression on his face that quickly melted as his eyes found hers and he stared down at her. As fascinating as she had found those parts of him that were so different from her own body, now she found herself completely mesmerized by so common a sight as his eyes. Blue, endless blue, so blue she feared she might drown in them.

"Have you any idea what you have done to me?" he asked her softly.

She shook her head, then lay back on the cot.

"Show me," she whispered in reply.

Arden lifted her arms to him, welcoming him to her. A voice inside her told her she was a fool, that he didn't love her, but she stilled it, telling herself instead that it didn't matter, that all that mattered was that she loved him.

Nothing else existed for her, not even the hurt and the

guilt she'd thought would overwhelm her when she'd wakened earlier. The memory of her resolve of that morning passed through her mind briefly, the resolve that she would never allow him to hurt her again. But at that moment she knew hurt had no part of what was between them. She was bound to him. Despite the knowledge that he didn't love her, still she was tied to him in ways that she could not understand but that were nonetheless stronger and more potent than any bonds could ever be.

She knew what she was doing, she told herself. She was not entering his domain blindly, but with both eyes open. If he did not love her, at least he still wanted her. And that, she told herself, would be enough if she could have no more.

He lowered himself to her, his body covering hers, warming hers, setting it adrift with a thousand tiny fires where his flesh touched hers. Arden closed her eyes, abandoning herself to the pleasure of his touch, to the surging liquid his lips released inside her where he kissed her breasts and her belly and her thighs.

She gave herself up to the throbbing surges he released within her, welcoming him eagerly when he slid inside her, pressing her body to his and gasping with the wondrous sensation of that first sweet thrust. She wrapped her arms around his neck and her legs twined sinuously around him, her actions guided by some knowing, adept stranger within her. She didn't question that knowledge. She simply accepted it as she accepted the rising tides that grew steadily stronger inside her.

Sky was not at all sure he understood what had released this strangely demanding creature he found in his arms. Whether it was fear for her father, or an effect of the attack the previous day, or something more, he did not know. Of one fact he was entirely sure, however, and

266

that was that her need was but a pale reflection of his own.

In the days since he'd come to realize that she might be a target of Constatin's group, he'd lived with one burning fear, that she might be snatched from him, that he'd never be able to prove to her how much he loved her. However horrendous the events of the previous day had been for her, it had had one positive result—it had given him the chance to show her that no one could love her as he did, and that nothing—not money, not social position—nothing was more important than that love.

It felt so right to him to hold her in his arms. He swore that he'd never let anything hurt her again, that he'd give his life willingly to keep her safe and happy. Whatever differences might exist between them, they paled beside the depth of feeling he had for her.

"Arden, I . . ."

She shook her head and put her fingers to his lips, stilling them before he had the chance to tell her that he loved her. She'd done it before, he realized, kept him from saying the words, and he wondered if it was because she didn't want to hear them, if she persisted with the charade that she intended to marry David Trumbull.

It didn't matter, he told himself. What she would not let him say aloud, he would tell her silently, with his body, tell her in such a way that she could not deny it, just as she would be unable to deny the fact that her feelings were an echo of his own. He would make her own body force her to admit to the truth.

He pressed his lips to hers and began to move inside her, taking as much pleasure from the response he roused in her as from the act itself. He moved with practiced expertise, pressing himself to her, feeling the heat rise within her. But he quickly realized that she answered each kiss with one of her own, that she held him to her

267

with what seemed the desire to melt into him, to become a part of him. If she had roused him with the intensity of those first few kisses, he now realized that that passion was shared between them and with the sharing had grown only more intense.

She was like a stranger to him, this creature he held in his arms, a stranger he had wakened with his passion, a passion that only seemed to grow stronger and more pressing for them both. When finally he felt her trembling in his arms, when he heard her low moan of pleasurable release, he realized he could control the flood no longer. He gave himself over to the sweeping tide, letting it wash over him and carry him with her.

Arden's breath came in ragged gasps, and she felt her heart pounding inside her as though it had determined to free itself of the walls that held it. She felt shattered, as though she'd broken into a thousand pieces, each one shiny and brilliantly glowing with its own tiny fire. She wished she could hold onto the feeling, to never let it end.

She stared up into deep blue eyes, Sky's eyes, and once again felt as though she might drown in them.

"Arden," he whispered as he stroked her hair.

The fires dimmed in the shadow of a growing panic. He's going to say this was a mistake, she thought, that he doesn't love me. Or worse, he'll make some joke, and once again show me that it means nothing more to him than a game. She felt a shiver of cold at the thought, and realized she could not let him say the words, at least not yet. She needed time to find the strength to bear them.

"Please," she begged him softly, "don't let's talk, not now. I can't bear it. Not thought, not words, not yet."

"We have to talk sometime," he told her.

She nodded, acknowledging that this was true. "Later, perhaps, or tomorrow," she said. "Just not now. I'm so tired now."

Even as she spoke, she reminded herself of the resolve she'd so easily abandoned. That had been foolish, she told herself, but not fatal. She knew what to expect and could guard herself from it, keep it from hurting her. But first she needed to sleep. After some rest, she assured herself, she would be able to face whatever she needed to face.

He stared into her eyes, studying what he saw there, telling himself that she could not hide her feelings from her eyes. And he saw what he was searching for in their dark green depths: passion, yearning, desire, all those things he wanted to find there. He leaned forward to her and kissed her gently on the lips, satisfied finally when she answered his kiss with tenderness.

But she said nothing more, made no admissions, and finally he shrugged, then lowered himself from her to lie beside her on the narrow cot. He held her close, letting his fingers drift through her hair.

"As you like," he whispered, placing a kiss on each eyelid. "Sleep now."

She complied gratefully, letting herself drift off, forgetting the fear of the dreams that had seemed so terror filled when she'd wakened, sure that while she was in his arms nothing so trivial as a dream could hurt her.

A few moments later he was lying beside her, holding her in his arms, wondering idly and with a hint of amusement how two people could find themselves comfortable on so small and comfortless a bed. Perhaps, he thought, people who love one another can find comfort anywhere.

The knock on the door was gentle, but enough to rouse Sky, who hadn't really been sleeping. He carefully extricated himself from Arden, leaving her soundly asleep on the cot. He pulled on his trousers as he crossed the room and pulled the door open a few inches to find Major Petsos standing in the corridor. He slipped outside the room, pulling the door closed behind him.

"I regret the necessity to bother you, Kirie Trask."

"Is something wrong?" Sky asked.

"My men have found someone in the ruins of the monastery stables," Petsos told him. "He is not a monk."

"Not Mr. Devereaux?"

Petsos shook his head. "No, this man is Greek. He hid from the Turks and somehow managed to evade them when the others were taken. But he was trapped by a fallen beam when the monastery was shelled, and it was only by chance that my men found him. It is a wonder he isn't dead. The doctor is surprised he has survived as long as he has."

Sky nodded, encouraging the officer, wondering if it was Constatin who had been trapped in the stable.

"Can I talk to him?" he asked. "Perhaps he can shed some light on what happened to Devereaux."

Petsos nodded. "That is the reason I have come to you," he said. "This man mentioned your Kirie Devereaux. I assumed you might wish to question him yourself."

With that, Petsos motioned to the left and the two of them started along the corridor.

"The doctor tells me you will be fit enough to travel tomorrow," Petsos offered. "I am delighted your wound was not serious."

"Not so delighted as am I," Sky assured him.

"You will not take my offer of passage to Athens?"

Sky shook his head. "Not until I've found Devereaux. We'll go back to Knossos if we can make our way there without encountering any more Turkish troops."

Petsos nodded. "In that case, you'll be glad to know my scouts tell me the Turks are massing in the south in

270

preparation for battle. If you keep to the northern road, you should be safe."

Sky nodded his thanks. Neither man seemed inclined to further conversation. The two of them walked in silence through the monastery hallways until finally they were at the door of the chapel, cleared now of benches and turned into an emergency hospital for the wounded.

"This way," Petsos said and led Sky through the long rows of cots. The scents of disinfectant and blood assailed them, and both men moved stiffly, both made acutely aware of the frailty of human life by the obvious pain of the men who filled the room.

Petsos stopped by a cot near the far wall of the chapel. A sharp finger of brilliant sunlight shone through a stained-glass window just above them, casting shadows of colored light on the face of the man who lay on the cot. Sky stared at him. It took him several seconds to recognize Kostas Spirtos.

The left half of Kostas's face was darkly bruised, and much of his body was encased in bandaging. His eyes were open, but he seemed not to see anything. Instead, he stared upward, at the ornately decorated ceiling of the chapel.

"Do you know him?"

Sky nodded. "His name is Kostas Spirtos."

At the sound of his name, Kostas's eyes moved and he suddenly seemed to waken. He tried to push himself forward, straining to talk. A thick sound came from him, but the words were unclear.

Sky knelt forward to him. "What is it?" he asked.

"They, they took them all," Kostas uttered in a hoarse, low-pitched croak. Sky had to put his ear next to Kostas's mouth to hear the words. "They discovered the monks were hiding him, and they took them all."

"Who?" Sky asked sharply. "Devereaux?"

271

"Constatin," Kostas murmured. "They knew about Constatin. They took them all."

"Where?" Sky demanded. "Where did they take them?"

"To the ships. To take them to Bodrum, to the prison."

"Devereaux," Sky hissed sharply, "did they take Devereaux, too?"

"All," Kostas answered and then fell silent, his eyes closing slowly.

When Sky turned away from Kostas, he found Doctor Georgandis behind him. "Poor fellow," the doctor muttered as he looked down at Kostas. "He won't live through the night."

"There's nothing you can do?" Sky asked as he straightened.

The doctor shook his head. "There is too much damage. I only wonder how he has survived this long."

Georgandis's eyes grew hard and angry, and Sky realized he had never quite accustomed himself to losing men to the hands of death. Strange, he thought, for an army doctor who sees so much death not to be resigned to the sight of the dying.

"He has helped you?" Petsos asked. "He knew if your Kirie Devereaux was here when the Turks reached the monastery?"

Sky nodded. "Yes, he was here," he said. "Kostas said the Turks took them to a place called Bodrum. Do you know of it?"

Petsos nodded. "It is an old fort on the Turkish coast. A number of years ago it was converted to a prison to house those Cretans who, for one reason or another, proved too troublesome for the Turks to be dealt with here on Crete." He grimaced. "Not nice. Your *Despinis* Devereaux and her father both have my sincerest sympathy."

Sky considered the major's words, then his expression,

which seemed to be even more informative. It was obvious that the prison at Bodrum was not known for its humane treatment of its inmates.

"I see," he said finally.

"I wish it were otherwise," Petsos said. "I think you should not encourage *Despinis* Devereaux to expect too much."

Sky nodded. "Thank you for your help."

Then he turned and walked out of the chapel as quickly as he could, trying not to think of the man he'd left dying on the cot, wishing he could keep himself from thinking of what was probably happening to Forbes as well.

He returned to the room, glad to find Arden still sleeping, and managed to undress and climb into bed beside her without waking her. Then he lay thinking, wondering how he would tell her her father had been taken to a Turkish prison, and wondering what he could do about it.

When she woke, Arden found him lying quietly beside her, staring at her. For a moment she feared he might demand the talk she'd managed to avoid, but he made no mention of it, apparently determined to let her have those few hours of peace she had asked of him. They climbed awkwardly out of the narrow bed, then laughed, suddenly nervous with one another. They dressed in near silence, treating one another with a curious mix of tenderness and caution, as though they were afraid to hurt one another, or perhaps be hurt themselves.

They spent a peaceful few hours lazing in the afternoon sunshine that filled the cloister, even eating a meal of coarse bread, surprisingly good cheese, and an excellent wine Major Petsos's aide provided for them from the monastery's larder. But as the afternoon wore on, Arden thought Sky seemed to withdraw from her. At first she thought he was simply telling her what she had so far refused to hear, that there was really nothing between them, nothing except the physical passion they were capable of rousing in one another. But she soon dismissed that reason, and decided instead that his wound had once more begun to pain him.

The sunlight was just beginning to fade into a muted twilight when she turned to find him sitting on a stone bench with his head back and his eyes half closed.

"Perhaps you should go back to bed, Sky," she suggested. "The doctor did say you ought to rest."

He seemed to have a bit of difficulty opening his eyes and concentrating on her words.

"Yes," he said finally, "maybe you're right."

He stood slowly, and Arden went to him, offering him her arm on which to lean. She helped him cross the cloister to the small room, aware that he was walking with painstaking care, as if he feared he might fall. He seemed more than grateful to fall wearily onto the cot.

Arden put her hand to his forehead, wondering why he'd become so weak when he'd seemed perfectly well only an hour or so before, thinking that the fever might have returned. His skin felt cool and dry to her touch.

"Shall I ask them to call the doctor for you?" she asked, worried about him and unable to think of anything else she could do.

"No," he replied. "I'm sure he has his hands full with the wounded soldiers. I'll just sleep a little and I'm sure I'll be fine." He put his hand to his shirt and started to unfasten the buttons, but after the first few his fingers seemed to falter.

Arden knelt in front of him. "Let me help," she offered.

She turned her attention to the remainder of the buttons, trying to keep herself from thinking about the feel of his bare flesh, warm beneath her fingers, aware

274

that, try as she might, each one seemed to take a bit longer as she progressed down the shirt front.

When she'd finally bared his chest, she began to pull her hands away. But suddenly he was leaning forward to her, and he put his hands on her shoulders to hold her. It bewildered her for a moment to realize that there was nothing weak or unsteady about his grasp, nothing that gave even the slightest hint that he was in the least debilitated.

He lifted her up onto the cot beside him, then pulled her close, his lips finding hers with impassioned longing. When he finally released her, it was Arden who felt herself weak and unsteady.

"I thought you felt ill," she murmured.

"Not ill, precisely," he told her as he brushed a kiss against her ear, and then one more, just below it, on her neck. "Just in need of some very special nursing, I think."

"Sky . . ."

There was something tremulous, something frightened about the sound of her voice. Sky wondered if what had happened between them earlier had been an aberration, a result of nothing more than fear and anxiety. Surely, he thought, she must know better, surely she realized that she loved him. Or perhaps he was simply imagining what he'd seen in her eyes, imagining it because he'd wanted it so much to be there. He released his hold on her.

He stared down at her, wondering if it was relief he saw in her eyes as she pulled herself away from him, and hating the thought that it might be. He almost expected her to stand, to run out the room, away from him. But she didn't. Instead she stayed where she was, sitting beside him, looking away from him, staring up at the crucifix on the wall above his head.

"What happens tomorrow?" she asked him finally.

275

"Tomorrow?"

"What happens tomorrow when we leave here? Where do we go? What do we do?"

He grinned at her. "Well, we could find a priest, or a justice of the peace, I suppose," he suggested.

How could he, she wondered, how could he continue to make a joke of it? Not that it wasn't her own fault for asking the question that way, for giving him the chance. She bit her lip, then steeled herself to face him.

"My father," she said firmly, pretending he hadn't said anything. "How do we go about finding my father?"

Sky sighed. He hadn't wanted to talk about this with her, at least not yet.

"We leave early in the morning. First we go back to Knossos and, with any luck, we'll find him waiting for us there." He wondered how he could say that to her so levelly when he knew it was a lie. He lied all too easily, he thought. Over the years he'd learned that lesson only too well.

"And if he's not there?" Arden pressed.

"Then you go off to the consul in Athens, to make the appropriate inquiries."

"You said yourself they won't do much good," she snapped.

"But it should be done. While you're in Athens, I'll see what I can do here in Crete."

"You'd send me off alone?" she asked, feeling a sinking feeling inside herself.

"There isn't much choice in the matter," he said. "Someone has to go to the consul."

"I could stay with you," she offered softly. "I could help you."

"You'd just be in the way," he told her. "I work best alone."

She stared at him, seeing the way his expression hardened. This was how he was doing it, she thought, telling her without telling her, sending her off to Athens to be rid of her. She felt as though she were going dead inside, as though she were dying and just leaving a shell behind.

She stood slowly.

"If that's the way you want it," she said slowly, and moved toward the door.

Sky watched her cross the room, realizing that he had hurt her but aware that it had been necessary, that if he was to do what he had been considering over the previous few hours, she could not safely go with him.

Arden, however, knew none of that. All she knew was that he wanted to be rid of her. She had enough pride left, she told herself, to honor that desire. One thing she would not do would be beg him to let her stay.

"I suppose I needn't go to Athens alone," she said, letting her tone grow sharp. "I suppose David could accompany me."

And those words sent a wave of cold washing over Sky, chilling him as nothing else could. "Yes," he agreed slowly. "I suppose he could."

Arden hesitated a moment, wishing he'd say something, wishing he'd tell her that he didn't want her to go with David, wishing he'd tell her he wanted her to stay with him. He didn't, and after a protracted moment, she realized he wouldn't.

"I think I'll go to my room," she murmured. Her throat felt tight and the words sounded hoarse to her own ears. She wondered if he could hear it, too. "It's getting late."

"Yes," he agreed. "We'll want to start early in the morning."

Chapter Fifteen

"Arden! Thank God you're safe!"

For a moment Arden was surprised by the amount of emotion in David's expression, for no other reason, she supposed, than that she was used to thinking of him as having only a limited capacity for feeling of any sort. Faced by his apparently unabashed relief at seeing her, she could not in good conscience pull away from his embrace despite the fact that at that moment his arms held absolutely no attraction for her.

She was, however, extremely uncomfortable standing there with his arms around her, a feeling that was only exacerbated by the fact that both Sir Arthur Evans and Sky were watching them, the former with an absent sort of paternalism and the latter with openly derisive amusement. She silently damned Sky, wishing he would betray at least a hint of jealousy, something she could interpret as a sign that he had at least a tiny spark of feeling for her. But she saw nothing in his expression except the hint of scorn that said only too plainly that David's technique of embrace was lacking, that Sky himself could perform that particular task with a great deal more flair.

She was relieved when David finally released her.

"Forbes?" David asked when she'd pulled away from

him and he'd had the opportunity to look around. "He's not with you?"

Arden told herself she really hadn't expected her father to have managed to avoid the Turkish army and found his way back to Knossos, but still David's question confirmed her worst fears and made her realize that part of her had been clinging to the possibility of that slim hope. She shook her head.

"No, he's not with us. We'd hoped he'd somehow managed to make his way back here." She looked to Evans. "He hasn't, then?" she asked in a wan voice. "Or to Spirtos's farmhouse?"

"No," David answered, his tone sharp, as though he resented the fact that she had turned her attention elsewhere. "We've seen nothing of him since the day after you left. I've been so worried about you, Arden. What happened?"

For a moment she thought to tell him, to make him understand just how completely her life had changed in the previous days. If nothing else, she now knew that the violence she'd witnessed, the things that had happened to her since the night Constatin had dragged her away from Knossos, had made her realize life was far too precious to be wasted with the foolishness of an ill-conceived marriage. She loved Sky and despite the knowledge that she meant nothing to him, still she knew she could never marry David. She'd made far too many mistakes of late. This, at least, was one she would not allow herself to blunder into as well.

Before the first words made their way to her lips, however, she realized she could not simply blurt it out, especially with others nearby. Surely she owed David more kindness than that. She would tell him, and soon, she decided, but it would have to be later, when circumstances were more fitting.

Sky noticed her hesitate and assumed her reticence stemmed from an attack of conscience over what had occurred between the two of them the previous afternoon. After all, she'd kept him at a distance all that day, and he no longer harbored any hope that she might resign herself to going alone to Athens and waiting there for him. She'd made it more than plain that she intended to allow David to accompany her there and then fallen into a cold silence which told him she considered what had occurred between them nothing more than a regrettable mistake.

They had left the monastery in the morning just after sunrise and ridden all day, for the most part without a word between them. For a moment he was almost tempted to tell David what had happened, to let him know just how virtuous a wife he intended to take. Instead, he told himself he didn't care, that they deserved one another.

He turned to Evans.

"The others," he asked, changing the subject and allowing Arden to leave David's inquiries unanswered, "Blake and Hobbs and the workers, what happened to all of them?"

Evans's expression grew grim. "I sent them away. After what happened at the tomb, I couldn't ask them to stay." He returned Sky's even stare. "You were right, Mr. Trask. I should have listened to you at the start. I don't think I will ever be free of the knowledge that my stubbornness cost four men their lives."

"But why didn't you go as well?" Arden demanded of both him and David.

Evans shrugged. "There was still work to be done, artifacts that had to be crated and stored. There are many priceless objects here. They couldn't be left lying about like so much cheap pottery to be stolen or destroyed."

"And I couldn't leave without knowing where you were, whether or not you and Forbes were safe," David interposed.

"How courageous of you, Trumbull," Sky said without making any effort to hide the derision he felt. "But now that Arden is returned to you, you can feel free to leave without staining your precious honor."

There was a moment of awkward silence as he and David stared at one another, their mutual dislike filling the air around them.

Evans broke the tension. "But what has happened to Mr. Devereaux?" he asked. He turned to Arden. "Wasn't he with you?"

Arden thought of the fleeting minutes she'd spent in her father's company, of the anger she'd felt with him for the way he'd accepted everything Constatin had told him. Now, not knowing when she'd see him again, she wished she'd at least had the chance to tell him she loved him.

"We were separated," she replied to Evans's question with pained reserve. "We believe he's in the hands of the Turkish authorities. Mr. Trask thinks I should go to the American consul in Athens and have them initiate inquiries."

Evans turned back to face Sky and raised a questioning brow, silently suggesting that that particular move would hardly produce reasonable results considering the current temperament of the Turks and the imminence of war between them and the Greeks. But he did not voice his opinions.

When he turned back to Arden, he nodded and said, "That is the most reasonable course, I suppose."

Arden wasn't quite sure if she felt disappointed or not by his calmly agreeing words. She wondered for a moment what she would have done had he suggested it would be more fruitful for her to remain on Crete and find other means of initiating an investigation to find

Forbes. But he didn't, and before she had the chance to ask Evans if he knew of any alternative means she might use to query the authorities, Sky had begun talking.

"I'll go to Heracleion now that I know Miss Devereaux is in safe hands," he said. "There are one or two people I met when I was first there who might be useful in finding Forbes in a less formal manner."

Arden turned questioning eyes to him. This was the first she had heard of these people who might know where her father had been taken by the Turks. And by the way Sky spoke, she had the feeling that he thought the possibility better than remote.

She was on the verge of telling him that she refused to go to Athens, of demanding that he take her with him to make his inquiries. But she quickly changed her mind as she considered his expression. It was fixed and remote as he stared at her, as he watched David put his hand to her arm.

"Then we won't detain you further," David was saying. From his tone, Arden knew his attitudes about Sky had not improved in the intervening days and realized David was anxious to see the last of him.

But Sky apparently had no intention of allowing David to dismiss him like a servant. He eyed Arden.

"Before you and your fiancée leave Knossos to go to Athens, you might tell Kirie Spirtos that Kostas was killed at Haghios Nicodemos. It will hardly be news that will bring him pleasure, but he deserves to know what happened to his son."

His words startled Arden. How he came into possession of that particular piece of information baffled her.

"How do you know that?" she demanded. "Did you see Kostas at the monastery?"

"I saw him. Major Petsos told me this morning before we left that he died last night."

This news, too, bewildered her. She could not imagine

when he might have seen Kostas if she hadn't.

"When?" she demanded. "And why didn't you tell me?" She was angry, she realized, angry that he'd kept things from her. "He might have seen my father. I ought to have been told. I should have seen him."

"I just told you, I spoke to him," Sky told her, his own voice edged with anger now.

"What did he tell you?" she demanded. "Did he know anything about my father?"

Sky shrugged. "Nothing," he said. He managed to stare into her eyes as he uttered the lie.

Arden returned his stare. He'd kept his news about Kostas from her. She wondered what else he knew, what else he had kept hidden.

Evans was talking now, saying there had been word of fighting at Cape Yoannis, asking if it was indeed true. Sky seemed to ignore him, staring for a long moment at Arden. Then he turned to Evans.

"Yes," he replied, "there was fighting there. And unless I miss my guess, it will spread. If you have any sense at all, you'll leave your pots and get out of Crete."

With that, he turned and walked away, leaving Arden and the two men to stare after him and mull over his parting words.

David seemed to shake himself awake. He turned to Arden, and his manner became suddenly brisk.

"I'll take you to the farmhouse," he said, putting his hand on her arm and starting toward the door. "You must be exhausted. You'll want to bathe and rest." He turned to Evans. "Sir Arthur, if you'll excuse us."

Evans nodded. "Certainly." He turned his glance to Arden. "I am delighted you've been returned to us unharmed, my dear," he said. Then, as though privately relieved that the distraction was finally at an end and he

284

could return to his work, he started toward a table littered with earthenware and stone figures and shook his head. "So much still to do," he muttered as they left.

Once outside the small barn that was serving as a temporary storage for the dig, Arden turned to David.

"I—I don't think I want to go to the farmhouse just now, David," she began.

"Just what does that mean, Arden?" he asked as he watched her eyes follow the fading trail of dust Sky's horse lifted behind it.

"I think he knows where Papa is," she said in a softly absent voice as she kept her eyes on Sky's diminishing form. "I think we should go after him."

"Don't be ridiculous. If he knew where your father was, he'd have told you."

She shook her head.

"No, no, he wouldn't," she insisted. "Not if he thought it might be dangerous."

David decided he didn't like the contemplative and torn expression her face had taken on as she watched Sky leave.

"He didn't seem concerned about danger when we set off to that damned monastery after you," he hissed, angry with her and not thinking about what he was saying.

She turned sharply and faced him. "What do you mean?" she demanded. "He came alone for me."

David grew suddenly confused. "We started off together," he said, trying to cover his mistake. "And then we separated, in case you came back here."

Arden considered him a moment, trying to decide if what she saw in his eyes was guilt or something else. In the end, she decided it didn't matter. Even if he had cared enough to set out after her with Sky, he'd returned here, caring more for his own safety, while Sky had persevered. She was bewildered with her reaction to that thought, wondering why Sky had continued on, determined to find her, when her own fiancé, the man who by rights ought to have had enough feeling for her to ignore his own well-being, had not considered the risk to himself one worth taking.

"I'm going after him," she said finally, and started off to where her horse had been left tied to a nearby tree.

"Don't talk nonsense, Arden. You can't do any such thing."

"Why not?" she demanded. "He's looking for my father. I have the right to go as well."

"Think of how it would look," David fumed at her and put his hand on her arm. "An unmarried woman, racing off after a man."

She shook off his hand. "I don't care how it looks," she replied.

"Well, you should." He caught her arm again, and this time held it firmly, not letting her pull away. "Or is it him, not your father that interests you so much that you'd go racing off in the darkness?" he asked. "Perhaps you might care to explain just what happened out there between the two of you during the last few days."

"You ask the question as if you had a right to an answer, David," she shot back, suddenly finding herself shaking with anger with him. Whatever she had done, she told herself, he had no right to question her this way, no right to treat her like a criminal. After all, he didn't own her. "You don't."

"You're to be my wife, Arden. I should think that gives me the right."

She shook her head. "No, David. It does not."

She pried his fingers loose from her arm and backed away from him, feeling suddenly as if his touch were something odious, something unclean. Whatever feeling of pity she might have had for him a few minutes before had completely disappeared.

His expression grew fixed and hard. "If you go after him, Arden, you may consider the ties between us permanently severed."

He stared at her, challenging her, obviously expecting her to back down and come meekly back to him. Arden found herself stifling a sudden urge to laugh as she realized he had freed her of the task of telling him she couldn't marry him. Perhaps, she thought, this way was best for both of them.

"If that's what you want, David. I just know I am going to do this. I am not asking for your leave or your approbation."

She hesitated only a moment longer, standing there, staring at him, looking for some hint of loss in his eyes and finding only aversion and the reflection of his offended sensibilities.

Finally, she turned away and started toward her horse.

"You gave yourself to him, didn't you?"

David's voice followed her, ragged with anger and disgust. She ignored it, telling herself she didn't owe him an answer, certainly not to that question. She took the horse's reins and climbed wearily into the saddle, hardly eager to return to it after the long hours of riding that day.

"Didn't you?" he shouted when she didn't answer him.

She turned to glare down at him.

"Good-bye, David," she said.

She turned the horse, put her boots to its flanks, and started after Sky.

At first Arden thought she'd simply catch up with Sky and convince him to take her along with him. But she'd hardly left the dig behind before she realized he'd simply send her back, that he obviously intended to do whatever it was he was planning to do alone. Instead she decided to follow him, keeping an eye on him until it was too late for him to simply dismiss her.

She didn't realize how hard it would be to follow Sky in the growing darkness. He rode at a regular canter, obviously eager to reach Heracleion as quickly as possible. She squinted into the near darkness, keeping him in front of her, yet not daring to get too close lest he notice her following.

It didn't take long before she realized she was exhausted. Her head ached from the strain of keeping him in sight, and her muscles felt the strain of the hours of riding. She had to keep herself tense, fearing she might lose control of her own mount. She realized it was only determination and sheer stubbornness that kept her in the saddle and doggedly following behind him.

But the road to Heracleion was well marked, if not exactly an easy one, and there was little traffic on it this late in the day. By the time it was full dark and the moon had risen to bathe the countryside in a silvery shimmer of moonlight, which simplified the job of keeping him in sight since she could not allow herself to get close enough for him to notice her, she began to recognize the outskirts of the city.

Before he reached the city proper, however, Sky turned off to the east, skirting the more populated areas and moving toward the less prosperous areas of shore that edged Heracleion. She wondered where he was going, who he could possibly know in such a place. She had, however, little opportunity to ponder her questions, for there was far more traffic on the road and she was forced to focus her attention on pursuing him.

It wasn't long before Sky dismounted in front of a stable. Arden quickly slid from her own horse and hurried into a narrow alley where she could hide and yet keep an eye on Sky. He handed over his mount to a burly

288

stablehand, depositing a few coins in the man's out-stretched palm before starting off toward the *taverna* that skirted the beach.

For a second Arden was in a quandary. She had no coin to pay for the feeding and shelter of her own horse, and she sorely regretted leaving him to fend for himself after the long ride. In the end, she tied him to a spindly stick of a tree in front of the stable, hoping the stable man would take pity on the animal and take him in. Then she hurried after Sky.

He seemed to be ambling thoughtlessly as he meandered along the narrow road that edged the beach, staring into the courtyards of a half dozen *tavernas* before he finally found one that seemed to satisfy him. Arden trailed along behind him, keeping as much as possible to the shadows. She found herself glad of her rumpled and soiled appearance, relieved that it seemed to discourage whatever interest the sailors who idled in the *tavernas* showed her. She allowed herself a small grimace as she realized she was not even so well turned out as to be considered an acceptable whore.

Eventually she saw Sky settle himself at a table on the far side of a *taverna* courtyard, seating himself at a table where a small man in rugged clothing sat nursing the contents of a glass on the table in front of him. The man looked up as Sky slid into the seat opposite and smiled at him, apparently not displeased to see him. In seconds they were deeply engrossed in conversation, leaning forward to one another like conspirators as they spoke.

Eager to learn what it was they were saying, Arden sidled through a thick stand of scrub bushes, keeping to the shadows, trying vainly to ignore the scratches the thorns left on her exposed arms as she moved. She had no idea who this man could be, but somehow she knew she had to find out what it was he and Sky were discussing with such intensity.

She crouched low and crept through the sand until she was just outside the wall of the *taverna*, a few feet from where the two of them sat. She settled herself on her haunches, squatting in the sand, and listened to their talk.

"Yes, we got word here that the Turks have taken Constatin along with the monks from the monastery," Sky's unlikely friend was saying. "But my informant does not think they know that they have him. Apparently the monks gave him robes so he could pretend to be one of the holy men. They believe in our cause. They will not give him away."

"I'd not have thought they'd treat a religious order with so little respect, rounding them up that way, shipping them off to prison," Sky mused thoughtfully.

The small man shrugged. "They somehow discovered the monks were harboring our people. I suppose after Constatin's small act of reprisal in Mallia, they were determined to catch him."

"A small act of reprisal?" Sky hissed with anger. "Is that what you call the murder of a squadron of men, Petropoulos?"

"Turks," Spiros Petropoulos replied heatedly. "If you are so disgusted by what we do, then why do you come here again looking for me?" The leader of the separatists who had first sent Sky to Mallia to see for himself what was happening on Crete began to fear he'd made a mistake by relying on his instincts and trusting this American.

"Because we can help one another," Sky told him.

"How?"

"I know where Constatin was taken. You will agree that information might be useful to you?"

"You know it is. He's one of my best men. I need him back." Petropoulos leaned forward across the table.

290

"You said we can help one another. What do you want in exchange for this information of yours?"

"To go along."

"You risk a great deal for your little newspaper stories, my American friend."

Sky laughed, but there was little humor in the sound of it. "I suppose I do," he agreed. "But the Turks took a friend of mine along with your Constatin and the monks of Haghios Nicodemos. I am told normal methods of petitioning to have him released will be fruitless. I intend to go with you on your expedition to free your man and bring my friend back as well." He stared at the other man's sharp, appraising dark eyes. "Do we have a bargain, Spiros?"

Petropoulos held out his hand. "We have a bargain," he said and solemnly shook Sky's. "Now, where did they take Constatin?"

"Bodrum," Sky replied.

"Bodrum?" Petropoulos mused softly. "I should have known. Then it is hopeless. Constatin and your friend, whoever he is, will rot in the worst Turkish prison there is, and neither will ever see the light of day again."

Arden drew a sharp breath. Petropoulos's words seemed to settle into her, hard and sharp and final. She had no doubt that her father was Sky's missing "friend," and the thought of him dying in a stinking Turkish prison left her weak and shivering with terror.

She was shaking, and she fell against the low stone wall, no longer able to keep herself stiffly quiet in the darkness of the shadows. She heard nothing, saw nothing except the image Petropoulos's words woke in her imagination. A wave of guilt swept over her, guilt that the cause for much of what had happened lay at her feet.

291

She neither heard nor saw the man approach until he was standing in front of her. It was only when she found herself staring dully at his legs that she realized he was there. Then he was leaning over her, grasping her arm and dragging her up, out of the shadows and into the circle of light cast by the *taverna* lamps.

"What have we here?" Petropoulos demanded, leaning over the wall at the sound of scuffling, watching as Arden was pulled clumsily to her feet. His tone changed to one of incredulity. "A woman?"

The man who held Arden looked up at Petropoulos.

"She was kneeling here, listening to your conversation," he said. "I thought I saw movement a while ago, so she's been here for some time."

Sky leaned forward and stared over the stone wall. His eyes met Arden's wide, frightened ones and he groaned.

"Tell him to bring her here," he told Petropoulos. "She's the daughter of my missing friend."

Arden sat staring sullenly at the plate of food Sky had ordered for her. She hadn't touched a bite, despite the fact that both Sky and Petropoulos were consuming their own meal with apparent relish. Neither man had spoken to her, and although Sky seemed determined to ignore her, she had seen Petropoulos pause several times and stare at her for a moment before he returned to his meal.

When he'd almost finished with his food, Sky finally turned to her. "Eat something, Arden. You haven't eaten all day."

It wasn't an invitation, she realized; it was an order.

"You still haven't told me how you intend to get my father out of that place," she said, ignoring his words. She leaned forward to Petropoulos. "What are you going to do?"

He shook his head. "Nothing. The prison at Bodrum is an old fortress. There's no way in." There was regret in his tone, but resignation as well.

"You can't be willing to let your man die there!" she hissed at him. "Or are you such a coward that you won't even try?"

As she expected, Petropoulos's head shot up and his eyes darted anger as he stared at her. If she'd learned little else recently, she had learned one does not impugn the courage of a Greek without suffering the consequences. She knew had she been a man, Petropoulos would have drawn the knife he wore sheathed in his belt. As it was, it took him several seconds before he managed to get his anger under control. Once he had, he turned to Sky, no longer deigning to address Arden.

"Perhaps you might instruct your friend's daughter in the niceties of passable manners," he suggested in a sharp tone.

Sky darted her an angry glance of his own before he replied, "I've felt the need of doing precisely that once or twice myself."

"Regardless of what you think of my manners," Arden interposed, "surely you can not consider leaving Constatin to die in a Turkish prison." Petropoulos seemed to make a point of ignoring her, but he finally turned to face her when she added, "Not after Turkish soldiers killed his brother."

"Theo is dead?" he asked softly.

Arden nodded. "I was with him."

Sky added, "They killed Theo and tried to rape Miss Devereaux."

This information seemed to mollify Petropoulos. His expression softened and he leaned toward her.

"*Despinis* Devereaux. Understand. This is not a decision I make easily. Constatin is not the only one of our

293

people imprisoned in Bodrum."

"All the more reason why you should try to free them," Arden interrupted.

He shook his head. "We have tried to get into the place. The two raids we made cost the lives of sixteen good men." He shook his head. "No, I have no more lives I can afford to lose. Not for your father. Not even for Constatin."

She nodded. "All right, I accept that the prison can't be stormed and entered by force. I know nothing of such things." She stared at Petropoulos. "And I can only assume you know a great deal about them. But people must go in and out of this prison. Food must be brought in. There has to be some way."

Petropoulos stared at her, obviously lost in thought. Both Sky and Arden sat in silence waiting for him to speak.

Finally Petropoulos leaned forward and stared directly into Arden's eyes.

"There might be a way," he said slowly. "The commandant of Bodrum is a man known for his appetites. Especially his carnal appetites." He considered Arden's features as the flickering lamplight played over them. "I think beneath that layer of dust you are a very pretty woman, *Despinis* Devereaux. And with your coloring, your pale hair, those green eyes, surely you are a temptation this Turkish commandant could not resist. Just what are you willing to do to see your father freed from Bodrum?"

Chapter Sixteen

"No!"

Sky's voice rose in an angry roar. Petropoulos and Arden both turned to him in surprise, as did a number of the other patrons of the *taverna*.

"I won't have her along," Sky hissed.

He had lowered his voice, and the other patrons quickly lost interest and turned back to their own conversations.

"You have nothing to say about my actions, Mr. Trask," Arden snapped back at him.

"We'll need her," Petropoulos reminded Sky. "It can't be done without a woman."

"Then we'll find another woman," Sky told him. "We can hire one. There must be a whore on Crete anxious to earn a few hundred drachmas."

"You don't have enough drachmas to get any woman on Crete to go to Bodrum," Petropoulos said. "They'd rather starve."

"Stop it!" Arden said angrily. She turned to Sky. "You have no right to tell me what I can or can not do," she hissed angrily at him. "You have no rights whatsoever concerning me." She turned back to Petropoulos. "I will do whatever you tell me I must do," she told him.

"It will not be pleasant," Petropoulos warned her.

"It doesn't matter as long as we get my father out of that place," she said.

Sky leaned forward to her. "Damn it, Arden," he said. "You're going to Athens, to the consul." His eyes narrowed. "I think you've forgotten what Trumbull would say were he here to hear you."

"I don't give a damn what David would say," she told him vehemently. "And I heard you yourself say it was useless to go to the consul." She fixed him with a determined glare. "I'm going with you."

"The lady seems to have made up her mind, my friend," Petropoulos said with a smile.

"The lady is too damned stubborn, and she doesn't know how to follow orders," Sky told him. His tone was angry, and he glared at Arden as he spoke. "She'll get us all killed."

This information at least seemed to interest Petropoulos. He sat back in his chair and considered Arden with a questioning stare, his eyes seeming to weigh what he saw, as though he could determine the value of her honor with only a glance.

"I will do precisely what you tell me to do," she quickly assured him, terrified now that he might see something that would make her appear lacking in his eyes, that he might agree to Sky's demand to leave her behind.

"I have the lives of my men to consider, *Despinis*," he told her, drawing out the words, letting her know just how important his decision was.

She pulled herself up, straightening her shoulders. One way or another she determined that she would not let them leave her behind.

"You can't leave me here. If you don't take me with you, I'll go to the authorities. I'll tell them everything I know about you and Constatin and your group."

"Arden!" Sky hissed at her.

Petropoulos's expression turned to one of anger. He grasped his glass so hard his knuckles turned white. Arden was afraid the thick glass would shatter in his hand.

"That was not amusing, *Despinis* Devereaux," he hissed at her.

"I told you I will do whatever I have to do to have my father freed, Kirie Petropoulos," she said. "I meant it."

Petropoulos loosened his grasp of the glass, then raised it and swallowed the last of the liquor it contained, all the while keeping his eyes on Arden's. When he'd emptied it, he dropped the glass to the table.

"You will do exactly as you are told," Petropoulos told her without taking his eyes from hers.

She nodded, more than willing to agree. "Just as you tell me," she said. "Whatever you tell me."

"Because if you don't, *Despinis* Devereaux," Petropoulos went on, "do not think I would hesitate to kill you simply because you are a woman. I would do it without a second thought."

Arden cringed at his words, somehow aware that he would do exactly what he said he would do. She said nothing, only nodded.

"You can't take her," Sky insisted one last time.

"I have no choice, my friend," Petropoulos told him, finally turning away from Arden to look at him. "The young lady has given neither of us any choice in the matter." He stood. "You will stay here. Don't try to leave. If you do, friends of mine will detain you. I'll return when I've made some arrangements." He turned back to Arden again. "I suggest that you eat your dinner, *Despinis* Devereaux," he said. "It may be your last."

Arden looked around at the wharf and the line of fishing boats tied to it. The night had turned intensely dark, with a bare, slim crescent of a moon. The stars seemed terribly bright against the black of the sky. The water was dark and faintly reflected the tiny pinpoints of light. There was the scent of sea air and fish, the sound of water slapping against the hulls of the fishing boats, and the occasional creak of planks stirring and settling with the pressure of the waves—night sounds by the water.

For a moment she wondered if the darkness and the night quiet would have, under other circumstances, made her consider the romance of the place. It was all so different, so foreign from what she thought of as her real life, from the life she'd lived in New York. But the thought faded quickly, usurped by other thoughts, thoughts of what she had agreed to do. They left her terrified and filled with revulsion, but even that could not shake her determination.

And then the darkness was behind her as Petropoulos lit a lantern and led the way through the boat down to the small captain's cabin. The scent of salt air and fish followed them, growing stronger in the enclosed space.

"You two will remain here," Petropoulos said as he pushed the door open and stood aside so they could enter. "I'll return before dawn with the rest of my men." He stared first at Arden, then at Sky, as though he were considering just how far he could trust the two of them. "I'm leaving a guard on deck, so I advise you not to try to leave."

"She was just trying to manipulate you, Petropoulos," Sky said as he wandered into the small cabin. "She has no intention of going to the authorities or anyone else about you. We can still leave her behind."

Petropoulos shook his head.

"I would like very much to believe you, my friend," he said to Sky, but let his eyes drift back to Arden. "But there are some matters I cannot leave to chance. I cannot convince myself to trust her entirely, even with your word to vouch for her honor. Besides, we agreed we need her."

"I agreed to nothing," Sky replied.

"It doesn't matter," Arden interjected as she entered the cabin. "It's settled. I'm going."

Petropoulos nodded. "As you say, it is settled," he agreed. He entered the cabin behind her, put the lantern down on a small desk, then returned to the door. "Until the morning."

He stepped back and drew the door closed behind him.

There was the sound of a key being turned in a lock, then footsteps receding. And then there was nothing but the careful creaking of the boat, the sound of the water slapping against the hull, and the quiet night.

Sky was the first to break it.

"I hope you're pleased with yourself," he muttered angrily at her.

"Not pleased," she said as she seated herself wearily on the edge of a narrow bunk bed. She was tired, far more tired than she ever remembered being in her life. "Satisfied."

He crossed to her and stood over her, glaring at her. "Do you have a death wish?" he demanded. "Is it that you want to get yourself killed?"

"I want to get my father out of that place," she retorted.

She stared up at him, her eyes angry and defiant. He had no right to question her or treat her like an incompetent fool, she told herself. He had no right to make her question herself.

He shrugged, and turned away.

"We might as well get some sleep," he told her. "You can take the bed."

Arden stared at him for a moment, wondering if she could make peace with him, wondering if she even wanted to. He had, after all, made his feelings clear enough, that he wished she'd go to Athens with David, that he wanted to do this alone, that he had no wish to continue their, their . . .

Their what? she mused. Had they had an affair? Was that the proper term to define the stormy relationship they'd shared since that night in New York when she'd tricked him with that billiards game? She'd always secretly thought an affair meant star-filled nights and breathless, hidden love, something slightly dangerous and wickedly wonderful. This dull need she felt for Sky, this wrenching pain that filled her when she looked at him or thought of him, none of that was the way it was supposed to be. Still, whatever word she used, she knew it was over, that it all lay in the past now. All she knew for sure was that she wished none of it had ever happened.

She kicked off her shoes, letting them fall to the floor. "Suit yourself," she told him, then lay down on the bunk and turned her back to him.

Sky stared at her back for a moment, at the line of her hip as it sloped to her thighs, at the tumble of her hair trailing down over her shoulders. Part of him wanted to go to her, to touch her, to make love to her. But even desire at that moment was dulled by the anger he felt for her.

He blew out the flame of the lantern and lowered himself into the cabin's single chair, telling himself he was tired enough to sleep anywhere. But the chair was hard and he could find no position that didn't cramp his long legs. He stirred uneasily, unable to make himself comfortable enough to doze off, unable to settle his thoughts enough to give himself the chance.

Arden lay in the darkness, listening to him stir, telling herself she didn't care if he spent the whole night awake, that in fact she hoped he was miserable. But there was no satisfaction for her in the knowledge that he could not sleep. Although she closed her eyes firmly, she, too, found herself unable to doze off.

Finally, she turned around to face him. The room was dark, but she could see the pale reflection of his eyes staring at her.

"You can sleep here," she told him, and edged herself tight against the cabin wall to make room for him. "There's room enough."

He shook his head. "I don't think that would be very wise, Arden," he told her.

"Why not?" she demanded. "I'm too tired even to notice if you're here," she added tartly, then turned back to face the wall.

Her words, he was forced to admit, nicked his pride. He would allow her almost anything except the possibility that she might be oblivious to him.

"What would your precious Trumbull think?" he asked, realizing he spoke the words out of pique, that if she felt herself free to hurt him, he ought to be able to return the hurt.

She could hear the acid note of anger in his tone, and she lay for a long moment, staring at the wall. When she answered, she kept her back to him, not wanting to face him, knowing he would be able to see the hurt in her eyes if she did.

"David's my concern, not yours," she told him.

"True," he agreed. "Whatever lies you tell him, they're all your affair."

"Yes," she whispered, wondering why that last word seemed so cruel to her, why it ate into her like acid. "It's my affair. It has nothing to do with you in any case."

He sat for a few seconds longer, as if he were trying to decide what to do. Arden could almost feel his eyes on her back, and she cringed away from them, frightened by her reaction, wondering why his anger hurt her so.

301

He apparently decided he might as well accept her offer. He pulled off his boots, then stood and crossed the narrow cabin in a single step. Arden felt the bunk shift slightly as he settled himself beside her.

She lay stiff and still for several minutes, only too aware of the warmth of his body close to hers and of the tension it roused in her. But she closed her eyes firmly, telling herself that she was a fool to let him affect her like this, that all that was in the past and she would not let it ruin what remained of her life.

Sky raised his hand, almost touching her shoulder, telling himself if he saw any softening in her he would pull her close, somehow put an end to the strange war they seemed incapable of ending. But she remained stiff and, despite the fact that they lay close, further from him than she had ever been. Finally he turned his back to her, telling himself he was a fool to care.

Arden first felt him turn away, and then the warm damp on her cheek of the tear she had not even known she'd shed.

Duly determined, she finally forced herself to sleep.

It was a shattering dream. The soldiers from the hillside near the monastery came to life again, chasing her, leering at her, calling out to her, telling her what they were going to do to her. But when she tried to run it was as though her feet were mired in quicksand, and as much as she struggled she did not move. She turned to see the soldiers coming closer, but now rather than guns in their hands they held out coins. She looked down at herself and found she was wearing a whore's clothing, a dress of cheap red and black lace which nearly bared her breasts. Shocked, she looked up to find her father and David standing behind the soldiers, and she called out to them to help her. They sneered and called her a whore, turning their backs on her as the soldiers reached out and put their hands on her.

She sat up, gasping for breath, pushing the phantom hands away, trembling from the feeling of them pressed to her skin, skin that was wet with the rank perspiration of her fear.

"Arden?"

Sky reached for her and pulled her down to him. She let him hold her close, not daring to fight him. Instead, she lay in his arms, trembling still, afraid that if she pulled away from him she would see them again, the faces leering at her and the hands reaching out for her, and even worse, her father staring at her, his expression filled with disgust.

And then somehow he was kissing her and she knew she ought to pull away from him. He would stop if she told him to, of that she was certain, but instead she found herself kissing him too, reaching for him in the darkness and pressing herself to him, sure he would chase away the ghosts that had pursued her in her dream, sure that when she was in his arms she had nothing to fear. As the dream faded the fear she felt was replaced by want, a desire that filled her and pushed away all thought, leaving behind only the need.

Neither of them spoke, for both seemed to realize that words would only rob them of the passion that now bound them. They held one another close, seeking only the liquid fire they ignited in one another.

Arden found her fingers fumbling with the buttons of his shirt until they managed to free them so that she might find the bared flesh of his chest. And Sky, filled now with a fire he had no desire to extinguish, reciprocated, unfastening her shirt and pushing it aside, then pressing his lips to her bared breasts.

She lay back and closed her eyes, giving herself up to the feeling, to the sweet liquid warmth he released inside her. She trembled at his touch, aware that her body ached for him. There was no time, no yesterday, no tomorrow, only this deep, searing need for him that was growing ever sharper inside her as she felt his lips and tongue against her breasts.

A voice in her mind tried to warn her that this was perhaps the most foolish act she had performed, that it could only bring her hurt. She stilled it quickly, telling herself she no longer cared, that if she was to play the whore when they reached Bodrum she had at least the right to feel, for one last time, the ecstasy he released within her. And then she pushed thought aside altogether and gave herself up to the waves that engulfed her, let herself be swept up by the tide.

And then somehow she was naked and he was kissing her, kissing her breasts and her belly and her thighs. She spread herself beneath him, eager for him, eager for the first sweet thrust of him inside her. She reached up to him, and he raised himself to bring his lips to hers. She pressed herself to him, wanting nothing more than to melt her flesh until it was part of his, wanting to feel herself one with him.

He kissed her, his lips and tongue finding hers until her mouth filled with the taste of him, and she knew nothing could ever be sweeter. Then he was inside her, and the feel of him was full with honey and magic. She held him there, pressing close, savoring it. Somehow at that moment she realized she was tied to him, tied by bonds that she knew would never be severed. No matter what happened, no matter if she would soon be parted from him forever, still she knew that for as long as she lived she would be part of him and he of her.

He began to move inside her, and she gave herself up to

the dance, pressing her hips to his and moving with him, letting it sweep her up on waves of pure, sweet passion. She floated on a fiery sea, clinging to him, wanting nothing more than for the feeling to last forever. And a small part of her stood back and told her to remember, for there would never be another time for this. No matter what happened at Bodrum, they would never be together like this again.

When the release came it was shattering, like a thousand tiny explosions inside her that left her helpless and trembling in their wake. She held herself to him, trembling and weak, and sure her heart would shatter in her chest. And then she felt his release, too, and somehow she knew he felt as she did, shattered and spent and yet somehow more alive than either had ever felt before. Their bodies, it seemed, could speak in concert, one with the other, in ways that made words seem clumsy and pale by comparison.

Sky held her, cradling her head in his hands, and stared down at her. He wondered what it was he saw in her eyes when he looked into them, wondered if it was only the play of the dim light he saw, or really a pledge born of love and passion.

He lay back, pulling her down on top of him, feeling the beat of her heart, a thick, sharp thud that mirrored his own. For a moment they were still, and he wondered why it seemed so different with her than it had ever felt with another, why this was so right between them when it was obvious that everything else was so wrong. He felt himself almost afraid to speak lest he break the spell, lest he remind them both of the things that divided them.

Arden put her head to his chest and closed her eyes, letting her ears fill with the rhythmic beat of his heart. She could sleep now, she told herself, without fear of the dream. As long as she stayed close to him, she was safe.

305

Sky ran his fingers through the silken folds of her hair and listened to the voice inside him, the voice that told him to tell her he loved her, that she could not marry David when she knew she loved him.

"Arden," he said softly.

She didn't stir, didn't move in his arms. He looked down and realized she had already fallen asleep.

He sighed. Perhaps it's better this way, he thought.

He lay still, staring up into the darkness, holding her gently in his arms.

Arden stood on the deck of Spiros Petropoulos's fishing boat and stared off into the radiant blue of a sky that was decorated with a scattering of fluffy white clouds. She'd risen early, extricating herself carefully from Sky's arms, and dressed in silence so as not to awaken him. She was not ready to face him, not ready to begin the battle once again and lose the peace that lovemaking had left with her. Instead she'd stolen out to the deck and watched Petropoulos and his men unfurl the sails and take the boat out of port in the first pale glow of dawn. It seemed an unnaturally peaceful beginning to what she knew would be a decidedly less than peaceful venture.

Despite the heat of the bright morning sun, there was a damp wind from the water that left her chilled and shivering. She hugged her arms to herself, wondering if it was really the wind that chilled her or her own fear.

"I hope you're pleased with yourself, Arden."

She didn't even turn to face Sky. She had a sick feeling in the pit of her stomach that had become all too familiar of late. She was terrified, and the last thing she wanted to do at that moment was to get into yet another argument with him.

"Please, Sky," she murmured, "let's not fight."

"I didn't come to fight," he told her. He put a rough woolen jacket around her shoulders. "You looked like you could use this."

She slipped her arms into the jacket, huddling into its warmth. She was more than a little relieved to find he had apparently forgiven her the sin of forcing herself upon him, for that and whatever other sins she had committed the night before. She wasn't sure she had the strength to do what Petropoulos had told her she would have to do thinking Sky hated her.

She finally turned to face him.

"Stolen booty?" she asked and lifted her arms, flapping the sleeves foolishly. She managed to venture a grin.

He shook his head. "Honestly borrowed from one of Petropoulos's men. Lest I need remind you, you're the one who's about to embark on a life of crime. I'm just along for the ride."

"A life of crime?" she asked.

"I assume a jailbreak is considered a crime, even in Turkey," he told her.

She nodded absently. "I suppose it is," she agreed. She looked down at the rough, dark wool that now enfolded her. The jacket's thick bulk reached nearly to her knees, and the sleeves hung well below her hands.

"Most becoming," she ventured.

"If you think that's attractive," he told her, "you should see the finery Petropoulos has for you to wear once the fun starts. I doubt any of those Cretan whores in whom you showed so much interest before we left New York owns anything nearly so alluring."

She grimaced, then turned her back to him and stared at the bright glitter of sunlight reflected on the water. That night in New York, when she'd been secure in the knowledge she was safe in her father's house, she'd

307

thought herself so smart, so sure of what she was about. That feeling was lost to her now, and she wondered if she'd ever feel even a hint of confidence in herself again. Just the thought of what Petropoulos had told her she would have to do left her weak kneed and uncertain. The knowledge that her father's freedom and the lives of the men on the boat with her would rest in her hands only made the terror inside her that much more pressing.

She mustn't allow herself to dwell on any of it, she told herself, at least not yet, not before she was forced to think of it. It could only make her feel worse.

Sky put his hands on her shoulders.

"You don't have to do this, Arden," he told her softly. "We can tell Petropoulos to turn back, to take you back to Crete."

His words startled her. She closed her eyes and wished it would all go away. She almost found herself wondering: if she wished hard enough, would life suddenly go back to the way it had been? Could there be some magic that could take her back? More than anything she wanted to open her eyes and find nothing had ever happened, that it had all been some terrible nightmare.

She opened her eyes, blinking into the sunlight. It was real, and she knew it. Running away from it wouldn't help, even if it was only in her imagination that she fled.

"No," she told him. "You know he won't, not now, not after the things I said, the threats I made." It was what she had intended when she'd made the threat, to force the Cretan's hand, to make him take her with them. She knew it, and knew Sky knew it as well. "Besides, I don't want to go back. I intend to help get Papa out of that place."

"You don't have to prove anything to anyone, Arden," he said.

His words brought a sudden constriction to her throat.

She knew the real reason she had forced herself upon him was simply that she felt so responsible for what had happened to her father. If she hadn't come, hadn't done everything she could, and something happened to Forbes, she knew she would never forgive herself.

It seemed almost as though he was reading her thoughts, as if he knew that more than anything she wished she could run away. It occurred to her that she was prepared for his anger and his sarcasm, that she had steeled herself to deal with that, but not this open kindness. She thought she could deal better with his anger. His kindness only made her feel weaker.

"I do," she whispered, suddenly finding it hard to speak. "I have to prove something to myself."

He put his arms around her, and she leaned back against him. She oughtn't to do this, she told herself. She oughtn't to let herself give in this way. She oughtn't to allow herself to need him.

Still, she didn't pull away. It was all she wanted, she told herself, to stand close to him this way, and look at the ocean and stare up into the limitless expanse of the sky. She wondered how much longer this peacefulness would last, how many more hours before Petropoulos would come to them and tell them they were approaching the Turkish coast and Bodrum. It couldn't be much longer, certainly not long enough to give her time to find courage she did not have.

She glanced up at the sails, seeing they were stiff with the wind that kept the boat cutting through the deep blue water. Such a strangely beautiful sea, she thought, wondering if there was water anywhere else that looked so temptingly clear, so inviting. The sky, the sea around her, the bite of the wind against her cheek—she seemed to see and feel all of it with a clarity that she'd never before possessed. The warmth of Sky's body close to hers left her tingling and aware, as though she'd never felt the press of his naked flesh to hers, as if they'd never shared the heat of passion.

She wondered if it was fear that heightened her perceptions, or the knowledge that when it was over, nothing would ever be quite the same again. It made her sad to think that even if Petropoulos's plan worked, even if they were to find Forbes in Bodrum and free him, still she had lost whatever chance she might have had with Sky.

It occurred to her that she had been given a chance for real happiness, not the sort her father wanted for her, not position or money or things she could hold in her hands, but real happiness, and she had foolishly pushed it away. Still, she knew it would do her no good to mourn her loss, especially when there was still so much she stood to lose.

"There it is, the prison of Bodrum."

Arden peered into the distance, making out the large gray structure on the coast against the far horizon. It was a dark, bleak structure rising high on a rocky promontory, a blot against the pleasant green of the rolling hills beyond.

"You can stay on deck a while longer," Petropoulos told her, "but I don't want you seen before the time is right. When I tell you, get below without an argument."

She nodded and assured him she would do as he ordered, and he left to tend to other matters. She stayed as she was, staring at the slowly growing gray structure on the horizon, watching it take on distinct form as guard towers and parapets appeared out of the blur of dull gray.

"Not a pleasing edifice, is it?"

She'd hardly noticed Sky near her, but she wasn't surprised to find him on deck and watching as well.

310

She shook her head. "No," she murmured. "Hardly pleasing at all." They were close enough now for her to clearly make out the sea wall, more than thirty feet tall, a completely unbroken expanse of huge stone blocks rising out of a narrow patch of sand edged by water beating against a stretch of sharp rocks. "I don't see how it can be done," she said. "It looks impossible."

"Petropoulos says it can be done, and I take his word," Sky replied. "We don't have much choice."

She nodded and turned away from the prison, scanning along the coast for the small huddle of buildings that were the town. In front of them were wharves where a dozen or more fishing boats were being tied up and unloaded of their day's catch. In all, it seemed a very unprepossessing place for so ill reputed a prison.

She turned to him suddenly and stared up at him. "You won't do anything foolish, will you, Sky?" she asked him. "You won't go and get yourself killed?"

"I'm not a foolish man," he replied with a grim smile. He turned his glance away from the gray pile of stone that was the prison to consider what he saw in her eyes and the smile disappeared. He put his hand to her cheek. "Would it really matter if I did?" he asked her softly.

She swallowed, trying to force away the constriction that had suddenly filled her throat. The thought of him dying terrified her, more even than the contemplation of what she was to do that evening.

"Yes," she murmured. "It would."

"To you, Arden?" he asked. "Would it matter to you?"

She nodded. "Very much," she admitted, wondering if she was just giving him another weapon to use in his game against her, but unable to deny the truth. "It would matter very much to me."

He considered her expression in silence for a moment,

then leaned forward until his lips were only inches from hers.

"Tell Petropoulos you can't do it, Arden," he told her. "Tell him we have to find another way."

"I can't," she whispered. "He already told us, there *is* no other way. And if I don't try, if Papa is in that place and dies there, I won't be able to live with myself."

Sky pulled away, dropping his hand to his side.

"It's time," Petropoulos shouted at her from the stern. "Go below and get yourself ready."

Arden nodded, then backed away from Sky. She could feel his eyes on her as she turned and made her way below.

Chapter Seventeen

Arden looked down at the extent of the cleavage revealed by the dress Petropoulos had found for her. She'd never felt quite so exposed. She tugged at the black lace, but to absolutely no effect. The limited amount of fabric in the bodice could cover just so much.

It was early still, and there were only a few soldiers and a handful of fishermen in the *taverna*, but they were staring at her with interest, probably wondering how much Petropoulos, playing the role of her procurer, would demand for an hour of her services. She tried to ignore them, tried not to think of the fact that she had suddenly come to accept the role of a whore.

"Under other circumstances I might find that gown a spur to my own baser instincts, Arden," Sky hissed at her under his breath. "Just now, however, I wish you'd pull your cape closed."

"Quiet," Petropoulos muttered angrily back at him. He looked around the dimly lit *taverna*, making sure no one had noticed the exchange. It would not do for his lure to appear to be anything but what he intended her to be. When he saw Arden fingering the cape, he added, "Let it be. A harlot displays her wares."

Arden colored slightly but obediently dropped her

313

hand. She darted a glance at Sky, who was reluctantly returning to a nearby table where three of Petropoulos's men sat talking and nursing glasses of *boza*. He, like the others, was dressed in sailor's rough clothing, thick wool pants, and a sweater. Unshaven and a good deal less than pristine, the men fit perfectly into the dingy surroundings of the *taverna* . . . just as did a whore, she thought. Just as did she.

Sky sat with the others and lifted his own glass of the rough liquor, but he didn't drink. Instead he kept his eyes on the table where Arden sat with Petropoulos. She could feel him watching her and found herself wondering what it was he thought. Probably disgust, she told herself, for what she was about to do. She pushed away the thought, telling herself that what he thought of her meant nothing to her. Unfortunately, she couldn't quite make herself believe it.

"Remember," Petropoulos told her. "Sit quietly. Act cowed, as though you're afraid of me." He was leaning close to her, his voice low, speaking so that only she could hear.

"I think I am afraid of you," she whispered in reply. She darted a glance at Sky and felt oddly comforted by the fact that he was watching her.

Petropoulos ignored her comment.

"When he comes in, the tavern owner will tell him about you. He'll come to see for himself, probably invite himself to sit with us. I'll tell him you're English, that I bought you from a white slaver in Morocco, that I'm taking you to Izmir, to a pasha with a taste for pale-skinned women. We mustn't act too nervous. You especially."

She nodded. "I know," she replied in a weary tone. "We've been through it a hundred times."

"And we go through it once more," he told her sharply. She turned to stare at him, to see the dark look in

314

his eyes that told her, just as he had told her a great many times already, that his life and those of his men depended on her. He seemed determined to impress upon her her responsibility even though it already weighed all too heavily upon her. "Once we've agreed on a price, I'll insist on keeping an eye on my valuable property. He'll agree to let me go as far as the prison gates, but he won't let me beyond them, so once you are inside you will be alone with him."

"I understand."

"If you keep your wits about you, we should all get out of there with whole skins, your father included. It all depends on you."

She nodded. She wished he wouldn't keep telling her how much the plan depended on her. It only made her more afraid and more sure she would not be able to do what he expected.

"Keep your wits about you," he repeated.

She nodded again, but could think of nothing to say. Instead she closed her eyes and tried not to think that she was sitting in a filthy *taverna*, waiting to be sold as a whore.

The *taverna* was suddenly much noisier and Arden looked up, hoping it would not be him, not yet. She was trembling inside, and her stomach had filled with a dull fear. She wanted more time to compose herself, to prepare for him.

But there was no more time.

"He's here," Petropoulos hissed at her.

She stared up at the newcomer, saw a large and burly man dressed in a blue uniform that was heavily decorated with a good deal of gold braid. He had dark hair, round dark eyes, thick lips, and a wide, wiry moustache.

"Eat!" Petropoulos commanded angrily.

Arden obediently looked down at the unpleasant brown puddle of stewed meat on her plate and pushed it

315

around a bit in an effort to satisfy him. A moment or two later the blue uniform was standing in front of their table. Arden, eyes down, kept nervously poking at the food on her plate.

He said something in Turkish, and Petropoulos replied, the conversation meaningless to her, merely coarse sounds. Part of her wanted to look up at the Turk, to see what sort of a man commanded a prison like Bodrum, but she dared not. She kept her eyes on the food as the two talked, until eventually Petropoulos shrugged his shoulders and waved a hand in reluctant invitation to the newcomer to sit.

The Turk called out to the innkeeper and then seated himself across from her.

"English, eh?" the Turk said, talking to Arden now, and smiling at her as he considered the charms unabashedly displayed by her low-cut gown.

She looked up for a moment, letting her eyes meet his briefly, then looked down again at the food on her plate.

"We don't get many English here, and never any English women."

"You wouldn't have one now had not a damned drunken mate let my boat founder in the shoals to the south and forced me to put to shore to make a few repairs," Petropoulos replied. "Luckily it won't take long. I'd hate to be forced to spend more than a night in this place." He looked around the dingy *taverna* and scowled. "One *taverna* in this town, and it's a sty."

The Turk nodded in agreement. "All of Bodrum is a sty," he agreed. "A civilized man has all he can do to make himself comfortable here." He sighed, obviously pained at the thought of all he was forced to forgo in the name of duty.

The innkeeper arrived, bearing a bottle and some glasses, which he set on the table.

"But I do what little I can," the commandant went on

316

as he reached for the bottle. "French cognac, not that local *boza*," he said as he poured liquor into the glasses. "My own liquor. I have it sent all the way from Istanbul." He pushed a glass to Petropoulos and one toward Arden, then raised his own. *"Serefe."*

He downed the contents in one swallow.

Petropoulos took the offered glass. *"Serefe,"* he repeated, and emptied his glass.

The Turk looked at Arden. "Will you not join me as well, my dear?" he asked and pushed her glass across the table.

Arden darted a questioning look at Petropoulos, then timidly ventured a hand toward the glass. But Petropoulos put his hand on hers and pulled it back roughly. Arden cringed and dropped her hands into her lap.

"The woman is being sent to Izmir," Petropoulos said, keeping his eyes on the Turk. "She has a very rich and powerful protector waiting for her there. I would not want to be accused of having allowed her to come to any harm while she was in my care."

"Ah, but you are forced to spend the night here in Bodrum," the Turk said, all the while fixing his eyes on Arden. "How cruel it would be not to allow her the few simple pleasures this backward place might provide."

He turned his glance then to Petropoulos while he removed a leather purse from his pocket and laid it pointedly on the table.

The conversation was once more begun in Turkish, but this time Arden knew what they were saying, knew they were haggling over the price Petropoulos would accept for an evening of her company. It went on for a long time, and Arden began to think Petropoulos was overplaying his role, that in his attempt not to appear too anxious to accommodate the Turkish commandant, he would completely discourage him.

But Petropoulos seemed to know what he was doing.

Each time he waved his hands and rejected an offer, the Turk turned to Arden and stared at her, and each time his breath seemed to come a bit harder and his resolution to grow stronger before he turned back to make a counter-offer.

Finally the bargain was struck, and the Turk pushed the leather purse across the table toward Petropoulos. Then he leaned forward to Arden. He took her untouched glass of cognac, the one Petropoulos had refused to let her touch.

"To a beautiful evening," he said, and he held it out to her.

Arden pointedly turned a questioning glance at Petropoulos. He looked away. She realized that it was her cue, that the bargain had been made. Now, she told herself as he had told her innumerable times, it all depended on her.

She reached for her drink.

The Turk wrapped his hands around hers as she accepted the glass. His hands felt hot and damp. For a second she wondered if he noticed the cold perspiration that clung to her hands, wondered if he could feel the fear that was so strong within her she could taste it.

"I fear we have not been properly introduced, my dear," he said in a voice that had grown suddenly throaty with excitement. "I am Commandant Soltan Muhammad Bildirjian."

Arden hesitated a moment, then slowly pulled her hand away from his. She raised the glass to her lips and sipped the cognac. It made a fiery trail in her throat, and she knew she could not afford to drink any more, that if she did she might become drunk. She wet her lips again with the cognac, pretending to take a second swallow, then looked up at him.

"Arden," she whispered when her eyes found his. "Arden Devereaux."

318

"It would be a great pleasure, my dear, to show you the one lovely spot in all of Bodrum." He put his hand on her arm and began to rise.

Petropoulos slammed his hand onto Bildirjian's arm. The Turk turned to look at him, surprise and the edge of anger in his eyes.

"That is valuable merchandise you are handling," Petropoulos hissed. "I am not so great a fool as to let you steal off into the night with it."

His remark seemed to amuse the Turk. "And where would I take her?" he asked. "Into the wilderness?"

Petropoulos smiled slyly. "You must remember, I must be sure she is safe. And secure."

Bildirjian returned the smile. "Then come along," he invited as he straightened. "You can enjoy the hospitality of Bodrum as well." He laughed, apparently amused by the possibility that anyone would choose to enter the prison. "There are those who would sooner forgo the honor, but if that is your fancy, come."

He reached again for Arden, smiling as he put his hand on her arm and helped her stand. He pulled her out from behind the table and then placed her hand on his arm. She allowed herself to dart a quick glance at Sky as she stood, then turned to the Turk and returned his smile. He led her through the smoky *taverna* to the door.

Petropoulos stood. He gave Sky and his men a quick signal with his hand, then followed along behind.

Sky and the men at his table hurriedly downed their drinks. Then they stood, dropped a few coins on the table, and left the *taverna* as well.

Arden quickly realized the prison of Bodrum had earned its reputation honestly. It was situated on a small jutting point of land with nothing but sheer, steep walls overlooking cliffs on three sides, not just on the side she

319

had seen earlier that day from the water. The fourth side, with the single entrance to the fort, boasted a rampart. She could see heavily armed guards patrolling the narrow, open field beyond. Nothing, she realized, could enter the prison unseen from this side, and the three other sides were simply too steep to be scaled without aid from inside.

There were two successive gates to the entrance, each with its own detail of guards, who made a great show of coming to attention and saluting as Bildirjian, with Arden on his arm, passed them. Petropoulos trailed along behind, the Turkish commandant apparently unaware of him. Once they were inside the open central compound of the prison, Bildirjian stopped and turned.

"As you can see," he said to Petropoulos, "the woman is well guarded here." He laughed, pleased with his joke. "You will remain here with the guards."

Petropoulos darted a glance at Arden, and she could see the warning in his eyes, the reminder that it was now up to her. She turned away as he nodded to the Turk.

"I'll want her returned to me at dawn," he told Bildirjian.

The Turk nodded, agreeing to the arrangement. "My men will be told to admit you," he said.

Petropoulos turned away, moving back to the gates. He disappeared into the darkness, and the two thick metal gates were pulled closed and locked behind him.

As Arden watched him leave, a sinking feeling grew inside her. She turned and stared up at the grim-looking towers, wondering in which one her father was imprisoned.

And then Bildirjian had his hand on her arm and was leading her away from the open space and into a narrow passage in one of the towers. She realized he was hurrying, eager for his night to begin. She was forced nearly to

320

run to keep up with him. She wondered if Bildirjian would simply drag her if she were to balk.

When he reached the door leading into the tower, however, he turned to her. Realizing she was flushed with the run, he seemed genuinely surprised.

"Is something wrong, my dear?" he asked.

She shook her head and smiled at him seductively. She wondered if he would think the flush came from the prospect of spending the night with him.

"I have never before been inside a prison, Commandant," she told him.

He nodded, willing to accept the explanation. "Certainly, my dear. But come . . . soon you will forget all that."

He pulled the door open and led her into a narrow corridor, brightly lit with half a dozen lamps and ending with a set of stone steps. He waved Arden ahead of him, and she began to climb.

The flight was a fairly long one and windowless. Arden could hear the distant sound of waves against rocks and realized this was the long, empty wall that faced the sea. She climbed quickly, delighted to hear Bildirjian huffing and straining as he hurried after her.

"Ah, here we are," he said when they reached the landing. He opened the single door and stood aside to let her enter. "*Hos geldanese,*" he said. "Welcome."

Arden almost laughed. Here, inside this huge pile of stone at the water's edge, Bildirjian had managed to create a den that could be compared only to a desert pasha's tent. The stone was covered with canvas, even the ceilings, and the light flickered from a dozen brass lamps suspended from above. The floors were covered with rugs, an endless number of them, one thrown haphazardly on top of another, a welter of sizes and colors and designs. A large pillow-covered divan was drawn up against the wall, and there were more piles of pillows placed haphazardly. On the far side of the room was a single narrow window overlooking the wharves and the town.

Bildirjian bustled in behind her.

"What do you think, my dear?" he asked, obviously expecting praise. "Hardly a dull stone prison, this, eh?"

Arden composed her expression and turned to face him. "It's quite," she hesitated, searching for the right word, "absolutely breathtaking," she offered with what she hoped was acceptable enthusiasm.

He seemed pleased enough with that. "Make yourself comfortable," he said, then shouted for his orderly.

Arden shuddered when the man appeared. Petropoulos hadn't told her to expect an orderly, hadn't told her she would be forced to deal with two men, not one.

The orderly was a small man with a narrow mustache and small, round eyes which he seemed unable to remove from their consideration of her breasts. She turned away from him and moved into the room, wanting only to get away from his eyes. Bildirjian spoke to him rapidly, barking out his words harshly, and the man hurried off, disappearing as quickly as he had appeared.

Bildirjian turned back to her once the orderly had left them alone.

"I've sent him for some cognac and some food. I noticed you hardly touched your dinner, not that I blame you. The food at that *taverna* is not fit for animals, and certainly not for so lovely a creature as yourself."

"How kind of you, Commandant," she replied. The thought of food at that moment set her stomach heaving, and she had to force herself to smile back at him.

"Please, you must not be so formal, my dear. You must call me Soltan." He crossed to her, standing behind her and putting his hands to her shoulders. "Let me take your wrap."

322

Arden smiled at him, but she put her hands to the cape, holding it firmly where it was, not ready yet to relinquish it or the small protection it provided her.

"If you don't mind, Soltan," she said, and smiled at him as she used his name, "the night air has chilled me. Perhaps a bit of the cognac you mentioned?"

"Certainly, my dear, certainly," he replied.

He spoke with his lips close to her. Arden could feel the heat of his breath against her neck. It began to grow warmer, and she realized he was leaning forward to her, intent on pressing his lips to her neck.

She took a step away from him. He reluctantly released her, but Arden had no thought that he would let her cling to her cape for very long. She knew he would expect her to provide him with the services for which he had paid, and that would require not only the removal of the cape, but the remainder of her clothing as well.

He shed his own jacket, and then settled himself on the divan, looking up at her as he sat.

"Will you not join me, my dear?" he asked, patting the heap of pillows beside him.

She smiled at him as she began to cross the room to him, wondering how she would do this, how she would keep herself from cringing from him with revulsion when he touched her. He reached up to her as she neared the divan and grasped her hands in his. Arden felt herself trembling inside as he pulled her down and she seated herself beside him.

She was allowed a short reprieve, however, as the orderly once again entered the room, this time bearing a huge tray. Bildirjian released her hands and motioned to the orderly to set the tray down on a table in front of the divan. Arden used the opportunity to inch herself away from him.

When the tray had been safely delivered, Bildirjian bellowed his dismissal at the orderly, and the man fled, obviously well aware of what his superior would do were he to long interrupt the evening. When he was gone, Bildirjian turned back to Arden.

Before he could touch her, she slipped off the divan and knelt in front of the low table on which the tray had been set. She lifted the bottle of cognac.

"May I pour for you, Soltan?" she asked in a throaty whisper.

He seemed pleased at the prospect. "Please, my dear," he replied.

She uncorked the bottle, filled the two glasses, and returned the bottle to the tray. Then she lifted one of the glasses, pressed her lips to it, and handed it to him.

He took the glass from her and reached for her, but she drew back just enough to be beyond his grasp as she took her own glass. She considered the amber liquid, then set it gently swirling in the glass.

He leaned forward, considering the distance she had managed to keep between them. His eyes narrowed, and he seemed to be skirting the edge of anger, but she smiled at him and raised her glass.

"To a memorable evening," she said, hoping as she made the toast that she would be able to look back on this night and remember it as the night she had helped to free her father from prison.

He nodded. "A memorable evening," he repeated, thinking, no doubt, she meant something entirely different.

He raised his glass to his lips and quickly emptied it of its contents. Arden lifted her glass, touching the cognac to her lips, wetting them with the liquid but only pretending to drink. All the while she kept her eyes on his, aware of the heat she saw in them, and the hunger. What she saw sent a shiver along her spine.

When she lowered the glass, she realized she had

avoided him for as long as he would allow.

He leaned forward, dropped his glass onto the tray, then reached for her, putting his hands to her shoulders.

"Surely you are warm enough now, my dear," he said as he pulled away the cape, "to do without this." A lecherous grin spread across his lips. "If not, I am sure I can remedy the situation."

He pushed the cape down, off her shoulders, and Arden let it fall to the floor. She held herself still, not daring to move, afraid that if she did, she would bolt for the door.

He seemed unaware of her lack of enthusiasm, his attention instead on what the removal of the cape revealed to his view. He was obviously more than pleased.

Arden felt his hands on her arms, lifting her, pulling her to the place on the divan beside him. She forced herself to smile at him, but when he leaned forward to her, she lifted the glass that she still held. Her hand trembled as she raised it, and a few drops of the amber liquid fell, one spotting the skirt of her dress, the rest splattering on the naked skin exposed by the décolletage of the dress. He eyed her as she raised the glass to her lips, but then his eyes fell to the fallen drops on her cleavage.

When she lowered the glass from her lips, he reached for it, taking it from her still trembling hand and putting it on the floor beside his feet. Then he leaned forward to her, pressing his lips to the fallen droplets and hungrily licking them up.

Arden closed her eyes and told herself he was not touching her, that it was just flesh he held and not really her. She told herself that if she kept herself apart, it didn't matter what happened in that room between them, that he could only touch that part of her she allowed him to touch.

325

And then he was putting his hands to her shoulders and pushing her backward and down to the pillows of the divan. And despite the things she had told herself, she still could feel his lips and his tongue and the anxious heat of his breath against her breast.

A sudden panic seized her and she put her hands to his shoulders, pushing against him with all her might. He seemed to ignore her, but she squirmed against his grasp, and he finally released her and sat back.

"What game is this?" he demanded.

She could see the sharp anger in his eyes. For a moment she felt herself freeze in fear, both for what he might do to her were he to become angry with her, and for the consequences to her father were she to fail. But it eased quickly, a fact which completely mystified her. She realized that she would be a victim only if she allowed him to make her one. She determined not to allow it to happen.

She pulled away from him and stood. But she smiled at him.

"There is no need to crush my gown," she told him. "Surely we can arrange matters so that will not be necessary."

She raised her hands to the buttons of her bodice and began slowly to unfasten them. She watched him, watched the way his eyes stared hungrily at the pale flesh the unfastened buttons revealed.

This, then, seemed to satisfy him for the moment, and he leaned back against the pillows and watched her slowly remove her clothing for him, prepared to accept this as part of the entertainment for which he had so handsomely paid.

"*Melahat*," he whispered.

She shook her head. "I don't understand," she replied with a breathy smile.

"*Melahat*," he repeated, his eyes following the slow

progress of her fingers with the buttons and the revelations it provided of what lay beneath the fabric of the gown. "It means 'beauty'." He drew in his breath in a great, hungry sigh. "You are a beauty."

Arden had freed the last of the buttons, and she slowly pulled away the bodice of the garish gown, presenting herself to him with deliberately provocative movements as she pushed the fabric down, first to her waist, and then over her hips. She let it fall to the floor so she seemed to be standing in a small pool of red and black, bared now, except for the laced trimmed corset and stockings.

He reached out a hand, intending to touch her, to pull her to him, but she deftly stepped out of the circle of her dress, using the movement to step back, until she was standing by the table.

"Now," she said, as she bent down to the table, letting him satisfy himself with the view she provided of her nearly naked breasts, "shall we finish our cognac, Soltan?"

She grasped the bottle and his glass, walking forward to him as she refilled it, glad to see he leaned back once again and accepted the offering of the liquor from her with no further indication of rushing matters to their inevitable conclusion. It seemed he had resigned himself to the fact that she had decided to seduce him. He gave every indication that he was perfectly satisfied with that prospect.

He seemed incapable of lifting his eyes from her, of thinking about anything except what she seemed willing to do for him. Arden smiled at him as she climbed up beside him on the divan, kneeling on a heap of pillows at his side and watching him empty the second glass of cognac as quickly as he had emptied the first.

She took the emptied glass from him, refilled it, and pretended to drink from it. She licked her lips, letting her tongue linger against them for a long, expectant moment

327

before she leaned forward over him and held the glass to his lips.

He drank yet again, but this time only a swallow. Then he pushed the glass away and reached out for her, his hands hot and anxious on her back and moving hungrily downward to her haunches.

Arden smiled at him as she slowly permitted him to pull her to him.

Chapter Eighteen

Arden could feel his hands, hot and anxious against her skin, and his lips hungrily seeking the warmth of her breasts. She closed her eyes as she allowed him to pull her down on top of him, telling herself as she had before that it was just flesh he touched, that he couldn't really touch that part of her she kept apart and clean from him if she did not allow it to happen.

But after a moment she opened her eyes and looked down at him, assuring herself that he was completely engrossed in his exploration. Then she carefully raised the hand that still held the bottle of cognac, keeping it out of his sight until she brought it down with all her strength, letting it strike his head.

He cried out, and his eyes looked up at her, for an instant round and wide with surprise. Then his hands dropped away from her to fall at his sides and his eyes fluttered closed. Arden pulled herself away from him, filled with disgust, disgust both for him and for what she had done.

She scrambled off the divan and stood, staring at him and listening to the thick thud of her heartbeat. There was a thin trickle of blood on his forehead and a dark red mark where he'd been struck. She glanced down at her shaking hands and saw she was still holding the bottle. It felt suddenly hot in her hands, as though the heavy glass was burning her fingers. She released her hold, letting it fall from her hand to the floor. The contents, what little remained, dribbled out and formed a damp puddle on the rug near her feet. The smell of the alcohol filled the air around her. The air was suddenly so thick with it her stomach began to heave.

She found herself rooted, staring at the Turk's still body, wondering if she had committed murder. Part of her said that if it was so, it had been necessary, but she could not quiet the voice inside her that insisted it was wrong, that she had no right to take a life. As much as she wanted to, she found herself unable to put her hand to his neck to see if there was still a pulse. Better, she told herself, to think he might still be alive than to know for certain she'd killed him.

She had no idea how long she stood staring at him, but eventually she shook herself and stepped back from the divan. It has only just begun, she told herself firmly. There was still a great deal to do.

She hurriedly lifted the clothing she'd left scattered on the floor and pulled it on, haphazardly fastening the buttons of the bodice. Her hands were still trembling, and she was far too frightened and nervous to notice that she mismatched several buttons in her haste. She only knew she had to get out of that room, away from the still body lying on the divan.

Finally dressed, she snatched up the cape and ran to the door.

She listened for a second, and then, satisfied there was no sound in the corridor, pulled open the door. She stood for a second and darted a quick glance along the hallway. A wave of relief filled her as she realized the way was empty. She stepped out and pulled the door closed behind her.

Lifting a lantern from its peg on the wall as she passed, Arden hurried to the narrow stairs at the end of the corridor. It was dark, and she held the lantern high, peering into the slim glimmer of light.

As she climbed, she silently repeated the instructions Petropoulos had given her: get to the roof of the commandant's tower. It will be unguarded, as it faces the sea. She prayed he was right. If not, she might well step out and find herself facing the barrel of a rifle.

The flight ended abruptly, with a heavy batten door that was barred with a thick wooden bar held in place with rusted metal brackets. That heartened her somewhat: if there were guards on the roof, it made no sense that their way out would be barred . . . unless, a nagging voice warned her, there was another way down from the tower.

She was forced to put down the cape and the lantern on the stair so that she could draw back the bar. The wood was rough and heavy, and it took all her strength to lift it. It made a dull, scratching sound as she pushed against it, a sound that seemed frighteningly loud, echoing down the narrow staircase and into the corridor beyond. She was sure the orderly would hear, sure he would alert the guards and send them to investigate. Her hands shook as she drew the bar away.

She stopped to listen for sounds of someone following and was rewarded only with the thick thud of her own heartbeat. She heaved a sigh of relief, gathered up the cape and the lantern, and pushed open the door.

She peered into the darkness. As Petropoulos had said, the roof of this tower facing the sea was unguarded. She stepped out onto the roof and drew the door closed. Then she crossed to the tower's edge, peering down when she'd reached the waist-high wall that surrounded it. There was the noise of the waves as they slammed angrily against the rocks far below. She could see nothing but darkness.

She dropped the lantern at her feet, then knelt with the cape in her hands. It only took her a few seconds to find the small hole in the lining, and she put her hands to it and pulled, splitting the fabric until she'd made a tear several inches long. She put her hand inside, pulled out a thin rope, and continued to pull until finally a small heap of the stuff lay in front of her. She found one of the ends and tied it to her wrist. Then she stood.

She looked over the wall a second time, searching for the narrow strip of beach by the prison wall. She could see nothing but blackness, and she felt the first stab of doubt, the fear that she might be alone, that no one had come as Petropoulos had promised they would. She imagined herself left to the mercies of Bildirjian or whoever found him. The prospect of dying in this horrible place grew all too real.

Her hands were shaking as she lifted the lantern, once, twice, then three times, the signal Petropoulos had given her. Then she lifted the heap of rope and threw it over the side.

The rope made a thick, dull sound as it struck the rock of the wall when it fell. This too, frightened Arden, made her fear someone would hear the noise and wonder what had caused it. But the silence that followed frightened her even more: it seemed to last forever.

She huddled down against the wall, shivering in the night chill off the water, her free hand on the end of the rope she'd tied to her wrist, waiting for something to happen. But the silence seemed to go on forever, and there was no tug on the rope, no sign of the response that Petropoulos had promised.

It seemed a lifetime that she knelt there in the darkness, clinging to the stone of the wall, waiting for the sound of footsteps on the stairs, for soldiers to suddenly burst out and find her there. When finally she felt the sharp tug she nearly shouted in relief to know she was not abandoned, that she would not have to face those soldiers alone.

She stood and began to pull up the rope. It was heavy now, far heavier than it had been when it had been coiled up and hidden inside her cape. And the more of it she pulled up, the heavier it became. When she heard the first sound of metal scraping against the stone, she leaned forward over the wall, holding the rope as far from her as possible, and continued to draw it up. By the time she'd come to its end and held the grappling hook in her hands, her arms were aching with the effort.

It was just as Petropoulos had promised—a thick rope, nearly three times the width of the narrow one she'd thrown down, was securely fastened to the hook and now trailed down the steep wall of the prison.

She fixed the grappling hook on the side of the wall, then tugged at the rope, telling those below that it was set. There was an answering tug, and then the rope stiffened.

She peered down, trying to see the men climbing, trying to urge them on, to hurry them with her thoughts. But there still seemed to be nothing except the darkness below, and she had to force away the thought that Petropoulos's men had somehow been caught, that it was Turkish soldiers who were making their way up the wall.

When the first man finally became visible to her as he neared the top of the wall, he seemed nothing more than a shadow clinging to the rope in the darkness. She wondered how he'd managed to climb that way, how he'd held onto the rope and dangled there in the night blackness, how he'd managed to keep from falling to his death on the rocks below. Her heart seemed to stop as he made his way slowly upward.

And then there was a hand reaching up to the top of the wall. Arden stepped back, leaving room, watching him swing himself up onto the wall and then over. Her heart

333

seemed to stop as she saw him in the dim light of the lantern, and she recognized the uniform of a Turkish soldier.

She put her hand to her mouth as a thin scream rose in her throat.

He looked at her, then rushed over and put his hand to her mouth, stifling the scream.

"It's me, Arden," Sky whispered.

She sighed with relief, then nodded, and he released her. He considered her for a moment, then turned away, helping the man who had been behind him on the rope over the wall, taking the second hook the man carried and fixing it against the wall so that there were now two ropes that could be climbed.

Arden kept her eyes on them, feeling herself slowly growing steady again. She couldn't allow herself to become so fearful again, she told herself. She had nearly given them away. Had Sky not stopped her, had she let the cry escape her, the guards would certainly have heard it.

And she had known: Petropoulos had warned her that his men would be dressed as Turkish soldiers. She had cringed at the words when he'd told her, wondering how the soldiers to whom those uniforms had once belonged had died so that they might be used by the Cretan separatists. Not for the first time she had wondered if she had traded her soul to the devil for her father's life. It had seemed a necessary trade at the time. She only hoped the price would not be greater than what she was prepared to pay.

At that moment, however, she told herself she could not allow herself to panic. She'd known about the uniforms, and had no real excuse for nearly calling down the guards on them by crying out. She still could ruin them all if she was not careful.

There were soon half a dozen men on the tower roof, all moving silently, stealthily in the darkness. One took the lantern Arden had brought, and she made out his features, realized it was Petropoulos. He nodded at her curtly. She wondered if he was aware of the mistake she'd nearly made, if he no longer trusted her.

Petropoulos led the way to the stairs, and the others began to follow. She watched them with a feeling of remoteness. She began to feel as though she lacked the strength to go on with them.

And then there was a hand on her arm.

"It's almost done, Arden," Sky whispered to her.

She nodded, grateful for his words and his touch. Together they followed the others.

They crept down the stairs, taking care to make as little noise as possible. Petropoulos extinguished the lantern and left it in the dark stairwell as they approached the lighted corridor where Bildirjian's apartment was. He stood aside, motioning to Arden to show them the way.

She glanced up at Sky, aware of his eyes on her, staring not at her face, but at the front of her dress. It was only then that she noticed the buttons that she'd fastened crookedly in her haste. She turned away from him, her hands automatically righting the buttons as she made her way to the front of the group of men.

Her mind filled with what she knew Sky must be thinking at that moment, with the contemplation of just what favors Bildirjian had enjoyed before she'd managed to get away from him. She saw herself as Sky must see her, as a whore, perhaps even a murdering whore. She felt herself awash in a wave of self-revulsion.

She reached Petropoulos's side and pointed to the end of the corridor. She started forward, to the lit stairwell

335

leading down to the courtyard, showing him the way. He nodded and started after her.

As she reached the head of the flight of stairs, she thought of how she'd been amused by the sound of Bildirjian as he had heaved his way up them at her heels, breathless with anticipation, only an hour or so earlier. The thought made her cringe now.

When they finally stood at the foot of the stairs, Petropoulos motioned her once more to the rear of the group. He put his hand to the door and cautiously drew it open. The courtyard was silently still, and they filed out, keeping to the shadows.

The guards at the far end of the courtyard by the prison gates gave no indication that they noticed them. Those who were on duty continued to peer out into the darkness outside the prison walls. The guards not on duty either slept or sat gambling at a table they had set up in front of their quarters.

Arden couldn't believe it was so easy, that they were simply going to walk into the prison proper and free her father without so much as a challenge. The courtyard remained still and silent as they reached the entrance to the first of the two large towers where prisoners were kept. No one turned, no one called out to them.

They climbed another flight of stone stairs, this one well lit but bearing evidence of a good deal more wear than the one that led to the interior of the commandant's tower. It wasn't long before they were standing at the far end of a long corridor lined with barred cells and murkily lit with only a few lanterns.

A guard sat at the far end, his attention on a plate of food on the small table in front of him.

Arden felt a hand on her arm as Sky pulled her out of the lamplight and into the shadows, out of the guard's view. He moved in front of her, covering her with his

336

body just as the guard looked up and saw the group of apparent soldiers at the end of the hall.

"What is it now?" he demanded, obviously less than pleased that his meal was being disturbed. He stood and peered at them, trying to make them out in the dim light. "Can't a man eat in peace?"

Petropoulos stepped forward.

"I have orders to bring a prisoner named Constatin to the commandant," he said.

The guard shook his head. "There's no Constatin in this block," he replied.

Petropoulos started forward, moving along the corridor toward him.

"Are you sure?" he asked. "I was told he was. I have the order right here." He put his hand into his breast pocket.

"Of course, I'm sure," the guard replied. He reseated himself and turned his attention back to his food. "Your orders are wrong."

Petropoulos was now standing beside him. "We all know orders are never wrong," he said, smiling down at the guard.

The guard looked up at him, for the first time really examining his face. His expression grew suspicious.

"Who are you?" he demanded. "I don't know you."

His hand reached to the pistol he wore holstered at his side.

Arden peered out at him from the shadows, sure they were all about to die.

The guard's suspicion came too late. Petropoulos slid behind him, moving quickly, reaching with one hand to grasp his chin, with the other for the knife he had hidden in the sheath inside his jacket. There was only an instant

337

as the guard recognized the danger, and then the knife was drawn across his throat.

Petropoulos released him, letting him slump forward over the table. Arden realized she was shaking as she watched the grisly scene, as she watched the body twitch in the guard's death agony and heard the dull gurgle of the blood seeping from his throat. She stared numbly at the bright red that slowly spread out on the rough wooden table, unable to move despite the fact that Petropoulos's men were moving forward, along the corridor, staring into the cells.

"Spiros?"

Petropoulos turned to a man who stood clinging to the bars of his cell and staring out at him. He was ragged and thin, and a thick uneven beard covered the lower half of his face. Petropoulos stared at him uncertainly for a moment, then smiled.

"Did you think we'd forgotten you, Achilles?" he asked.

He began to rifle through the guard's pockets and quickly drew out a key ring. He threw it to one of his men, who opened the door of the filthy cell Achilles occupied, embracing him as he stumbled out of it, then moved on to open the doors of the other cells.

Achilles stood, staring at Petropoulos.

"I was beginning to wonder," he replied softly. "We were all beginning to wonder."

Petropoulos approached him. "We tried before," he said.

"I know," Achilles replied. "We mourned those who died for us."

The two men stood facing one another for a moment longer, and then Petropoulos crossed to the other and embraced him.

"Brother," he murmured in pained relief.

Sky moved forward, and Arden trailed along behind him. He stood at Petropoulos's side, glaring with rage.

"You let your own brother rot here?" he hissed in anger. He nodded toward Arden. "You let her risk her life for you when you were too much of a coward to do it yourself?"

Petropoulos colored but said nothing.

"Sky." Arden put her hand on his arm. "It doesn't matter. Papa is all that matters."

Sky stared at Petropoulos, but managed to swallow his anger. He turned to Achilles.

"A man named Devereaux—he was brought here with a friend of yours, Nikolas Constatin, and the monks from Haghios Nicodemos."

Achilles was staring at Arden with a look of disbelief on his face.

Sky put his hand on his arm and shook it.

"Do you hear me?" he demanded. "Devereaux . . . the monks from Haghios Nicodemos."

Achilles nodded, then smiled at Arden. "You will excuse me, please, *Despinis,*" he said. "It has been a very long time since I have seen a woman, any woman. And now to see an angel in this place, it has unsettled me."

"Have you any idea where they might be holding my father?" she asked him. "They brought him here with the monks."

"I know of no one by the name of Devereaux," he replied. "But they brought the monks here. They're being held in the other tower."

"But my father . . ." Arden protested.

"Might be among them," Achilles interjected. "One man in a robe looks much like another." He looked up at Petropoulos. "Did you say they had Constatin as well?"

Petropoulos nodded.

"Then the monks may have disguised them," Achilles said.

"You know a good deal for a man in a cell," Sky told him, his tone arch.

Achilles smiled. For all the time he had spent in the filthy cell, he gave no indication he was cowed. He moved to the door of the cell and tapped against it rhythmically.

"A man can say a great deal without speaking any words," he explained. He turned to his brother and his expression grew suddenly sober. "It won't be easy. The guards' quarters are beside the entrance to the tower."

"I don't suppose you have an idea?" Petropoulos suggested with a smile.

Achilles grinned. "You know me well, brother." He turned back to Arden. "I've had little else to think about," he explained, "than finding a way to escape, should the opportunity arise." He turned to one of the other prisoners who had been released. "You, Petro, take the keys and four men and see how many others you can release. When it's done, go to the cellars. You know what to do." He was in charge, obviously the first leader of the separatists, obviously still in the habit of commanding others.

Petro nodded, collected the keys, and nodded to four others, motioning to them to follow him.

"Now," Achilles said, and he rubbed his hands together with obvious pleasure at being once again in the midst of some action, "let's see what we can do about freeing some holy men."

They were following Achilles down a flight of stairs into what appeared to be complete blackness. The single lantern sent out a feeble glow that barely managed to light the way a few feet beyond them. The darkness seemed to drink in the dull glow and swallow it.

"We'll be directly below the guards' quarters," Achilles warned them. "No noise at all from here on."

He finished speaking and turned to move forward without waiting for a response from the others, assuming they would do as he'd told them.

Arden clung to Sky's arm. She found the further she walked into the darkness, the stronger her fears grew. Shadows rose up out of the darkness, threatening, frightening.

"What if he's not here?" she whispered to Sky. "What if they haven't brought him here with the rest?"

He had no answer for her, nor did she really expect one. But he put his hand around her waist, holding her close, and she found the contact comforting despite the doubts that plagued her.

"Shh!"

The reprimand came from Petropoulos, and Arden cringed at the sound of it. If Petropoulos had only used her to free his brother, if indeed her father was not imprisoned in Bodrum as well, he might very well decide her usefulness had come to end. She wondered just how ruthless the Cretan was, if he'd merely kill her and Sky to be rid of them if that act suited his purpose.

They must be, she realized, in the cellars to the old fort. The air was dark and thick with damp, and there was the scent of rot about it. She wondered what she would see if there was more light than the thin fingers that extended from the single lantern, wondered what sort of hideous instruments of torture were hidden here and what vile creatures took their refuge in the unremitting darkness.

Something brushed against her cheek, and she put her hand to her mouth to keep herself from screaming in fear. She drew back in sudden terror, nearly falling as she tried to back away from whatever had reached out for her in the darkness. Had Sky not been beside her, had he

341

not had his hand on her waist, she would surely have fallen to the filth of the floor.

He drew her close to him, steadying her, brushing away the cloud of spiderwebs that clung to her cheek and her hair. She forced herself to swallow the panic, knowing she must not give in to it.

She nodded her thanks to him and they started forward again, after the others. Arden thought with horror what it would be like to be left behind in this awful place. It would be like being left alive in a tomb, she thought.

It seemed an eternity there in the near absolute darkness. They moved slowly, carefully, taking great pains not to bump into any of the objects that littered the place, crates mostly, large and dark in the shadows. They all knew they could not afford to make any noise that could be heard in the guards' quarters above. It seemed to Arden that they had been walking through the darkness forever, and that they would never leave it.

Finally Achilles led them to a flight of stone steps and they once again began to climb. There was a moment of near terror as Arden found herself behind a shut door and there were sounds coming from the other side, voices of the guards whose quarters they were skirting. But the door stayed firmly closed as they crept silently past it, and eventually Arden felt her heart steadying itself inside her.

And then they were climbing again until they found themselves on a landing beside another of the stone cells like that from which they'd freed Achilles and his men. Arden couldn't help but peer into the cell through a narrow slit in the wall. A half dozen men were inside, lying on the floor or sitting with their backs against the wall. The dark robes they wore were wrinkled and spotted with dirt, and there were dark bruises on their cheeks and eyes and occasional bloody gashes. Their expressions were dull and glazed. None moved, none lifted his eyes to meet hers. As she peered from face to face, Arden found herself dreading the thought that one of these men might be her father.

But none was. Petropoulos moved forward, darting a glance into the corridor beyond, and a moment later rejoined them.

"There are no guards," he announced as he motioned the others forward. "They've left the prisoners alone for the night."

Achilles and the others followed, but Sky seemed uncertain.

"It's too easy," he muttered. "It shouldn't be this easy."

Despite his reluctance to release her, Arden bolted forward, staring into the cells that lined the long central corridor as Achilles and Petropoulos prowled about in search of keys with which to open the cell doors.

The occupants of the next three cells were identical to those she had seen in the first she'd looked into, all glassy eyed and nearly indifferent to the sight of a woman staring in on them from the narrow windows in the cell doors. She moved on to the next, aware of a feeling of dread that had begun to grow inside her. She almost had to force herself to look in on the occupants of the next cell.

When she did she almost couldn't believe her eyes: he was sitting in the corner, staring dully at the wall. He was wearing a monk's robes, and his spectacles had disappeared, but it was her father.

"Papa," she breathed, almost unable to speak for the lump in her throat.

She could see the bruises on his cheeks, and there was a bloody cut on his lower lip.

He stirred and looked up at her. There was fear in his eyes.

"Arden?" he mouthed, but no sound came from his lips.

Then he scrambled to his feet, nearly tripping over the

343

legs of the others in his haste. He was breathless as he fell against the door. His hands grasping the bars in the windows, and he stared out at her.

"Oh, Papa," she murmured.

"Get out of here, Arden," he whispered, his voice hoarse with emotion. "Get out before it's too late!"

It was the fact that there were no guards that galvanized Sky. He could accept the possibility that luck might have accounted for their having made it so far without encountering any resistance, but it seemed impossible to him that all those cells filled with prisoners had been simply left unguarded.

He realized it was fruitless to try to get Arden away. She was intently peering into the cells, searching for Forbes, and there was absolutely no possibility that she might allow him to draw her away before she'd made a thorough search. But he also realized that they were in a very vulnerable position, that they would be taken all too easily if somehow the Turks had been warned, if they were waiting to spring a trap.

He darted another glance at Arden and then quickly returned to the stairwell, taking the steps three at a time until he was once again behind the door that led to the guard's quarters. He heard noises there, the sharp tap of boots against the floor, the low sounds of orders being hoarsely whispered. They were definitely not the sounds he would have expected to come from quarters where the men were turning in for the night.

He backed away, down the first few steps that led back to the cellars. He realized it would be nothing less than folly to try to warn Petropoulos and the others. All he would be doing was giving the Turks another prisoner and eliminating any possibility they might have of getting away.

344

Instead he concentrated on what he had seen in the cellars. There had been the dim forms of crates and casks in the darkness, of that he was certain. That meant the area below was being prudently used for storage. He prayed he wasn't wrong as to what they contained.

There was a noise behind him, and he pressed himself into the shadows as the door from the guard's billet was drawn open. He darted a quick glance and saw the first of the guards file out of the barracks and start up the stairs.

There was no more time to lose, he realized, as he darted down the steps into the cellars. If there was to be any hope for any of them to escape, he had to act quickly.

Arden stared at Forbes in disbelief.

"We've come to get you, Papa," she told him. "To get you out of here. It will be only a few minutes. Petropoulos will find the keys and we'll get you out of this terrible place."

Forbes shook his head. "No," he croaked and stared out, craning his neck to peer to the end of the corridor. "There's no time. You have to go—*now*."

Arden stared at him in disbelief. Could this be her father, she wondered, the man who was always so sure of himself, so confident? It seemed as though a stranger had invaded her father's body, a frightened, anxious stranger. Surely this couldn't be Forbes.

"What have they done to you, Papa?" she asked, her voice low and mournful. She was on the edge of tears.

He looked back to her face and his expression grew cross as he realized she had made no move to leave.

"Get out, Arden," he hissed at her. "Before they have you, too."

"It's too late for that, I'm afraid."

Arden turned to the corridor and froze. Commandant Soltan Muhammad Bildirjian stood at the end of it, staring along its length at her. There was still blood on his forehead, and a huge, red bruise. But none of that was nearly so frightening as the angry look of hatred in his eyes.

There was a moment of shuffling indecision as Petropoulos and his men stared, then started for the far end of the corridor. But this way, too, they soon found was blocked.

Soldiers poured into the corridor, rifles raised and aimed. They were trapped.

Despite the movement around her, Arden was rooted, unable to move. She darted a second look at Bildirjian, but her gaze drifted to the man who was moving through the group of soldiers behind him until he stood at the commandant's side. He returned her stare in silence.

Then he smiled at her.

"Hello, Arden," he said with obvious pleasure in his voice.

Arden swallowed, then managed to find her tongue.

"David?" she murmured in disbelief.

Chapter Nineteen

"*David?*"

There was confusion in Arden's voice, and dismay. She couldn't understand how he'd come to be there, and for some reason it frightened her. But what was even more terrifying was that he seemed completely at his ease among the Turkish soldiers, that Bildirjian seemed to treat him as a comrade.

"Drop your weapons," Bildirjian shouted at Petropoulos and his men. "Immediately! You have exactly ten seconds until I give the order to my men to shoot you down."

Petropoulos had little time to hesitate. He nodded to his men as he withdrew his pistol from its holster and let it fall to the floor. The others followed suit.

Bildirjian smiled, pleased with the situation, as the soldiers stepped forward to gather up the weapons and roughly take hold of the Cretans.

"I think," Bildirjian said to Petropoulos, "you will be a very useful guest."

Petropoulos cocked a brow skeptically.

"I think you can give me some information," Bildirjian told him.

Petropoulos's eyes narrowed. "I know nothing," he said.

The commandant nodded and walked forward, stopping at Arden's side. "I know," he said. "You are simply a poor, struggling procurer, seeking a customer to whom you might peddle a little pale flesh." He touched his hand to Arden's cheek. "But there is a reward for the man who set the bomb at Mallia, and I mean to have it. I know he was taken along with the rest at Haghios Nicodemos. So far these foolish monks have not proved cooperative, and my men seem to dislike dealing with them in the usual manner." He looked at Arden, then back at Petropoulos, and his eyes grew hard. "You, I think, will not make them quite so squeamish. In fact, I am sure they will be quite pleased with the opportunity to work on a Cretan who walks in here wearing one of their own uniforms. One way or another, I assure you, you will be happy to tell me which of these monks is not really a man of God." He clasped Arden's cheeks and pressed them, pulling her face up so that she was looking at him. "Don't you think your friend here will be willing to tell me who set that bomb?"

She said nothing, and he dropped his hand. Two red marks remained on her cheeks from the pressure of his fingers.

"Put them in a cell," Bildirjian ordered his soldiers. "I'll deal with them in the morning." The soldiers herded the Cretans toward a cell at the far end of the corridor. Bildirjian turned back to Arden. "For now, you and I have unfinished business, my dear," he told her.

In panic, she let her eyes drift to David's. He was standing behind the Turkish commandant, staring at her, considering the fear he saw in her eyes.

"David?" she whispered, her tone pleading.

Bildirjian turned to him. "I promised you a few moments with her first," he said. "Take them."

David took her arm and pulled her to the far side of the

corridor. He looked down at her, at the whore's dress she was wearing, and smiled.

"I see you're now dressing the part, Arden," he said in a vicious tone.

She ignored the anger she saw in his eyes. "What's happening, David?" she asked him.

"I would think that's more than obvious," he told her. "You and your friends are being imprisoned for attempting to release unlawfully men detained by the Turkish government. And I am earning myself a powerful friend."

She shook her head. "How? Why?"

"Did you think I'd let you ruin my career?" he hissed at her. "Wasn't it enough for you that you went off after that filthy reporter, turning your back on me as though I were nothing, nobody? Hadn't you taken enough without leaving me to carry the blame, to have the authorities ban me from my work?"

"Your career?" she repeated in a numbed voice as she slowly began to understand what it was he was telling her. "You gave us up to the Turks for the sake of your career?"

He shook his head and smiled at her, a cruel, humorless smile.

"For that and for the pleasure of contemplating what little joy Trask will have of you when the commandant is done with you. That is, if he lives long enough. I think our friend Bildirjian has some special plans for him as well."

She couldn't believe the words he was saying, couldn't believe the look of satisfaction that filled his eyes as he spoke them.

"Monster," she hissed. Nothing else seemed appropriate.

And then she thought about Sky. She didn't remember

having seen the guards take him away with Petropoulos and the rest of his men. For a second she was filled with a pale hope that somehow he'd managed to get away, that his death, at least, would not be on her conscience as well. But then she realized she'd been so dazed by the sight of David standing at Bildirjian's side, she really couldn't be sure if he'd been shoved into one of the cells along with the rest.

She turned and darted a look at the cell door, now firmly shut and locked, wondering if Sky was there with the rest. But she didn't have long to consider the matter.

David put his hand on her shoulder and pushed her roughly toward Bildirjian, who waited with obvious impatience for David to be done with her.

"Here's your whore, commandant," David said in a vicious tone. "Enjoy her."

Sky fumbled for a few moments in the darkness, the beginnings of a plan forming in his mind. He told himself that he was no tactician, that he wrote about wars, that he did not participate in them, and that he was not even remotely suited for what he was about to try to do. Still, he knew he had no choice, not if he had any hope of freeing Arden and Forbes and the others.

Then he heard a sound and saw, as his eyes adjusted to the nearly nonexistent light, a half dozen shadows moving about among the crates.

"Petro," he called out softly, remembering that Achilles had sent one of the released prisoners to do something in the cellars and hoping it was that man.

The movement ceased suddenly and there was only silence to answer him.

"Petro," he called again, this time a bit louder. "I'm Trask. I'm with Petropoulos."

350

Again there was no answer, but there were noises, sounds and movement that told him he was being surrounded. He realized that if he had made a mistake, if it was not the man Petro, then he would probably soon be dead.

There was a sudden spark of light as a match was struck and a lantern lit. Sky found himself squinting into the unexpected glow.

The lantern was raised, spreading the light, and Sky recognized the man Achilles had called Petro standing only a few feet from him. He considered Sky in silence for a long moment, at first concentrating on the Turkish uniform and the holstered pistol, then staring at his face before he nodded.

"I remember you," he said. "Where are the others? Have they gotten out of the prison yet?"

"By now they're probably in the Turks' hands," Sky replied. "We have to find a way to get them out."

Petro shook his head. "No . . . it is not possible. There are too many of them. They will find soon that we are missing as well." He looked suddenly stricken, crushed, as though his last hope had been destroyed. "They'll come for us, too."

Sky darted a look around at the twenty or more men who were with Petro in the dark of the cellar. "Achilles told you to do something down here," he said. "What did he want you to do?"

Petro pointed to the heaps of crates littering the cellar floor.

"Supplies," he said. "And ammunition. For many years this place was a fort, and much was left here when they turned it into a prison. We were to set it afire, cause an explosion."

"Do you think the powder and ammunition are still good?" Sky asked.

351

Petro nodded. "They use it for target practice, and the occasional firing squad," he said grimly.

Sky smiled grimly. It was just as he'd hoped.

"Then an explosion should be as good a way to catch them off guard as any other," he said. He looked up at the wooden supports of ceiling which were old and brittle. "But not here," he said. "We could bring down the whole of the tower."

"Isn't that what we want to do?"

Sky nodded. "Eventually," he agreed. "But first we need some time to get Petropoulos and the rest out. We don't want to kill our own people." He pointed into the darkness at the far end of the cellar. "Does the cellar extend as far back as the other towers?"

Petro nodded. "Yes," he replied. "All the way to the commandant's tower. But the only access is here, the one that leads down from the guard's billet. And the one from the smaller tower, the one where we were held."

"Then we set our fire back there, beneath the commandant's tower," Sky told him. "We make the first explosion a small one, just enough to set the stores beneath the second tower afire. If we spread out the casks of ammunition in the second tower, the fire will spread slowly, setting off a series of small explosions as it works its way back here."

"There's no time," Petro told him. "They'll find the dead guard soon and then come looking for us."

"Then the sooner we get to work, the better," Sky told him grimly. "Tell the others what to do," he ordered. "Now."

Petro hesitated a moment longer, but he was a good soldier, accustomed to following orders. Petro called to the others, barking out orders to find barrels of ammunition and carry them to the far end of the cellar.

"*Ghlighora!*" Sky added. Quickly.

Sky heaved a barrel of ammunition to his shoulder and

led the way, aware of the ragtag group of men behind him following suit. This wouldn't be simple, he realized. These men were weakened by their stint in prison and no longer sure of themselves. And he could not help but think of Arden, and about what the commandant would do to her.

He had but this one chance to get her away from this place, and it was a poor chance at that. Still, if he did not succeed, he knew he would sooner die in the attempt rather than try to escape without her.

Sky knelt and stared at the makeshift fuse he'd manufactured out of rags and a little of the oil from the lantern. He wondered if it would work, if it would give them enough time, or even stay lit long enough to set fire to the ammunition crates. He turned to Petro.

"Once we get outside, you and your men stay hidden. The explosion should distract the guards long enough for you to get the gates open and get outside."

Petro nodded. "We'll make our way to the beach and wait for you and the others."

"There are a half dozen fishing craft pulled up on the beach. Get as many as you can into the water and make ready to sail." He looked at Petro thoughtfully. "I don't suppose you have any qualms about stealing a few fishing boats, do you?"

"I'd steal the milk from an orphan's cup to get out of this hellhole."

"If it looks like we aren't going to make it, don't try to be heroes. You might as well save yourselves."

Petro strared at Sky for a moment in silence, considering the import of his words. He wondered why this outsider should risk his own life to save his and those of his fellows.

"We'll make that decision when the time comes,"

Petro replied. "Are you sure you don't want any help?"

Sky shook his head. "I think it'll be easier if I'm alone," he said. "The uniform should buy me a little time, at least."

There seemed to be nothing left to say, and Sky carefully lit the end of the fuse, watching the damp rag sputter into smoky flame.

"Let's get out of here," he muttered as he pushed himself to his feet and started through the dim cellar toward the stone steps leading up to the guard's quarters.

Petro was at his heels, and the two of them found the other released prisoners at the foot of the stairs, waiting anxiously. Sky took the stairs first, leading the way up, assuring himself that there were no guards waiting for them.

When he found himself behind the guard's billet, he found the place deserted. He hissed down to Petro, motioning that the way was clear. Then he turned, leaving them to their own fate as he started to climb the stairs to the cells in the tower above.

Bildirjian grabbed Arden's arm, letting his fingers bite into the flesh, oblivious to the fact that he was hurting her, or perhaps inwardly savoring it.

"We had begun something, hadn't we, my dear?" he asked. "A glass of cognac to warm away the night chill, and then some private amusement, that was the evening's agenda, wasn't it?"

He put his free hand to her breast and roughly kneaded it. She shuddered at his touch and tried to pull away, but he twisted her arm and held her firmly.

"David, please," she begged in desperation, turning to him, searching for some pity, some movement that meant he would help her.

But he was smiling at her, obviously pleased with the

tortured sound of her voice, with the terror he saw in her face, and with the sight of what Bildirjian was doing to her.

"It was your choice, Arden," he told her.

Then he turned his back on her and followed the guards who were marching down the corridor to the stairs.

Bildirjian pulled her close to him and pressed her body against the wall with his own.

"Your friend is gone now, my dear. You've had your cognac, and you no longer seem plagued by the night cold, so we'll dismiss the preliminaries, shall we?"

"No!" she screamed as he put his hands to her skirt, pulling it up until he found the soft skin of her thigh with his hand.

"Arden! Arden!"

Forbes's voice sounded as terrified and as stricken as her own.

"Papa!" she cried out, but sobs muffled the word.

Bildirjian stopped for a moment and considered what the cries meant.

"It would seem one of our silent monks is not really what he pretends to be," he said.

He stared down at her, then pulled her away from the wall, dragging her to the door of Forbes's cell. Forbes stared out at him with stricken eyes.

"Which one of them set the bomb in Mallia?" Bildirjian thundered at Forbes. "Tell me now, or I'll rape her here, in front of you."

Forbes was shaking, his fear almost keeping the words from his lips.

"Constantin," he whispered. "It was Constantin."

Behind him one of the monks came suddenly to life, pulling away the cowl of his robe, letting it fall away from his face as he sprang to his feet.

"*Coward*," he hissed as he threw himself at Forbes.

355

"Papa!" Arden screamed as she watched Constatin put his hands to her father's throat.

Bildirjian smiled. "So now I have you," he said to Constatin. He nodded toward Forbes. "Go ahead. Kill him. It will save me the effort."

Constatin dropped his hands and stared out at Bildirjian through the bars on the door.

"You're the enemy, not him," he hissed. "Go to hell."

The commandant turned back to face Arden. He smiled with malign pleasure.

"Come, my dear," he said as he reached for her. "We've some entertainment to provide for your father."

Arden's ears filled with the sound of her own scream.

Sky kept his cap pulled down low as he let the soldiers pass by him on the stairs. Much to his surprise, they walked past him without taking any notice of him at all. He realized they thought the escape attempt had been quashed and there was no longer any need for caution.

When he saw David Trumbull walking with the soldiers, Sky nearly exploded in rage. That was how the Turks had known, he told himself: Trumbull had warned them. Sky held himself in check, knowing he could not afford to give himself away yet, that to give in to his emotions would mean alerting the guards, and that could lead only to disaster for them all.

He felt himself cringe when he heard Arden's scream, but he knew it was not yet the moment for him to act, that there was still nothing he could do to help her but race to the top of the stairs and stand ready.

And then there was the rumble and the roar of the first explosion deep in the cellars at the far end of the fortress. He knew the moment had come. He hoped the noise would confuse the guards long enough so that Petro and the others had time to get away.

He raced into the corridor even as the tower trembled slightly in the wake of the explosion. He hardly noticed it, nor the deafening sound. All he saw, all he heard, was Arden's scream as Bildirjian grabbed at her.

"Let her go!"

The Turk looked up, disoriented by the noise and the tremor of the blast. He saw Sky standing at the far end of the corridor, pointing a pistol at him.

"I suppose you're another of the fools who came with some idea of breaking the prisoners out," he hissed. "It can't be done."

"I wouldn't be too sure," Sky replied. "That explosion was only the first of a series that will bring down this whole place. Let her go now or you'll find yourself buried under a ton of rubble."

Bildirjian shook his head and pulled Arden roughly in front of himself, holding her against his chest.

"If it comes down," the Turk shouted, obviously not believing, "then we all die here. Or do you think you can kill me without hurting her? Drop your weapon before I call the guards."

Sky swore silently at himself, wondering if he'd been too cautious, if perhaps the fire would die and not spread to the ammunition stored below the second tower. What stupidity had let him think he knew enough about that sort of thing to bet his life and Arden's on the outcome?

Sky took careful aim and held the pistol steady. "I'm aiming right between your eyes," he said. "Let her go."

"Go to hell," Bildirjian shouted at him.

"Oh, he will, commandant, I'm sure he will."

Sky heard the click of a pistol being cocked, felt the cold metal of the barrel pressed close to his neck.

"Lower the gun, Trask."

Sky had no choice but to do as David demanded.

357

"I'll leave you to your amusement, commandant," David said as he dropped the key ring into Bildirjian's outspread hand. But he couldn't leave, not without looking into the cell one last time and gloating at Sky. "Pleasant dreams, Trask. I daresay you won't have many more nights to enjoy them."

He started down the corridor, leaving Arden to stare at his back as he disappeared down the stairs. Bildirjian let her watch him go, taking pleasure from the hurt and dismay he read in her expression as it became ever more obvious to her that David had simply abandoned her to his less than tender hands.

"We have to see to the damage your friend has done, my dear," he told her once David had disappeared. "And then I will see to you." He, too, started down the corridor, pulling Arden behind him.

His progress was halted by the second explosion. This one was louder and much stronger, strong enough to shake the walls and cause the floor to tremble.

Realizing Bildirjian had been unsettled by the force of the blast, Arden squirmed against his hold, fighting against the solid bonds of his arms. She had no real thought that she could free herself of him, but she hoped to make him lose his balance, to do something that would at least give her a chance. His arms tightened around her, forcing the breath from her, but still she struggled, kicking out wildly.

And much to her amazement her heel somehow managed to strike his shin a good, sharp blow. The hurt obviously caught him off guard, for he stumbled and fell backward.

But he didn't release his hold of her, nor did he fall far. He landed against the door to the cell in which he'd just locked Sky. He jerked her roughly, trying to quiet her as he regained his balance, angry with this second hurt she had managed to inflict upon him.

She gasped against the force of his arms and hands tightening against her abdomen, barely able to breathe. But then Bildirjian made a garbled, strangling sound and his hold on her loosened. She squirmed in his arms, surprised when his hands dropped away and she found herself unexpectedly free of him. She turned and saw him struggling with the hands that reached through the bars of the cell door, hands that were on his throat and forcing the air from him. He struggled wildly for a moment longer, then went slack.

"Get his pistol, Arden," Sky shouted at her. "And the key. *Quickly*."

She did as he said, putting her shaking hand to retrieve Bildirjian's pistol. Then she put her hand gingerly to his pocket. He lay quiet, still unconscious, but she feared he might come to at any moment, and her hands trembled as she rifled through his pocket. Finally she found the key ring and withdrew it.

"Petropoulos's cell first," Sky told her. "Then this one."

She ran down the corridor, opening the door to the cell where Petropoulos and his men were imprisoned, freeing them.

Achilles grasped the key ring as he stepped out.

"Allow me," he said, and took the ring from her shaking hands.

And then Sky was suddenly free. He took the pistol. She fell into his arms as Petropoulos quickly made his way along the corridor, opening the doors, releasing the imprisoned monks from Haghios Nicodemos, her father and Constatin among them.

Sky pushed her away and turned to Achilles.

"We have to get out of here. Unless that fire extinguished itself, this whole place will soon be rubble."

Achilles nodded, calling to his brother and his brother's men, organizing them into groups to take

359

charge of the still confused monks. But Arden noticed none of it. All she saw was her father, all she felt was his arms holding her.

"*Papa*," she breathed.

"What madness brought you here?" he asked, but there was no anger in his words, only joy to be outside the cell and to see Arden was safe.

"Talk later," Sky ordered him, pushing both him and Arden past the still heap of Bildirjian on the floor, urging them toward the stairs. "We have to get out of here."

Forbes nodded, entirely willing to accept whatever orders would mean escape. He'd seen more than enough of the inside of Bodrum.

Sky took Arden's arm and Forbes followed along behind, moving quickly down the stairs. The stairwell behind them was soon filled as the others descended behind them.

Achilles turned to Sky. "I don't suppose you have an idea how to get past the guards?" he asked.

Sky shook his head. "I was hoping you did," he said.

"My plan had the explosion taking out the guard's billet first," Achilles told him ruefully.

As though to punctuate his words, the roar of a third explosion tore through the air. This was the strongest, shaking the walls and the stairs beneath their feet. Behind them the monks struggled to keep from falling forward and tumbling on those in front. Huge cracks appeared between the stones of the walls. All around them there were tearing sounds as the rock shifted from where it had lain for centuries.

Arden ran, barely aware of anything save the guiding pressure of Sky's hand at her waist. They passed through the guards' quarters unchallenged. In front of them the guards were racing into the courtyard, well aware of the disaster the shifting floor beneath them heralded, with

360

no thought to stop the fleeing prisoners until their own lives were safe.

Even as they dashed through the billet and out into the torch lit courtyard, Arden could hear the first screeching noise as stone slid along stone to tumble and fall. She turned to watch as the smallest of the towers, the one in which Bildirjian's quarters had been, crumbled into a heap of fallen gray stone.

Now it was no longer necessary to think of facing the guards. The remaining ammunition was initiating a series of explosions that shook the ground, making those that had come before seem weak and paltry by comparison. Prisoners and guards alike fled, streaming out of the gates and into the darkness of the night as the prison of Bodrum began to tumble behind them.

Fortunately Petropoulos's men kept their wits about them. They herded the still dazed prisoners down to the beach, to the fishing boats that were floating just offshore, where Petro and the others who had fled with him were waiting. They splashed through the water, reaching the boats and heaving themselves over the sides, determined not to lose this last chance for freedom.

But the run was not without casualties. Behind them the soldiers had managed to recover themselves. They gave chase until they stood just outside the trembling walls of the prison, firing at the frenzied, fleeing crowd as they scrambled along the beach.

"Go, Arden!"

Sky pushed her on, then turned to help a wounded man onto his feet. Arden ran blindly for a moment more, her ears filled with the sound of shots being fired and the cries of pain as one of the fleeing Cretans was struck. When she turned back, she saw a dozen or more men being half dragged through the sand and into the water by their comrades.

She stopped, searching for her father and for Sky in the melee.

"Run, Arden."

It was Sky's voice, and she saw him struggling through the sand behind her. Constatin was hobbling beside him, his leg spurting blood from a wound in the thigh. She hesitated, then ran back to him.

"No," he shouted at her. "Get to the boat."

She refused to turn away from him. "Papa," she said. "I don't see him."

"He was in the lead, with Achilles."

She turned back to face the water, searching among the dark forms splashing through the shallows. But the night was too dark. She could see nothing. Sky motioned her forward, and she obeyed, confused now by the noise of rifle fire and the shouts and the darkness. Salt water splashed up at her and wet her face, leaving the grit of salt on her lips. The weight of her soaked skirts dragged at her, and she had to struggle to move forward through the surf.

And then there was a final explosion, this one deafening in its force. Arden turned back to see flames, until then enclosed in the cellars, suddenly burst out of their confinement, sending shafts of light leaping into the blackness of the night sky. The two still erect towers of Bodrum stood for a moment, dark pillars amidst a sea of glowing flame. And then they seemed to simply crumble, the stone caving in on itself, until all that was left were the flames leaping higher, shining more fiercely, as the fire consumed whatever could burn.

It took Arden a few seconds to realize that the rifle fire had ceased, that the soldiers, those who had not been trapped by the falling stone and the flames, now fled for safety.

Petropoulos began to direct the loading of the boats.

urging the escaped monks to hurry before the scattered Turkish garrison could regroup. As each of the fishing boats filled, he assigned a crew of his own men and sent them off into the darkness of the night sea.

"Arden!"

She couldn't believe it was her father's voice, her father's face staring down at her from the deck of Petropoulos's boat. Behind her, a pair of hands found her waist and lifted her, and suddenly she was in the boat and wrapped in her father's arms.

"Well, it seems you've done what you set about doing, Arden."

She pulled away from his arms to find Sky standing behind her and Constatin sitting with his back against the rail. They were both smiling, their expressions plain in the light of the fires from the prison behind them on the shore.

"I think we may be able to use you, *Despinis* Devereaux, that is, if you find yourself in need of occupation."

Arden stared at him, at the bloody hole in his leg and the self-satisfied way he smiled at her. And suddenly all she could see was red. Since the first moment she'd set eyes on this man, it seemed that she'd been dogged by a trail of thick, red blood, first his brother's, and then more and more of it from a seemingly endless parade of ghastly wounds. She had had enough of it, more than enough to last a lifetime. It sickened her to realize he could lie there bleeding and still contemplate the shedding of more blood.

"Damn you," she hissed. "*You* started this. If it hadn't been for you, my father would never have been taken to this place. Can't you be done with it? Hasn't there been enough bloodshed?"

He obviously did not like the tone she used with him,

nor the fact that she could so easily criticize what he held to be a holy cause. His expression grew angry and his expression hard.

"Never enough," he said. "Not until Crete stands independent will there be enough."

"Even your own brother's blood?" she demanded. "Does it mean nothing to you that the Turks killed Theo?"

She realized that he hadn't, until that moment, known, and hated herself for saying it that way. She watched him grow pale at the news of his brother's death.

But his expression did not soften. "All the more reason to fight," he replied through tight lips.

Sky put his hand on Arden's arm. "You can't preach reason to a zealot, Arden," he said. Then he turned to Petropoulos. "Let's get out of here."

Petropoulos darted a last glance back at Bodrum. There was no sign of any attempt to stop them, but he had no doubt there would be soon enough. He called out to his men to set the sails.

"I think there's one more matter to be settled first."

They all turned to the figure who slowly stepped out of the shadows at the aft of the fishing boat. He drew back the cowl of the monk's robe that obscured his features and carefully raised his hand. The light of the flames of the fires that consumed the prison reflected off the pistol he was holding.

"You can't go quite yet," he said as he pointed the pistol at Sky's heart.

"Oh, God, no," Arden murmured as she recognized David's features leering crazily at her from beneath the monk's hood.

Chapter Twenty

"Give it up, Trumbull," Sky told him. "It's over."

David leered, his face oddly skeletal as he stared out at them from beneath the dark cowl.

"You know, Trask, part of me agrees with you. I tell myself the game's over. You played it quite well, incidentally, far better than I expected, actually. It took a good deal of ingenuity to arrange those explosions to give you the time to find Arden and the rest and get out before bringing the place down on you." He smiled, suddenly the academic don, considering the work of a talented but yet unproved pupil.

Sky told himself he had to keep David talking; as long as he was still talking, he wasn't using the pistol. That, he hoped, would give them time to think of some way past him, some way to overpower him.

Sky knew he still had the pistol Arden had taken from Bildirjian holstered at his side, but he realized it might have gotten wet as he'd pulled Constatin through the water to the fishing boat. There was a good possibility that it was useless. To reach for it now with David's pistol pointed at his heart and find himself holding nothing more useful than a piece of cold metal would be inviting death.

"I pride myself on my gamesmanship, Trumbull," he said conversationally. "Of course, I've always been intrigued by the challenge of games." He moved a step closer to David, and smiled pleasantly.

Arden stared at the two of them in disbelief. She didn't understand Sky's intention, nor could she believe she was hearing correctly. How could the two of them stand there, she wondered, calmly discussing the events of the past twenty-four hours as though it had been nothing more than sport? Could everything that had happened to them since they'd landed in Bodrum have happened simply because these two men wanted to best one another, wanted to show the other who could play a game with greater expertise? Could it have been nothing more to Sky than another chance to prove his own superiority as he had taken great pains to do with her?

"This isn't a game," she shouted in a sudden spurt of raw anger. "It's people's lives!"

David's eyes drifted slowly to meet hers, and his expression grew thoughtful.

"No, it isn't a game," he agreed. "And despite Trask's valiant effort, I'm afraid I can't allow him to leave the field victorious." Despite his words, there was no trace of regret in David's tone. "I *certainly* cannot allow any of you to return to Crete."

"And how do you propose to stop us?" Constatin demanded. "You can't kill all of us."

"No I can't," David agreed. "I could probably shoot two, maybe three of you before someone could get to me, but that would mean I would die as well, and that is not my intention." He grinned humorlessly. "It is certainly convenient that my friends can do what I am unable to do."

"Friends? What friends?" Forbes asked. "You have no friends here."

"I'm shocked, Forbes. Where is the hail-fellow-well-

366

met who seemed so determined to have me marry his daughter?" David's eyes narrowed as he spoke to Forbes, and by the time he mentioned Arden he was spitting his words. When Forbes looked away in embarrassment, he suddenly brightened. "But I do have friends," he went on, "the friends who brought me." He seemed to be enjoying himself suddenly, as though the prospect of seeing their fear amused him. His eyes darted to the jutting point of land where the burning prison stood. "Here they come now."

He nodded toward the small cape where the still burning remains of the prison stood. Illuminated by the light of the flames was the prow of a Turkish battleship just rounding the point of land. It was closing fast to the place where the fishing boat foundered, its sails still limply hanging, in the water.

"You can't be serious," Arden cried. "You can't mean to give us back to them?"

David shrugged. "I haven't much choice," he said with no apparent emotion. "I have my career, my good name to think about. If I let you return, I am quite sure you'd sully both."

"Your career and your name!" she murmured in disbelief. "I can't believe you'd send us to a Turkish prison for the sake of your name."

But when she stared up at David, she realized that that was precisely what he intended to do. Her life and those of the others meant nothing to him. He would watch them all die without a qualm so long as he wasn't inconvenienced, as long as he went about his life in precisely the way he wanted.

She wondered that she had never realized that his lack of emotion, his veneer of calm, hid beneath it an absence of something basic, something intrinsically human. She was filled with disgust as she remembered that only a few weeks had elapsed since she'd agreed to marry him. She

367

couldn't believe she hadn't been able to see what he really was the moment she'd met him, that she'd been so easily fooled by the studied, polite veneer.

David ignored her and smiled at Forbes. "Surely you understand, Forbes," he said. "You understand the importance of a man's name. After all, it seemed to mean a great deal to you to have your own tied to it." He turned his glance back to Arden, and his smile disappeared. His eyes grew sharp, and he glared at her in a sudden spurt of vengeful anger. "Unlike you, slut. I offered you the honor of my name and you spit on it. Bodrum was too good for you. You deserve to die."

Forbes grew red at his words. "How dare you speak that way to my daughter, you, you . . ."

"Shut up, old man!" David shouted at him, stopping the flow of Forbes's words with a movement of the hand that held the pistol. "I've put up with as much of your driveling babble as I intend to. Look at you, a tradesman who only just washed the printer's ink from his filthy fingers. Do you think because you have a little money you can dictate to me?"

Petropoulos ignored the little drama being played out on the deck in front of him. Instead he'd centered his attention on the growing form of the closing Turkish ship. He could see her guns being trained on his boat. He knew what would happen if he didn't make a move to get the yawl out of the range of those guns, and he knew he had to make it quickly.

He came to an abrupt decision. "I'm not going to stand here and wait to be boarded."

David turned his pistol toward the Cretan. "That's just precisely what you are going to do," he said. "Move and you die."

Petropoulos bared his teeth. "Then kill me, coward," he snarled as he charged forward.

David floundered, his attention distracted by the

unanticipated attack, his certainty shaken. He'd not expected to find them prepared for any more resistance, not after the bloody race along the beach. He turned, aiming his pistol at Petropoulos.

Sky took advantage of the instant of David's indecision. He charged forward, striking out at David. He reached for the pistol, deflecting it with his arm as he pushed David back. Startled and off balance, David let the pistol fall from his hand, but not until after he'd inadvertently fired.

Arden screamed. Her first thought was that Sky had been shot. But then she saw him wrestle David down to the deck. She fell to her knees and scrambled for the fallen pistol.

David didn't put up much of a fight. He had no skill to match all Sky had learned through diligent practice in an often dangerous profession, and he quickly ceased struggling. Sky dragged him to his feet.

"That damned ship is closing fast," Petropoulos shouted.

He darted forward, crying out to his men to haul up the sails. But the sails were no sooner set than the Turkish ship fired a warning shot directly across the prow of the yawl. The ball fell into the water just feet in front of them. It was close enough to make the small vessel rock with the concussion.

"Heave to," came the shouted order from the Turkish ship after the ball was fired. "Heave to, or we will open fire on you."

David seemed delighted. "Now what are you going to do?" he laughed at Petropoulos. "It's too late for you."

Petropoulos took the pistol from Arden's shaking hand and gave it to Constatin. "Keep an eye on him," he said. "If he moves, shoot him."

Constatin gave every indication that the prospect delighted him. "A pleasure," he replied. He leaned back against the rail, shifting his injured leg slightly to make himself more comfortable, and pointed the pistol at David. "I might not even wait for him to make the move."

Petropoulos nodded to Sky and Forbes. "Come with me," he ordered. "We have a little surprise for those Turks."

The men quickly crossed to the starboard rail. Petropoulos moved with a determined stride to a canvas-draped heap. He grasped the edge of the heavy canvas and pulled it away.

Arden stared at the long, dark form the canvas had obscured.

"A cannon?" she murmured to Constatin, her voice tight with disbelief.

He grinned. "Spiros was never one to avoid an opportunity for a good fight," he told her with a hint of glee.

"Let them get close," Petropoulos told the men as they tamped the powder. "Close enough so we give them a mortal blow."

"They won't just sit there," Sky said as he readied the fuse. "They'll return fire."

"And we'll run from it," Petropoulos replied. "This yawl may look like a lumbering scow, but she's deceiving . . . if the gods are with us, we may get out of here yet."

He called out orders to his men, speaking softly now, as he didn't want his words to carry across the water. The sailors ran to his bidding, preparing to shorten the yawl's sails to turn and flee at his order.

"There's going to be a battle," Arden murmured.

This prospect, like that of shooting David, seemed to give Constatin pleasure. He grinned at her in anticipation.

"That there is, *Despinis*. Perhaps you'd better go below."

Arden had no time even to consider his suggestion. The Turkish ship had turned broadside, the men on her deck ready to board the yawl. Petropoulos, obviously deciding the time had come, pointed to the cannon.

"Now!" he shouted.

Sky ignited the fuse. At the same time Petropoulos's sailors pulled the sails tight, turning them into the wind. The yawl had begun to pull away even before the cannon-ball found its target in the side of the Turkish ship.

The ball struck, opening a wide hole in the hull. But what happened then proved that Petropoulos's gods had decided to smile on him. Beside opening a hole in the hull, the ball struck a magazine. There was a tearing explosion, and thick, dark smoke poured from the hole. The men on deck, waiting to board the yawl, felt the brunt of the explosion's force. They were thrown into panic. Petropoulos's men used the time to good purpose, tightening the sails as the yawl gained speed and drew away from the Turkish ship.

And then all was a confusion of noise and bright flames. The Turkish ship returned fire as her crew recovered from their moment of shock. The night stillness was filled with the deafening dissonance of both rifle shot and cannon.

Arden shrank from the noise and the light, but there was no way she could turn away from Constatin's scream of pain. She turned to find him staring down at the puddle of blood spurting from the bullet that had struck him in the back.

And then there was the sound of wood splintering as one of the cannon shots struck the fleeing yawl's mizzen-mast.

There was a moment when the split mast seemed to shudder. Then it fell, snapping lines and causing the yawl

371

to list with the impact. There was an instant of havoc as the wounded yawl shuddered and shook, trying to find its equilibrium. There were cries of pain from the men it struck as it fell. And Arden, clinging to the rail behind her to keep from being thrown over the side, looked on in horror as she saw Sky fall beneath the weight of the mast.

She screamed. For a moment that seemed to last forever, all she could do was scream with the horror of the thought that he was dead. And then her eyes fell and she saw the pistol that had fallen from Constatin's hand to the deck between them.

David saw it, too.

It seemed as though it was happening too slowly to be real. There was the pistol, lying on the deck beside Constatin's still body, and there was David, diving forward to retrieve it.

Arden fell forward on her hands and knees, scrambling toward the pistol, not really thinking about what she was doing, only knowing that she could not let David reach it before she did. But she had been numbed by the sounds of battle around her, numbed by the shock of seeing Constatin die in front of her, by her fear for Sky. David fell forward, pushing her back as he reached for the pistol.

Filled with an unseen fury, she scratched out at him, reaching for his eyes. He had brought the Turkish ship after them. He held all responsibility for what that encounter had wrought. Only one thought mattered to her at that moment, and that was that he could not do this horrible thing and not pay.

She felt a wave of satisfaction as her nails dug into the skin of his cheek. He drew back, momentarily stunned, shocked by the ferocity of her attack, or perhaps by the fact that she would fight back.

And in the second he pulled away, she rolled away from him and found the pistol.

"Get back," she screamed.

She pulled back, away from him, and scrambled to her feet. She aimed the pistol carefully, putting both hands to the butt trying to steady it, but still it shook.

He lay for a moment where he was, staring at her, then slowly pushed himself to his knees.

The yawl steadied itself in the water, determining the blow it had received was not fatal. The mainsail tightened with the wind and the boat started forward, the end of the fallen mast trailing behind her in the water.

"You're not going to shoot me, Arden," David told her confidently. "You aren't going to shoot anyone."

"I will," she shouted at him.

He shook his head. "It doesn't matter anymore. You're going to get away."

It was true. The Turkish ship, crippled by the hole in her side, was taking on water and beginning to list. And despite the fallen mizzenmast, the yawl was pulling away, its main mast tight to the wind. There was still the sporadic sound of rifle shots being fired at them, but they were half-hearted, a last angry protest as the Turks realized their prey had been lost.

David got slowly to his feet, keeping his eyes on her as he stood. "Put the pistol down, Arden. You're not going to shoot me," he told her in a tone that implied she had no choice but to obey.

The pistol shook in Arden's hands. He's right, she thought . . . she couldn't shoot him. If nothing else she'd seen far too many deaths in the preceding days to want to be the cause of yet another.

"Go," she said, her voice a tight whisper. "Swim back to your masters. Maybe they'll give you a medal for the men who've died because of what you've done tonight."

She let her hand fall to her side and turned her glance

to the fallen mizzenmast, to the place on the aft deck where Sky lay beneath the shaft of wood. For a moment she thought her heart would break. And then it started pounding again, pounding with hope and relief. Sky was moving, pushing against the fallen mast. She started forward, David already forgotten, thinking only of getting to Sky, of helping him.

Arden wasn't the only one to find a newfound hope. David saw her lower the pistol and he lunged, knowing full well that this was his last chance, that in a few moments longer they would be out of range of the Turkish vessel.

He caught her by surprise, grabbing her arm and swinging her around as he grasped the hand that held the pistol. Then he took a handful of her hair, winding his hand in it and pulling it back until she cried out in pain.

"I've not quite done with you, Arden," he hissed. "Not you nor your father nor Trask. The rest are outlaws to both the Turks and the Greeks. To go back to my life, all I need do is kill you three."

He began to pull her hand that held the pistol, trying to force her to turn it on herself.

Sky had been stunned by the weight of the falling mast striking his side. He'd had the breath knocked out of him, and he now lay with his leg pinned beneath the weight of the mast, but he was far from dead.

But when he turned and saw David threatening Arden with the pistol, he felt none of the pain in his side or his leg, only fear. He reached to the holster and withdrew Bildirjian's pistol, pointing it as David overpowered Arden, wrestling his pistol from her hand.

He knew he had one chance and only one. If he missed, or if the pistol had gotten wet enough for it to misfire, neither he nor Forbes nor Arden would live long enough to see the Turkish coast disappear behind them. With Petropoulos and his crew distracted, it would take only moments for David to complete what he had begun, slip over the side, and swim for shore.

Arden struggled against the pressure of David's arm, trying to hold the hand in which he now grasped the pistol. Part of her knew the effort was useless, that it would only be a matter of a few seconds before he overpowered her, before he held the pistol to her temple and fired it. But still she struggled, the hope kindled by the sight of Sky's stirring body refusing to simply give up and accept death.

Then there was the sound of a shot and a scream of pain. David's hand flew back, the pistol falling away in a shower of droplets of red. He released her, too busy with his own pain to think of her. She fell to the deck, grabbing up the fallen pistol and flinging it with all her might over the side.

Petropoulos appeared at her side, drawn by the sound of the shot and the cry. There was fire in his eyes as he stared at David, then down at Constatin's still body. He reached for the knife in his belt.

"Prepare to die, coward," he hissed as he drew the blade.

Arden felt a sudden wave of revulsion. After all she'd seen, the thought of David's body lying with that knife in his chest was too sickening to contemplate. Despite the wrong he'd done, still she couldn't face that.

"No," she shouted to Petropoulos. "There's been enough killing."

Petropoulos hesitated, then nodded toward the rail. "Go," he shouted at David. "If you can swim to shore you have your life. Go now, before I change my mind."

David eyed the receding shoreline, not at all sure he could manage the swim against the powerful current. But when he turned back and looked at Petropoulos's determined expression, he realized he had no choice. Still nursing his injured hand, he swung himself over the side and into the dark waves.

Arden didn't even watch him start his swim. She turned and ran to where Sky lay pinned to the deck by the fallen mast.

Petropoulos stood by the rail for a moment longer, watching as David oriented himself in the water and then started the long swim for shore. Then he turned and joined Arden.

"That was a nice shot," he said as he began to heave the mast upward. "Shooting a gun out of a man's hand is not exactly easy."

Sky dropped the pistol onto the deck and, with Arden's help, pulled himself back, out from under the weight of the shaft.

"Don't ask me to do it again," he said as he pulled himself free.

Petropoulos dropped the end of the mast with a grunt of effort. "I should have killed him," he added.

Arden looked out at the dark water and shook her head. "No," she said. "He can't go back, not to Boston nor Greece, nor anywhere else that matters to him. He's lost his career and his precious name. Living without them is a punishment worse than death to someone like him."

Petropoulos did not seem convinced. "Well, maybe the sharks will get to him before he reaches shore," he muttered.

Arden turned back to face Sky. She suddenly found her throat had grown tight, and she didn't know what to say to him.

He pushed away the rumpled hair that had fallen across her cheek and stared at her. Then he smiled and she fell against him.

He grunted in pain and she drew back.

"I've hurt you!" she said.

He put his hand to his side and considered the hurt he felt as he explored his ribs. "Nothing that won't mend," he told her. He smiled as he saw the look of concern in her eyes. "It seems racing around after you, Miss Devereaux, is not a very healthy pursuit."

"Not like going into battle for a story."

Sky looked up to see that Forbes had approached, accompanied by the rest of Petropoulos's men. For a moment he wondered just how far David Trumbull would have gotten in his pursuit of Arden had it not been for Forbes pushing her to him.

Then he turned his attention back to Arden. He knew then that it really didn't matter what Forbes wanted for her. The only thing that really mattered was what she wanted for herself. He had only to show her that what she wanted was what he wanted.

"Arden," he told her softly. "I have been shot trying to save you from your own folly. And now it would seem I have a few broken ribs as payment for my affection. I am not about to take any more punishment. I think in high time that you accept the fact that you are in love with me and are ready to marry me."

Arden stared at him wide eyed.

"No games?" she whispered, not really sure she could believe he meant what he was saying.

He put his hand once again to her cheek. "No games," he told her firmly. "I love you, and I know you love me. If your father disagrees with those simple facts, he can fire me. I promise you, we won't starve. Now say you'll marry me."

She swallowed, then nodded. "I'll marry you," she repeated.

"You could add the words 'I love you,'" he suggested. "They are usually considered appropriate at this point in the proceedings."

"I love you," she said with a smile.

Then he pulled her face to his and kissed her. It was a long, slow, pleasantly exploratory kiss, one that promised them both a great deal.

When finally he lifted his lips from hers, he seemed oblivious to the others around them, staring at them with wryly knowing grins.

"Now," he said softly, "I suggest you help me below. I have injuries that need tending."

She smiled, then scrambled to help him to his feet. Neither of them noticed the Turkish coast sink away behind them as they crossed the deck.

For an instant Forbes started after them, angry that Sky could take his daughter from him with such apparent ease. But then his own common sense told him Arden was no longer a little girl, that she would no longer simply bend to his will. And for the first time he realized that perhaps that was not such a bad thing.

He turned back to the rail and stared out at the darkness and the sea.

"Will you go on with it?" he asked Petropoulos.

He leaned over the rail and silently considered the darkness of the night sky. There had been times, back in Bodrum, when he'd never thought to see the sky again. It seemed a wonder to him that he'd never realized just how beautiful it was.

Petropoulos stood silent for a moment at his side, staring at the canvas-wrapped object that was Nikolas Constatin's body.

"I don't know," he said finally. "It's been a long time since I've really thought about what it is we are doing. Now that I do, I fear I may have lost sight of what it was we all wanted when we began."

"You and Constatin?" Forbes asked.

Petropoulos nodded. "Me and Constatin and Achilles and I don't even know how many others. I've forgotten some of their names. That's the most frightening part, oddly—to realize I've forgotten their names."

"There've been many deaths," Forbes said softly.

"Too many," Petropoulos murmured. "Maybe it's time to listen to the Greeks. They are, after all, our brothers. Perhaps it's better to live in your brother's house than to die trying to build your own."

"There are still the Turks," Forbes said.

Petropoulos nodded. "And we are still facing a long fight. But now that the Greeks have joined us, I know we will win."

Forbes turned to him. "I know it too," he agreed.

Petropoulos smiled and put his hand to Forbes's shoulder. "And you, do you still have battles to fight, my friend?"

"Battles?" Forbes asked.

"It does not require an oracle to see that your daughter loves Skyler Trask. In fact, even a man as unobservant as I can see what is in front of my own eyes. I cannot help but wonder if what I heard a few moments ago means that you are not pleased with her choice."

Now it was Forbes's turn to grow pensive.

"If you'd asked me a few months ago, I'd have told you I knew what was best for Arden, and it wouldn't have been Skyler Trask. But tonight I find myself wondering if it wouldn't be nice to have a son-in-law who has a flair for the newspaper business, one who can take over the *Sun* when I feel the urge to retire."

Petropoulos snorted in amusement. "Then you will not fire him from his job?"

Forbes shook his head. "No, certainly not. I didn't bear the cost of bringing him here to let him off without writing the stories he owes me. You said yourself there will be a long battle." He grinned. "I think I might even ask for one about a daring escape from a Turkish prison. It would please the readers."

Petropoulos laughed outright. "And that is, after all, your business."

Forbes suddenly sobered. "Perhaps David Trumbull was right," he said, "perhaps I am nothing more than a tradesman with a little money."

"Is that such a bad thing?" Petropoulos asked.

Once again a smile edged its way to Forbes's lips. "I used to think so, but now I realize it's quite a good thing to be, after all."

"A man should be pleased with what he is," Petropoulos said.

Forbes smiled as he stared out at the dark sea.

"I think you're right," he agreed. "It may not be an easy lesson to learn, but I think you're right."

"Ow. That hurt."

Arden stopped, nearly dropping the scissors she'd used to cut away the remaining roll of bandage. She looked up at Sky, her expression stricken. She was just finishing wrapping his injured ribs. She couldn't understand how she had hurt him.

"I'm sorry, Sky," she murmured.

Sky took the roll of bandages and the scissors from her hand and dropped them on the table.

"I think you'd better help me to lie down, Arden," he suggested.

She put her arm around his waist and helped him to the narrow bunk. They'd lain together in that bunk only the night before. Somehow it seemed almost a lifetime away to her.

But as he sat, she realized he was not in quite as much pain as he had led her to believe. He was smiling at her, and there was no hint in his expression that he was suffering.

"I don't suppose you would like me to finish undressing you, would you, Sky?" she asked.

He grinned and nodded. "I think you'd better," he replied.

She gave him a seraphic smile as she reached for his belt. She carefully freed the buttons of his trousers and then looked up at him, aware that all pretense was now useless.

"Are you in much pain, Sky?" she asked slyly.

"More than mere words can express," he replied as he felt her hand warm against him.

She looked up at him and smiled. "Perhaps we could relieve it," she suggested.

He put his hands to her shoulders and pushed away the fabric, baring her breasts and pulling her close to him.

"I wonder if Petropoulos would perform a wedding at sea," he said softly as he pressed his lips against the warm flesh of her neck. "After all, he *is* a captain."

She pushed the red and black lace dress down to her hips, then wriggled out of it, letting it fall to a heap on the floor at her feet. Then she stared down at it.

"Not exactly my idea of a wedding gown," she said.

He pushed her away, holding her at arm's length. His eyes narrowed.

"You don't intend to wear white, do you?" he asked.

She shrugged. "No one need know except you and me," she told him. "Besides, that's the proper way, isn't it?"

He laughed. "And you would never want to be thought improper, would you, Arden?"

She pretended shock. "Me? Never."

He grew pensive. "And the prospect of a sample of the honeymoon a bit early?" he asked. "That wouldn't by any chance seem indecorous?"

She leaned forward and pressed her lips to his, parting them in invitation to the willing probe of his tongue.

"If you feel strong enough, love," she whispered in a

low, breathy voice when he lifted his lips from hers.

He laughed and pushed her down to the pillows.

"You forget," he said. "I'm a very good healer."

She smiled up at him. "Show me," she said.

She put her hands to his shoulders, then slipped them behind his neck and pulled him down to her.

She spread herself beneath him, and he smiled as he slid inside her. She moaned softly with pleasure at the sweetness of that first hungry thrust. She gazed up at him, staring at his eyes, finally sure that what she saw in them was what she'd wanted to see in them from the moment she'd met him.

He held himself still and returned her stare.

"I love you," he whispered. "I'll never stop loving you."

"And I love you," she replied, no longer afraid of what that admission could cost her. "I fell in love with you that very first night, when you warned me about playing games. I was simply too afraid to admit it, even to myself."

"And now?" he asked.

"Now I'm no longer afraid. As long as you hold me I'll never be afraid again."

It was true, she realized, what she had told him. She no longer feared the power over her that her loving Sky gave him. In the previous hours she'd learned to trust him, and the trust had forced away her doubts. She only wondered that she had held on to the fear for so long.

He began to move slowly inside her, and she welcomed the flood of passion that swept through her, willingly offering herself up to it. It rose within her with surprising speed, shattering her, leaving her dizzy and adrift as she let it claim her.

He grew still and held her, cradling her in his arms. She found herself clinging to him, breathless and trembling.

"What happened?" she asked him in bewildered amazement.

He smiled down at her, then leaned forward to let his lips find hers.

"A beginning, love," he whispered as he once again began to move inside her. "The start of a very long honeymoon."

She smiled up at him. "Very long?" she asked.

"Decades," he promised. "Five or six of them at the least."

Arden pressed herself close to him. It was, she decided, a perfectly lovely prospect.